Praise for *The Art of Being Normal*

Winner of the Waters~~tones~~ ~~James~~ ~~Children's~~ ~~Book~~
Sunday Times Chi~~ldren's~~ book.
~~Shortlisted for the~~ the due date.

'A life-changing and life-saving book' *Philip Pullman*

'A sensational, heart-warming and life-affirming debut'
Juno Dawson

'The sort of book I hope will change lives. Amazing'
Non Pratt

'Please, please, please read *The Art of Being Normal*!
I want to scream from the rooftops about it!' *Lucy Powrie*

'Impressive and affecting' *Guardian*

'Passionate and gripping . . . a powerful tale of a
teenager's struggle with identity' *Telegraph*

'Heart-warming, and ground-breaking' *Independent*

'Life-affirming' *Marie Claire*

'A compelling story with a ton of heart' *BuzzFeed*

'Incredible and heartbreaking' *Express*

'Life-affirming, powerful and heart-warming' *BookTrust*

'A revelation' *Books for Keeps*

'Wow' *Fiona Noble, The Bookseller*

Praise for *Paper Avalanche*

One of *The Times'* Biggest Children's Books of 2019

'Pacy, instantly absorbing' *Guardian*

'Relatable characters and well-crafted dialogue
make this a thoroughly engaging read'
Financial Times

'Poignant, thought-provoking and intensely readable,
this is UK YA writing at its best' *The Bookseller*

Praise for *All About Mia*

'Absorbing, hilarious . . . witty and touching'
Guardian

'This zingy rites of passage novel is filled with
warmth and insight' *Financial Times*

'Mia is a chaotic, charming character and one of
the most irresistible teenage voices I've read in a
long time' *Fiona Noble, The Bookseller*

'A tumultuous but poignant tale about family, friendship
and being a sister' *Sun*

Foreword

In the summer of 2010, I was offered two days of admin work at the Gender Identity Development Service (GIDS), a highly specialized NHS clinic for young people struggling with their gender identity. My task was simple. I was given audio typing equipment and a stack of cassette tapes and instructed to type what I heard. I put on the headphones and pressed 'play', unaware that the case notes I was about to listen to would one day inspire the book you are now holding in your hands.

I ended up staying at GIDS for two years, acting as the team's administrator. During this time, I typed up hundreds of cases. Some of the stories I heard were sad and painful; some were uplifting and full of hope. Some service users had been living in role for years; others were at the very beginning of their transition. Some young people were surrounded by love and support, while others were dealing with hostility and ignorance, often from within their own families. Although no two cases were the same, there was one thing that united all the young people I came across – the desire to be accepted.

I began writing *The Art of Being Normal* in spring 2012. I had no plan, no plot, no title, certainly no idea it would be published one day. All I knew was that I wanted to write a story that somehow captured the bravery and brilliance of the young people I was encountering on a daily basis. During my time at GIDS, I was fortunate enough to be able to sit in on group therapy sessions. These were held during the school holidays and were an opportunity for service users to meet and socialize in a safe and supportive setting. I sat in the corner and watched as bonds were built and friendships forged. GIDS had brought these young people together, but there was so much more to their interactions than a shared struggle around their gender identity. In much the same way, the more I wrote, the more I realized that I didn't want the book to be defined by a single issue. Yes, *The Art of Being Normal* is about gender identity, but it's also about friendship and family, fancying someone for the first time and not fitting in – subjects I think we can all relate to in some way, no matter what our age or experience.

In the five years since *The Art of Being Normal*'s publication, I've received hundreds of messages from trans teenagers, and my heart sings with every single one. Nothing compares to hearing that its existence has helped a young person feel seen, or given them the strength to come out to their family. I suspect *The Art of Being Normal* will always be my most special book for this reason alone.

If you are about to discover David and Leo's story for the first time, welcome. I hope you enjoy getting to know them even as half as much as I enjoyed creating them.

Lisa Williamson
January 2020

LISA WILLIAMSON

THE ART OF BEING NORMAL

David Fickling Books

31 Beaumont Street
Oxford OX1 2NP, UK

Also by Lisa Williamson:

All About Mia
Paper Avalanche
Malala (Yousafzai) – First Names Series

Co-written:
Floored

The Art of Being Normal
is a
DAVID FICKLING BOOK

First published in Great Britain by
David Fickling Books,
31 Beaumont Street,
Oxford, OX1 2NP

www.davidficklingbooks.com

Hardback edition published 2015
This edition published 2020

978-1-78845-133-8

1 3 5 7 9 10 8 6 4 2

David Fickling Books supports the Forest Stewardship Council (FSC), the leading
international forest certification organisation. All our titles that are printed
on Greenpeace-approved FSC-certified paper carry the FSC logo.

MIX
Paper from
responsible sources
FSC® C104723
FSC
www.fsc.org

DAVID FICKLING BOOKS Reg. No. 8340307

A CIP catalogue record for this book is available from the British Library.

Typeset in Sabon by Falcon Oast Graphic Art Ltd.
Printed and bound in Clays Ltd, Elcograf S.p.A

For Isla

1

One afternoon, when I was eight years old, my class was told to write about what we wanted to be when we grew up. Miss Box went round the class, asking each one of us to stand up and share what we had written. Zachary Olsen wanted to play in the Premier League. Lexi Taylor wanted to be an actress. Harry Beaumont planned on being Prime Minister. Simon Allen wanted to be Harry Potter, so badly that the previous term he had scratched a lightning bolt on to his forehead with a pair of craft scissors.

But I didn't want to be any of these things.

This is what I wrote:

I want to be a girl.

2

My party guests are singing 'Happy Birthday'. It does not sound good.

My little sister Livvy is barely even singing. At eleven, she's already decided family birthday parties are tragically embarrassing, leaving Mum and Dad to honk out the rest of the tune, Mum's reedy soprano clashing with Dad's flat bass. It is so bad Phil, the family dog, gets up from his basket and slinks off mid-song in vague disgust. I don't blame him; the whole party is fairly depressing. Even the blue balloons Dad spent the entire morning blowing up look pale and sad, especially the ones with 'Fourteen Today!' scrawled on them in black marker pen. I'm not even sure the underwhelming events unfolding before me qualify as a party in the first place.

'Make a wish!' Mum says. She has the cake tipped at an angle so I won't notice it's wonky. It says 'Happy Birthday David!' in blood-red icing across the top, the 'day' in 'birthday' all scrunched up where she must have run out of room. Fourteen blue candles form a circle around the edge of the cake, dripping wax into the butter cream.

'Hurry up!' Livvy says.

But I won't be rushed. I want to do this bit properly. I lean forward, tuck my hair behind my ears and shut my eyes. I block out Livvy's whining and Mum's cajoling and Dad fiddling with the settings on the camera, and suddenly everything sounds sort of muffled and far away, a bit like when you dunk your head under water in the bath.

I wait a few seconds before opening my eyes and blowing out all the candles in one go. Everyone applauds. Dad lets off a party popper but it doesn't 'pop' properly and by the time he's got another one out of the packet Mum has opened the curtains and started taking the candles off the cake, and the moment has passed.

'What did you wish for? Something stupid, I bet,' Livvy says accusingly, twirling a piece of golden brown hair around her middle finger.

'He can't tell you, silly, otherwise it won't come true,' Mum says, taking the cake into the kitchen to be sliced.

'Yeah,' I say, sticking my tongue out at Livvy. She sticks hers out right back.

'Where are your two friends again?' she asks, putting extra emphasis on the 'two'.

'I've told you, Felix is in Florida and Essie is in Leamington Spa.'

'That's too bad,' Livvy says with zero sympathy. 'Dad, how many people did I have at my eleventh?'

'Forty-five. All on roller skates. Utter carnage,' Dad mutters grimly, ejecting the memory card from the camera and slotting it into the side of his laptop.

The first photo that pops up on the screen is of me sitting at the head of the table wearing an oversized 'Birthday Boy' badge and pointy cardboard party hat. My eyes are closed mid-blink and my forehead is shiny.

'Dad,' I moan. 'Do you have to do that now?'

'Just doing some red-eye removal before I email them over to your grandmother,' he says, clicking away at the mouse. 'She was gutted she couldn't come.'

This is not true. Granny has bridge on Wednesday evenings and doesn't miss it for anyone, least of all her least favourite grandchild. Livvy is Granny's favourite. But then Livvy is everyone's favourite. Mum had also asked Auntie Jane and Uncle Trevor, and my cousins Keira and Alfie. But Alfie woke up this morning with weird spots all over his chest that may or may not be chicken pox, so they had to give their apologies, leaving the four of us to 'celebrate' alone.

Mum returns to the living room with the sliced cake, setting it back down on the table.

'Look at all these leftovers,' she says, frowning as she surveys the mountains of picked-at food. 'We're going to have enough sausage rolls and fondant fancies to last us until Christmas. I just hope I've got enough cling film to wrap it all up.'

Great. A fridge full of food to remind me just how wildly unpopular I am.

After cake and intensive cling-film action, there are presents. From Mum and Dad I get a new backpack for school, the *Gossip Girl* DVD box set and a cheque for one hundred pounds. Livvy presents me with a box of Cadbury Heroes and a shiny red case for my iPhone.

Then we all sit on the sofa and watch a film called *Freaky Friday*. It's about a mother and daughter who eat an enchanted fortune cookie that makes them magically swap bodies for the day. Of course everyone learns a valuable lesson before the inevitable happy ending, and for about the hundredth time this summer I mourn my life's failure to follow the plot of a perky teenage movie. Dad drops off halfway through and starts snoring loudly.

That night I can't sleep. I'm awake for so long, my eyes get used to the dark and I can make out the outlines of my posters on the walls and the tiny shadow of a mosquito darting back and forth across the ceiling.

I am fourteen and time is running out.

3

It's the last Friday of the summer holidays. On Monday I go back to school. I have been fourteen years old for exactly nine days.

I'm lying on the sofa with the curtains closed. Mum and Dad are at work. Livvy is at her best friend Cressy's house. I'm watching an old episode of *America's Next Top Model* with a packet of Maryland double-chocolate-chip cookies balanced on my stomach. Tyra Banks has just told Ashley she is not going to be America's Next Top Model. Ashley is in floods of tears and all the other girls are hugging her even though they spent almost the entire episode going on about how much they hated Ashley and wanted her to leave. The *America's Next Top Model* house is nothing if not brutal.

Ashley's tears are interrupted by the sound of a key turning in the front door. I sit up, carefully placing the packet of cookies on the coffee table beside me.

'David, I'm home,' Mum calls.

She's back early from her meeting.

I frown as I listen to her kick off her shoes and drop her keys in the dish by the door with a clatter. I quickly grab the crochet blanket at my feet, pulling it up over my body and tucking it under my chin, getting into position just before Mum walks into the living room.

Immediately she pulls a face.

'What?' I ask, wiping cookie crumbs from my mouth.

'You might want to open the curtains, David,' she says, hands on hips.

'But then I won't be able to see the screen properly.'

She ignores me and marches over to the window, throwing open the curtains. The late afternoon sun floods the room, making the air look dusty. I writhe on the sofa, shielding my eyes.

'Oh for heaven's sake, David,' Mum says. 'You're not a bloody vampire.'

'I might be,' I mutter.

She tuts.

'Look,' she says, gesturing towards the window. 'It's beautiful out. Are you seriously telling me you'd prefer to lie on the sofa in the dark all day?'

'Correct.'

She narrows her eyes before perching on the sofa by my feet.

'No wonder you're so pasty,' she says, tracing her finger down the side of my bare foot. I kick her away.

'Would you rather I lie in the sun all day and get skin cancer?'

'No, David,' she says, sighing. 'What I'd *rather* is see you doing something with your summer holidays other than staying indoors watching rubbish all day. If you're not watching TV, you're holed up in your room on the computer.'

The phone rings. Saved by the bell. As Mum stands up the blanket snags on her ring. I reach to grab it but it's too late, she's already looking down at me, a quizzical expression on her face.

'David, are you wearing my nightie?'

It's the nightie Mum packed to take to the hospital when she had Livvy. I don't think she's worn it since; Mum and Dad usually sleep naked. I know this because I've bumped into them on the landing in the middle of the night enough times to be scarred for life.

'I thought it might keep me cool,' I say quickly. 'You know, like those long white dress things Arab men wear.'

'Hmmmmm,' Mum says.

'You'd better get that,' I say, nodding towards the phone.

I keep the nightie on for dinner, figuring it'll be less suspicious that way.

'You look like such a weirdo,' Livvy says, her eyes narrowing with vague disgust.

'Now, Livvy,' Mum says.

'But he does!' Livvy protests.

Mum and Dad exchange looks. I concentrate really hard on balancing peas on my fork.

8

After dinner I go upstairs. I take out the list I made at the beginning of the summer holidays and sit cross-legged on the bed with it spread out in front of me.

Things to achieve this summer by David Piper:

1. Grow my hair long enough to tie back in a ponytail
2. Watch every season of Project Runway in chronological order
3. Beat Dad at Wii Tennis
4. Teach Phil to dance so we can enter Britain's Got Talent next year and win £250,000
5. Finish my geography coursework
6. Tell Mum and Dad

I had one glorious week of being able to scrape my hair into the tiniest of ponytails. But school rules dictate boys' hair can be no longer than collar length, so last week Mum took me to the hairdresser's to have it all cut off. Points two and three were achieved with ease during the first two weeks of the break. I quickly realised four was a lost cause; Phil isn't a natural performer.

Five and six I've been putting off in turn. I've practised six plenty. I've got a whole speech prepared. I recite it in my head when I'm in the shower, and whisper it into the darkness when I'm lying in bed at night. The other day I sat my old toys, Big Ted and Mermaid Barbie, on my pillow and performed it for them. They were *very* understanding.

I've tried writing it down too. If my parents were to look hard enough they'd find endless unfinished drafts stuffed in the drawers of my desk. Last week though, I actually completed a letter. Not only that, I very nearly pushed it beneath Mum and Dad's bedroom door. I was right outside, crouched down by the thin shaft of light, listening to them mill about as they got ready for bed. All it would take was one push and it would be done; my secret would be lying there on the carpet, ready to be discovered. But in that moment, it was like my hand was paralysed. And in the end I just couldn't do it and went racing back to my room, letter still in hand, my heart pounding like crazy inside my chest.

Mum and Dad like to think they're really cool and open-minded just because they saw the Red Hot Chili Peppers play at Glastonbury once and voted for the Green Party in the last election, but I'm not so sure. When I was younger, I used to overhear them talking about me when they thought I wasn't listening. They'd speak in hushed voices and tell each other it was all 'a phase'; that I would 'grow out of it'; in exactly the same way you might talk about a child who wets the bed.

Essie and Felix know of course. The three of us tell each other everything. That's why this summer has been so hard. Without them to talk to, some days I've felt like I might burst. But Essie and Felix knowing isn't enough. For anything to happen, I have to tell Mum and Dad.

Tomorrow. I'll definitely tell them tomorrow.

Right after I've finished my geography coursework.

I climb off the bed, open my door a few centimetres and listen. Mum, Dad and Livvy are downstairs watching TV. The muffled sound of canned laughter drifts up the stairs. Although I'm pretty sure they'll stay put until the end of the programme, I place my desk chair under the door handle. Satisfied I won't be disturbed, I retrieve the small purple notebook and tape measure I keep locked in the metal box at the bottom of my sock drawer. I position myself in front of the mirror that hangs on the back of my bedroom door, pull my T-shirt over my head and step out of my jeans and underpants.

An inspection is due.

As usual, I start by pressing my palms against my chest. I will it to be soft and spongy, but the muscle beneath my skin feels hard like stone. I take the tape measure and wrap it around my hips. No change. I go straight up and down, like a human ruler. I am the opposite of Mum who is all fleshy curves – hips and bum and boobs.

Next, I stand against the doorframe and measure my height. One hundred and sixty-eight centimetres. Again, no change. I allow myself a tiny sigh of relief.

I move downwards to my penis, which I hate with a passion. I hate everything about it: its size, its colour, the way I can always feel it just *hanging* there, the way it has a complete mind of its own. I discover it has grown an entire two millimetres since last week. I check it twice, but the tape measure doesn't lie. I frown and write it down.

I move up closer to the mirror, so the glass is only a couple of centimetres away from my nose and I have to fight to stop

11

myself from going cross-eyed. First, I run my fingers over my chin and cheeks. Some days I swear I can feel stubble pushing up against my skin, sharp and prickly, but for now at least the surface remains smooth and unbroken. I pout my lips and long for them to be plumper, pinker. I have my dad's lips – thin, with a jagged Cupid's bow. Unfortunately I appear to have inherited pretty much Dad's everything. I skip over my hair (sludge brown and badly behaved, no matter how much product I use on it), eyes (grey, boring), nose (pointy-ish) and ears (sticky-outy), instead turning my head slowly until I am almost in profile, so I can admire my cheekbones. They are sharp and high and pretty much the only bit of my face I like.

Last of all I inspect my hands and feet. Sometimes I think I hate them most of all, maybe even more than my private parts, because they're always there, on show. They're clumsy and hairy and so pale they're almost see-through, as if the skin is thin pastry stretched over spidery blue veins and long bony fingers and toes. Worst of all, they're huge and getting huger. My new school shoes are two whole sizes bigger than last year's pair. When I tried them on in Clarks at the beginning of the holidays I felt like a circus clown.

I take one last look in the mirror, at the stranger looking back at me. I shiver. This week's inspection is over.

4

'Leo!' my little sister Tia calls up the stairs. I close my eyes and try to block her out. It's hot. It's been hot for days now. The thermometer that hangs in the kitchen says it's thirty-three degrees. I've got all the windows and doors open and I'm still dying. I'm lying on my twin sister Amber's bunk sucking on a raspberry ice pop. It has turned my tongue bright blue. Dunno why. The last time I checked raspberries were red.

At night I sleep on the bottom bunk because Amber reckons she gets claustrophobic, but when Amber's not around I like to hang out on her bunk. If you lie with your head at the end closest to the window, you can't see the other houses or the rubbish bins or the mad old lady from across the way who stands in her front yard and just yells for hours on end. All you can see is the sky and the tops of the trees, and if you concentrate really hard you can almost convince yourself you're not in Cloverdale at all.

'Leo!' Tia yells again.

I sigh and sit up. Tia is my little sister. She's seven and a complete pain in the neck. Mam let her have a pair of high heels for her last birthday and when she's not watching telly she clomps round the house in them, talking in an American accent.

Tia's dad is called Tony. He's in prison, doing time for handling stolen goods.

My dad is called Jimmy. I miss him.

'Leo, I'm hungry!' Tia wails.

'Then eat something!'

'We've got nothing in!'

'Tough!'

She starts to cry. It's ear splitting. I sigh and heave myself off the bunk.

I find Tia at the bottom of the stairs, fat tears rolling down her face. She's short for a seven-year-old and paperclip-skinny. As soon as she sees me her tears stop and she breaks into this big dopey smile.

She follows me into the kitchen, which is a mess; the sink piled high with dishes. I search the cupboards and fridge. Tia's right, the kitchen is bare and God knows what time Mam's going to be back. She left just before lunch, saying she was off to the bingo hall with Auntie Kerry. There's no money in the tin so I take all the cushions off the settee and check the inside of the washing machine and the pockets of all the coats hanging in the hallway. We line up the coins on the coffee table. It's not a bad haul – £4.82.

'Stay here and don't answer the door,' I tell Tia. She'll only slow me down if I take her with me.

I put my hoodie on and walk fast, my head down, sweat trickling down my back and sides.

Outside the shop there's a bunch of lads from my old school.

Luckily they're distracted, mucking around on their bikes, so I pull my hood up, fastening the zip to the top so all you can see are my eyes. I buy crumpets, Tizer, washing-up liquid and a chocolate Swiss roll that's past its best-before date.

When I get home I stick the *Tangled* DVD on for Tia and give her a pint glass of Tizer and a slice of the Swiss roll while I wash the pots and stick a couple of crumpets in the toaster. When I sit down on the settee she scampers over to me and plants a wet kiss on my cheek.

'Ta, Leo,' she says. Her mouth is all chocolaty.

'Gerroff,' I tell her. But she keeps clinging on, like a monkey, and I'm too tired to fight her off. She smells of the salt and vinegar crisps she ate for breakfast.

Later that night I put Tia to bed. Mam is still out and Amber's staying over at her boyfriend Carl's house. Carl is sixteen, a year older than us. Amber met him at the indoor ice rink in town last year. She was mucking about, trying to skate backwards and fell and hit her head on the ice. Carl looked after her and bought her a cherry flavour Slush Puppy. Amber said it was like a scene from a film. Amber's soppy like that sometimes. When she's not being soppy, she's as hard as nails.

I'm watching some stupid action film on telly with lots of guns and explosions. It's nearly finished when the security light outside the front door comes on. I sit up. I can make out shadows behind the swirly glass. Mam is laughing as she tries and fails to get her key in the lock. I hear a second laugh – a bloke's. Great. More fumbling. The door finally swings open and in they fall, collapsing on the stairs giggling. Mam lifts her head up and notices me watching. She stops giggling and clambers to her feet. She puts an unsteady hand on the doorframe and glares.

15

'What you doing up?' she asks, kicking the door shut behind her.

I just shrug. The bloke gets up too, wiping his hands on his jeans. I don't recognise him.

'All right, our kid?' he says, holding up his hand in greeting, 'I'm Spike.'

Spike has inky black hair and is wearing a battered leather jacket. He has a weird accent. When he says he's from 'here, there and everywhere', Mam starts laughing like he's said something really hilarious. She goes off to the kitchen to get him a drink. Spike sits down on the sofa and takes off his shoes, plonking his feet on the coffee table. His socks don't match.

'Who are you then?' he asks, wiggling his toes and putting his hands behind his head.

'None of your business,' I reply.

Mam comes back in, a can of Strongbow in each hand.

'Don't be so rude,' she says, handing Spike his can. 'Tell Spike your name.'

'Leo,' I say, rolling my eyes.

'I saw that!' Mam barks. She takes a slurp of her cider and turns to Spike.

'Right little so-and-so this one is. Dunno where he gets it from. Must be from his father's side.'

'Don't talk about my dad like that,' I say.

'I'll talk about him how I like, thank you very much,' Mam replies, rummaging in her handbag. 'He's a good-for-nothing bastard.'

'He. Is. Not.' I growl, separating each word.

'Oh really?' Mam continues, lighting a cigarette and taking a

16

greedy puff on it. 'Where is he then? If he's so bloody marvellous, where the bloody hell is he, Leo? Eh?'

I can't answer her.

'Exactly,' she says, taking a triumphant swig of cider.

I can feel the familiar knot in my stomach forming, my body tensing, my skin getting hot and clammy, my vision fogging. I try to use the techniques Jenny taught me; roll out my shoulders, count to ten, close my eyes, picture myself on a deserted beach, etcetera.

When I open my eyes Mam and Spike have moved on to the settee, giggling away like I'm not even in the room. Spike's hand is snaking under Mam's blouse and Mam is whispering in his ear. She notices me watching and stops what she's doing.

'And what do you think you're looking at?' she asks.

'Nothing,' I mutter.

'Then get lost will ya.'

It's not a question.

I slam the living room door so hard the entire house shakes.

5

Family legend goes that Mam's waters broke as she was waiting to collect a chicken bhuna, pilau rice and peshwari naan from the Taj Mahal Curry House on Spring Street. Family legend also goes that she was still clutching the naan when she gave birth to Amber an hour later. I took another half an hour. Auntie Kerry says I had to be dragged out with forceps. I must have known that I was better off staying where I was.

My first memory is of my dad changing my nappy. Amber reckons you can't remember stuff that far back, but she's wrong. In the memory I'm lying on the living room floor and the telly is on behind Dad's shoulder, and he's singing. It's not a proper song, just something made up and silly. He has a nice voice. It's only a short memory, just a few seconds, but it's as real as anything.

After that, the next memory I have is knocking Mam's cup of tea off the coffee table and scalding my chest. I still have the scar. It's the shape of an eagle with half of one wing missing. I was two and a half by then, and Dad was long gone. I wish I could remember more about him but I can't – that one memory is all I've got. I've tried searching for him on the internet of course, but there are hundreds of James Dentons out there, and so far I haven't found the right one.

I wonder what he'd think if he could see me now – standing in front of the bathroom mirror wearing an Eden Park School blazer over my T-shirt.

It's the following night, and the last day of the summer holidays. Mam called in sick for her shift at the launderette this morning and spent the day in bed with a 'migraine'. She must be feeling better now though, because ten minutes ago I saw her leave the house and climb into a rusty white car, Spike behind the wheel. Not that I care.

I stare at my reflection, at the smart-looking stranger staring back. It's the first time I've tried on my blazer since the beginning of the summer holidays, and it's weird how different it makes me look. There are no blazers at Cloverdale School, just yellow and navy sweatshirts that go bobbly after one wash. When I modelled the blazer for Mam she burst out laughing. 'Bloody hell, you look like a right ponce!' she said, before turning up the telly.

I straighten the lapels and relax my shoulders. I ordered the size up so it's a bit baggy on me. I don't mind though; this way I can fit a hoodie underneath. It smells different to my other clothes – expensive and new. It's burgundy with thin navy stripes and a crest on the right breast pocket with the school motto – *aequitatemque et inceptum* – stitched underneath. The other day, I went to the library and looked up what it meant on the computer. Apparently it's Latin for 'fairness and initiative'. We'll see.

Mam and I went to the school for a meeting back in the spring. Eden Park itself was exactly how I'd imagined it, all green and lush with tree-lined streets and little cafés selling organic-this and

19

homemade-that. And even though Eden Park is a state school, just like Cloverdale, the similarities stop there. Not only did the place look different that day, with its smart buildings and tidy grounds, it felt different too; clean and neat and ordered. About a million miles away from Cloverdale.

My therapist, Jenny, came with Mam and me to the meeting. Mam put on this stupid voice that I know she thinks makes her sound posh. She always uses it when she's around doctors and teachers and trying to be on her best behaviour. We met with the Head Teacher, Mr Toolan, Miss Hannah, the Head of Pastoral Support, and Mrs Sherwin, the Head of Year 11. They asked lots of questions, then me and Mam waited outside while they talked with Jenny. A few times pupils walked past us and gave us funny looks. They looked rich. I could tell by their neatly ironed uniforms and shiny hair and Hollister backpacks. Me and Mam must have stuck out like a sore thumb.

After loads more talking and questions, I was offered a place for Year 11. Jenny was really excited for me. Supposedly people move house just so they can be in the catchment area for Eden Park. Jenny reckons it'll be a 'fresh start' and 'an opportunity to make some friends'. Jenny's obsessed with me making friends. She goes on about my 'social isolation' like it's a contagious disease. After all these years she still doesn't get that social isolation is exactly what I'm after.

'Leo?'

I step out into the hallway. Tia's bedroom door is ajar as usual, so she can see the landing light.

'Leo?' she says again, louder this time. I sigh and push open her door.

Tia's room is tiny and a complete wreck, clothes and cuddly toys everywhere and crayon scribbles all over the walls. She sits cross-legged under the duvet cover she inherited from Amber. Once covered in a Flower Fairy print, it's now so faded and worn that some of the fairies are missing faces or limbs, ghostly white smudges in their place.

'What do you want?' I ask wearily.

'Will you tuck me in?'

I sigh and kneel down next to Tia's bed. She beams and shimmies into a lying-down position. Snot clings to her tiny little nostrils. I pull the duvet up under her chin and turn to go.

'That's not proper,' she whines.

I roll my eyes.

'Please, Leo?'

'For Pete's sake, Tia.'

I crouch back down and begin tucking the duvet underneath her, working all the way down her spindly little body until she looks like a mummy.

'How's that?' I ask.

'Perfect.'

'Can I go now?'

She bobs her head up and down. I get up.

'Leo?'

'What?'

'I like your jacket.'

I look down. I still have the blazer on.

'Oh yeah?'

'Yeah, it's well nice. You look really handsome. Like Prince Eric from *The Little Mermaid*.'

I shake my head. 'Ta, Tia.'

She smiles serenely and shuts her eyes. 'You're welcome.'

6

'David!' Mum yells up the stairs. 'Time to get up!'

I turn on to my stomach and pull a pillow over my head. A few more minutes pass before my bedroom door creaks open.

'Rise and shine,' Mum singsongs, creeping across the carpet and peeling back the duvet.

I snatch it back and pull it over my head, making a cave for myself.

'Five more minutes,' I say, my voice muffled.

'No way. Up. Now. I won't have you making Livvy late on her first day at big school.'

I heave myself out of bed and look in the mirror. I look awful – sweaty and pale with dark circles under my eyes and crease marks across my cheeks. I never sleep well the night before the first day back.

By 8.30 a.m. I'm sitting in the passenger seat of the car. Livvy is posing for a photograph on the doorstep while Mum weeps behind the lens. Livvy is very photogenic; everyone says so. Mum and Dad often joke her real dad's the milkman. No one *ever* makes similar jokes about my parentage.

'You're going to take after your dad,' aunts and uncles always tell me knowingly, as if it's some sort of compliment I ought to be grateful for. I don't know what they're thinking; Dad's hardly Brad Pitt.

Livvy cocks her head to one side and smiles angelically. The way the sunlight hits her, I can see the outline of her bra through her blouse. She already wears a 32A. She and Mum went shopping for it in the summer holidays, coming home with a plastic bag from Marks and Spencer, acting all giggly and secretive.

'Look after her, David!' Mum says as she drops us off outside the school gates, her eyes still wet.

As we start to walk up the drive, I place a protective hand on Livvy's shoulder. Immediately she grunts, shaking it off.

'Don't walk so close to me!' she hisses.

'But you heard Mum, I'm meant to be looking after you,' I point out.

'Well don't. I don't want people to know we're related,' she says, quickening her pace. I let her go, watching as she strides confidently towards the lower school entrance, her long hair flying out behind her.

'Nice,' I mutter to myself, recalling a time when Livvy used to follow me round the house, sweetly begging me to play with her.

I hear two voices calling my name. Immediately I grin

and spin round. Essie and Felix are heading towards me, waving madly.

Essie is tall (almost a head taller than Felix) with messy black hair that she dyes at home herself, green eyes and stupidly long legs. Beside her Felix is immaculate as usual, his fair hair combed into a neat side parting and his face tanned from the Florida sun.

I skip towards them and we collide in a messy group hug.

'When did your little sister get so fit?' Felix asks as we separate.

'Ew, don't be such a perv, she's only eleven!' I cry. At the same time Essie punches him on the shoulder, sending Felix staggering back a few steps.

'Ow!' he cries, clutching his shoulder and letting out a comedic yowl.

'Er, hello? Girlfriend? Right here?' Essie says.

Felix and Essie got together at the Christmas ball last year. I left the dance floor to go and buy a packet of crisps and a can of Coke and by the time I returned, they were chewing one another's faces off to an Enrique Iglesias song. I didn't even know they fancied each other so it all came as a bit of a surprise. Felix and Essie claim it was as much of a shock for them ('I blame Enrique,' Essie often says, usually when Felix is annoying her).

'How was Maths Camp?' I ask Felix. Felix goes every year. I can't imagine anything more hideous.

'Awesome,' he replies cheerfully.

'I missed you both so badly,' I say, as we head towards

the upper school entrance, instinctively falling into step with one another. 'My birthday party was beyond miserable without you.'

'Don't talk to me about miserable,' Essie says. 'I've been in step-monster hell for the past six weeks. Can you believe she tried to make me take my nose ring out?'

'Oh God, don't get her started,' Felix moans. 'It's all she talked about last night.'

I stop walking.

'You guys hung out last night? Why didn't you call me?'

Essie and Felix exchange looks.

'It was kind of boyfriend/girlfriend hanging out,' Essie says. 'If you know what I mean.'

'Yeah,' Felix echoes, turning a bit red and pushing his glasses up his nose. I notice his skin is peeling around his hairline.

'Oh, right,' I say. 'Never mind.'

We keep walking.

Although I'm obviously thrilled my two best friends in the entire world are in love, I still can't help but get slightly freaked out by the idea of them 'together'. I don't know if they've had sex or anything yet and I haven't asked. Which bothers me. Up to now, we've always told each other everything and all of a sudden one topic, and a pretty major one at that, is unofficially off limits. To me anyway.

This year I'm in form 10C. I get there early so I can reserve a seat near the front, as close to Mr Collins as possible, even if that means sitting next to Simon Allen, who inexplicably stinks of plasticine. At least this way I can guarantee people like Harry Beaumont and Tom Kerry won't be sitting anywhere near me. For about the thousandth time I wish I was in the same form as Essie and Felix, but they're both in 10H, next door, light years away.

Bam! The spitball strikes me hard on the back of my neck. I twist round in my seat. Harry is pretending to tie his shoelaces. Everyone around him is sniggering. I peel the spitball off my skin and flick it on to the floor where it lands with a dull splat. It's fat, moist and heavy. He's been practising.

'Hey, Freak Show!' he calls.

I pretend not to hear him. 'Freak Show' has been Harry's nickname for me for years. A lot of other kids call me it too, but Harry's the one responsible for its longevity.

'Aw, c'mon, Freak Show,' he says, coaxingly. 'That's not very polite is it? I'm making an effort to have a nice conversation with you and you've got your back turned to me.'

I sigh and twist round in my seat again. Harry has got up and is now lounging on Lexi Taylor's desk while she giggles like a hyena behind him. Lexi is Harry's current girlfriend. She thinks she's super-hot because apparently modelling bridesmaid dresses in the fashion show at the Eden Park Summer Fair last year somehow makes her Naomi Campbell.

'Was that your little sister I saw you arrive with this morning?' he asks.

'What's it to you?'

'No need to be touchy! I was only asking.'

I sigh. 'Yes, she's my sister. Why?'

'It's just that she looked, well, almost normal.'

Laughter ripples across the classroom. Harry basks in it, a slow grin spreading across his face. I try not to let my irritation show.

'So what I'm trying to work out is this,' he says. 'Which one of you is adopted?'

Mr Collins breezes into the classroom, oblivious. 'Welcome back everyone! Harry, on a chair please.'

Harry slides off the desk, smirking.

'I reckon the smart money's on you, Freak Show.'

7

Lunch time. I take a can of Coke from the fridge and put it next to the plate of lukewarm congealed macaroni cheese already on my tray.

'Well, I heard he got expelled,' a Year 11 girl with frizzy brown hair in front of me is saying.

'Who?' her friend asks.

'The new kid in 11R.'

'Expelled? What for?' someone else asks.

'I don't know. It must be something bad though. I've heard it's almost impossible to get expelled from Cloverdale.'

I've heard of Cloverdale School. It's on the other side of the city and has a reputation for being really rough and scary, always in the papers for failing its Ofsted inspection or kids trying to set fire to it.

'I know why he got expelled,' one of the boys chimes in proudly. 'Apparently he went mental in a DT lesson and chopped off the teacher's index finger with a junior hacksaw.'

There's a collective gasp. Apart from the frizzy-haired girl who says, 'I'm not surprised. You can tell he's a bit crazy, just look at his eyes.'

I follow their gaze to a boy sitting alone at a table in the far corner of the dining room. He has messy light brown hair and is glaring at a plate of chips. I'm too far away to tell if his eyes are 'crazy' or not.

'How has he ended up here, then?' someone else asks.

'I dunno. All I do know is, I'm not going to go anywhere near him,' another boy says. 'To have got expelled from Cloverdale he must be a proper maniac.'

I pay for my food and find Essie and Felix at a table in the corner. I pass the popular kids in the centre of the room, shrieking and laughing and showing off – the star attractions. Their hangers-on are eating at the surrounding tables, forming a protective barrier, leaving the more out-there groups to populate the outer tables. Over in the opposite corner, the emo kids huddle around an MP3 player, listening intently, bobbing their heads in time to the music, hair in their eyes. A few tables over, the clever, nerdy kids are passionately debating the next *Star Wars* movie.

Essie, Felix and I don't fit into any particular group. Essie reckons this is a good thing. It was Essie who came up with our name – the Non-Conformists (or the NCs for short), not that anyone ever calls us that.

'Hey, Davido,' Essie says as I slide into my seat. 'We're discussing which has more nutritional content, today's delicious macaroni cheese,' she leans in and sniffs at her plate, 'or a can of dog food.'

'I vote for the dog food,' Felix says cheerfully, his mouth full, spraying pumpkin and tahini millet ball crumbs in all directions. He's allergic to pretty much everything so his mum prepares him a macrobiotic lunch every day.

'I vote for the dog food too,' I say, unfolding a paper napkin. 'I once tasted some of Phil's Pedigree Chum and it wasn't actually all that bad.'

'You did what?' Felix says, putting down his carton of carrot juice.

'How have we not heard this story before?' Essie demands.

'Mum caught me eating from Phil's bowl one morning,' I say. 'I guess I must have just been really hungry. In my defence I was only about three at the time.'

'And this is precisely why we love you, David Piper,' Essie says. 'Pass the salt, will you?'

I can't quite pinpoint the moment Essie, Felix and I became best friends. I only know we somehow gravitated towards one another like magnets, and by the end of our first year at primary school, I couldn't imagine the world without the three of us in it together.

As I pass the salt to Essie, my eyes fall on the new boy. He's sitting two tables away, picking at his food. Up closer, he doesn't *look* crazy. In fact, he's sort of cute-looking with a snub nose, sandy brown hair falling across his forehead and the most incredible cheekbones I think I've ever seen.

I lean in.

'Hey, do either of you know anything about the new boy in 11R?'

'Only that he got expelled from Cloverdale and is meant to be a violent lunatic,' Felix says, his voice carelessly loud.

'Sssssshhhh, he might hear you!'

I peer over Felix's shoulder but the boy is still having a stare-out competition with his chips.

'I feel bad that he's all on his own,' I say. 'Should I ask him to sit with us?'

Felix raises his eyebrows. 'Did the words "violent" and "lunatic" not raise even the faintest alarm bells?'

'Oh, don't be so boring!' Essie says. 'Anyone who has got an official screw loose is more than welcome at our table. Go for it, Mother Teresa, spread some NC love.'

I hesitate, suddenly afraid.

'If you're keen, you do it,' I say.

'I don't want to scare him off,' Essie says. 'A lot of men are intimidated by strong women.'

Felix and I roll our eyes at each other.

'No, definitely best you go, David,' she continues. 'You're nice and unthreatening.'

'Gee, thanks,' I say in an American accent, pushing back my chair and making my way over to the boy's table.

'Hi,' I say, hovering at his side.

I notice a red 'free school meals' token poking out from under his tray. The boy doesn't respond.

'Er, hi?' I repeat, worried he hasn't heard me.

He sighs heavily and slowly angles his head to look up at me.

'I'm David Piper,' I say, extending my hand. 'Nice to meet you.'

The boy ignores it and takes a swig from his can of Coke instead, wiping his mouth on the sleeve of his blazer. My hand hovers awkwardly in midair. He finally looks at it before sighing again and shaking it once, firmly.

'Leo Denton,' he says gruffly.

He raises his eyes to meet mine, and I have to catch my breath for a moment, because, wow, those Year 11 kids were totally wrong. Leo's eyes aren't crazy at all; they're beautiful, hypnotic, like looking down a kaleidoscope almost – sea green with amber flecks around the pupil and just really intense, like they could see into your soul or something.

'Can I help you?' Leo asks.

I realise I'm full on staring.

'Er, yes, sorry,' I stammer, dragging my eyes away from his. 'It's just that me and my friends over there . . .'

I point over to Essie and Felix. Helpfully, Essie has plastered her top lip to her gums and Felix has flipped his eyelids inside out.

'Er, well, we were wondering if you'd like to eat lunch with us?'

I hold my breath. Leo is looking at me like I've got two heads.

'No thanks,' he says finally.

'We're not weird, honestly,' I glance back at Essie and Felix. 'Well, we are a bit . . .'

'Look, thanks, but no thanks. I'm done anyway.'

And with that, Leo pushes away his tray, picks up his can of Coke and heads for the door.

I amble back to our table.

'He wasn't interested,' I report.

'What?' Essie cries, outraged.

I shrug and sit down.

'Psychopaths do tend to be loners,' Felix muses.

'He didn't seem very psychopathic,' I point out.

'They never do,' Felix replies loftily.

I crane my neck to look out of the window, but Leo has already disappeared from view.

'Olsen alert! Olsen alert!' Essie starts to hiss.

'Where?' I say, turning my attention back to the table, instinctively sitting up straight.

'Behind you. Over by Harry's table.'

I slowly turn round in my seat. And there he is. Zachary Olsen. Otherwise known as the love of my life.

I have loved Zachary Olsen ever since we shared the same paddling pool, aged four. The fact I was once in such close proximity to his semi-naked body is sometimes too much to bear. The fact he clearly has no recollection that our semi-naked bodies ever shared a paddling pool in the first place is even worse. Zachary is everything I am not – a half-Norwegian love god complete with shaggy blond hair and tanned six-pack. He's captain of the football *and* rugby teams. He's crazily popular. He *always* has a girlfriend. He basically stands for everything we Non-Conformists claim is wrong with the world. And yet I am utterly in love with him.

Unfortunately he doesn't appear to know I'm alive.

Today he has his arm slung around Chloe Hollins's shoulder, indicating she is his current girlfriend (death to Chloe) and laughing at something Harry has just said. Even Zachary's fraternising with the enemy does little to dampen my love for him. He could probably torture kittens and rob old ladies at gunpoint and I'd still adore him.

I watch as he and Chloe saunter out of the canteen, looking totally smug and sexy. Essie reaches across and gives my hand a squeeze. Which says it all really. I am a hopeless case. In about a billion different ways.

8

My first day at Eden Park School goes more or less to plan. Apart from some Year 10 kid who tries to talk to me at lunch, no one comes near me all day. Not that I'm invisible exactly. All day kids have been staring at me. At first I can't work out why, but then I notice the way they're staring at me. They're scared. So I play up to it. I act the hard man and stare right back, and every time they chicken out first. Who cares *why* they're scared. As long as they leave me alone, I don't give a toss what they think.

The bell rings for the end of the day. The corridor is packed but as I walk down it, kids scramble to make way for me, parting like the Red Sea. It's as if I have a glowing protective shield around me, like I'm some new breed of super hero. It would actually be pretty funny if it wasn't so strange. I'm almost at the end of the corridor when this girl appears out of nowhere and bashes right into me.

Her eyes spring open in surprise and I can't help wondering what kind of idiot walks around the place with their eyes closed.

'Jesus, sorry!' she laughs, lowering the massive pair of red headphones she's wearing so they're hanging round her neck. 'I was totally not looking where I was going. Are you OK?'

She reaches out and puts her hand on my arm. When she doesn't remove it straight away I have to force her to by folding my arms. If she guesses that's what I'm doing, she doesn't show it. She has black curly hair that shoots out in all directions, and light brown eyes almost the exact same shade as her skin. Basically, she's gorgeous. I quickly chase the thought out of my head.

'It's just that I was listening to the most amazing song,' the girl continues, 'I'm literally obsessed with it. Want to hear?'

She thrusts the earphones at me.

'No thanks,' I mutter, squeezing past her, careful my body doesn't touch hers.

'Hey!' she calls after me.

Reluctantly I turn round and raise my eyes to meet hers. Her lashes are stupidly long, Disney-Princess long. I hate that I notice this.

'You're new, right?'

'Yeah, I'm new,' I say reluctantly.

She breaks into a fresh grin.

'Well in that case, welcome to Eden Park School, new boy.'

I arrive home to discover Spike's bashed-up white Peugeot parked at a funny angle outside our house, as if he's abandoned it at the scene of a crime. He stayed over again last night. This morning his Homer Simpson boxer shorts were drying on the washing line and the bathroom sink was full of black stubble. If I blurred my eyes, the hairs looked like tiny ants trying to crawl out of the plughole.

36

I push open the front door. Spike is sitting on the settee with Mam perched on his knee. He's whispering in her ear and she's giggling like a little girl. His hand is on her bum.

I slam the door shut. It makes the two of them jump. Mam glares at me and straightens her mini skirt.

She's always going on about how she's as skinny now as she was when she was fifteen, and insists on wearing the skimpiest of clothes to prove it. It's her eyes that give the game away – dead and tired, like life's sucked all the sparkle right out of them.

'All right, mate?' Spike says over her shoulder. He takes in my blazer and lets out a whistle. 'Bloody hell, what are you wearing kid? You go to Hogwarts or something?'

I ignore him and wander into the kitchen. I open the biscuit tin. It's empty apart from half a soggy custard cream.

'Excuse me, Spike's talking to you,' Mam barks after me.

'It's the Eden Park School uniform,' I say, replacing the lid.

'Eden Park, eh? Very swish,' Spike replies. 'Clever clogs, are you?'

I shrug.

'Just don't go getting ideas above your station,' Mam says. 'Just because you're wearing a fancy blazer it don't mean you're above us.'

'Like I would dare,' I say.

'What did you say?' she asks sharply.

'Nothing. Can I go now?'

'Please do, you miserable little sod.'

I find Amber sitting on her bunk, brushing her clip-in hair extensions.

'Why aren't you round Carl's?' I ask.

'Argument,' she says. 'I found a load of texts on his phone from some tart from the ice rink.'

'Oh.'

Carl and Amber have a massive argument at least once a fortnight.

I sniff. The room smells rank – of chemicals and mouldy biscuits.

'Bloody hell, Amber, it stinks in here!'

'Keep your hair on, it's only fake tan,' she says.

Amber reckons she'd rather die than be 'all gross and pale'. When I was a kid I used to tan in the summer, but my legs haven't seen the sun in for ever and these days they're so white they're almost fluorescent.

'Well it smells nasty,' I tell her, wrinkling my nose.

'Soz,' she replies breezily.

'So how was school?' she asks as I hang up my blazer and take off my tie. I drop to the floor and start to do my daily press-ups, banging them out fast.

'All right.'

'Are all the kids well posh?'

'Some are.'

'Do they all have names like Tarquin and Camilla?' she asks, putting on a posh voice.

'Not really.'

'Did you make any friends?'

She's relentless. I pause mid press-up to look up at her.

'You're as bad as Jenny.'

'Well, did you?'

38

I think of the girl I saw in the corridor this afternoon, the one wearing the headphones.

'Nah,' I say. 'I'm only there for a year. No point.'

Amber makes a face, but doesn't push it. I flip onto my back and start to do my stomach crunches. I hear the bathroom door opening and closing and the shower being cranked on. A few seconds later Spike starts singing an old Elvis song. When he goes for the top notes he sounds like a strangled cat.

I crawl over to the wall and give it a thump.

'Shurrup!' I yell.

'Oh, leave him be,' Amber says with a yawn.

'You're joking aren't you?'

'He seems harmless enough.'

'He's a tool, Amber.'

'He's not that bad. Tia likes him.'

'Tia likes everyone.'

'He's better than the last one at least,' Amber points out.

'Not hard,' I snort.

Mam's last boyfriend did a runner with our telly. But then Mam's boyfriends always do a runner eventually. She'll drive Spike away before too long, just like she did Dad. Not that I'd care if Spike did one. Dad is the only one I care about.

9

My first lesson after lunch on Tuesday is English, one of my least favourite subjects. I prefer subjects with wrong or right answers, formulas and rules.

I get there early, choosing a desk next to the window about halfway back. I sit down and begin to unpack my stuff on the desk.

'Hey, do you have a pen I can borrow? Mine has totally just leaked all over me!'

I look up. It's her. The girl with the headphones, sitting at the desk right in front of me. She's twisted round in her seat so her elbows are resting on my desk, her chin cupped in her hands.

'So, do you?' she asks.

'Do I what?' I ask stupidly.

She rolls her eyes and laughs. 'Do you have a pen?' she asks again, separating each word for me.

'Oh yeah, course I do, hang on.'

I fumble in my pencil case, trying to find the least chewed pen I can. I feel her eyes on me as I hand over a black biro.

'Thanks, new boy! Oh God, how rude am I? I haven't introduced myself properly. I'm Alicia Baker,' she says, offering her hand for me to shake. 'Excuse the inky hands.'

'I'm Leo Denton,' I say, shaking her hand once then dropping it.

'Oh, I know who you are,' she says.

The teacher, Miss Jennings, claps her hands to get our attention. Alicia smiles at me before turning round to face the front of the class.

Shit.

I'm not here to meet girls. Girls let you down. They trick you, manipulate you. Girls can't be trusted. Fact. But at the same time I can't ignore this strange feeling in my belly, a bit like when I used to dive from the ten-metre board at the swimming baths. As Miss Jennings takes the register, Alicia turns round and sneaks another look at me over her shoulder. I look away fast, pretending I haven't seen her and fix my eyes on the clock above Miss Jennings's head, so hard my vision goes all blurry.

I blink. Miss Jennings is saying my name.

'Denton? Leo Denton?' she asks, frowning, her eyes searching the room.

'Er, yeah, here, miss,' I say, raising my hand. Half the class turn round in their seats to look at me.

'Stay awake please, Mr Denton,' she says through pursed lips, unimpressed, before continuing down the register.

The rest of the lesson is taken up with handing out books, filling in forms, listening to Miss Jennings talk. I try really hard to concentrate, focusing on Miss Jennings's skinny red lips moving like my life depends on it.

The bell finally rings. As I'm packing up my things, I can feel

41

Alicia watching me. I look up. She's smiling again. She has a dimple in each cheek. Her teeth are crazy white. I really wish she wouldn't.

'Laters, daydreamer,' she says, grinning as she puts her headphones on before linking arms with some blonde girl and gliding out of the classroom.

At lunch time I can't face sitting in the canteen so I buy a takeaway sandwich instead and eat it on the steps outside the science block. It's quiet here, away from the football pitch and other main lunch time hangouts. It's also overlooked by the staff room so I can relax knowing no one would dare mess with me here. I finish my sandwich fast. Our entire family wolfs our food down like we might never eat again. I wonder whether speed-eating is in our DNA and if Dad is the same.

I look over my shoulder. Apart from a couple of goth kids sitting at the very top of the steps, there's no one around. I take my wallet from my pocket and slide out the photograph of Dad.

It's a full-length shot of him standing next to a red Ford Fiesta. He must have just finished washing it because it's really shiny and there's a bucket of soapy water at his feet. I wish it was at a different angle because then I might be able to read the number plate, but the photo was taken side-on, with Dad leaning up against the passenger window. He has his arms folded across his chest and is grinning proudly at the camera. He has good teeth – white and straight. I must take after him because Mam's got horrible teeth, all crooked and yellow from a lifetime of fags. He's tall with sandy brown hair, just like mine. It's too far away to really see whether I've got his eyes or nose or anything else. On the back there's a date written in Mam's scratchy handwriting. Seven months before Amber and I were born.

One New Year, tipsy on cheap white wine, Auntie Kerry let it slip that Dad was a carpenter. I like the idea of that, of him working with his hands and making beautiful things from scratch. Kerry also let it slip that she reckons he might have gone down south to live by the sea, but no one seems to know this for sure. Any time I ask questions, people clam up or get angry and the subject is always closed before it even gets started.

Behind me, the two kids are getting up. I shove the photo back into my wallet as they pass.

10

It's Friday morning. English again. As I walk up the aisle I try not to look at Alicia. I'm almost at my seat when I make the mistake of glancing down at her. And there she is, smiling away again, totally oblivious to what it's doing to my head, messing with it.

Miss Jennings dims the lights. We're watching a film version of *Twelfth Night*, the play we're studying this term. At first I try my hardest to concentrate on the film, but after a few minutes I find myself drifting and my eyes staring at the back of Alicia's head. She usually wears her hair down but today it's up and I can see her neck. I imagine kissing it. The thought makes me feel hot all over. I try to wipe it from my brain, like it never existed. I take a deep breath and try to keep my eyes on the screen.

Outside it's raining and the classroom is warm. I lay the back of my hand against the window. The condensation feels good – cool and wet. When I take my hand away, it leaves a print behind. Next to it I draw a circle with my index finger. Miss Jennings looks up from her marking. I pull my damp hand into my lap and wipe it on my trousers.

A second later Alicia twists sideways in her seat and adds eyes and a smiley face to my circle. Before I can stop myself I'm leaning forward, and adding sticky-out ears and a tuft of hair. And I can just tell, by the way the muscles in her neck contract, that Alicia is smiling.

'Ahem?'

I look up. Miss Jennings is staring right at us, her eyebrows raised. Alicia lets out a tiny giggle. I fight my lips from curling into a smile and know I have to pull myself together.

For the rest of the lesson I force myself to look at the screen and nowhere else.

By the time the bell rings, my and Alicia's smiley face has begun to run and slide down the window, the eyes all droopy, the smile now a frown. As I pack away my things, I can sense her watching me. Distracted, I drop my pen. I bend down to pick it up, but Alicia is faster.

'Here,' she says, pressing it into my hand.

'Thanks,' I reply, jamming the pen into my bag.

I wait for her to move off, but she doesn't. Instead she perches on the edge of my desk, swinging her legs and continuing to watch me.

'Leo?' she says.

'Yeah?' I reply, zipping up my bag and not meeting her eyes.

'Can I ask you a favour?'

I swallow hard.

'What kind of favour?' I ask slowly.

'It's just a tiny one, I promise,' she says, biting her lower lip. 'It's just that I've entered this singing competition online and the winner gets the chance to meet a team of top record execs, but I need way more votes if I'm going to make it through to the final. So, I was just wondering whether you'd vote for me? I've been pestering everyone else on Facebook and Twitter, but I couldn't find you.'

My skin prickles as I picture Alicia searching for me online.

'I think it's really cool by the way,' she adds.

I frown.

'That you're not on Facebook, I mean,' she continues. 'I wish I wasn't on there a lot of the time. It can do your head in sometimes, you know?'

I don't answer her.

'You, er, sing then?' I ask instead.

'Oh, yeah,' she says, looking at her feet, shy suddenly. 'I write my own stuff too, and post videos online, you know, on YouTube and stuff.'

'Oh, right, cool,' I murmur.

'So you'll vote for me then?'

'What do I have to do?'

'Give me your hand.'

Before I can say or do anything, she's grabbing my hand and turning it over in hers. Her skin is soft and her nails are short and neat, and painted with clear polish. I let my hand go limp and hope she doesn't clock my own bitten-down nails. She scrawls on the back of my hand with a biro, the nib of the pen dragging at my skin. When she's done, she pauses. I have to fight the urge to yank my hand away. She looks up.

'Freckly hands,' she says.

'Eh?'

'I've always wanted freckles,' she continues. 'My gran reckons they're kisses from the sun. Cute huh?'

I shrug.

Alicia taps the back of my hand with the pen.

'Well, that's the website. I'm listed as Alicia B.'

'Alicia B,' I repeat.

'To vote for me, you just have to click on my name and watch my video. I'm about halfway down I think.'

'OK.'

'Amazeballs. Thank you, Leo, I really appreciate this.'

It's only then she lets go of my hand.

After school, instead of going straight home, I head to the computer lab. Apart from one other kid and the teacher on duty, it's empty.

I take a set of headphones from the stack at the front and sit down at one of the monitors in the back row. I type the web address printed on my hand into the URL bar. I scroll down until I find Alicia B and click on her name.

Alicia's face flashes up on the screen. She's sitting on the end of a bed cross-legged, a guitar on her lap and her face frozen in a smile. I press play.

'Hi! I'm Alicia B,' she says directly to the camera. 'This is a song I wrote called "Deep Down with Love". I really hope you like it and if you do, that you'll vote for me! Thanks!'

She begins to sing. And she's amazing, better than anyone on *The X Factor* or *Britain's Got Talent*. I watch the video a couple more times, even though I'm only allowed to vote once. I'm about to go when I remember her talking about posting stuff on YouTube, so I type in Alicia B and up come loads and loads more videos. Some are of her singing songs by people like Adele or Leona Lewis. But it's her own music I like the best, all these songs with really sad lyrics about love going wrong. At the end of each one she always waits a few beats before breaking into a big smile to remind you it's all pretend.

Because I'm pretty sure Alicia Baker is the sort of girl who breaks hearts, not the other way round.

When I get home, Spike is in the kitchen reading the newspaper and eating toast.

'What are you doing here?' I ask.

He has his feet up on the table. One of his socks has a hole in the toe.

'Hello to you too,' he says cheerily.

'Where's Mam?'

'She's got a shift down at the launderette then she's having her nails done with your auntie Kerry. They're having a girly night.'

'That still doesn't explain why you're here,' I say.

'I offered to pick Tia up from school and make you kids some dinner.'

'Right.'

I open the bread bin; it's empty. I glance over at Spike's plate. There must be five slices on there at least.

''Ere, have some of this,' Spike says quickly, noticing my frown. 'It'll keep you going.'

'No thanks.'

'Don't be daft. I can't eat all this anyway. What's yours is mine, our kid.'

'I'm not "your kid",' I say under my breath.

I go into the living room and turn on the telly. It's one of those programmes about people looking for houses abroad. I can feel Spike watching me. I look over my shoulder. He's got up from the kitchen table and is leaning against the doorframe, balancing the plate of toast on his palm.

'Bloody lovely,' he says, nodding towards the screen. 'Ever been to Spain, Leo?'

'No.'

'Fantastic place,' he says. 'Although I always say you can't beat Thailand. Bloody beautiful country. The nicest people too. God, the times I had in Thailand, kiddo,' he says, letting out a low whistle. 'People are always telling me I should write a book about my travels, you know.'

'Then why don't you?'

I don't usually stick around to listen to Spike but when I do, this is how he talks. Like he's had all these grand adventures; Britain's answer to Indiana Jones, only he never goes into any detail, he's always really vague about it, as if he's making it up as he goes along.

The other day he left his wallet on the coffee table and I had a quick nose through it. His driving licence says his name is Kevin. So much for Spike. The address on it is somewhere in Manchester. Apart from that there was a bit of cash, some receipts and a folded-up strip of photos of him and Mam taken in one of those passport photo booths. In the first shot they were grinning at the camera, in the second doing bunny ears behind one another's heads, in the third and fourth, they were snogging. Rank.

Spike comes to sit next to me.

'Slice?' he offers. 'Go on.'

The toast drips with butter. It smells amazing. In spite of myself I take a slice, but only cos I'm starving. I rip it in half and stuff the smaller piece into my mouth, swallowing it down whole. It scrapes the back of my throat.

Spike takes a bite and munches for a few seconds, his lips smacking against one another.

'Actually, Leo, I'm glad your Mam's out tonight. I think we got off on the wrong foot maybe. This might be a good chance for us to have a proper chat, you know, man to man.'

'Thanks, but no thanks,' I say, swallowing my other bit of toast in one go and standing up.

''Ere, Leo, wait, will ya?'

I turn. Spike is looking up at me. With his floppy hair and droopy eyes, he reminds me a bit of the spaniel Kerry had for a bit, until it weed in her underwear drawer and she took it to the RSPCA.

'I'm really keen on your mam, you know that don't you, kiddo?' he says.

I just shrug. The idea of anyone being into my disaster zone of a mother seems pretty unlikely to me.

'She's a special lady, Leo, and I know it's early days and that, but if things work out, and I hope they do, I'm going to do right by you and your sisters. I'm not like the others, I'm not going to bugger off the minute things get a bit rough.'

'Whatever,' I say, looking out the window. 'I'm fifteen. In a few years, I'll be out of here anyway.'

'Of course, mate. I'm just saying, that's all. I know it must be hard for you and Amber, not having a dad around and that.'

I spin round. 'Keep my dad out of this. You don't know anything about him.'

50

'Now steady on, kiddo, I might know more than you think,' Spike says, holding up his hands.

'You know bugger all,' I spit, heading for the door.

'Leo,' Spike calls. 'Oh, come back, mate! Leo!'

I slam the front door behind me.

As I stomp across the garden I hear one of the upstairs windows open and Tia's thin little voice calling my name. I ignore it and keep walking.

I know exactly where I'm going.

I'm heading for the old Cloverdale baths.

It's still light when I arrive so I lie on my back on the bottom of the empty pool with my hoodie propped under my head as a pillow. Above me, the fading sunlight shines through the glass roof and warms my face. Already I feel a bit calmer. I spread my fingers out. The tiles beneath me feel cool and sort of damp, which is odd because there hasn't been any water in here for a couple of years now. It still smells of chlorine though. I like breathing it in, taking big gulps and letting it fill up my lungs and nostrils.

When they announced they were going to close down the Cloverdale swimming baths a few years ago, everyone made a big fuss and signed a petition, but it did no good; the council went ahead and closed them anyway. They're building a new leisure centre about a mile away apparently, with a gym and café and Zumba classes. It won't be the same though.

I used to swim here when I was a kid. On sunny days like today, you'd get blinded doing the backstroke. But I liked it best when it was raining. I used to love how it got really dark and the water would thunder on the roof and you could imagine you were swimming down the Amazon in the middle of some tropical storm.

51

Gav used to bring me and Amber here on a Saturday morning while Mam stayed in bed and slept off her hangover. Gav was Mam's boyfriend at the time. He taught us to swim in the shallow end – backstroke and front crawl. Amber never liked it much. She didn't like getting her hair wet and would cough and splutter every time she got water in her mouth. But I loved it. Gav used to say I was a natural, a proper water baby.

I liked Gav. He was one of the better ones. Of course he was too soft and let Mam get on at him all the time, until one day he must have finally had enough because he left the house in the morning and never came back.

Even though I haven't been in the water for five years now, I miss the way swimming made me feel – calm and in control. I miss the muffled sound of voices when my head was underneath the water. Sometimes I think life would be about a thousand times easier if I could do everything under water, with no one bothering me, everyone's words distorted and far away, and me just under the surface, fast and untouchable.

As I lie there, Spike's words keep echoing around my head: 'I might know more than you think.' Part of me wishes I'd stayed and asked him what he meant. But then Spike would only have Mam's story and who knows what crap she's been telling him.

No, the only person who can really tell me the truth is long gone.

11

At lunch time on Monday, the canteen is packed, the majority prepared to put up with the stench of boiled cabbage and burnt parsnips in exchange for warmth. Essie, Felix and I look over at Leo who is wolfing down a plate of chips.

'I wonder where he goes?' I ponder, watching as he deposits his empty tray and heads for the door.

'To howl at the moon?' Essie suggests.

'Ha bloody ha.'

'Why do you care anyway?' she asks.

Through the glass, I watch as Leo strides across the play-ground. He doesn't wear a coat and I can see his breath in the air.

'He must be freezing,' I murmur, frowning and craning my neck as he disappears round the corner. The weather turned over the weekend. According to the newspaper it's set to be the coldest September on record since the 1940s.

'Who are you, his mother?' Essie says.

Essie is in a horrible mood because she's just found out her mum is going skiing for Christmas, leaving Essie and her younger brother to spend the holidays with their dad and his wife again.

'I was just speculating,' I mutter, poking at my food with my fork.

'Did I tell you he's in my maths class?' Felix asks.

'Are you serious?' I say.

I can't help but be surprised that Leo is in the advanced class too. Immediately I feel ashamed for judging him so quickly. I mentally add 'good at maths' to the irritatingly sparse list of facts I know about him, made all the more irritating because I haven't quite worked out why I'm so interested in the first place.

'What's he like in it?' I ask.

'No wielding of weapons so far,' Felix says. 'In fact, he hardly says a word. He can obviously do the work though.'

'I can't believe you didn't tell me sooner,' I say.

'What is it with you and this kid?' Essie asks. 'You're like fascinated with him.'

'No I'm not. I just find him interesting, that's all. Don't you?'

'Moderately,' Essie says with a yawn.

'You're just annoyed he didn't jump at the chance to eat lunch with us that time,' I say.

'No, I'm not, although based on that alone, the boy clearly has no taste.'

She narrows her eyes at me. 'You don't fancy him do you?'

'Just because I find someone interesting does not mean I fancy them.'

'It's OK if you do. I'm just surprised, that's all. I didn't think bad boys were your type. Poor Zachary,' she says, sighing, 'ousted by the new boy.'

'I do not fancy Leo Denton,' I say, probably a little too loudly because the girls sitting at the next table peer over their shoulders at us with rare interest.

'I don't fancy him,' I repeat, in a low hiss.

'OK, OK,' Essie says, holding up her hands in mock-surrender. 'I believe you.'

'Thank you,' I say.

'Although thousands wouldn't . . .' she adds, smiling wickedly.

I don't see Leo again until after school. As Mum drives home past the bus stop, I spot him slumped against the shelter, his hands shoved in his pockets, kaleidoscope eyes staring out into space. It's so strange, because the feeling I get when I look at him is totally different to how I feel when I see Zachary around school. I don't have butterflies or feel like I'm about to vomit. I'm still capable of speech. I don't turn the colour of a tomato. And yet I definitely feel something. I just haven't worked out what the *thing* is yet, and it's driving me mad.

Every evening when he gets home from work, Dad sits down in his favourite armchair and reads the newspaper while drinking a cup of milky tea. Today I position myself on the sofa opposite him and pretend to study my French vocabulary for Madame Fournier's test tomorrow morning. I'm pretending because what I'm really doing is watching Dad's face for clues – a telltale raise of the eyebrows, a furrow of the brow, perhaps a smile; some sort of hint of disapproval or otherwise. Because on page twenty-three of the newspaper there is an article about a teenage girl in America who has just been elected homecoming queen at her school. I'm not really sure what a homecoming queen does, apart from wear a crown and sash, ride in a parade and wave at people. But that's not the bit of the story I'm interested in. Because the girl in the article, in her glittery evening gown and high heels, was born a boy.

As he reads, Dad's face remains frustratingly unchanged.

I peek over the top of my vocab list as he takes yet another noisy slurp of tea, and leisurely turns the page.

'Anything interesting?' I ask casually.

'Not really,' Dad replies with a yawn.

After half an hour he's finished. He sets the newspaper down on the arm of the chair, and trots off to the kitchen to rinse his mug. As soon as he is out of the room, I swipe the newspaper and run upstairs, two at a time, slamming my bedroom door behind me.

My bedroom is my sanctuary. Last year, for my thirteenth birthday, Mum and Dad let me paint it any colour I liked. The shade I really wanted was a gorgeous hot pink, but I was too afraid to ask for it. After much thought I ended up going for a deep red instead, which, according to Essie anyway, is very 'womb-like'. Dad prefers to refer to my bedroom as 'the cave', in a deep gravelly voice he thinks is hilarious. My walls are decorated with framed prints, mostly black-and-white shots of New York City, or vintage film posters, and photo collages of Essie, Felix and me through the ages, the three of us changing remarkably little, except perhaps for Essie's ever-evolving hair colour.

I turn on the fairy lights that loop their way around the entire room, and clamber on to my bed, spreading the newspaper out in front of me on the duvet. I turn to page twenty-three and let out a sigh. The page is dominated by a photograph of the beaming homecoming queen; black hair cascading down her tanned shoulders. She is officially beautiful. My finger traces the contours of her face and the curves of her body in its sparkling dress. According to the article she is sixteen. She looks older, twenty-one maybe. Could I look like that in two years? I try to imagine myself on the school stage, wearing a glittering ball dress and smiling serenely as I wave down at my cheering classmates, Zachary (crowned homecoming king, naturally) on my arm, gazing at me adoringly. But the image fails to form properly in my head. It feels silly and fake, like a half-hearted game of Let's Pretend.

Taking a pair of scissors from my desk, I carefully cut out the article. Lying on my stomach, I reach under my bed and pull out my bulging scrapbook.

A tenth birthday gift from a distant great-aunt, my scrapbook represents four years of careful curation. At the front, the pages are populated with postcards, sweet wrappers and cinema tickets glued neatly on to its black pages. After a while I started gluing in anything I found interesting or beautiful

– a peacock feather collected on a school trip to Newstead Abbey; a tissue imprinted with a pink lipstick pout, swiped from Mum's dressing table; pictures of beautiful women snipped out of magazines. My favourites are the old film stars – Elizabeth Taylor dripping with diamonds, Marilyn Monroe on a beach in a gleaming white swimsuit, Audrey Hepburn wearing long black gloves and pearls. These days, my movie stars mingle with clippings from newspapers and medical journals, statistics and tables, facts and figures.

I open the scrapbook on the most recent page. It smells sweet from the perfume sample I glued in last week. I let my eyes fall shut and bury my nose in the pages for a moment, inhaling deeply. On the opposite page I carefully glue the article into place, smoothing it down so there are no bubbles or creases.

I glance at my phone. Twenty minutes until dinner. Just enough time for an inspection. I shove my desk chair under the handle of my door and turn on some music to make the process more bearable. I pick out Lady Gaga's *Born This Way* album, cranking up the volume to maximum.

I'm finished and reaching for my underpants when the door handle begins to rattle.

'David?' Livvy calls over the music. 'Let me in!'

'Hang on!' I yell, pulling on my bathrobe, tying the belt tightly round my stomach. I turn off the music and remove the chair from under the door handle. As the door begins to open I realise my inspection notebook is lying open on my pillow. In a panic I pick it up and chuck it into my school bag before leaping back into the centre of the room.

Livvy enters cautiously, wrinkling her nose as she spots me standing ramrod straight, wearing my bathrobe hours before bedtime.

'Didn't you hear us yelling you to come for dinner?'

'Obviously not.'

'Why did you have something up against the door?' she asks, frowning at my desk chair.

'I was changing.'

'Like any of us are interested in watching you get changed.'

I make a face. She returns an uglier one.

'David! Livvy!' Mum calls from downstairs. 'Dinner's getting cold.'

I move to go but Livvy stays put, her eyes narrow with suspicion.

'Go on then,' I say, gently nudging her towards the door. 'You heard what Mum said, dinner's getting cold. I'll be down in a sec.'

Reluctantly, she lets me usher her out of the room and onto the landing.

12

That night I fall asleep on my bed surrounded by my French notes. I have feverish dreams where I find myself in the body of Madame Fournier; only I can't speak French, and have to hide in the stationery cupboard.

I oversleep the next morning, only waking up when Phil jumps on my bed, slobbering all over the duvet. In a stupor I stumble about the bedroom, pulling on my school uniform, trying to tame my sticky-up hair, throwing books and folders into my school bag, before clattering down the stairs and into the car, my eyes still sticky with sleep.

The morning doesn't get much better. First period is PE, a subject at which I do not excel. It's the only lesson I share with Zachary and hardly a chance to shine, although an excellent opportunity to look at his legs. This term we are doing rugby. Ordinarily my and Felix's tactic (Felix too is terrible at sports, not to mention almost completely blind without his glasses) is to keep as far away from the ball and the other players as possible. But today an overly enthusiastic trainee teacher is covering the lesson and forces us into the scrum. The low point is Simon Allen sitting on my head.

In French the test goes spectacularly badly. When I hand in my paper at the end of the lesson, Madame Fournier is already frowning, as if she can predict my failure.

In maths we are studying standard form. Mr Steele may as well be speaking Elvish for all I understand. Unable to keep up, I end up spending most of the lesson doodling. It takes me by surprise when I realise the hunched-over figure I've drawn in the corner of my page looks more than a bit like Leo Denton.

By lunch time I am thoroughly exhausted. Harry, Tom and Lexi are behind me in the canteen queue, Harry and Tom taking turns to flick my ears, making Lexi squeal with laughter every time.

'Very mature guys,' I say, trying to sound as bored as possible.

'Oh c'mon, lighten up, Freak Show,' Harry says. 'It's just a bit of fun.'

He flicks me again on the right earlobe, hard. I flinch. The three of them crack up laughing.

I fix my eyes on the back of the head of the kid in front of me and concentrate on staying very still, trying to resist the urge to abandon the queue altogether. Occasionally, if I ignore him for long enough, Harry gets bored and moves on to a fresh victim.

'Where are your friends? Beauty and the geek? No, wait,

hang on, let me rephrase that, this is Essie Staines we're talking about after all; where are the mutant and the geek?' he crows.

'What did you call my friends?' I ask, annoyance propelling me round to face him.

'The mutant and the geek,' Harry replies innocently. 'Got a problem with that, Freak Show?'

I bite down hard on my lip.

'So where are they? Off mutating somewhere?'

'They're at band practice,' I say.

'Oooooh, band practice,' Harry says in a lisping high voice.

I turn away from him. Up ahead the dinner ladies are ladling out food in what seems like slow motion.

'God, this queue is killing me,' Lexi says, sighing. 'Entertain me, Harry?'

'Isn't being in my company entertainment enough?' Harry asks. Lexi giggles.

'Hey, how about a quick round of Snog, Marry, Throw Off a Cliff?' Tom suggests.

'Go on then,' Lexi says. 'Anything to break this tedium.'

'Let me go first, I've got an amazing one for Lex.'

'Go on then, Tommy-boy,' Harry says. 'Do your worst.'

'OK,' Tom says. 'So here are your choices, Lexi. Mr Wilton . . .'

'Gross!' Lexi squeals. Mr Wilton teaches maths and is at least seventy.

'Mr Stacey . . .' Tom continues.

Lexi squeals again. Mr Stacey teaches English and is a

complete perv. There's a rumour he tried to get Caitlin Myers drunk on the Year 12 trip to Toulouse last term.

'And finally, 10C's very own . . .' I hear Tom perform a drum roll on his thighs. '. . . David Piper.'

Lexi dissolves into a fresh wave of giggles.

'Genius!' Harry exclaims, high fiving Tom. 'Pure genius, mate!'

I try to concentrate on the menu, debating sausage and mash versus vegetarian lasagne.

'So c'mon then, Lex, the man has spoken, what's the verdict?' Harry says.

'Easy,' Lexi replies. 'I'd snog Mr Stacey, cos at least you'd know he'd be into it, I'd marry Mr Wilton, cos he might die soon and I'd get all his money in the will, and I'd throw Freak Show off the cliff.'

'Aw, poor Freak Show!' Harry says.

'Like I care,' I say under my breath, reaching for a bottle of water.

'What did you say?' Harry asks.

I place the bottle on my tray, take a deep breath and turn all the way round to face him.

'Do you honestly think I care whether Bubble Brain here wants to throw me off a cliff or not?'

Tom stifles a giggle.

'What did you call me?' Lexi asks, her face suddenly bright red.

'Bubble Brain,' I say, sounding about a thousand times more confident than I feel. There's a line with Harry and I have a feeling I'm teetering dangerously on the edge of it.

'Harry, are you going to let him speak to me like that?' Lexi demands, pouting.

Harry walks round me in a slow circle. I can feel my heartbeat speed up. He stops behind me, his body pressed up against mine, his chin resting on my shoulder. I can feel his breath warm on my cheek. It smells of cigarettes masked with polo mints.

'Apologise to my girlfriend,' he growls in my ear.

I consider my options. I could, of course, do what Harry has asked, and apologise to Lexi. This would probably be the most sensible option in the long run. However, it would also haunt me for days. I'd wake up in the middle of the night in a cold sweat thinking of all the kick-ass things I *could* have said. Alternatively, I could channel my inner-Essie and reel off the long list of Lexi's other 'attributes' in addition to being a bubble brain. This would be the most satisfying option but potentially very dangerous indeed. What I don't consider is what I actually end up doing, possibly the most dangerous option of all.

'I'm waiting, Freak Show,' Harry whispers, his breath tickling my ear.

I jerk my shoulder upwards, the bone connecting with Harry's jaw with a loud crack. I spin round. Harry has both hands clasped over his mouth, his eyes bulging with shock.

'You made him bite his tongue, you total freak!' Lexi cries, rushing forward and putting her arms round Harry. He shakes her off and charges at me. I stagger a few steps backwards, hesitating before pushing him back. I must catch him off guard because he loses his footing and goes stumbling into a screeching Lexi. He straightens up and pushes me again, harder this time, his eyes flashing angrily. The force of the push sends me flying into the kids behind me. My backpack drops from my shoulder and falls to the floor. I bend down to pick it up, but Tom gets there first, scooping his foot underneath it and kicking it to Harry who proceeds to dribble it round in a circle.

'Beaumont, don't be such a child,' a Year 11 girl says.

For a second I think Harry is going to listen to her because he stops and picks up the bag. As he moves toward me, I hold out my hands to take it from him. But at the last second a huge grin spreads across his face and he chucks it over my head to Tom instead. As it's sailing through the air as if in slow motion, I remember.

My inspection notebook is in there.

Panic floods my chest.

'Give it back,' I say to Tom.

'Give it back,' he imitates in a high-pitched squeak.

'You could at least ask nicely,' Harry says.

'Give it back, please!' I say, urgency creeping in to my voice.

'Now that's much better,' Harry says. 'But you know what, Freak Show? We're not done yet.'

He chucks the backpack to Lexi this time, who shrieks with delight before throwing it to Tom.

'Look, just give it back!'

I'm yelling now. But they keep throwing and I'm piggy in the middle, jumping helplessly. Tom throws the backpack to Harry. It arches high over my head. I reach for it, my fingers just grazing the shoulder straps, before it lands in Harry's arms. Instead of throwing it back to Tom, he holds it to his chest, rocking it like a newborn baby, a fresh grin on his face.

'You know what I think? That the lady doth protest too much,' he says, slowly undoing the zip.

No, no, no.

'Harry,' I say in a low whisper. 'I'm begging you, just give it back.'

'You're begging me, are you?' he says. 'How very, very interesting.'

Not taking his eyes off mine, he turns the backpack upside down. The contents clatter out. My pencil case springs open, pens and pencils scattering in all directions. Half a bottle of water comes tumbling out after it, a packet of chewing gum, my keys, books and folders, paper floating innocently to the ground like over-sized confetti. And finally, my purple notebook. I drop to my knees to pick it up but Harry is one step ahead of me, snatching it up in one swift movement.

'Now what do we have here?' he announces to the growing audience. 'Does Freak Show keep a diary? Dear Diary, why am I such a weirdo loser?' he recites in a high voice.

More and more kids are gathering to watch. I look around for a teacher or dinner lady, but I can't see anything over the heads of the small crowd that circles us.

Including Zachary Olsen.

Suddenly I feel very dizzy.

'Give it a rest, Harry,' someone says, possibly the Year 11 girl again. But Harry's on a roll. He's having too much fun to even consider quitting now. He opens the notebook at random. His eyes dart down the page, widening with excitement, like he can't quite believe his luck.

'Harry, please,' I say, glancing sideways at Zachary who is frowning slightly. But it's useless; nothing's going to stop Harry now.

'Guys, guys, listen to this!' he cries. 'Eighth March. Height – one metre, sixty-five centimetres, Adam's apple – small but visible,' he looks up at me, shaking his head. 'What the hell is this, Freak Show?'

I lunge towards him, trying to make a grab for the notebook, but Tom gets hold of my arms, pinning them behind my back.

'Get off me!' I yell, twisting against him and kicking my legs. One of my kicks connects with his left shin. He swears under his breath and wraps his arms all the way round my chest instead, tight, so I can barely breathe. He's taller than me, and broadly built.

'Pubic hair – coarser, more wiry!' Harry continues to crow. 'Bloody hell, listen to this! Penis length – six and a half centimetres!'

There's an explosion of laughter. I'm screaming now, at the top of my lungs, thinking maybe if I make enough noise I can drown Harry out. At one point I think I can hear someone telling him to stop, but over the din I can't be sure.

'Shutupshutupshutup!' I chant, my eyes squeezed shut. Perhaps if I don't open them I can pretend this is all a horrible dream; that Zachary Olsen isn't standing a metre away from me listening to Harry recite the fluctuating size of my penis. I can feel water building up under my eyelids, threatening to spill. But I can't cry in front of them. I won't.

The punch shuts us all up.

It sounds unreal, like a sound effect from an action film. I open my eyes. Harry is on the floor, blood gushing from his nose, his eyes wide with shock. At first I think maybe I've had some kind of out of body experience and I'm the one responsible. But then I realise Tom's arms are still around me. I trace Harry's eye line. Standing over him is Leo, the kid from Cloverdale School, staring at his fist like it doesn't belong to him.

13

Mr Toolan's office is different to how I remember it – smaller and darker. In the centre there is a large and messy desk covered with paperwork and coffee cups. Framed photographs of his wife and grown-up kids, tanned and good-looking, on skiing holidays and at graduation ceremonies sit to the left of his computer screen. A half-eaten sandwich sits to the right. Behind the desk, Mr Toolan is looking at my file and frowning.

My left leg is jiggling up and down. Most of the time I can disguise how I feel, rearranging my face and body to throw people off the scent. But my left leg manages to override my brain every time.

Mr Toolan puts my file down on his desk and sighs. 'I'm not going to sugar-coat this, Leo. This is not a good start.'

I flex my hands. My knuckles are red and tingly.

'I hoped *never* to see you in this office and yet barely two weeks into your first term, here you are. And for hitting another pupil no less,' Mr Toolan continues.

I look down at my shoes. I'm still wearing last year's pair. They're scuffed at the toes and the laces are starting to fray.

There's a knock at the door. It's Miss Hannah, Head of Pastoral Support.

'I came as soon as I heard,' she says, slipping into the seat beside me.

'Are you going to kick me out?' I ask. They're the first words I've spoken since I arrived.

Mr Toolan and Miss Hannah exchange looks.

'How about you tell us what happened first?' Mr Toolan asks.

I clear my throat and lean forward in my chair.

'This kid was getting picked on you see, really getting laid into. And no one was standing up for him, not properly anyway. Like, there were loads of kids standing around watching but none of them did anything, they all just let it happen.'

'So at this point why didn't you alert a teacher? Why did you take it upon yourself to sort it out with your fists?' Mr Toolan asks.

I close my eyes. But it's still a blur. All I can see are flashing images; the kid's face, the one who came over to me in the canteen last week, all hurt and humiliated, on the verge of tears, then the other kid, the one I punched, looking all smug and proud. The next thing I remember is me standing over him as he lay on the floor, blood pouring from his nose, and a couple of teachers grabbing one arm each and marching me out of the canteen. Everything in between is hazy.

'Well?' Mr Toolan says.

I open my eyes.

'I dunno, sir. I just . . . lost it, I suppose.'

'Well "losing it", as you put it, is simply not acceptable behaviour.'

I look at my feet again.

Mr Toolan takes off his glasses and rubs his eyes. He has red marks either side of his nose. I glance at Miss Hannah, trying to work out exactly how much trouble I'm in, but she refuses to meet my eye.

Mr Toolan puts his glasses back on and props his elbows on the desk, his chin resting on his clasped hands.

'Do you know why I accepted you as a pupil here, Leo? When several other schools had been reluctant?'

'No, sir,' I say.

'It was not just your clear aptitude in mathematics that secured you a place here, I saw something special, something worth taking a chance on. I saw a young person who wanted to work hard and keep his head down.'

'And I do! Look, sir, you weren't there, you didn't see what really happened. He was asking for it!'

Mr Toolan holds up his hand to silence me. I grip on hard to the wooden arms of the chair, so hard my knuckles turn from red to bright white.

'Leo, I don't think you're comprehending the seriousness of the situation. You're fortunate Harry's nose wasn't broken.'

He's the fortunate one, I want to say. But I'm skating on thin ice already. I take a deep breath before speaking.

'Look, sir, I get that I maybe shouldn't have hit him. And if I could turn back time, I wouldn't have. But you didn't hear what he was saying to that kid, he was destroying him and it just wasn't right!'

'I don't care, Leo,' Mr Toolan interrupts. 'The bottom line is, Eden Park pupils do not physically attack their peers, end of story. Do you understand me?'

'But, sir—'

'Do you understand me, Leo?' Mr Toolan repeats.

My nails dig into the arms of the chair, anger still hot and bubbling in my belly.

'Yes, sir.'

The room is suddenly very quiet apart from the ticking of an unseen clock.

'So are you going to expel me?'

Mr Toolan sighs. 'No, I am not going to expel you, Leo. You will be in detention for the next month, starting tomorrow, and on probation for the remainder of your time here. If you take even a step out of line, I will have no choice but to take more permanent action. Does that sound fair?'

All I can do is nod my head.

He begins to scribble in my file.

'That's all, Leo. You're dismissed.'

I nod and stand up. My left leg is still trembling.

Outside Mr Toolan's office, Harry is sitting with his head resting against the wall and a massive wad of tissue held to his nose. Some blonde girl is practically straddling him as she coos in his ear and strokes his hair.

'Maniac,' she spits over her shoulder as I pass.

I give her the finger. Her eyes bulge but she doesn't say anything else.

On the other side of the glass, in the secretary's office, the notebook kid, whose name I can't remember, is writing his statement. When he notices me, he breaks into a smile and waves.

'Thank you!' he mouths.

I ignore him, pushing open the door to the empty playground.

Afternoon classes have already started. The fresh air hits my face – cold and sharp.

I haven't been expelled. But I've got to be extra careful now. Any more slip-ups and I'm out. Mr Toolan is right; if I got expelled from Eden Park, no other school would touch me with a bargepole. I'd end up in one of those pupil referral units with all the other maniacs and dropouts. I'd never get into sixth form college after that, never mind university. I'd be stuck in Cloverdale for ever. Good grades from Eden Park are my ticket out. I need to keep my head down, need to keep in control. But at the same time the unfairness of it all burns in my chest.

Miss Jennings must know about my visit to Mr Toolan's office because when I slip into English over half an hour late she just looks up from her marking and nods. I can feel my classmates watching me as I make my way up the aisle to my seat. I try my best to appear cool and live up to the reputation they've built for me. I sit down and take out my creative writing folder. After a few moments, Alicia twists halfway round in her seat. She is wearing different earrings today, tiny silver ladybirds in place of her usual gold hearts.

'I heard about you,' she whispers.

I try to read her face. I get the feeling Alicia Baker might not be the sort of girl who gets turned on by violence.

'Oh yeah?' I say, trying to sound nonchalant.

'Yeah, defending that Year 10 kid.'

'Oh that. Stupid of me. Dunno what I was thinking.'

'It wasn't stupid at all. I think it was sweet of you.'

I swallow.

'Yeah?'

She nods.

'Mr Toolan didn't think so,' I say. 'Detention for a month, starting tomorrow.'

'Harsh.'

'Tell me about it.'

I don't mention the probation.

Miss Jennings looks up. We both look down at our books. She frowns, but returns to her marking.

'For what's it's worth though, I mean it,' Alicia continues to whisper over her shoulder. 'It was well sweet of you to do what you did. Not enough people stand up for the underdog round here. That Harry Beaumont kid is a right dickhead too. It was about time someone gave him a taste of his own medicine.'

She checks the front of the room before twisting all the way round again.

'Leo, can I ask you something?' she says, playing with the silver chain around her neck.

'Er, yeah, OK.' I say, shifting in my seat.

'Why did you really move schools? There's that stupid rumour going round, about you chopping off a teacher's finger, or something crazy like that, but I don't believe it for one second.'

Over the past few days I've overheard snatches of the same rumour. I have no clue where it came from, but figured there was no harm in letting it fly; anything to reinforce my image as the tough guy from the wrong side of the tracks.

'So why don't you believe it?' I ask carefully.

'Because. You're not like that.'

'What makes you so sure?'

'Oh, I don't know, let's just say I'm a very perceptive person,' she says, smiling.

74

I don't smile back.

'So come on, what really happened?' she asks.

I check the front of the room. Miss Jennings is talking to Lauren Melrose.

'Come on, you can tell me. I won't blab it around, I promise, cross my heart and all that,' Alicia says, running her finger across her chest.

But Alicia doesn't know what she's signing up for. The truth is bigger than she could probably ever imagine.

'OK,' I say, leaning in for effect. 'But you really can't tell anyone.'

'Your secret is safe with me,' Alicia replies solemnly, mimicking my action and moving in closer. God, she smells good. All the time my mind is whirring for something to say.

'The thing is,' I begin, my voice lowered. 'I got in with a bad lot at my old school. And I could see how stuff was going to go for me, you know, if I stayed. And, well, I didn't want that for myself, so I got a transfer.'

'You can do that?'

'Under special circumstances, yeah.'

Alicia sits back. 'Wow, that's a pretty grown-up decision to make.'

I shrug, as if it's no big deal.

'Why don't you tell people that then?' she asks. 'Why do you let them go round making stories up about you getting expelled?'

I shrug. 'None of their business. I figure they can think what they like. The most important thing is that I know the truth, you know?'

I look down at my fingers. There's a splodge of ink on the pad of my right index finger. I can feel Alicia watching me.

'Miss Baker, is there a problem?' Miss Jennings calls.

Alicia rolls her eyes at me and turns to face the front of the class. I dare to breathe out.

'I voted for you by the way,' I say, when the bell rings ten minutes later and we're packing away our stuff. 'In that singing competition.'

'You did?' Alicia asks.

'Course. You were great.'

'You really think so?'

'Definitely. Best on there by miles,' I find myself saying.

'Aw, thanks Leo,' she says, pink and pleased.

And it feels sort of good to have made her feel good.

'You know who you remind me of?' I continue. 'This singer my gran used to like when she was alive. Shit, I've forgotten her name now, Ella something . . .'

Alicia grips hold of my arm.

'Oh my God, not Ella Fitzgerald?' she whispers.

'Yeah, that's it.'

'Ella Fitzgerald is like my inspiration!' Alicia says, her eyes shining. 'You honestly think I'm like her, Leo?'

'I said so didn't I?'

She beams.

'Leo?'

'Yeah.'

'Can I ask you something else?'

'Er, OK,' I say, putting on my backpack.

'How come you don't do PE? It's the only other class we have together and you're always on the bench.'

I am totally aware PE is the only other class I share with Alicia and how good she looks in that tiny pleated skirt and tight polo shirt.

'Knee problems, from a football injury a few years back,' I lie smoothly, in the swing of things now.

'That must be hard, not being able to play any more,' she says, the classroom emptying around us.

'It's not great, but what can you do? It's not like I was good enough to play professionally or anything,' I say with a modest shrug.

She pauses and folds her arms.

'You're interesting, Leo Denton, do you know that?'

And Alicia is looking at me as if I have all these layers and the whole time our eyes are locked together. And for a moment I forget all about Harry Beaumont, and Mr Toolan and being on probation, and my million other problems. Even the voice in my head, the one warning me to make a run for it and that girls are no good, is fading by the second. Because everything is cancelled out by my heart going wild in my chest, like it's going to burst out of me and dance right across the room.

14

When I come out of Mr Toolan's office, Felix and Essie are waiting. They jump up from their chairs and fling their arms around me like I'm a soldier returning from battle. I get a big mouthful of Essie's hair. It tastes of her perfume and chemicals.

'Oh my God, are you OK?' she cries, holding me at arm's length, inspecting me for injuries.

'I'm fine,' I say. 'What are you guys doing here? Shouldn't you be in art by now?'

'Art, schmart,' Essie replies.

'What the hell happened, dude?' Felix asks over her.

I start with the ear flicking and end with Leo getting carted off to Mr Toolan's office, a mixture of anger and bewilderment on his face.

'But why was your inspection book in your bag in the first place?' Felix asks. 'I thought you kept it locked away?'

'It wasn't on purpose,' I say grimly, 'believe me.'

'Did Harry see much of it?' he asks.

'Just a few pages I think.'

'That's something at least.'

'I still can't believe that Cloverdale kid punched Harry Beaumont!' Essie interrupts, shaking her head in wonder. 'Was it amazing? I bet it was amazing!'

'I don't know. I had my eyes closed,' I admit. 'It sounded pretty amazing though. It was a proper punch, really loud. And Harry's nose was bleeding loads afterwards.'

'Awesome,' Felix says, his eyes dancing. Harry broke Felix's glasses back in Year 8 and Felix has been patiently waiting for his comeuppance ever since.

'You should totally invite him to have lunch with us,' Essie says.

'Who? Harry?' I ask.

'No, you idiot!' she cries. 'What's-his-name! The junior-hacksaw wielding maniac!'

'You mean Leo?' I reply. 'I thought you said he'd had his opportunity?'

'But that was before he stood up for you and punched Harry Beaumont in the face!' Essie exclaims. 'The boy deserves a medal!'

'Fine, I could ask him in detention I suppose. I don't know if he'll say yes though.'

'Hang on a second, detention? How come *you* got detention?' Felix demands. '*You* were the victim!'

'For making Harry bite his tongue,' I say, rolling my eyes. 'A week. For what it's worth, Harry got a week too. Leo got an entire month apparently. For a single punch. That's pretty harsh, don't you think?'

Essie shrugs, swinging her legs. 'You know what Mr Toolan's like, always banging on about how we're "young ladies and gentleman",' she says, imitating his deep voice.

'Essie's right,' Felix adds, 'he has a really low tolerance for physical violence.'

'Psychological torture on the other hand . . .' Essie says. 'God, things are messed up in this place sometimes. If the teachers had any sense, they would have socked Harry in the face themselves years ago. Eurgh, he's such an animal.'

We sit in silence for a few moments.

'It is strange though, when you think about it,' Felix says.

'What is?' Essie asks.

'That the school would accept Leo as a pupil in the first place. They make out places here are like gold dust and yet Mr Toolan, who prides himself on running such a "peaceful" school, goes and lets in some kid with a history of violence. That's weird, right?'

'I suppose,' I say.

'And what's weirder still is this,' Felix continues. 'Do either of you know what a junior hacksaw actually looks like?'

Essie and I shake our heads. I don't think either of us paid particular attention back in DT in Year 7, far too busy messing about with the glue gun when Mr Hampton wasn't looking. Felix takes out his phone and after a few seconds of tapping, passes it over to me and Essie. We peer at the picture on the screen.

'*That's* a junior hacksaw?' I say. The saw on the screen is a flimsy little thing, nothing like the massive weapon I'd envisaged Leo swinging about the corridors of Cloverdale School.

'It looks like it could barely saw a Kit Kat in half, never mind a finger,' Essie scoffs.

'Exactly, my friends,' Felix says, folding his arms, sitting back in his chair and looking rather proud of himself. 'Exactly.'

15

The next day, the air fizzes with gossip. Harry's nose has swollen to almost twice its normal size and has turned a deep purple. Even more brilliant is the fact that, so far anyway, the revelations in my notebook appear to have been overshadowed by the news that someone finally punched Harry Beaumont. The fact that this someone is the alleged maniac from Cloverdale School is just the cherry on top. Not that the contents of my notebook have been entirely forgotten. As I walk between lessons I notice a load of kids making weird shapes with their hands. It takes me a few seconds to work out they're indicating roughly six and a half centimetres between their thumbs and index fingers. And even though I'm not exactly thrilled by this, I'm mainly just grateful no one has worked out why I was writing all this stuff down in the first place.

I tell Mum I'm helping out with the costumes for the school musical for a week to cover my detention. Essie, a wizard at forgery, agrees to sign my planner. I pay Livvy ten pounds not to tell Mum. She frowns but takes the cash, and I'm thankful yesterday's events do not appear to have registered on the lower school gossip mill yet.

As we eat lunch, Essie declares it, 'the best day at school since that time in Year 9 when Mrs Clarey let off the loudest fart in the history of farting during our English SAT and the whole exam room completely lost it.'

I look for Leo in the canteen, but he's nowhere to be seen.

After school I head to detention. I haven't had one since I was in Year 8, when Essie, Felix and I tied ourselves together for Children in Need and caused a mass pile-up at the bottom of the stairs in the art block. This is my first solo offence and I can't help but feel a little bit badass as I sign in with ancient Mr Wilton.

Two sullen Year 9 girls are sitting in opposite corners of the classroom with matching tear-stained faces. I slide into a seat in the front row and take out my maths homework and pencil case. A few seconds later Harry walks in, his nose looking even more purple than it did a few hours ago. He glares at me before making his way to the back of the room. A few seconds later Leo enters. His eyes sort of float over me as he walks past and chooses a seat by the window. He slumps down deep in his seat, so low his chin is almost level with the desk.

'Welcome, everyone,' Mr Wilton growls. 'Your one hour detention starts now.'

He starts a stopwatch, sits down behind his desk and promptly falls asleep.

I try to do my homework, but I can't concentrate. Harry is listening to music through his headphones and must have it turned up to the maximum because I can clearly hear the lyrics and tinny bass line. To my left Leo has a copy of *Twelfth Night* propped open. I don't think he's reading it properly though. I can just tell by the way his eyes are staring at the same spot on the page, like they're about to burn right through the book. He must notice me watching because he looks over sharply. Quickly I pretend to scowl at a maths problem in my book. I try not to look again.

The rest of the hour creeps by, the hands of the clock dragging their way round the face. Finally Mr Wilton's stopwatch starts beeping. I begin to pack away my things. As he passes, Harry knocks my pencil case off the edge of the desk, sending it clattering open.

'Laters, Freak Show,' he calls over his shoulder.

I sigh and drop to my knees. My pencil sharpener has burst open and there are shavings everywhere.

'Why does he call you that?'

It takes me a moment to register that Leo is speaking to me.

'Sorry?' I say, blinking up at him.

'Freak Show. Why does he call you that?'

I consider my answer. Leo punched Harry in the face for me, which surely indicates he's on my side to at least some degree. I'm assuming he also heard Harry spout the contents of my notebook before punching him, which also bodes well. But at the same time, I can't help but feel cautious.

'It's kind of historical,' I say, scooping the shavings into my hand and tipping them back into my pencil case.

Leo frowns. 'How do you mean?'

'Harry's been calling me that since we were, like, eight years old,' I reply, standing up and shoving my pencil case into my backpack.

'But why?'

'I don't know. Because I'm different?'

'Isn't everyone?'

'Not at Eden Park School.'

I pull on my coat and we begin to walk down the deserted corridor.

'So you just let him?' Leo continues.

'It's not a case of letting him . . .' I say. 'Let's just say it's complicated.'

Leo raises an eyebrow but doesn't say anything else.

'Harry Beaumont is kind of the unofficial king of Year 10,' I say.

'But why? He's a dickhead.'

'He's on the football team and runs the one hundred metres for the county. Oh, and he's on the Ball Committee, which automatically grants him god-like status around here.'

'Ball Committee?'

'You didn't have balls at Cloverdale?'

Leo lets out a single laugh. 'No.'

'We have two, one before Christmas and one in the summer. And Harry is in charge this year. He's promising a snow machine at the Christmas one. Whoop-de-doo.'

'And people care about this stuff?'

'They really do.'

Leo shakes his head.

'At least I'm not alone when it comes to dealing with Harry's abuse,' I add brightly. 'He has it in for pretty much anyone who doesn't fit the mould. Yesterday was just my turn, that's all. Thanks by the way, for knocking his lights out. Much appreciated.'

'Don't mention it,' Leo says, pushing open the main doors.

We step outside. It's begun to rain. I fish in my backpack for my umbrella.

'Want to come under?' I ask as I open it up.

'No thanks.'

We begin to walk down the drive.

'You shouldn't let him,' Leo says after a moment.

'Pardon?'

'Harry. You shouldn't let him call you that.'

'It's only another two years. Then, if my parents let me, I'm going to a sixth form college in the city rather than stay on here, and Harry will be a figment of my imagination.'

'So until then you're just going to put up with it?'

'I know it sounds really pathetic, but it's honestly just easier to try and ignore Harry. You never know, he might get bored eventually. Hey, it would be different if I knew I had a personal bodyguard on hand to beat him up every time he gives me grief, but I have a feeling yesterday was probably a one-off . . .'

'Yeah,' Leo says quickly. 'I'm on probation so probably best I keep my head down.'

I look over at him in surprise.

'You're on probation? Just for what happened yesterday?'

'Yeah,' Leo says. 'Er, new policy I think. Zero tolerance or something.'

'Oh, right. God, I'm sorry.'

Leo shrugs. 'Not really your fault, is it?'

He doesn't say it with a whole lot of conviction though.

The rain is falling faster now, hammering down on the fabric of my umbrella. I try again to coax Leo under, but he pretends not to hear me. His eyes look even greener in the eerie grey light. It's funny, but the rain sort of suits him.

We reach the gates just as the number fourteen bus comes juddering up the hill.

'That's me,' Leo says, taking his bus pass out of his pocket.

'What's Cloverdale like?' I blurt.

He gives me a sharp look.

'Why do you wanna know?'

'It's just you hear all this stuff about it so I was curious . . .'

Leo sighs. 'You really want to know what Cloverdale is like?'

I nod eagerly.

'It's a shit-hole,' he says. 'Pure and simple. See ya.'

I watch as he breaks into a jog towards the bus stop, his blazer flying out behind him like a cape.

16

As I make my way to the back of the upper deck of the bus, I replay the conversation with David in my head. It's so messed up. This Harry kid repeatedly gets away with picking on all these kids, and here I am with four weeks' detention and probation; my entire future at Eden Park School at risk, just because I actually stood up to him. I feel angry just thinking about it. Like I want to find out where Harry lives and punch him again, only harder this time. A familiar feeling bubbles in my chest like hot lava. I remember describing it to Jenny once. She wrote something down in my file with this little frown on her face.

'Volcanoes are unpredictable, Leo, uncontrollable,' she said. 'They erupt. We need to work at keeping the one inside you dormant, or at the very least, from causing as little mass destruction as possible.'

I'm so agitated I get off the bus three stops early so I can walk the rest of the way and cool off.

I'm walking across the bridge, when a car drives past and I do a double take. It's a beaten up red Ford Fiesta. Before I have the chance to think, I'm bolting after it, running so hard I think might explode, splattering blood and guts all over the pavement. I finally catch up with it at the traffic lights, peering inside, my chest heaving up and down. The driver is an Indian lady wearing a bright pink sari. There are a couple of kids in the back. The lady doesn't notice me but one of the kids presses his face up against the window, squishing his nose against the glass and crossing his eyes at me. I stare back until the lights change and they speed away.

It was stupid of me to even think it could be Dad behind the wheel. He's long gone from here, I know it. I can feel it in my bones.

Sometimes, if I can't sleep at night or I'm bored on the bus or in lessons, I imagine this parallel universe where Dad is still around. In it he takes me to football games, helps me with my homework and calls me 'son', like he's really proud of me. He makes Mam nicer too; younger, prettier, happier. Parallel-universe Mam always remembers to buy loo roll, cooks massive roast dinners on a Sunday and laughs a lot. With Dad around, our house isn't a pig sty. It's spick-and-span and if things get broken, they get mended or replaced. I try not to think about it too much though, there's no point when it's all just a stupid fantasy anyway.

When I get home, Spike and Tia are sitting on the settee watching cartoons with the curtains closed. The sink is full of dirty plates and mugs and there's a new kidney-shaped stain on the carpet.

More and more of Spike's belongings keep appearing around the house: a rusty old toastie maker in the kitchen; a set of weights in the lounge; a book of 'inspirational' quotes; tattered and dog-eared, propped up behind the toilet rolls in the bathroom. It's like his crap is mutating on a daily basis.

'Leo!' Tia squeals the second she spots me, jumping up and running over to me, chucking her skinny little arms around my waist.

'Watcha, kiddo!' Spike says.

I roll my eyes and wish he would just call me by my actual name for once.

Tia is still wrapped around me, her cheek pressed against my belly, her feet balanced on mine.

'Dance with me?' she begs.

'No. C'mon, gerroff, T,' I say. Reluctantly she lets go of me, her lower lip sticking out in a sulk.

'Where's Mam?' I ask Spike.

'Upstairs. Getting ready for bingo with Kerry later,' he replies.

'Surprise, surprise,' I mutter, going into the kitchen and opening the cupboards. As usual they're bare apart from an ancient can of tuna and half a packet of stale cream crackers. I can't remember the last time Mam did a proper supermarket shop.

'Big jackpot going. You never know, tonight might be her lucky night,' Spike says, rubbing his hands together. 'Imagine that, eh, kids? Your mam a millionairess?'

'Like Kim Kardashian?' Tia asks.

'Exactly like Kim Kardashian,' Spike says.

I shake my head. Who are they kidding? I open the fridge. Something in there stinks, I don't know what. I shut it again.

'I was thinking, how do you kids fancy fish and chips tonight?' Spike asks. 'My treat.'

Tia lets out this big gasp. 'Really?'

'Yeah, why not. Leo?'

Part of me wants to say 'no', just to rain on his smug parade.

But already I have the smell of fish and chips in my nostrils and I'm practically drooling.

'Whatever,' I say.

'Fish 'n' chips, fish 'n' chips,' Tia chants, jumping up and down on the settee.

'What about Amber? She'll want some too, I bet.' Spike says.

'She here?' I ask.

He jerks his head upwards.

'Ask your mam if she fancies anything while you're at it,' he calls after me as I trudge up the stairs.

I bump into Mam on the landing. She has a pink towel wrapped around her body and another on her head, turban-style. Both are stained from the bleach she uses to dye her roots every few weeks. Her skin looks waxy and pale without its usual layer of make-up.

'You're late,' she says, adjusting her towel under her armpits. Her arms themselves are scrawny and bird-like.

'Like you care,' I reply.

'Oi, I heard that,' she snaps.

'You were meant to,' I say, trying to push past her.

She grabs hold of my sleeve and pulls me back so we're facing each other. I'm only a few centimetres taller than her, but because she's so skinny it feels like much more.

'I've told you once, and I'll tell you again,' she says, getting in close so I can smell her breath – toothpaste and fags. 'Just because you're going to that posh school now, it don't mean you're any better than the rest of us, all right?'

'What? Wanting to do well is a crime, is it?' I ask.

'There you go,' she says. 'Mouthing off again. The sooner

91

you finish your exams and start earning your keep, the better.'

'What, like you?'

Her mouth flaps open, but she doesn't say anything. Mam never holds down a job for long. She's been at the launderette since May – a bit of a record for her.

Mam's gaze lingers over my blazer.

'What does that mean anyway?' she asks, prodding at the embroidered crest and screwing up her face.

'Like you actually want to know.'

'What? I'm not allowed to ask my own kid a question now?'

'It's the school motto,' I say reluctantly. 'Latin for "fairness and initiative".'

She lets out a short laugh.

'Fairness? Well, that's where they're going wrong. Because life isn't fair, Leo, and the sooner people are taught that, the better off they'll be.'

She folds her arms, like she's proud of herself. I could open my mouth to argue with her, try and explain that's not what the motto is saying, but I can't be bothered. Because even though she got that bit wrong, she's right about one thing – life *isn't* fair.

'Are we done?' I ask.

She just shakes her head and sweeps past me, into her bedroom. A few seconds later the roar of the hair-dryer starts up.

I rub my face with my hands before pushing open my own bedroom door to find Amber sitting on her bunk, painting her toenails Barbie pink.

'Spike's going down the chippy. You want anything?' I ask. I realise I forgot to ask Mam. Not that she would want anything anyway. She seems to survive just fine on cider and nicotine.

'Just a couple of saveloys for me, ta,' Amber says, leaning forward to blow on her toes.

'That's it? No chips?'

'No thanks, I'm cutting out the carbs.'

Amber's always on some sort of crazy diet.

'You're mental,' I say, tugging off my tie. 'If you get any skinnier there'll be nothing left of you.'

'Whatever, I'm huge,' she says, pinching at a non-existent roll of fat on her stomach. 'By Hollywood standards I'm practically obese. Why're you so late?'

'Detention,' I admit.

She sits up straight. 'You're joking?'

'Nope.'

'What'd you do?'

I tell her all the bits I remember, finishing with Mr Toolan's warning – one more step out of line and I'm out.

'Jenny's going to go ape-shit,' Amber says.

I groan. There's no way Mr Toolan isn't going to tell her. And I've got an appointment with her on Friday. What shit timing. I can already picture her face; all sad and disappointed, which is somehow way worse than her being angry.

'What are you going to do?' Amber asks.

'Nothing much I can do except try and keep out of trouble from now on.'

'So this kid you stood up for, who is he?'

'No one.'

'That's too bad. I thought you were going to say you'd finally got yourself some mates.'

'Why is everyone so bloody obsessed with me making friends?'

'Because. It's normal,' Amber says.

I look up at her. 'Normal? And since when have I been normal, Amber?'

Because 'normal' kids don't have six files' worth of notes on them. 'Normal' kids don't see therapists. 'Normal' kids don't have mothers like mine, who tell you life isn't fair with messed-up glee, like the unfairness of life is pretty much the only thing they know for sure. I've spent my whole life being told I'm the complete opposite of 'normal'.

Normal. I say it over and over again as I pace up and down on the flimsy rug, agitation gushing down my arms and legs, making me want to lash out and go wild. Amber leans down and grabs hold of my shoulder.

'All right, bad choice of word. I'm sorry. Calm down, Leo.'

I shake her off, but stop pacing.

'Here, come up,' she says, moving across to make room.

I pause before climbing up the ladder to join Amber on her bunk. We sit cross-legged, our knees touching, the top of my head brushing the ceiling. I'm still trembling.

'I just don't get why you're so against the concept of opening up to someone,' Amber says softly. 'Having some kind of meaningful relationship with someone who isn't your sister or your therapist.'

I almost open my mouth to tell her about Alicia, just to shut her up, but at the last second I stop myself.

'I just don't want you to let what happened in February dictate the rest of your life.'

I stiffen. Amber never mentions February. It's an unspoken rule between us. What happened that day was enough to taint the whole month; turn it dark and murky. My eyes fall shut and all of a sudden

I'm back in the woods, the cold on my body, tears pouring down my face, puke in my mouth. I open my eyes. My breathing is fast and raggedy.

'Sorry,' Amber says. 'I didn't mean to upset you. Come here.'

She puts her arms around me. I let her. My breathing begins to return to normal.

'I just want you to be happy, little bro. Move on and that,' she whispers into my hair.

'I know,' I say. 'Just let me do things my way, OK?'

She sighs. 'OK.'

By the time we make it downstairs, Mam is getting ready to leave, a slash of red lipstick across her mouth, lighter in hand.

'Be lucky!' Spike yells after her.

She totters down the path with one arm raised, her fingers crossed. For someone so convinced life isn't fair, she plays an awful lot of bingo.

We eat dinner on our laps in the lounge while watching repeat episodes of *Total Wipeout* on the telly. Spike and Tia laugh like drains the whole time. Amber nicks half my chips. She doesn't mention February again.

17

In Thursday's detention, the two Year 9 girls have gone, so it's just Harry, Leo and me. Harry is already there when I arrive, sprawled in his chair at the back of the room, his rubbish music playing again. The swelling has gone down a bit, but the nose itself has turned a pleasingly disgusting shade of yellow. I can't help but smirk a little as I sit down. I'm taking out my history homework when Leo comes in. I mouth 'Hi'. He hesitates a moment before mouthing 'Hi' back, a frown on his face the whole time.

Mr Wilton sets his stopwatch and promptly falls asleep again, his snores loud and immediate.

Unable to concentrate on my homework, I rip a piece of paper out of the back of my book and begin to sketch Mr Wilton, snoozing away in his chair. I exaggerate his bushy eyebrows and rounded belly. I draw a thought bubble above his head and in it, a busty girl in a bikini, pouting, with her hands on her hips. I fold the page up into quarters and aim it at Leo's desk. It lands a few centimetres away from his right hand. He picks it up and smoothes it out on the desk. For a second I'm certain I detect a change in his face; not quite a smile, but something in that direction. But just as quick, his expression is blank again and he's refolding the piece of paper and pushing it to the very edge of his desk.

Finally the stopwatch goes off. Mr Wilton groggily dismisses us, although Harry is already out the door before he's finished speaking, his footsteps thundering down the corridor. Leo goes to hand me back the picture.

'Keep it,' I say.

'You don't want it?'

'I drew it for you.'

Leo frowns.

'What I mean,' I say quickly, 'is that it's just a sketch, nothing special. Keep it. Or throw it in the bin. Whatever.'

Leo gives me a weird look but tucks the picture inside his copy of *Twelfth Night* anyway.

'It's good, you know,' Leo says, as we walk down the corridor.

'Sorry?'

'The picture you drew. It's pretty good.'

I smile shyly. 'Thank you.'

'You taking art for GCSE?' he asks.

'No. Textiles.'

'What? Sewing and that?'

'Yes, although I can barely thread a needle, much to Miss Fratton's dismay. I'm more into the design side of things, fashion and stuff. What about you? Are you into art?'

'Nah. I'm shit at all that stuff. Can't draw to save my life.'

'What are you good at?' I ask.

'Maths,' Leo says without hesitation. 'Numbers.'

'I'm awful at maths,' I say. 'It's my worst subject by far. Anything with right or wrong answers I'm generally rubbish at. Funny how everyone's brain is wired so differently, isn't it?'

'Hmmm,' Leo mutters, looking at the ground.

We're halfway down the driveway when I spot Mum's car parked just outside the school gates.

I swear under my breath. I'd told her I'd get the bus home.

'What?' Leo asks.

'Nothing.'

I consider pretending I've forgotten something and turning round but Mum has already noticed me.

'Yoo hoo! David!' she calls, getting out of the car and waving.

'That your mum?' Leo asks, nodding towards her.

'Unfortunately,' I reply.

From the back seat of the car, Phil clocks me and starts going mad, bouncing up and down on the seats.

'You've got a dog,' Leo says, his eyes lighting up in a way I've never seen before.

'Oh yeah. That's Phil.'

'Phil? What, as in short for Philip?'

'I know, lame right? Blame my dad. He has a thing about

giving all our pets human names. Our goldfish are called Julie and Dawn, and our last dog was called Graham.'

'But that's cool,' Leo says, 'way better than calling a dog something dumb like Fluffy or Lucky.'

'I suppose so. It's a bit embarrassing though, when you take him off his lead in the park and you yell "Phil" and about half the men there turn round.'

'What breed is he?' Leo asks.

'We don't know. We got him from a rescue centre about four years ago. We think there might be some Jack Russell in him, maybe some spaniel. We're not really sure though. He's a total mongrel.'

'Nah, he's cool-looking.'

We reach the car.

'Hi, darling,' Mum says, pushing her sunglasses up on her head, 'thought you might appreciate a lift home after all your hard work.'

I can sense Leo looking at me quizzically.

'Hi there,' she says, leaning over me and extending her hand out to Leo, 'I don't think we've met before. I'm Jo, David's mum.'

'Leo,' Leo replies, shaking her hand.

'Nice to meet you, Leo. Are you working on the musical too?' Mum asks.

'Musical?' Leo says with a frown.

'Yeah, er, Leo's working backstage, building scenery,' I say quickly, widening my eyes at him. 'Aren't you, Leo?'

'Yeah, backstage,' Leo echoes, thankfully taking my cue.

'What show is it they're doing this year?' Mum asks,

directing her question at Leo. He shoots a panicked look at me over her shoulder. I try to mouth the words *Oh! What a Lovely War* at him but it's too late; Leo is already telling Mum we're doing *Grease*.

'Oh brilliant!' Mum says, 'I love *Grease*! God, I had such a crush on John Travolta when I was younger, I thought he was a right fox. David, you must remind me when it's on, so I can get some tickets.'

'OK,' I say, hoping Mum will have forgotten by the time December rolls round.

Phil is going crazy now, running round in circles on the back seat. I open the door. He bounds out onto the pavement, jumping up first at me, then at Leo.

'Phil!' Mum says sharply. 'Get down!'

'No, it's OK,' Leo says, 'I love dogs.'

'Hello, boy!' he says, kneeling down so his face is level with Phil's, rubbing his ears, which Phil loves. Knowing he's on to a good thing, Phil rolls onto his back so Leo can scratch his belly.

'You've got a friend for life there now, Leo,' Mum says.

Leo just grins, not taking his eyes off Phil for a second. He looks totally different with a smile on his face – softer and less intense.

'Can we give you a lift home?' Mum asks after a moment.

Leo gives Phil a final belly rub and straightens up.

'Thanks, but I live kind of far away.'

'Whereabouts?' Mum asks.

'Er, Cloverdale,' Leo says, looking at his feet.

'That's not so far,' Mum says. 'Come on, jump in.'

'Nah, honestly, it's fine,' he says, backing away, 'my bus is due any time.'

'It's really no bother, Leo. I've got to nip and get some bits from the supermarket anyway so it's only a little detour. Go on, save yourself the bus fare.'

'Yeah, go on,' I add.

Phil licks Leo's hand.

'Er, all right,' Leo says. 'Thanks.'

Leo insists on sitting in the back with Phil.

'Are you sure?' Mum asks as she starts the car. 'It's awfully dog-hairy back there.'

'No. I like it,' Leo says, as he massages a blissed-out Phil's ears.

'Do you have dogs of your own?' Mum asks.

Leo shakes his head.

'Do you want one?' I ask, 'Phil doesn't eat that much.'

'David!' Mum scolds.

'Only joking.'

'Do you have any other pets, Leo?' Mum asks.

'Some hamsters once.'

'What were their names? Can't be as bad as our pets,' I say.

'Cheryl. My sister named that one,' Leo says, 'after Cheryl Cole, and, er, Jimmy.'

'Who did you name Jimmy after?' I ask.

'My dad,' Leo says quietly.

'Wasn't that really confusing though? Bet your dad and Jimmy the hamster didn't know whether they were coming or going.'

'My dad doesn't live with us.'

'Oh. Sorry.'

Leo just looks out the window.

'What happened? To the hamsters, I mean,' I add quickly.

'Cheryl died. Jimmy escaped.'

'Oh. That sucks.'

'Shall I put on some music?' Mum says with artificial brightness, fiddling with the knobs on the radio. It blares out really loudly for a moment and makes Phil jump, sending him cowering under Leo's arm.

'Actually, David,' Mum says, 'I might have the *Grease* soundtrack knocking about somewhere. Have a look in the glove box. I'm quite in the mood for it now.'

A few seconds later the car is filled with John Travolta and Olivia Newton John belting out 'Summer Nights', Mum singing along tunelessly. I look through the rearview mirror. Leo is staring out of the window, his forehead knotted into a frown, his left hand resting gently on Phil's head.

Twenty minutes later we pass a dilapidated 'Welcome to the Cloverdale Estate' sign. I sit up a little straighter. Mum flicks the interior door locks on. I wince and hope Leo didn't notice.

'You'll have to guide me from here, Leo,' Mum says, turning down the music.

Leo leans forward between the front seats and gives her directions.

I watch as Cloverdale creeps by. It's nothing like I imagined. From the way people talk about it, I expected drug dealers on every corner, mass shootouts, a dead body or two at least, but there's virtually no one in sight. Everyone must be indoors, hiding behind identical sets of net curtains.

The estate is like a never-ending maze, the same formation of skinny little brown brick houses, over and over again. Finally, we turn into Leo's street – Sycamore Gardens according to the graffitied sign.

'This is me,' Leo says.

'Which house?' Mum asks.

'Er, that one, number seven. But here is fine,' Leo says.

'Okey dokey.'

Number seven is the scruffiest looking house on the street, with peeling paintwork and a jungle-like front garden, the grass almost waist-high.

'Thanks for the lift,' Leo says as Mum turns off the engine.

'You're very welcome,' Mum replies.

Leo gives Phil a final belly rub before thanking Mum again and climbing out of the car. He slams the car door shut behind him and walks away, his back immediately hunching over. Mum goes to turn the key in the ignition.

'Wait a sec,' I tell her, opening the door and jumping out of the car.

'Leo!' I call. 'I just wanted to say thanks,' I say, catching up with him. 'You know, for not letting on to my mum about me being in detention. And for covering for me about the school musical.'

'Oh, that. That's OK.'

'It's just that if she knew I had detention she'd want to know why and stuff so . . .' I let my voice trail off.

'Yeah, I get it,' Leo says, folding his arms. But of course he doesn't get it, not properly.

Behind him, the curtains at number seven open for a moment, a misty face appearing at the glass, before falling shut again.

'Your mum's waiting,' Leo says, nodding towards the car. I glance behind me. Mum taps her watch.

'Well, have a good evening,' I say.

'Yeah. You too.'

He turns and makes his way across the trampled strip of grass that substitutes for a garden path.

'Let's just make sure he gets in all right,' Mum says as I get back in the car.

We sit and watch as the scratched front door of number seven bangs shut behind him.

18

When I enter the living room, Tia is lying on the sofa watching *Frozen* for at least the hundredth time, a dreamy expression on her face. Through the doorway, I can see Amber in the kitchen kneeling down next to the washing machine.

'All right?' I say, wandering in.

'Not really. Mam's left a flipping tissue in her pocket again. Everything's covered in white fluff.'

'Where is she?' I ask.

'Down the pub with Spike.'

'Right,' I say. 'What's in the oven?'

'Pizza.'

'What kind?'

'Pepperoni. Not sure there's enough for all three of us though. We might have to do some toast as well.'

'Thought you were off the carbs?'

'Beggars can't be choosers,' Amber says, sighing and shoving everything back in the washing machine again.

'You're home early,' she says, adding soap powder to the drawer.

'Got a lift.'

'Yeah, I saw.'

'Then why are you asking?'

'Who is he?'

'Who?'

'Who do you think? The boy you were talking to outside.'

She slams the soap drawer shut and turns on the machine.

'Just a mate.'

'Thought you didn't do mates,' she says with a smirk.

'I don't. He's no one. Just a kid from detention. His mum dropped me off.'

'Nice car they've got,' Amber says. 'They rich?'

'I dunno, I suppose.'

I should have said no to the lift, followed my instincts and got the bus. I saw David's mum lock the car doors when we drove into Cloverdale. And the way David looked at the estate, gawping like he was a kid on a theme-park ride. Not that I blame them. I bet they live in really nice house, with three bathrooms and a huge kitchen with one of those big shiny fridges you see in American sitcoms, and a massive garden with a proper lawn and flowerbeds and matching patio furniture.

I pour myself a glass of water and flop down on the sofa next to Tia. She's murmuring along with the lines from the film. She could recite the script in her sleep, easy. I take a sip of water. It tastes funny. Metallic. I should have run the tap for longer.

I try to relax and think of something nice. Alicia pops into my brain. I try to shove her away, replace her with something else, but nothing works. I give in, closing my eyes and picturing her face. Alicia in her bedroom, her hair falling around her face, guitar on her knee, smiling and singing a song just for me.

Yeah, that's better already.

First thing the following morning I have an appointment with Jenny at the Sunrise Centre. The Sunrise Centre is kind of a misleading name. The building itself is made from grey concrete and the walls inside are painted this really cold mint-green colour that makes you feel chilly even on a boiling hot day. They put posters and paintings up on the walls and stuff, but there's still no getting away from the fact that it's a depressing place for kids with 'problems'. Mam used to come to my appointments with me but stopped as soon as I was old enough to get the bus here on my own. When she does come she talks in her silly posh voice and sucks up to Jenny, acting like I'm not even in the room. She only comes now if Jenny asks her to, which suits me just fine.

I've been coming to appointments here ever since I was seven years old so Jenny knows me pretty well by now, or at least thinks she does. It's weird though because I hardly know anything about Jenny, apart from the fact she probably has a cat cos there's always cat hair all over her tights. Sometimes I try to ask her personal questions, but she always manages to avoid answering them and then turns them round and asks me *why* I'm asking and before I know it, I'm answering yet another question. It's pretty annoying. On the whole though, Jenny is all right. When I was younger I used to get mad a lot and storm out of the room or shout at her. Once I threw her pot plant out of the window. It smashed on the bonnet of someone's car and set the alarm off. Jenny was all cool and business-like about it, which somehow was way worse than if she'd just screamed at me.

I wait in the Adolescent Department reception. Jenny's running late. I bet Mr Toolan has called her by now. There are two other kids also waiting, a boy and a girl. The boy plays on his phone. The girl reads a magazine. None of us speaks. It's an unofficial rule. I glance at the clock.

Jenny pops her head round the door.

'Leo?'

She's wearing her blank friendly face, but she's not fooling me. There's no hiding the tightness in her lips and disappointment in her eyes. I fling the magazine I was half-reading back onto the pile and follow Jenny into her room.

Jenny's room is small and narrow with the same mint-green walls. In the centre there are four chairs arranged around a small square coffee table with a box of tissues set upon it. You always know you're in for a good time when there's a box of tissues on permanent standby – and this is no ordinary box, it's a *jumbo* box. Jenny closes the door and we sit down.

'So, how's it going, Leo?' Jenny asks, taking a gulp of tea.

'Is that a new jumper?' I ask.

Jenny looks down. 'No, not particularly.'

'It suits you.'

'Thanks. So, what's been happening? How's school?'

'Where'd you get it from?'

She puts down her pen and looks at me.

'Leo, we're here to talk about you, not my wardrobe choices.'

I shut up after that and go into a bit of a sulk. I'm suddenly not feeling in a very chatty mood.

'I had a call from Mr Toolan on Tuesday,' she says, setting down her mug.

Here we go. 'Oh, yeah?'

'Afraid so, Leo. He said you hit a fellow pupil. Do you want to tell me about it?'

'He deserved it.'

'Oh, Leo,' Jenny sighs. 'We've worked on this. You can't go lashing out at people like that, whether they "deserve it", or not.'

'But he was bullying another kid.'

'I know,' Jenny says gently. 'And I appreciate you were trying to help, but surely you can see you went about this the wrong way.'

'Maybe,' I mutter, pulling at my tie and curling it round my index finger.

'I'm just disappointed, Leo. Eden Park is such a great school. I'd hate to see you waste this opportunity.'

There's a long pause.

'How about those techniques we practised?' she asks. 'Are they helping?'

I don't answer.

'Look, Leo, the bottom line is you can't go around punching people, no matter how much they annoy or anger you. No excuses.'

I just shrug and look out of the window. The sky is filled with dull white clouds.

Jenny sighs. 'How is everything else going?' she asks, changing tack. 'How are you getting on with the other pupils?'

I shrug again. 'OK.'

I can't help but think about Alicia.

On Wednesday she gave me half her stick of chewing gum, and

yesterday, when I was walking to history, she called me over and made me listen to a song on her headphones. Because we were sharing, our cheeks were almost touching and Alicia kept glancing at me every few seconds to check my reaction, like it was important to her that I liked the song too. I told her I did.

Not that I'm going to share any of this stuff with Jenny. She'll only go making a big deal out of it, and ask me about a billion extra questions I don't want to answer.

'Have you found anyone there you feel you can trust? Who you can talk to when things get confusing or difficult?'

'Nope,' I reply, drumming my nails on the wooden arms of my chair.

Jenny shifts position in her chair.

'I know you find it hard to trust your peers, and I understand your caution, Leo, I do, but you can't live your entire life in this hard shell, no matter how much you think you want to. I'm concerned about your social isolation.'

Social isolation. Again. She's bloody obsessed with it.

'I do fine by myself,' I say firmly.

Jenny lowers my file onto her lap.

'Friends isn't a dirty word, Leo.'

I look her in the eye.

'It is to me.'

'I just want to see you participating in a positive way, Leo.'

'Participating?' I ask, screwing up my face. 'Participating in what?'

Jenny sighs again. 'In life, Leo. I want you to start participating in life.'

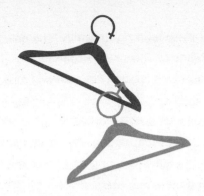

19

After leaving Jenny's I miss the bus and am late for English.

'Where have you been?' Alicia whispers over her shoulder as I slide into my seat behind her.

'Er, doctor's appointment,' I say.

She frowns.

'For my knee,' I add quickly, congratulating myself on my quick thinking.

'How is the old knee?' she asks.

'It's getting better actually.'

'Glad to hear it.'

And she smiles like she really means it.

That afternoon, I'm the first to arrive in detention. I slouch into the same seat I sat in yesterday, but struggle to get comfortable. A few minutes later Harry arrives, heading straight for the back of the classroom. Then David, giving me a quick wave as he slides into his seat. I nod back. Today we're joined by two boys from Year 8. As I try to get through the rest of *Twelfth Night*, I can feel one of them looking at me, staring at me with his mouth open, like I'm a waxwork at Madame Tussauds or something. I turn my head sharply and fix him with a glare. His eyes widen with fright before he looks away.

I still can't concentrate. Out of the corner of my eye, David is bent over his work, his left hand propping up his forehead. Every few seconds he lets out a sigh or groan. I watch as he rips a page out of his book and tosses it aside, his face all pink. I sit up a little straighter. I recognise the cover of the maths textbook he's working from. It's one I completed a few years ago.

In front of me, Mr Wilton is snoring. I look over my shoulder. Harry has his eyes closed and the two Year 8 boys are sulking. I stand up and cross the aisle, sliding into the seat next to David. He looks up in surprise. I look at his page. It's a mess of scribbles and crossings-out.

'You're making this way more complicated than it needs to be,' I say.

'I am?' David whispers.

'Big-time. Once you've got the formula straight, simultaneous equations are really simple to solve.'

'For geniuses like you and my friend Felix maybe,' he says miserably.

'Nah, I'm serious. Let me show you.'

I pick up David's pen.

'So, simultaneous equations are two equations with two unknowns. So the first step is to try to eliminate one of the unknowns. You with me?'

'I suppose so.'

'For example, here we need to work out the value of y. So we

112

add the two equations to eliminate the y. Like this . . .'

I begin to write, David leaning in to watch.

'See, once you've done that it's clear what the total value of x is. Then all you need to do is divide that by, what?'

David peers at the page.

'I don't know.'

'Yes, you do. Just take your time. The answer's there, you just need to unpick it.'

He continues to stare at the page, his face getting redder and redder.

In front of us, Mr Wilton stirs. We lower our voices.

'Just relax,' I whisper. 'It'll come.'

'Five?' David whispers back doubtfully.

'Exactly. Which leaves us with the value of x.'

'So y equals 1, and x equals three?' he asks slowly.

'Bingo.'

'Really?'

'Yep.'

'But that's really simple.'

'Told you. Wanna try another?'

On Monday I'm in detention doing my geography homework when a folded-up piece of paper comes sailing through the air and lands on my desk. I glance over at David. He's looking straight ahead although his lips are twitching as if resisting a smile. I open it up. It's another drawing. This time it's of a dog that looks a bit like Phil. Next to the dog is a speech bubble containing the words 'Bow wow, bow wow, woof, woof, BARK!' and an asterisk guiding me to a footnote in the bottom corner – 'Doggy Translation: I aced my maths homework!!! Mr Steele almost fainted. Thanks a trillion. David x.'

I look up. David is smiling hopefully. And even though the note is well cheesy, I can't help smiling back.

The next day I get to English to discover Matt, the kid I usually sit next to, is off school with glandular fever.

'We're going to be working in pairs today, discussing the symbolism in *Twelfth Night*,' Miss Jennings announces. She puts me into a three with Alicia and Ruby, the girl who sits next to Alicia. Ruby's OK; a bit annoying, but OK.

I keep my cool, nodding casually as Alicia and Ruby turn their chairs round so they're facing me. Alicia's knee touches mine for a second.

'God, I've got such a hangover,' Ruby announces, flopping her head on the desk.

Alicia rolls her eyes. 'You've always got a hangover. It's like Tuesday, Rubes. Who gets that messed up on a school night?'

Ruby gives Alicia the finger from under her veil of bleached blonde hair. 'Leave me alone. I am in a very delicate state right now,' she says, her voice muffled.

Alicia just shakes her head and grins at me.

'You don't drink then?' I ask.

'Not during the week. Coming to school with a hangover is not my idea of fun.'

I wonder where Alicia drinks at the weekend, what she drinks, whether she's got a boyfriend who buys them for her. I watch out of the corner of my eye as she opens her copy of the play, smoothing out the pages with the palm of her hand.

'I know it's not cool, but I really love this play,' Alicia says.

'Oh yeah? What do you love about it?' I ask.

Alicia scrunches up her face to think.

'The humour I guess. And the love story, the way everything is a big muddle, but it all comes together right at the last minute. And the way you sort of know that that's going to happen the whole way through, but when it happens you're still really happy about it, even though you knew it was coming. If that makes sense?'

I nod encouragingly.

'But most of all,' she continues, leaning forward in her chair, all excited, her eyes sparkling (and her excitement is catching because I'm leaning forward too, even though I couldn't give a toss about the play, apart from the fact that Alicia likes it so much). 'I love that it has a really kickass heroine. I mean Viola is just so brave and bolshie. I love that. And when you consider this was written like a gazillion years ago, it's even more amazing.'

'Even if her part would have been played by a bloke at the time?' I ask, remembering what Miss Jennings told us the other day about the all-male casts back when Shakespeare was alive.

'I reckon. I mean, the fact a character like her got written all those years ago is big enough. How confusing would that be though? A guy playing a girl pretending to be a guy?' Alicia laughs.

'I hadn't thought about it like that,' I say.

There's a pause and I can feel Alicia's eyes still on me, the air between us sort of thick and hazy.

'Are you going to Becky's party?' she asks slowly.

'I didn't know she was having one,' I reply.

This isn't quite true. Becky Somerville is in my form and has such a big mouth you'd have to be living on Mars not to have heard her go on about it.

'Yeah, next Saturday,' Alicia says, tracing her finger up and down the spine of her copy of the play.

'Oh, right. Cool.'

'So, now you do know about it, do you think you might go?' Alicia asks, twirling one of her corkscrew curls round her finger.

I clear my throat and shrug. 'I dunno. Parties aren't really my scene.'

'What do you mean, parties aren't your scene?' Alicia squeaks. 'That's like saying food isn't your scene, or breathing isn't your scene. I mean, who doesn't like parties?'

I look down, cursing myself for saying something so dumb. Alicia's right – normal people *do* like parties.

'I'm just not great at crowds,' I add. I regret my words straight away because I know I'm making it worse, blowing it big-time with my weirdness.

'That's too bad,' Alicia says.

'Anyway, I'm not invited,' I add. 'I don't think Becky is my biggest fan.'

Becky treats me like most of my other classmates seem to, with this mixture of fear and fascination, like I'm an exotic animal escaped from the zoo that may or may not be dangerous. Everyone apart from Alicia. Alicia doesn't act like she's scared of me one bit.

'Becky just hasn't taken the chance to get to know you yet, that's all,' Alicia says. 'Cos if she did, she'd think totally differently, I know it.'

I shrug and look at my hands. There's a long pause.

116

'You know, I was the new kid once.'

'Yeah?' I say, looking up.

'Yep. Back in Year 8. My parents moved up here from London halfway through the year.'

'And how was it?'

'Hideous.'

'Really?'

I can't imagine Alicia's life being anything but golden.

'Uh-huh. In case you haven't noticed, Eden Park isn't the most diverse of schools. You can count the number of black kids here on two hands. I felt like I was walking around with a flashing light on my head half the time. Plus, everyone had friends already; I was a year and a half too late. And there were all these cliques, and rules about who could sit where in the canteen, and looking around I just couldn't work out where I was supposed to fit in. For the first few weeks I ate my lunch on the toilet and cried myself to sleep every night,' she laughs.

'So what changed?' I ask.

'Well, I forced myself to eat in the canteen for a start. Then I joined drama club and choir, smiled inanely at everyone I encount- ered, etcetera. And eventually I discovered there were lots of nice people, I just had to put myself out there in order to find them. Having my braces removed probably helped too. It's kind of hard to exude confidence when you have a mouthful of metal. And I mean metal. My braces were epic.'

She laughs again.

'And for what it's worth, your rep around school is kind of badass,' she adds. 'I think I was known simply as the black mute girl for most of my first term.'

She tucks a loose curl behind her ear and grins. I like what it does to her eyes.

Alicia clears her throat.

'Look, Becky says I can bring someone,' she says. 'To her party I mean.'

Heat creeps up my neck.

'Oh yeah? Who you bringing then?'

She takes a deep breath before looking me straight in the eyes.

'Well, no one at the moment.'

'Oh, right,' I say, swallowing hard.

Ruby (who I'd forgotten was even there) raises her head off the desk and rolls her bloodshot eyes.

'For God's sake, you two are making me die. Leo, Alicia is trying to ask you out, you utter dickhead. Just say you'll go with her to Becky's party, please? Before I bang your stupid heads together.'

She plonks her head back down on the desk.

I look at Alicia who is hiding behind her hands. When she lowers them, her cheeks are all flushed.

I open my mouth to say something, but nothing comes out. What Ruby is proposing is full-on. But there's something stopping me from talking myself out of it; something way louder and stronger that the usual voice inside my head.

'So, what do you think?' Alicia asks, biting her lower lip. 'Do you want to?'

'Er, yeah, OK then.' I find myself saying, my steady voice fighting my motoring heartbeat and sweaty palms.

'Cool.' she says.

There's a pause before she bursts into giggles. And suddenly I'm doing something I haven't done in forever, and it's like I'm having this weird, out-of-body experience – because I'm laughing too.

20

'Congratulations,' I say to David that afternoon, as Mr Wilton's stopwatch beeps to signal the end of the day's detention. 'That's you done, isn't it?'

'I guess so,' David says. 'It hasn't been all that bad though, not really.'

'Nah.'

'Maybe I should break the rules more often,' he adds with a grin. 'Look, I'm sorry you've got another three weeks.'

'Don't worry about it.'

David clears his throat. 'Leo, I was, um, thinking, wondering really, whether you'd consider tutoring me in maths. You know, properly.'

'Can't you ask someone else?' I ask, frowning.

'My friend Felix maybe, only he's not very good at explaining things in basic terms. He sort of forgets that not everyone is a genius like him.'

'I dunno. I'm not sure I'll be much good at it either.'

'Oh yes you would,' David says. 'You were brilliant the other day. For the first time in ages maths actually made some kind of sense.'

'Whatever,' I say, rolling my eyes.

'I'm serious.'

'I dunno if I have the time.'

'Go on. I'll pay you.'

'Don't be stupid.'

'I mean it. Please?' David adds. 'It would really, really help me out.'

I hesitate. The truth is, I kind of enjoyed helping David out the other day, way more than I would ever have guessed. I liked watching things click into place for him, him being all proud at being able to solve stuff by himself.

'Just a couple of times a week,' he adds. 'And if it doesn't work out we can stop any time. No pressure.'

I sigh. 'OK, fine.'

He lets out a whoop and for a second I'm scared he's going to hug me.

'Thank you, thank you, thank you!' he chants, 'I'll be a model pupil, I promise.'

I shake my head. 'You're pretty mental, you know that?'

David just beams back at me. I continue to shake my head, turning away to pack up my stuff.

'Oh, another thing,' David says. 'Are you free tomorrow lunch time?'

'Why?' I ask over my shoulder.

'Do you want to have lunch with me, Essie and Felix?'

'Why?' I repeat, turning back to face him.

'Because. We want to get to know you better.'

'I kind of do lunch alone,' I say.

'Oh, please? It'll be fun.'

And I don't know whether it's because of Alicia and the party, or what, but I find myself saying yes.

The following day it's wet outside and the canteen is crowded and stuffy. As I weave my way through the tables and chairs, I pass Harry on the middle table.

'Psycho!' his little blonde girlfriend spits.

If only she knew. I ignore her and keep moving.

'You came,' David says happily as I set down my tray.

'I said I would, didn't I?' I mutter, sitting down on the seat beside him. Across from me, David's two mates, whose names he's told me, but I've totally forgotten, are watching me with wide eyes.

The girl has a mass of messy black hair. Her chin rests on clasped hands, her fingernails, stubby and bitten, painted with chipped black nail varnish. She dwarfs the boy beside her, who I recognise from advanced maths. He's small and slight, and maybe the neatest looking kid I've ever seen. Seriously, he looks like the type of kid who irons his own underpants.

Suddenly the girl leaps into motion.

'I'm Essie,' she says, leaning across the table to shake my hand. Her voice is all husky and theatrical.

'Felix,' the boy adds.

'Leo,' I say.

'Oh, we know who you are,' Essie purrs. 'You're like the most famous boy in the school right now.'

I shrug and open my can of Coke. It fizzes over the top and I have to slurp down the foam quickly to stop it spilling all over the table.

'So, why did you really get expelled from Cloverdale?' Essie says as I set my can back down.

'Ess!' David hisses.

'What? That's what we all want to know, isn't it?' Essie says.

'But you don't just come out with it!'

Essie pouts and rolls her eyes.

'Let me apologise for my girlfriend, Leo,' Felix says. 'She has a tendency to get a little, how can I put it? Overexcited.'

'You make me sound like an untrained puppy dog,' Essie grumbles.

'If the shoe fits, darling,' Felix says, patting her on the hand.

'You two go out?' I say, not even bothering to hide my surprise.

'Yes. Why, do we not look like a couple?' Essie demands.

'I dunno,' I say, squeezing tomato ketchup on the edge of my plate. 'What makes anyone look like a couple?'

I think of me and Alicia; how we might look walking down the corridor together, my arm slung round her shoulder, hers round my waist. The thought alone churns up a load of butterflies in my stomach.

'They reckon women are meant to go for men who remind them of their dads,' Essie says. 'How messed up is that? Luckily Felix is *nothing* like my father.'

'It's just the whole Oedipus complex thing in reverse,' Felix says, nibbling on what looks like a piece of cardboard. 'According to Freud, all men want to kill their dads and shag their mums.'

'Gross,' I say, stabbing a chip into my ketchup.

'Unless you've got a fit mum,' Felix adds.

'Felix!' Essie and David cry in unison. Essie rips up her bread roll and starts hurling bits at Felix's head, David quickly joining in.

'Gluten-intolerant! Abuse, abuse!' Felix cries, shielding his head.

They're bonkers. Officially. All three of them.

'You still haven't told us why you got expelled,' Essie says, having run out of bits of bread roll to throw.

'What makes you think I was expelled?' I ask carefully.

'There! Told you so!' Felix cries triumphantly, slapping his hand down on the table. 'I told you that rumour was rubbish!'

'But if you didn't get expelled, why did you leave Cloverdale?' David asks.

The three of them lean in towards me in unison.

I tell them the same story I told Alicia. When I'm done they slump back in their seats, disappointed.

'How very dull,' Essie says. 'I much prefer the junior hacksaw thing.'

'Sorry,' I reply with a shrug.

'How did you learn how to punch someone like that, then?' David asks. 'You were like Jason Statham or something!'

'My dad taught me,' I lie.

'Jimmy?' David says, looking pleased with himself for remembering. Hearing someone else say my dad's name unexpectedly like that makes me feel really strange.

'Yeah,' I murmur. 'Jimmy.'

Just then Essie starts hissing and I'm glad of the interruption.

'Olsen alert!' she says, jerking her head wildly to the left.

David immediately goes bright red.

'What's an Olsen?' I ask.

'You mean who,' Felix says. 'Zachary Olsen. Over there.'

David goes redder still. I follow his gaze to a tall blond boy standing in the queue. I look back at David. His eyes have gone all droopy and misty-looking.

'You fancy him?' I ask.

'Try head over heels in love with him,' Essie supplies in a noisy whisper.

'Ess!' David cries, his face practically purple by now.

'Hey, it doesn't bother me,' I say, holding up my hands. 'I mean, I'd already worked out you were gay if that's what you're worried about.'

David peers at me. His face has begun to calm down a bit.

'And you're OK with that?'

'What? You think I'm some kind of homophobe? Because any boy from Cloverdale has got to be a Neanderthal, right?'

'Of course not,' David says, flustered. 'You just never know . . .' He lets his voice trail off.

I sigh. 'Look, I don't care who you fancy. It's none of my business if you like boys.'

'Does that mean you're straight then, Leo?' Essie asks.

Felix rolls his eyes towards the ceiling.

I put down my can of Coke and look her in the eyes, which are a very pale blue, and lined with crusty black eyeliner.

'As a matter of fact, it does,' I say. 'You ask a lot of questions, you know that?'

'Curiosity is one of the permanent and certain characteristics of a vigorous intellect, Leo,' she recites.

'Samuel Johnson,' I reply, not missing a beat.

Essie blinks at me. 'Sorry?'

'The quote. It's by Samuel Johnson, right?'

'You know Samuel Johnson?' Essie asks, her mouth practically hanging open.

'Course,' I say.

This is sort of true. It's one of the quotes from Spike's book that lives in the bathroom. In spite of myself I've started reading it while sitting on the toilet.

'Don't judge a book by its cover, eh?' I say.

Essie opens her mouth then shuts it again.

'English idiom, exact origin unknown,' I add, popping a chip in my mouth. I can't help glancing at David. He's grinning like a lunatic.

21

The following Tuesday I'm queueing alone in the canteen when I hear someone say Leo's name. My ears immediately prick up. I glance behind me. It's a group of Year 11 girls, their heads bent together in a gossipy huddle. I angle my body sideways so I have a better chance of hearing them, and pretend to study the chalkboard menu on the wall above their heads.

'I'm telling you, Leo Denton is taking Alicia Baker to Becky's party on Saturday,' one of the girls, a tall redhead says. 'Ruby Webber told me.'

Alicia Baker is in Year 11, same as Leo. She always plays the female lead in the school musical, and every Christmas she's selected to sing the first verse of 'Once in Royal David's City' in the carol concert.

'Lucky Alicia, he's well cute,' one of the other girls, a petite blonde, says wistfully, curling a piece of hair round her index finger.

'Yeah,' another girl agrees. 'I love the strong silent type. And a bit of rough is always sexy.'

They all burst into giggles.

'But isn't he meant to be insane or psychotic or something?' the redhead points out. 'Clare Boulter reckons she saw him coming out of the Sunrise Centre last week.'

The Sunrise Centre is on the outskirts of the city centre. It's for teenagers with mental health issues. A girl in 10B who self-harmed in the school toilets used to have appointments there. But why does Leo, I wonder. My mind is racing.

'Plus he's kind of short, don't you think?' the redhead continues.

'With eyes like that, who cares?' the blonde replies.

It was only a few weeks ago they thought that exact pair of eyes was 'crazy'.

'What do you want, love?' The dinner lady is talking to me, ladle in hand, a weary expression on her lined face.

'Sorry?' I stammer.

'What do you want?' she repeats.

I blink, suddenly unable to focus on the words written on the chalkboard.

'Come on, I haven't got all day,' she says.

'Er, pizza please,' I say.

The dinner lady shovels a thick slice onto my plate.

I find a table in the corner and sit down. But my appetite has gone and I only manage to eat half my lunch.

All the way home I can't help thinking about Becky's party. Not that I'd get an invite to a Year 11 party in a million years. I don't even get invited to Year 10 parties.

When I get in I slump down on the sofa with my laptop and before I can stop myself, my fingers are typing Leo's name into Facebook. I can't find him. He's not on Twitter or Instagram or Pinterest either. I google his name but the closest I can find is a load of stuff about some Cloverdale girl called Megan Denton who won a load of swimming trophies once.

'What you looking at?'

I jump. Livvy is leaning over the back of the sofa, her long hair brushing my arm.

I slap the lid of my laptop shut.

'Nothing,' I snap. 'What do you want anyway, sneaking up on me like that?'

'Mum wants you to help with dinner,' she says.

I remain still, my hands flat against the warmth of my gently whirring laptop.

'Go ahead, I'll be there in a few seconds,' I tell her.

'Weirdo,' she replies.

The following day, I meet Leo in the library at lunch for our first tutoring session. I want to ask him about Becky's party, but can't find a suitably casual way of dropping it into a conversation about factoring quadratic equations. In fact I want to ask him lots of things.

As he leans across to pick up my pen, I get a whiff of soap and aftershave, and when the sun hits him at a certain angle, I can see a cluster of fine light brown freckles across his nose I've never noticed before. Both things make me feel strange.

'Hey guys, can I interrupt?'

We look up. It's a girl called Rachel from my textiles class, a friend of Lexi's. She's holding a clipboard edged with tinsel and wearing a Santa hat and a plastered-on smile.

'Can I interest you in Christmas Ball tickets?' she asks.

'No, thank you,' Leo and I murmur in unison.

'Are you sure?' Rachel asks. 'It's going to be the social event of the year. We'll be transforming the school hall into a winter wonderland. Harry Beaumont is even hiring a snow machine. I promise you, you do not want to miss it.'

'I'm OK at the moment, thanks,' I say.

'Me too,' Leo adds.

Rachel's smile quickly morphs into a pout.

'Suit yourselves,' she says snootily, adjusting her Santa hat before stalking away.

'What's the big deal about this ball?' Leo asks. 'There are posters for it everywhere and it's not even happening for another two months.'

'Christmas Ball fever hits earlier and earlier every year,' I say.

'Do you ever go?'

'Ess, Felix and I always say we're not going to, but then at the last minute we end up caving in and buying tickets.'

'And what's it like?'

'Oh, you know, hideous. Harry struts around like he's cured the world of famine or something. There's always a massive bowl of really disgusting non-alcoholic punch. And the DJ is super-obnoxious and refuses to play requests, yada yada yada . . .'

'So why do you always go if you have such a bad time?'

'Oh I don't know. I guess each year there's this flimsy hope that maybe this one will be different. Stupid, right?'

Leo frowns. 'Do people take dates and stuff?'

'A lot do.'

Leo clears his throat. 'C'mon, let's finish this equation. You're really close to solving it.'

As we're packing away our things, Leo's wallet slips from his grasp and I drop to my knees to retrieve it. It has fallen open and in the section where you can insert a photograph, there's a picture of a handsome guy with the same sandy brown mop of hair as Leo.

'Who's that?' I ask, peering closer.

'It's my dad,' Leo says, holding out his hand. Reluctantly I pass him the wallet.

'You look just like him,' I say, standing up.

Leo nods slightly.

'Do you get to see him much?' I ask.

Leo shakes his head, shoving the wallet deep into his back pocket.

'Will you see him at Christmas?'

'I doubt it.'

'How come?'

'Look, he left when I was a baby, I haven't seen him since.'

Now it makes sense why Leo acted so weird when I asked about his dad in the car the other week.

'But you must at least know where he is?' I ask.

'Nope.'

'But doesn't he have to pay, I don't know, Child Support or something?'

'God knows,' Leo says, putting on his backpack.

'Haven't you tried looking for him? Like on the internet? Surely he's on Facebook or something.'

'Course I have,' Leo snaps. 'Do you think I'm an idiot?'

'Sorry.'

Leo sighs. 'All I know about him is his name and the fact he was a carpenter. I don't even know his date of birth.'

'You're kidding?'

'Nope.'

'Wow.'

'Yeah,' Leo says, his voice flat.

'Do you miss him?' I ask.

Leo looks thoughtful. 'Every day.'

As soon as the words leave his lips, he looks as if he regrets them, like he's shared too much on the subject.

'Mental, right?' he adds with a bitter laugh.

'It doesn't sound mental at all,' I say quickly. 'It sounds human.'

Leo shrugs, a far-off look in his eyes.

'Why did he leave?' I ask.

Leo grimaces. 'They all leave. Without fail. It's what Mam does best, her party trick.'

I want to ask more questions, but Leo is looking up at the clock.

'I've got to get going to registration. I'll see you.'

I watch as he jogs out of the library.

As I pack up my things, I try to imagine my dad leaving

me when I was a baby, but it's impossible. I've seen the end-less photograph albums of him in hospital scrubs, beaming away as he holds his firstborn child in his arms, or asleep on the sofa with me, tiny and wrinkled, curled up on his chest. He would never have left me and Mum, ever. What must Leo's mum have done to drive away her baby's father, never to return, I wonder. Something terrible. Something unforgiv-able. I shiver.

As I climb out of the car after school, Mum lets out a gasp.

'Your trousers are halfway up your ankles, David,' she says.

The moment we get inside, I run upstairs and lock my door. Mum is right. I've grown two centimetres in height in less than two weeks. At first I think it's impossible so I measure myself again. And again. But the pencil marks don't lie. When I write it down in my notebook my hands are trembling and the letters come out all wobbly. If I can grow two centimetres in the space of two weeks, how many might I grow in six weeks? Or ten?

On Saturday morning Mum insists on taking me into town to buy a couple of new pairs of trousers.

'You're growing up so fast,' Mum says, as we pull into a space in the underground car park. 'You watch, you'll end up taller than your dad!'

Apparently Dad was always one of the shortest kids in the class until, in the space of less than a year, he had this crazy growth spurt aged fifteen, and shot up to one metre, ninety centimetres pretty much overnight. This is fine if you're a guy. If you're a girl, it's a disaster.

Mum and I head for John Lewis. It's too warm and bustling with shoppers.

In the lift there's a buggy with twin babies in it. A boy and a girl.

'How old are they?' Mum asks their parents.

'Coming up to eleven months,' the mother replies.

'Such a fun age!' Mum says. 'They're gorgeous.'

'They're a handful!' the father chimes in, and everyone laughs as if he's just made an absolutely hilarious joke. I inspect the babies. The girl is asleep. She is all in pink. The boy is awake and chewing on a soggy rice cake. He wears denim dungarees with a tractor embroidered on the pocket and his free fist is clutching a toy car. He eyes me wearily. I bet already his parents assume he's going to be a typical boy; that his favourite colour will be blue or black or red, that he'll play football and like cars and trucks, that one day he'll get married and have babies. And even if he's not typical, even if he likes ballet or baking cakes or kissing boys instead of girls, they'll still imagine that their little boy will grow up to be a man. Because why wouldn't you? As we leave the lift, the boy and I eyeball one another until he is wheeled out of sight.

In the school uniform department Mum flips through the racks of trousers, every so often holding a pair up against me and muttering to herself.

I wander across to the racks of school skirts – pleated, flared, long, short. I reach over and trail my fingers over them, feigning uninterest as I do so, just in case Mum glances across and notices what I'm doing.

In the fitting rooms, I try on four identical pairs of navy trousers.

'He's having a growth spurt,' I hear Mum confide to the sales assistant in a stage whisper as she waits on the other side of the curtain.

The fitting room light is bright and harsh, not like the dim light I use in my bedroom for inspections. The whole time I'm changing I keep my back to the mirror.

Afterwards we head to the food court for lunch and eat at Yo! Sushi. We sit side by side on high stools in front of the conveyer belt. I coach Mum on her chopstick technique. She lets me have two portions of the chocolate mochi for dessert.

'This is fun,' she says, filling up her glass with fizzy water from the tap built into the bar we are sitting at. 'We should do this more often.'

My mouth is full so I just nod.

'We're all so busy these days,' she continues, 'Dad and I with work, you and Livvy with school. I don't feel like you and I have had a proper chat in ages. You know, proper mother–son time.'

She pauses and sets down her glass. I feel her eyes settle on me, studying me. I dab the chocolaty corners of my mouth with a napkin.

'Everything is all right at the moment, isn't it darling?' she asks slowly.

'Of course it is. Why do you ask?' I reply, keeping my eye

on a portion of cucumber rolls snaking their way round the conveyer belt, tracking their progress.

'You've just seemed a bit preoccupied lately.'

'It's just that school is really busy,' I say lamely.

'You would tell me, wouldn't you, if something wasn't OK, or if there was something you wanted to get off your chest. Because your dad and I would understand, you know.'

I swallow. Because here it is; my opportunity to come out with it. Six little words: I. Want. To. Be. A. Girl. But they don't come out. They stay stubbornly lodged in my throat, choking me into silence. Because the thing Mum is trying to get me to tell her isn't what she's been preparing herself for. Because Mum is expecting me to tell her I am gay. I suspect she's been working up to this moment for years; ever since I requested my first Barbie for Christmas, tore around the house in my first pair of fairy wings, wrapped a towel round my head and pretended it was a mane of long hair. She's probably been rehearsing her response for months now, practising in the mirror the right balance between surprise and acceptance. She's certainly dropped enough hints, initiating passionate pro same-sex marriage debates around the dinner table and making constant references to her gay second cousin, Craig, who lives in Cardiff with his boyfriend, Aaron. But she and Dad have got the signals all wrong, just like Leo got it wrong in the canteen the other day. Because I'm not gay. I'm just a straight girl stuck in a boy's body. But how do I go about telling them that?

'David?' Mum prompts, her eyes big and questioning, full of hope.

'No, Mum,' I say, finally finding my voice, 'I'm fine. Honestly.'

She looks disappointed for a second, but hides it quickly, reaching up and tucking a strand of hair behind my ear.

'Well, I'm glad to hear it,' she says, patting me on the hand.

As we're paying the bill, a flash of gold catches my eye. I glance across to Nando's on the opposite side of the food court. Alicia Baker, Ruby Webber and a few other Year 11 girls are squeezed into a booth surrounded by masses of shopping bags. Alicia has produced a shimmery gold top from a plastic Top Shop bag. She holds it up against her torso as the other girls nod their approval.

'Ready to go?' Mum says brightly.

'Sure,' I murmur, dragging my eyes away from Alicia and her friends.

That night, I am home alone. Livvy is sleeping over at Cressy's. Mum and Dad are going to dinner at the house of one of Dad's colleagues. Essie and Felix are having a 'date night'.

'Nothing fluffy or romantic,' Essie assures me over Skype, as Felix lolls on the bed behind her, 'just boyfriend–girlfriend time, you know.'

But I don't know. Not really. I've never had a boyfriend or girlfriend (unless you count going out with Leila Shilton for three days when we were six, which I don't). I've never kissed anyone. I've never even held hands. I've probably exchanged a grand total of ten words with Zachary in the past five years. I'm a complete relationship novice. It doesn't help that tonight is the night of Becky Somerville's party and across town in Cloverdale, Leo is getting ready to take Alicia, and I feel like everyone in the entire world is in a two-some except for me.

Mum clearly feels guilty about leaving me because she orders me a massive pepperoni pizza all to myself and sends Dad to the shops to buy a tub of my favourite Ben and Jerry's Phish Food ice-cream. I wave them off from the door, waiting for ten minutes before heading upstairs.

In my bedroom I drop to my knees and drag out the large box I keep buried under the piles of shoes and coats at the bottom of my wardrobe. Its contents are the result of years of careful sourcing. At the bottom are items that no longer fit but I cannot quite bring myself to throw away – the fairy wings Auntie Jane bought me when I was five (I didn't take them off for a week), the pink nightie I swiped from beneath my cousin Keira's pillow one Christmas, Essie's hated confirmation dress, white and frilly, donated happily. On top of these lie charity shop finds, smuggled into the house under my coat; then cocktail dresses and poly-ester trouser suits from the 1980s stolen from the back of Mum's wardrobe under the cover of darkness; more rejects from Essie.

Tonight I select a dress that belonged to Essie's mother when she was going through her hippie stage back in the mid-nineties, before Essie was born. It's long, floaty and tie-dyed, and covered with tiny mirrors. I take off my boy clothes, discarding them in a pile on the floor, before slipping it on over my head. I lift up the skirt to my nose and inhale deeply. It still smells of incense, sort of warm, like gingerbread, mixed in with stale perfume and sea salt.

Next I put on my wig. I bought it online earlier this year with money left over from Christmas, running upstairs with it before Mum and Livvy had the chance to demand what was in the mysterious cardboard box tucked under my arm. It's a shiny shoulder length bob, a slightly darker shade of brown than my real hair. I absolutely love it.

I sit down at my desk and take out my make-up bag. Most of it I've bought with my pocket money, other bits I've stolen from Mum, or inherited from Essie. I empty it all out, lining it up neatly on my desk, the array of colours. I've been watching lots of online make-up tutorials lately. I position my laptop beside me and search for my favourite; a girl from Texas called CeeCee, who is probably the closest I've ever seen to a real-life Barbie doll. She delivers her tutorials in a hypnotic thick Southern drawl. Together, step-by-step, we apply foundation, concealer, blusher, eyeliner, smoky eye-shadow. The smoky eyes in particular are harder than they look and it takes four attempts before I get my right eye to match my left. I sit back and take in my whole face – the smooth complexion, the hint of girlish blush, my eyes, thick with mascara and mystery. To finish, I take out my favourite lipstick – Diva Red – and drag it across my lips.

The doorbell rings, making me jump. I go into Mum and Dad's bedroom and peek through the curtains. It's the pizza delivery guy. I'd completely forgotten about him. For a moment I consider answering the door as I am, as a girl.

The thought fills me with excitement and fear. But the fear wins out and I'm quickly wiping my mouth on the side of my hand, smearing it blood-red, and pulling my bathrobe on over my dress. As I'm going downstairs, I rip off my wig and shove it into my pocket. I open the front door a crack, just wide enough to pass over the ten-pound note and receive my pizza, keeping my head down so the delivery man doesn't clock my made-up face. With the door safely shut, I put my wig back on and remove my bathrobe, draping it over the banister.

I take my pizza into the kitchen, collect napkins and pour myself a glass of Coke. Usually I enjoy catching sight of my reflection in the toaster or kettle, feeling the swish of material around my legs, but tonight, for some reason, I feel flat. I eat my pizza in front of the TV, followed by the ice cream, the entire tub in one go. I feel like I'm faking the enjoyment though, eating for the sake of it. I don't have that many chances to dress up undisturbed at home and when I do it's the normal everyday stuff I like doing best – loading the dishwasher, making toast, watching TV. But not tonight. Tonight I feel strange, like everything is off-kilter, like I'm a big fat fraud. As I load the dishwasher, my body leaden and tired, I feel a fat tear roll down my cheek. Horrified, I wipe it away. It leaves a watery black smear on my hand. It's only nine o'clock, hours before my parents are due home, but I trudge upstairs anyway, remove my dress and wig and scrub my face clean, the remnants of make-up washing down the plughole in a dirty rainbow. I take a shower in the dark, change into a fresh pair of pyjamas and get into bed.

I almost go to Skype Essie and Felix, but at the last second remember it's their date night and they're probably rolling around naked right now, their thoughts far away from me.

As I lie there in the darkness, unwanted images of Becky's party keep popping into my head. In my mind it is dark and smoky, full of sweaty bodies sighing and swaying, pressing up against each other in slow motion. There's a dull ache in my belly. I realise my pillow is wet. I turn on to my side so I'm facing the wall. What's wrong with you? I ask myself angrily. Then it hits me, I'm lonely. I'm so lonely it physically hurts. The realisation makes me feel even worse. Like I've been tricking myself into putting on a brave face this entire time. I roll on to my front, pull my pillow over my head and recite my French vocabulary in my head over and over and over, until, finally, I must fall asleep.

22

'What you doing, Leo?'

I turn round. Tia is standing in the doorway to the bathroom wearing the Hello Kitty pyjamas she's been in all day.

It's Saturday night. Becky's party starts in just over two hours.

'What does it look like? I'm doing my hair.'

'But you never do your hair.'

I ignore her and pick up a tub of Spike's hair stuff. I take a sniff before scooping some out with my finger and running it through my hair.

Tia sits on the edge of the bath, her toes not quite reaching the floor.

'Where are you going?'

'A party.'

'Can I come?'

'No.'

'Why not?'

'Because it's a grown-up party,'

'But you're not a grown-up. You're only fifteen.'

'Fine, it's a teenage party then, just for teenagers.'

'Oh. Will there be pass the parcel?'

'No.'

'Will there be jelly and ice cream?'

'I doubt it.'

'How can it be a party without jelly and ice cream?'

I ignore her. Spike's hair gunk has made the front of my hair look all greasy. I dunk my head under the taps and try to wash it out.

'Leo?' Tia says, pulling at my sleeve.

'What?' I yell over the running tap.

'If it turns out there is jelly and ice cream, will you save some and bring it back for me?'

I turn off the taps and straighten up, water dripping down my forehead, and look at her hopeful little face.

'Sure.'

On the way out of the bathroom I bump into Mam on the landing. She's just got in from her shift at the launderette and looks red-faced and tired.

'What's got into you?' she says accusingly.

'What do you mean?' I ask.

'Acting all chirpy,' she says, narrowing her eyes, like acting chirpy is the sin to end all sins.

'Dunno what you mean,' I say, breezing past her.

She's right though, I've been in a good mood all week. Things that usually annoy me – Amber using up all the hot water in the morning, Tia leaving her cereal bowl in the sink, Spike's singing, pretty much everything Mam does – all this stuff washes over me.

As I pull on my hoodie and check my reflection one last time, the familiar little voice pops into my head, warning me not to get carried away. I ignore it. Because Alicia is different, I'm convinced. She's not like the girls at Cloverdale School, made bitter and mean by the things they've seen. No, Alicia is fresh and hopeful. And tonight I get to spend the entire evening with her.

Alicia's house sits off the main road behind a pair of massive gates. It's big and symmetrical, with a huge front door twice the width of ours and loads of windows. As I walk up the driveway it seems to get even bigger, looming over me. I reach to press the doorbell and realise my hand is trembling slightly. I shake it hard. Now is not the time for nerves. Tonight is all about being calm, cool, tough.

A tall black man, who I assume must be Alicia's dad, answers the door. His skin is glossy and smooth and his teeth gleaming white, like Alicia's. Just like the house, he towers over me.

'Can I help you?' he asks, his voice deep and velvety.

I clear my throat but my voice still comes out sounding all funny. 'I'm here to pick up Alicia?'

'I'm sorry, young man, but you must be mistaken, my daughter is forbidden to date boys until she is at least twenty-one. On your way now, please,' he says, shooing me away and making to shut the door.

'Oh, right, sorry,' I stammer, confused.

'Dad!' Alicia screeches. I look over his shoulder and there she is, standing on the staircase behind him with her hands on her hips, wearing dark blue jeans and a gold top.

'Don't listen to a single word he says!' she calls.

Her dad breaks into a wide grin. 'Only joshing with you, Leo!' he laughs, punching me on the arm. 'Come in, come in!'

I'm ushered into the hallway. It's huge. We don't even have a proper hallway at home, just a space at the bottom of the stairs that's forever littered with shoes and bits of unopened post. But Alicia's hall is as big as our lounge, if not bigger. I wipe my feet hard on the doormat, not wanting to dirty the cream carpet. Alicia's mother appears from the kitchen, wearing a striped apron. She looks like a mum from a TV advert – all glowing and perfect. She takes hold of my shoulders and kisses me on each cheek, telling me how nice it is to meet me.

I'm struck that both Alicia's parents know my name, meaning Alicia must have spoken about me at least a bit.

'Leo, please excuse my super-embarrassing parents. They mistakenly think they're hilarious,' Alicia says as she pulls on her coat, ushering me out of the front door.

'Back by midnight, please,' her dad says, tapping his watch.

'Yes, Dad,' Alicia says, rolling her eyes.

In all the commotion I haven't had a chance to look at her properly. It's only now, standing on the front doorstep as she wraps a long pink scarf round her neck, I get the opportunity. She has her hair fastened up with a few curls pulled loose so they frame her face and she's wearing make-up. She looks amazing.

'You look really nice,' I say.

She smiles, 'And so do you, Leo Denton.'

My stomach does a flip-flop.

Shit.

There is no question which of the houses in Becky's street is having the party. At number twenty-six, the music is already pumping and I can make out the shadowy forms of party-goers through the

145

curtains. We arrive to find Becky in the hallway greeting each of her guests with a high-pitched squeal and/or perfumed hug. She's wearing a glittery pink dress that makes her look like a fairy on top of a Christmas tree. When we walk in she shrieks especially loud.

'OMG, I'm so beyond excited you're here!' she cries in this bizarre American accent, a bit like the one Tia speaks in when she's watched too much Nickelodeon. Becky's greeting to me is a casual, 'Hi, Leo,' and a slow look up and down, a hint of a smile on her lips.

'Here, let me take your coats,' she says, holding out her arms.

Even though it's sweltering, I keep my hoodie on. Alicia takes off her scarf and coat and gives it to Becky.

'God, I love your top,' Becky says. 'Let me see the back.'

Alicia does a little twirl. Her top ties round her neck and reveals her smooth brown back. From what I can tell, I don't think she's wearing a bra. I swallow.

'Go through to the kitchen,' Becky says, waving us through. 'My mum's ordered like twenty pizzas.'

Becky's mother is the spit of Becky, with the same moon-face and drawn-on eyebrows. The kitchen tops are piled high with pizza boxes. I help Alicia find a vegetarian slice before finding some ham and mushroom for me.

'Now, make sure you get a drink from Becky's dad!' Becky's mum says. 'We've got beer, wine, alcopops, whatever you want. I'm not one of those strict mums. I was young once, believe it or not!'

Becky appears in the doorway.

'Mum!' she says through gritted teeth. 'Aren't you and Dad meant to be leaving?'

'Calm down, darling, I'm just making sure everyone's fed and watered.'

'Well hurry up!'

Alicia and I grin at each other.

Becky's dad is behind the breakfast bar, playing barman. Bottles of spirits and mixers crowd the work surface and a load of cans of beer and bottles of WKD and Smirnoff Ice sit in a plastic bowl full of ice in the sink.

'What can I get you?' he says, ignoring me and looking straight at Alicia. She leans forward to inspect the drinks selection and I swear Becky's dad glances at her boobs.

'A Smirnoff Ice, please,' Alicia says brightly.

'Can of Foster's,' I chip in.

'Coming right up,' Becky's dad says, winking at Alicia. He makes a big show of tossing the bottle in the air and catching it, like he's a cocktail waiter or something. He even takes the top off with his teeth and spits it out into the bin, pausing like he expects us to applaud him. The whole time he keeps his eyes on Alicia.

'Enjoy, darling,' he says, handing the bottle over to her. Almost as an afterthought, he pushes a can of beer towards me, his gaze still lingering on Alicia.

We make our way out of the kitchen with our drinks, balancing our pizza on flimsy paper plates. The living room is packed with kids. The iPod deck is blasting Kanye West. It's weird seeing everyone from school out of uniform. This is the first time I've moved amongst them in this way, body parts brushing as Alicia and I make our way through the living room. Some openly stare at us, whispering as we pass.

Alicia heads for the conservatory where it's a bit quieter. We set our drinks down on a plastic picnic table in the corner, but remain standing up, Alicia swaying in time to the music. As I take my first bite of pizza, tomato sauce oozes over the side of my slice and lands on my hoodie.

'Leo!' Alicia cries out.

I swear under my breath as Alicia gropes about in her bag for a tissue. She manages to scoop up most of the sauce, gently dabbing at the rest. When she's finished she steps back, satisfied, and smiles at me, this gentler version of her usual megawatt grin. And for a moment it's like we're the only two people at the party. But then we're interrupted by some of Alicia's mates, chucking their arms around her, complimenting her on her top, the way she's done her hair, and they are just the first of a steady stream of visitors.

As Alicia receives her subjects, I sit down in one of the picnic chairs and just watch her – the way she laughs at jokes that aren't funny, how she leans in and listens intently as secrets are shared, nodding thoughtfully, saying all the right things. At one point she catches my eye and gives me this reluctant little shrug as if to say sorry.

Around nine o'clock, Becky's parents finally leave, making a big show of saying goodbye.

'We're just over the road if you need us! Back at midnight!' Becky's mum calls as Becky practically shoves her out of the door.

'Becky's so lucky,' Alicia says when we're finally alone again. 'My parents wouldn't let me have a party without them being there in a million years. And they definitely wouldn't let me have all that booze.'

'Nah, my mam wouldn't either,' I say.

'Becky's dad was a bit weird, wasn't he?' Alicia says, screwing up her face.

'Yeah, I didn't like him. He was well pervy.'

'You reckon? I thought he was a bit dodgy but I wasn't sure.'

'Nah, it wasn't right,' I say. 'The way he was looking at you. He must know you're only fifteen.'

Alicia leans forward, so that her breath tickles my ear.

'Nearly sixteen,' she whispers.

I swallow and I think Alicia must notice because she breaks into a giggle and punches me on the arm.

'You're a proper gentleman, you know that, Leo Denton?'

I'm about to answer her when a Rihanna song comes on and Alicia lets out this excited little scream and jumps up, grabbing me by the hand. I've drunk two cans of Foster's by now and as I stand up I feel a bit woozy. Alicia seems fine though, swigging from her third Smirnoff Ice as she tugs me towards the music.

'I don't really dance,' I'm saying, but Alicia either can't hear, or she's choosing to ignore me. We're in the centre of the lounge now, sweaty bodies surrounding us. Someone has turned the music up and the house feels like it's bulging, fit to burst from the booming bass line. Alicia is jumping up and down, more strands of hair falling free, flying around her face.

'C'mon, Leo!' she yells over the music. 'Dance with me!'

I look around. Everyone is moving, flinging their arms around and laughing. I don't even know where to start.

'Just do what I do!' Alicia says, grabbing hold of my hands. And maybe it's the beer, or maybe it's the fact it's with her, but I start to dance. And it's not so bad. I'm not so bad at it. I'm just about getting into it when a new song comes on. It's another R&B number, but slower this time, sexy, and immediately Alicia starts grinding up against me, her bum rubbing against my crotch. I back away a few steps and she turns round in surprise, frowning slightly. Quickly I mime, 'do you want a drink?' and she relaxes into a smile and nods, before continuing to dance.

I go to the toilet first, relieved to find it free. Next to the toilet itself there's a full-length mirror. What's that all about, I wonder. What kind of weirdo wants to watch themselves take a dump? Becky's pervy dad, I bet. I wash my hands. My face is very pink. I splash cold water over it, try to cool down.

When I return to the lounge, fresh drinks in hand, Becky has turned the music down and is in the centre of the room, wobbling about on her glittery pink heels.

'Games time!' she calls, trying to usher everyone into a circle. Alicia is already sitting cross-legged on the floor. She pats the spot next to her, but before I can make a move towards it, her mate Ruby plonks herself in the space. Alicia offers an apologetic shrug. I sit down where I am, between Matt and some girl with curly brown hair I recognise from school, but whose name I don't know. Out of what seems like nowhere, Becky produces an empty wine bottle and everyone goes 'ooooohhhhh!' like we're at a pantomime.

'This game needs no introduction,' Becky crows. 'It's that retro party classic, Spin the Bottle, people!'

There's lots of whooping.

'You know the rules, if the bottle points to you it's time to get down and dirty!'

Yet more whooping.

'As the birthday girl, I get to spin first.'

Becky crawls into the centre of the room, flashing her knickers to the crowd. I take a nervous sip of beer and go to stand up.

'Where do you think you're going, Denton?' Becky barks.

'I was gonna sit this one out,' I say.

'Oh no you don't,' she says. 'Joining in is compulsory, right, Alicia?'

Alicia blushes.

Reluctantly I sit down. Across the circle Alicia smiles at me. I fake a smile back.

Becky spins. As the bottle turns people clap and yell. I hold my breath, willing it to spin past me. It rests on a kid from my form called Liam. He shuffles on his bum into the centre of the circle. Becky grabs hold of his face with both hands and shoves her tongue down his throat. Everyone screams. I try to catch Alicia's eye across the circle but she is too busy screaming herself, fingers over her eyes. Becky eventually lets go of Liam. Their mouths are all pink and clown-like from friction and smudged lipstick.

'Not bad,' she reports to the circle at large. 'Six out of ten maybe.'

Liam's face turns as pink as the lipstick smeared on his chin. It's his turn to spin. I fixate on the bottle, praying for it not to stop on Alicia.

Couple after couple assemble in the centre of the circle, the girls reporting back on the boys' performances like it's an exam – 'A for effort', 'eight out of ten', 'needs practice' etcetera, the boys slinking back to their places triumphant or humiliated. Every spin, I will the bottle not to land on me or Alicia, holding my breath as it inches past each of us. All the time, I keep telling myself they'll get bored soon and the party can get back to normal.

'One last spin!' Becky announces, answering my secret prayer.

I dare to relax a little, convinced luck is on my side. This is why it all feels like a weird dream when suddenly people are yelling my name and I look down and the neck of the bottle is pointing right at me, like the barrel of a gun. I blink, look up. Ruby is kneeling in the centre of the circle, her head cocked to the side.

'I'm not waiting all night,' she says coyly. I nod and in what feels like slow motion I edge into the circle on my knees. All the time the whole party is chanting, 'Leo, Leo!' and I feel like I'm in the Colosseum in Rome, only instead of being fed to the lions, I'm being fed to Ruby Webber. She's leaning forwards now and I can see down her top. I've never noticed her tits before – how big they are, how round, how if she leans forward much more they might spill out of her top altogether. But none of this matters, because even though Ruby is fit and all that, she isn't Alicia. I edge closer still, someone leans across and ruffles my hair, telling me to go for it.

I glance across and there she is. Gorgeous Alicia. Chewing on her thumbnail. We lock eyes for a second and she smiles this sort of brave smile as if to say it's OK. Around me everyone is roaring. Ruby smiles and closes her eyes. I take my chance and kiss her very quickly, just a peck, our lips hardly making contact. Her eyes spring open.

'Is that it?' she asks, annoyed and amused all at once.

Around her everyone boos.

I shrug and glance across at Alicia. She is sitting up straight and biting on her lower lip. Becky strides into the circle and puts her hands on my shoulders.

'I have a feeling lover-boy Leo here is saving himself for a certain someone,' she crows. A load of the girls dissolve into knowing giggles.

Becky claps her hands together, 'Right, time to spice things up a bit. A new game!'

She goes into the hall and opens the cupboard under the stairs with a flourish.

'We'll spin again and the lucky couple gets ten minutes of heaven – in here!' Becky says.

She bounces back into the living room as everyone shuffles in to tighten up the circle, 'Your turn, Leo.'

I take a deep breath and spin the bottle. It seems to turn for an eternity until, finally, it begins to slow, coming to a stop pointing slap-bang at Becky. Everyone starts whooping. Becky shouts them down, holding up her hands in surrender.

'Sorry, guys, I'm exempt from this round, birthday-girl rules and all that, which means I get to pass to my left, and lo-and-behold, who is sitting to my left but Miss Alicia Baker!'

Alicia blushes furiously. Becky pulls her to her feet and practically frog-marches the two of us into the hallway while everyone claps and cheers, chanting our names.

'Get in there, my son!' Matt says, his eyes wide and excited on my behalf. I manage a cocky grin in return.

'Go on then!' Becky barks. We squeeze in to the cupboard, nestling between the household debris. It smells damp and fusty, of rained-on camping gear and stale sleeping bags.

'Enjoy!' Becky sing-songs as she slams the door shut and turns out the light, plunging us into darkness. A moment or two later the music starts up, the bass line thudding once more. Alicia and I shift around a little, trying to get comfortable.

'You OK?' I ask gruffly.

'Yeah, fine. You?'

'Yeah.'

Silence. Alicia breaks it.

'I'm glad you didn't snog Ruby properly.'

I swallow. 'Me too.'

More silence. I hear her take a deep breath.

'In case you haven't worked it out yet, I really like you, Leo Denton.'

I feel this weird rush in my chest.

'And I really like you, Alicia Baker.'

I imagine Alicia grinning in the dark, her dimples deepening and I'm suddenly desperate to touch them, to explore every single bit of her. I feel for her hand in the dark and find it and she's wrapping her fingers tightly round mine. And then we're kissing. Just like that, our lips like magnets. And it's amazing. Not only that, it's so easy, like the easiest thing in the world. And probably the nicest. At first it's soft, a bit tentative, like our lips are having a polite little conversation, but then it's more urgent, hungry, almost like we're feeding off each other. My arms go around her and hers around me. And I forget about everything. I forget about the fact an ironing board is sticking into my back, I forget about Becky and everyone else at the party just centimetres away from us, I forget about Mam and Tia and Spike and Amber and Harry Beaumont and David Piper and his crazy friends, I even forget about Dad. All I can think about is kissing Alicia and my hands on her bare back and how this is the best moment of my life bar none. And she's making all these *mmmmmm* noises and then she's kissing my neck and breathing, 'Oh, Leo,' and my God, I'm so turned on it's unreal. And then she's putting my hand on her boob and I'm about to explode. It feels so amazing, and the fact that she's put my hand there, that she wants

154

it there, blows my mind. And then her hands are making their way under my layers, under my hoodie, then my shirt, then my T-shirt, searching out skin.

'You're proper ripped, Leo, you've got like a full-on six pack!' she whispers, excitement in her breath, her hands warm against my stomach. All those hours of sit-ups have paid off. I try to enjoy her reaction, but I can't ignore the familiar anxiety building in my belly. I try to block it out but the anxiety pushes through, like a sprinter accelerating to win the race, and my entire body tenses up. I pull away.

'Leo, are you all right?' Alicia asks.

'Course,' I lie.

'No you're not. What's wrong?'

'Nothing.'

'Do you not fancy me or something?'

'Course I do!' I almost yell, because the idea of her not realising how much I fancy her is mental. 'I fancy you loads.'

'Then why have you stopped?'

'It's not you,' I begin.

'What? It's not you, it's me?' Alicia says. 'Jesus.'

'It's not a line!' I say, taking hold of her hands in mine. 'Listen to me, I like you so much I could burst, and I want to do stuff with you. God, I want to do everything with you. But not here, not in Becky Somerville's flipping cupboard under the stairs. You're too special for that,' I say, the words tumbling out of my mouth in a mad panic.

Silence. I bite down hard on my lip.

'You promise you fancy me?' Alicia says in a small voice.

'God, Alicia, I fancy you so much it makes me dizzy.'

155

It's the right answer because Alicia lets out this really cute little giggle.

There's a thump on the cupboard door.

'One more minute!' Becky yells.

I lean in to kiss Alicia. She kisses me back. Our arms go around each other. I can feel my anxiety shrinking away. I'm back in control.

For the rest of the evening, Alicia and I are glued to each other's side. For a bit we dance, but mostly we sit on the settee, Alicia's legs draped over mine, and talk. Alicia tells me about wanting to be a singer but her parents really wanting her to be a doctor, how much she adores her little brother who has Down syndrome, about her old life in London. I tell her about sharing a bedroom with Amber, about the funny stuff Tia comes out with sometimes, about my gran dying when I was twelve and how I still miss her. And it sort of feels good, to be sharing stuff with her, even if I'm carefully editing the bits I'm prepared to share as I go along.

I walk her home. We kiss on the doorstep as the grandfather clock inside strikes twelve. As we break apart Alicia says, 'Leo, you know the Christmas Ball?'

'Yeah.'

'Look, I know it's ages away, but do you want to go together?'

'Er, yeah,' I say. 'Why not.'

She breaks into a massive grin and kisses me. And it's amazing all over again.

'Alicia,' a man's voice calls from inside.

'My dad,' Alicia says, rolling her eyes. 'Bang on time.'

She kisses me once more before darting inside.

For a few seconds I'm frozen to the spot, finally able to digest what has just happened.

Alicia likes me. As in, *really* likes me. My entire body is buzzing. I feel epic, alive, like all my nerve endings are on fire. The little voice tries to interrupt, to remind me about how huge this is, how dangerous, of all the things that could go wrong. But for tonight I'm gonna ignore it, drown it out with thoughts of Alicia. And it works cos the entire five miles home I think of nothing and no one else.

23

It's Sunday night. I'm meant to be doing my maths home-work but I can't concentrate. Instead I'm lying on my bed watching YouTube videos on my laptop. The one I'm watching right now is about a boy who lives in America. He has a gravelly voice and stubble on his chin and you'd never guess in a million years that he used to be a girl until he pulls up his T-shirt and shows you something called a chest binder that looks like a thick white crop top and flattens down his breasts. He's waiting to have chest surgery when he turns eighteen. It's frustrating to think that beneath the binder he has exactly what I want, and that all the things I hate about my body, he'd swap in a heartbeat. If only we could.

I can hear a sound coming from the bathroom. I press pause and listen.

It's Livvy, calling out for Mum, quietly at first but quickly growing more and more urgent. I get up and head on to the landing. I knock gently on the bathroom door.

'Mum?' Livvy says.

'No, it's me, Liv. Are you all right?'

'Get Mum.'

'But what's up?'

'Just get Mum!' she practically screams.

I race downstairs and find Mum on the sofa watching *Master Chef* with Dad.

'Livvy says she needs you. She's in the bathroom,' I say breathlessly.

Mum frowns and gets up. I follow her up the stairs.

She knocks on the bathroom door.

'Livvy, sweetheart?' she calls. 'It's Mummy.'

Livvy opens the door a crack and Mum squeezes in, leaving me to hover on the landing. After a few seconds I hear Mum let out an excited little squeal and Livvy giggle. The door opens and Mum reappears, her face all pink and pleased.

'Mum, what's going on?' I ask.

'Nothing, David. Get on with your homework,' she says, shooing me away.

I continue to hover as Mum dashes into her room, returning a few moments later with a green packet of Always sanitary towels in her hand.

Then it dawns on me. Livvy, my baby sister, has started her period.

Mum ducks into the bathroom, locking it behind her. I can hear her speaking to Livvy in a low voice. A moment later I hear Livvy let out another giggle. Slowly I back away, torn between wanting to listen in and running as far away as I can.

I shut my bedroom door and sit down on the edge of the bed, wondering how many more moments like this I am going to have to witness; private, female moments from which older brothers are automatically excluded. I try to focus on what Essie told me about her periods – about the stomachaches and spots and greasy hair, how she feels permanently furious with Felix; but it does little to help.

Later I go downstairs to discover Livvy lying on the sofa with a hot water bottle resting on her tummy as Mum strokes her hair. I make an excuse about being tired and leave the room.

That night I can't sleep. All I can think about is how I'll never experience what Livvy's experiencing tonight. It's a biological impossibility so unfair it makes my entire body throb.

The next morning, instead of having cereal and toast for breakfast, Mum makes pancakes topped with strawberries and maple syrup in 'Livvy's honour'. Livvy sits at the head of the table like a queen, smiling serenely upon her subjects. Glossy-haired and clear-skinned, she shows none of the symptoms so gorily described by Essie. Trust Livvy to show early signs of breezing through puberty.

'My baby, all grown up,' Mum beams as she pours Livvy a second glass of ceremonial orange juice.

Dad kisses Livvy on the cheek. 'This better not mean you'll be bringing home boyfriends soon!' he says with a grin and a conspiratorial wink in my direction.

Livvy rolls her eyes. 'Daaaaaad, don't be so lame.'

I can tell though, she's pleased.

'Do you want more pancakes, David?' Mum asks, registering my presence at the table for the first time. And even though I am still hungry and could easily eat at least another two, I say no and excuse myself from the table so as not to let them see the tears in my eyes.

Essie and Felix notice something isn't right the moment they see me at school.

'David, what's wrong?' Essie demands.

Her question opens the floodgates. Quickly she and Felix guide me round the corner to the old abandoned bike sheds where I perch on one of the railings and sob like a baby.

'What on earth has happened?' Essie asks, kneeling down in front of me, while Felix rubs my shoulder.

At first I can't talk because I'm crying too hard but eventually I manage to choke out an account of my awful weekend, culminating in the news of Livvy's period.

'Oh, David,' Essie says, standing up and hugging me.

'It just sort of hit me, all at once,' I say between gasps, my speech all jerky. 'That things aren't going to magically fix themselves. They're only going to get worse, way worse.'

'Not necessarily,' Felix says. 'You don't know what's going to happen.'

'Yes I do. I'm a disgusting mutant who is only going to get more disgusting and more mutant-like. Did you know I'm a size nine shoe now?'

'Kate Winslet is a size nine,' Felix says quickly.

'How the hell do you know that?' Essie asks him.

'I don't know, I just do. Paris Hilton's feet are even bigger apparently.'

'Okay, you're creeping me out now,' Essie says.

Their bickering sort of helps me calm down.

'I just feel so . . . lonely,' I say.

'Don't say that. You've got us,' Essie says, tugging on my tie. And she's right, I do. But they've also got each other.

That lunch time I meet Leo in the library. Although talking to Essie and Felix helped a bit, I'm still feeling weird and empty from my monumentally rubbish weekend, like a bit of me might be missing or broken. I'm certainly not in the mood for trigonometry. Beside me Leo is waiting patiently for me to complete the next problem. He seems more relaxed. I wonder why.

'How was the party on Saturday?' I ask.

'What party?' Leo asks slowly, keeping his eyes on the page.

'Becky Somerville's. Didn't you go? I thought the whole of Year 11 was there.'

'Oh *that* party. It was all right,' he says with a shrug, 'nothing special.'

'Oh,' I say, doodling a star on my page. 'That's funny.'

'How so?'

'It's just that I heard it was really amazing.'

I watch his face carefully, alert for clues, certain he's not giving me the full story.

'David?'

'Yes?'

'The hypotenuse?'

'Sorry?'

'Which side of the triangle is the hypotenuse?' he asks, prodding at the page with the end of his pen.

'Er, that one,' I say, pointing aimlessly.

'No, that's the adjacent side. C'mon, you know this stuff, David.'

'Clearly I don't,' I say, frustration building in my belly.

Leo sighs.

'Look at it again.'

I try to look at the page but I can't concentrate properly. The more I try to focus the more the page blurs, the words and shapes beginning to dance in front of my eyes. I can't help it, I'm mad at him, even though he technically hasn't done anything wrong, which somehow seems worse.

'Which one is the hypotenuse?' Leo repeats.

'I don't know,' I say, horrified to discover a film of tears forming in front of my eyes.

'Yes you do. You're not trying. Just relax and concentrate.'

But I can't. I'm too blinded by aimless frustration to focus my thoughts.

'C'mon, David. This is easy.'

'I said I don't know,' I yell, throwing down my pen. 'I don't know, OK?'

I expect Leo to flinch, but he stays perfectly still, his face unreadable.

'David,' he says wearily, like I'm some toddler throwing a tantrum.

I stand up, grabbing my books and shoving them into my backpack.

'David, stop being an idiot and sit down.'

'Why should I? I clearly *am* an idiot. You said as much.'

'No I didn't. Look, let's try again. We can start at the beginning.'

'I'm not in the mood, OK. Let's just call it a day.'

I throw a five-pound note down on the table and stalk out of the library.

Leo doesn't come after me.

24

The rest of October passes in a blur. Despite David storming out of our maths session, we continue to meet. We clear the air but he seems different – quieter and more preoccupied. Sometimes I feel bad taking his money in return for my help, but it's clear he can afford it. Besides it means I have the cash to treat Alicia right.

My detention finally comes to an end. At the same time, all the drama round me hitting Harry seems to have died down. Harry still snarls at me in the corridor, but only when there's a crowd around. For once in my life, things actually seem calm. *I* seem calm.

It's the Friday before Halloween, and Alicia is having dinner with her family. I roam around the house, restless and impatient, counting down the minutes until I see her tomorrow.

'Will you stop pacing up and down like that, Leo?' Amber demands. 'You're like a caged animal or something.'

'Sorry,' I mutter, lying down on my bunk.

I still can't keep still though; even lying down, and after a moment Amber's head appears upside down, her hair brushing the bunk-bed frame.

'What's your deal, Leo?' she asks. 'You've been acting well weird lately.'

'I don't have a deal,' I lie, swatting at her ponytail.

My phone beeps.

'Who's that?' she asks.

'None of your business,' I reply.

Amber narrows her eyes but returns to her bunk.

I turn on to my side so I can get my phone out of my back pocket. It's a text from Alicia:

Missing you xoxo

I roll onto my back and break into this goofy grin, thankful Amber can't see me. Because it's the sort of grin that would give me away in seconds. Cos she's right, I am behaving differently. I can't help it.

I've told Amber I'm tutoring David on the nights I see Alicia so I don't have to spill the beans. I don't know why, but talking out loud about her to anyone feels wrong, like it might jinx things. I want to keep Alicia and me in a precious bubble, safe from the outside world, for now at least. But despite this, I can't ignore this niggling feeling of guilt. Most of the time I can keep it buried, but every so often Alicia will smile at me, or tell me some cute little secret, and the guilt creeps up and slices me in two, so sharply it almost takes my breath away. I know I'm skating on thin ice, but at the same time I just can't bring myself to stop.

The following night, Saturday, we go to the cinema to watch a

Halloween screening of some bizarre horror film from the 1970s. The whole way through she holds on to my hand really hard, her nails digging into my flesh during the especially gruesome bits. It sort of hurts after a while, but I don't care.

After the cinema I walk her home, even though it's pouring down with rain. By the time we reach her front door we're totally drenched. But it's like neither of us have even noticed.

'You know what I was thinking tonight?' she asks. 'In between screaming like a five-year-old girl of course.'

Jesus, she looks good wet.

'No. What?' I ask.

'How you are totally unlike any boy I've ever dated.'

I stiffen. Although I know Alicia's been out with other boys, I don't like to dwell on the fact for more than a few seconds. I have to keep reminding myself that she's with me, but it's hard when I'm pretty sure she could have any boy she wanted.

I continue to frown.

'That's a positive thing,' she insists. 'I like that you're your own person, that you don't care about being popular or being hard or showing off. You're different. And I like different. I like it a lot.'

She rubs her wet nose against mine in an Eskimo kiss. And I get this weird feeling of déjà vu. Then I remember, Mam used to kiss me and Amber like that when she tucked us in at night. I'd completely forgotten about that until now.

'Do you want to come in?' Alicia asks, her voice suddenly all husky and grown-up sounding. 'My family are out.'

I pull away from her and make a big show of looking at the time on my phone.

'Jesus, I would love to, you have no idea how much. But it's getting kind of late. My mum will be off her rocker if I don't get home soon.'

It's a lie. Mam is out with Spike tonight, due back God knows when. But Alicia doesn't know that. She nods, disappointed.

'You do still fancy me, don't you?' she asks, half joking, half serious.

I groan. 'Course I do. I just want things to be special, you know?'

Alicia pouts a little but nods.

'You're right,' she says. 'I just really, really like you, Leo.'

'Tell me about it,' I reply, grinning.

She blushes and giggles. And I know I'm off the hook.

We kiss once more before saying a final goodnight.

As I walk home, even though I'm still buzzing, the same thought keeps popping up and ruining my mood. How much longer can this go on?

On Thursday I cancel my maths session with David so I have time to go home and change before taking Alicia to the annual Guy Fawkes bonfire and fireworks display in Eden Park. I've never been before. Until this year Eden Park was a faraway land I had no real concept of, beyond knowing I didn't belong there. I have a feeling the Eden Park display will be very different from the unofficial Cloverdale ones where kids run riot across the estate, chucking fireworks at each other, the constant wail of fire engines in the background.

Remember, remember, the fifth of November. The rhyme pops into my head as I near the park. Alicia is already there when I arrive, wearing a red bobble hat that makes her look really cute and waving a sparkler. When she sees me she drops the sparkler and comes running over, throwing her arms around my neck. It still takes me back when she does this; the way she's so uninhibited about who sees us, like she's proud to be with me.

As we walk through the gates, although I'm pretty sure no one from Cloverdale will be here, I pull my navy beanie hat down low over my head.

In the centre of the park a huge bonfire is ablaze. Even from here I can feel its warmth on my cheeks. To the left there's a small funfair and a cluster of food stalls.

'Let's go on the big wheel!' Alicia says, dragging me towards the lights.

She pays for our tickets and we clamber up a set of rickety steps and into the first available seats. A boy not much older than us takes our tickets and pulls a bar down onto our laps. Almost immediately we swing upwards. Alicia lets out a squeal and clutches my arm.

'Sorry to be such a big kid,' she says, her eyes shining. 'But I love all this stuff.'

Our car jerks higher still and the noise below us begins to fade as we creak steadily upwards. I look over the side, at the tops of heads of the people milling around below us. Beside me Alicia gazes down at them, this look of wonder on her face, and in that second I decide I could look at her for days on end and never get bored.

At the top, our car swaying gently as more riders are let on and off down below, Alicia lets out a sigh.

'It's so peaceful up here,' she says. 'I love it.'

'I know what you mean,' I reply. 'It's like I can breathe properly up here, if that makes sense.'

'It makes total sense,' Alicia says, taking my bare hand and tucking it under her mittened one.

We go round a few more times. But it's being at the top I like best, where, for a few seconds, I imagine Alicia and I are the only people on the planet.

'Where's Cloverdale from here?' she asks.

I twist round and try to get my bearings.

'I dunno, er, that way I guess,' I say, pointing off to the right.

'Will you take me there some day?'

'Where? Cloverdale? You don't want to see Cloverdale, believe me.'

'But I do,' she insists, jiggling my arm. 'I want to see where you live, see your bedroom, meet your sisters, your mum.'

'Nothing much to see,' I say casually. 'And Mam, she works a lot, she's hardly ever in . . .'

'You're not ashamed of me are you, Leo?'

I make a face. 'As if.'

'Then what's the problem?'

'There isn't one.'

I try to imagine Alicia in our cramped front room, perched on the edge of the settee, drinking a cup of tea. Suddenly Mam is invading the picture, swaying about with a fag dangling between her fingers, a can of cider in the other hand. Then Spike is in on the act, wandering in wearing nothing but his cartoon boxer shorts, burping and farting and scratching. Before I know it, Tia's there too, gazing up at Alicia like she's one her beloved Disney Princesses and asking a ton of dumb questions. All three of them are like ticking time bombs, liable to ruin everything at any time with no warning. And this is without Amber to factor in.

'They do know about me, don't they?' Alicia asks, leaning away from me.

'Course they do,' I lie. 'I haven't stopped going on about you!'

She relaxes into a smile and snuggles back up against me.

'Tell me more about your mum, Leo. You never talk about her.'

I frown and scratch my head, trying to work out how to best describe my disaster zone of a mother.

'She's difficult,' I say eventually.

'Difficult how?'

'She's one of those people whose mood sort of affects the whole house, you know? Like if she's in a good mood, it's like we can all relax, but if she's in a bad one, everyone knows it and feels it.'

'Why is she like that do you think? I mean, there must be a reason for her acting that way?'

I shrug. 'I dunno. It's just how she's always been. It's Tia I feel most sorry for, when she's not driving me up the wall at least. She doesn't know whether she's coming or going with Mam blowing hot then cold all the time.'

'Sounds tough,' Alicia says, stroking my hand.

'It's OK. I mean, it could be worse. It's not like she beats us or starves us, or anything. She's just not your typical mother I suppose.'

Understatement of the year. My cheeks feel suddenly hot. I always get nervous when I feel I might have said too much. For a few seconds we sit in silence, the air hazy with smoke from the bonfire.

'Leo?' Alicia says, as our car rocks back and forth.

'Yeah?'

'After the fireworks tonight, do you want to come back to my house?'

I swallow. 'Won't your parents be there?'

Alicia grins triumphantly. 'Nope. They're at a charity dinner

171

tonight. Won't be back until late. And my brother's staying over at my nana's so we'll have the entire place to ourselves.'

She leans in close so her breath tickles my ear lobes. 'So what do you say?'

Instead of answering properly, I kiss her. And it's a great kiss, full of longing and lust and emotion and all that. But something else too. Fear.

After the big wheel, we buy hot dogs and pink candy floss on sticks. I hit all the targets at the shooting gallery and win Alicia a giant cuddly canary.

As we're making our way towards the fire, our mouths and fingers sticky from the candy floss, I hear someone call my name. My first instinct is to freeze up, terrified it's someone from Cloverdale. But then I connect the voice to its owner. David.

'Hey,' I say, as David weaves through the crowds towards us, Essie and Felix behind him. In skinny jeans, fur-lined parka and a rainbow striped scarf trailing on the ground, he looks different from when he's in school uniform – less awkward.

'Hi, Leo. Having a good night?' he asks. He seems nervous.

'Yeah, thanks. You?'

'Yeah, good.'

He looks from me to Alicia and back again. I clear my throat.

'Er, guys, this is Alicia. Alicia, this is David, Essie and Felix.'

Alicia nods enthusiastically.

'I've seen you all around school,' she says. 'Nice to meet you properly.'

A silence quickly descends, all the more pronounced by the racket going on around us.

'Well, this is nice and awkward,' Essie says loudly, reaching

172

forward and swiping a handful of candy floss from my stick. David elbows her.

Alicia turns to me and tugs at the drawstring on my hoodie.

'We should get moving if we're going to get a good spot at the front,' she says.

'Right,' I say. 'Er, see you guys at school, yeah?'

'Yeah, see you at school,' the three of them echo.

Alicia links her arm through mine. As we edge towards the crowd, I glance over my shoulder. Essie and Felix have wandered over to the Hook a Duck stall but David is still looking in our direction, a very slight frown on his face. For a second our eyes meet. He smiles tightly before darting over to join them.

At eight o'clock the fireworks begin. I've never really been bothered, but I guess I just never looked at them in the right way before, because tonight, listening to Alicia gasp and sigh as they splutter and crackle over our heads, I'm a complete fireworks convert.

It's almost enough to distract me from the anxiety in my belly that shows no signs of going away.

25

'You sure they're not going to be back until late?' I ask as Alicia unlocks her front door.

'I promise you. They go to this dinner every year, and every year they get back at stupid o'clock. Dad's even taken tomorrow off work because of it. Free bar and all that. Seriously, we've got hours.'

'Right,' I say, following Alicia into the dark hallway, trailing the stuffed canary on the ground behind me.

I almost persuaded Alicia we should head to Nando's with Ruby and Liam and a few other kids from our year. Not that I particularly wanted to go, but I knew by the time we'd got there and ordered and eaten and argued over the bill, it would probably be too late to go back to Alicia's. But Alicia had made up her mind, whispering something in Ruby's ear before dragging me away from the safety of the crowd.

'You want a drink?' she asks, taking off her coat.

'Er, yeah, please. Water's fine, or Coke if you've got some.'

She rolls her eyes. 'I meant a real drink.'

She takes my hand and leads me through a door off the hallway and into the living room. She flicks on the lights and opens a large glass cabinet containing at least twenty bottles of different spirits.

'Vodka OK?' Alicia asks, peering at the label of one of the fuller bottles.

'Sure.'

She pours us each a glass of clear liquid. We take a sip in unison. It burns the back of my throat and I have to fight to keep myself from coughing.

'Let's take the bottle up with us,' Alicia says, beckoning for me to follow her out of the room and up the stairs.

It's not the first time I've set foot in Alicia's bedroom. But this is the first time I've done so without her parents milling around downstairs and a strict door open, lights on policy in operation.

Alicia shuts the door and turns on a lamp, casting a soft pink glow across the room. She turns her back and bends to plug her iPod into its dock. Seconds later the room is filled with soft, jazzy music. My head starts to pulse.

'Ella Fitzgerald,' she says, smiling and setting down her empty glass.

I nod.

She holds out her arms. Wordlessly, I move towards them. Our lips meet, mine buzzing with alcohol. This is good. Kissing is distracting, safe. Only then Alicia's foot is hooking round my ankle and leading me towards the bed.

'I've still got my shoes on,' I say.

'Don't worry about it,' Alicia murmurs, falling on to the bed and taking me with her.

'But they're dirty.'

'I said, don't worry about it.'

I try to concentrate on the kissing again, cupping her face with my hands and concentrating on how amazing her lips feel against mine, how soft her skin is, her little sighs.

'Leo,' she whispers between kisses, 'have you got . . . a . . . you know?'

'Er, no, I haven't, sorry,' I say, my body flooding with relief. 'I didn't think . . .'

'That's OK, I've got it covered.'

'Great,' I lie, the relief exiting my body just as fast as it entered.

We continue to kiss. Alicia's hands snake under my hoodie and T-shirt, my body tensing up the second they do. And suddenly we're back in Becky's cupboard under the stairs. My breath quickens and I feel dizzy and hot as Alicia's fingers continue to creep upwards. I sit up, panting.

'What's wrong?' she asks.

'Nothing. Just thirsty,' I reply.

She pours me a second glass of vodka. As I take a sip, Alicia wriggles out of her top and jeans so she's wearing just her matching bra and knickers, pink and satiny, and arranges herself on top of the duvet. I gaze across at her. She looks so sexy and amazing. And all I want to do is touch her, smell her, be with her. But I know I can't.

I let her pull me down on the bed again. She crawls on top of me so she's straddling me and at first we're just kissing but then she's fiddling with the buttons on my jeans. I push her away and sit up, my heartbeat going wild.

'Is it your first time? Is that it? Because it's mine too. We're in this together,' Alicia says, kneeling up on the bed. She looks so beautiful I want to cry.

176

'It's not that,' I say.

'Then what is it? Because every time I touch you, you go totally weird. You claim you fancy me loads, but every time things get heavy, you push me away.'

'I do fancy you. Shit, Alicia, I think I might even love you.'

'And I think I might love you too. So what's the problem?'

The enormity of what she's just said makes my head hurt. I love Alicia. Alicia loves me. I should be walking on air right now. But I'm not. Because I know I'm on the edge of wrecking everything.

'There isn't a problem,' I say desperately, 'I just can't do this. Not tonight.'

'But why?' she pleads. 'What's the big secret? We're boyfriend and girlfriend, you should be able to tell me everything.'

'Even if it means you'll end up hating me?'

'Don't be stupid,' she says. 'I couldn't hate you, Leo.'

'You don't know that.'

'Yes, I do.'

I stare at her, beautiful Alicia, her eyes full of fear and hope all mixed up together.

'Just tell me, Leo. I don't want us to have secrets.'

My heart feels like it's going about ten thousand miles per hour.

'You don't know what you're letting yourself in for,' I begin.

'For God's sake, Leo, I'm a big girl,' she interrupts. 'Whatever it is I can handle it. Just tell me.'

'Maybe you should get dressed first,' I say.

Alicia frowns but climbs off the bed and pulls on a turquoise robe with a Chinese dragon embroidered on the back. She ties the belt round her waist and returns to the bed, sitting cross-legged on the duvet. I hesitate before perching on the edge next to her. She shuffles round on her bum so she's side-on to me.

'What I'm about to say is going to sound really crazy,' I say, looking straight ahead. 'So you've just got to promise me that you'll let me get to the end, OK?'

I dare to look at her. Her face is serious, her eyes unsmiling for once.

'OK?' I repeat.

She fixes her eyes on mine. 'I told you, Leo, whatever it is I can handle it.'

I could still make a run for it, but if I do I know I'll lose her for certain. And maybe, just maybe, there's a tiny chance she won't get totally freaked out by what I'm about to say.

I close my eyes. I can hear Alicia breathing next to me and I can tell she's nervous about what I might be about to say.

'You know how I've been pulling away from you and stuff, when we get, you know, intimate,' I begin.

Intimate. It seems like such a stupid word all of a sudden. Stiff and formal. It couldn't communicate how I feel when I'm doing stuff with Alicia in a million years. Alicia reaches across and takes my hand in hers. I have to resist the urge to pull it back into my lap. Instead I try to ignore her thumb gently massaging the palm of my hand as I continue to talk.

'Well, there's a reason I've been acting that way, pulling away and stuff. And you've got to believe me when I say it's nothing to do with you, OK?'

Alicia squeezes my hand as if to say go on, and I know I can't put it off any longer. Suddenly I feel dizzy, like if I opened my eyes, Alicia's bedroom would be spinning at one hundred miles per hour. I take a deep breath.

'OK, the reason I've been acting so weird is because I'm not who you think I am.'

I feel Alicia's grip on my hand slacken ever so slightly.

I need to say it now, quickly, like ripping off a plaster, before I can change my mind.

'I wasn't born Leo,' I say, my voice growing quieter and quieter, so I'm almost whispering.

Ella Fitzgerald has stopped singing. The room is silent.

'I was born a girl.'

I keep my eyes closed as Alicia's hand shoots from mine.

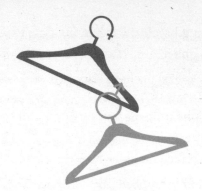

26

The day after the fireworks display in Eden Park, Leo doesn't eat lunch in the canteen.

'Are he and Alicia Baker going out then?' Essie muses as she picks the carrots out of her chicken pie with her fork.

'How should I know?' I reply.

'It certainly looked like it last night,' she says. 'They were all over each other.'

'Like I said, I don't know,' I say irritably.

Essie and Felix exchange looks. I pretend not to notice.

That afternoon, when Mum picks Livvy and me up after school and we drive past the bus stop, Leo is nowhere to be seen.

I don't see Leo the following Monday either.

On Tuesday, I wait in the library until five o'clock but Leo fails to appear for our maths session.

*

During morning break the following day, I spot Alicia Baker with Ruby Webber and Becky Somerville outside the tuck shop.

'Alicia?'

She doesn't hear me at first. I cough and repeat her name, louder this time.

She turns to face me. Her eyes are all bloodshot.

'Yes?' she says, looking through me like I'm a ghost.

'Er, is Leo poorly? I haven't seen him all week.'

Becky Somerville puts a protective arm round Alicia's shoulder.

'No, she hasn't. And she doesn't want to either.'

'Becky, don't,' Alicia says quietly.

'Why? What's he done?' I ask, looking from Alicia to Becky.

'Only gone and broken my best friend's heart!' Ruby interjects, shoving an unwrapped Snickers bar into Alicia's hand.

'Guys, stop it,' Alicia says, looking at her feet.

'What happened?' I ask.

'Like she's going to tell you! Alicia is too upset to even talk to us about it,' Ruby says, stroking Alicia's hair. 'That's how heartbroken she is.'

'But when she is ready to tell us,' Becky says. 'Leo Denton is going to wish he'd never been born.'

Alicia closes her eyes.

'Guys, I said stop,' she says softly.

'Not that it's any of your business,' Ruby snaps at me. 'Now, if you'll excuse us.'

She tosses her hair over her shoulder and together she and Becky link arms with Alicia and steer her away from me.

I stare after them. The last time I saw Leo and Alicia together they were snuggled by the bonfire, looking totally loved-up.

This doesn't make any sense.

After school I head to the admin office where Miss Clay, one of the school secretaries, confirms Leo has not been in school since last Thursday – the day of the fireworks display in Eden Park.

I head to the library, sit down at our usual table and try to complete some of the maths problems we were working on last week, but I can't concentrate. Without Leo, the numbers twist about on the page, mocking me, and after twenty minutes I give up and go home.

I would ring Leo, but I don't have his mobile number. I suggested exchanging numbers several times, but he always resisted, making an excuse or changing the subject. I consider asking Alicia whether she has it, but when I see her at school the next day she's flanked by Becky and Ruby – her unofficial bodyguards.

This is how, on Thursday after school, I find myself boarding the number fourteen bus bound for Cloverdale. Luckily Mum thinks I'm meeting Leo for tutoring, so I've got a few hours to kill before she sends out a search party.

The journey takes what seems like for ever, quickly leaving behind the tree-lined streets of Eden Park and heading south for unfamiliar territory. We pass Cloverdale School, its grounds dark and empty. The building itself resembles a fat office block marooned in the centre of a concrete car park. Behind the school, I can just about make out a tangle of trees, the only greenery in sight. When we stop a bunch of Cloverdale kids clamber on to the bus, rattling past me and up the stairs, and I can't help but feel glad I chose to sit downstairs, near the driver.

A few minutes later a robotic voice announces the next stop is Cloverdale Estate – East Side. I haven't a clue which side of Cloverdale Leo lives on, so I figure this is as good a place as any to get off and press the bell.

Although at least five other people get off the bus at the same stop as me, they quickly scatter, disappearing down alleyways, or into waiting cars, swallowed up by the estate, and within a minute I am all alone.

Cloverdale is even quieter than I remember it. I glance over each shoulder before taking out my iPhone and waiting for the GPS signal to kick in. I type in the name of Leo's street – Sycamore Gardens, and begin to walk, following the pulsing blue cursor on the screen. The route takes me past a small parade of shops in the centre of the estate, some of them already shut up for the day, thick metal grilles pulled down over their windows. Others are unoc- cupied altogether, just empty shells with faded signs and whitewashed windows. The only shop open for customers appears to be a small supermarket at the far end of the parade. Half the window is boarded up, shards of broken glass glinting on the concrete paving slabs like glitter.

Outside the shop, a group of boys wearing the Cloverdale School uniform of grey trousers and navy and yellow sweatshirt are mucking about, shouting and throwing crisps at each other. I look down to check my Eden Park blazer is not visible beneath my coat, and slide my iPhone into my pocket. I suddenly regret not postponing my mission until the weekend, when I could have come in the daylight with Phil at my side. Not that he's a very effective guard dog, plus he gets sick on the bus, but still, it would have surely felt less scary than this.

It's dusk when I finally enter Sycamore Gardens. I identify Leo's house immediately by its overgrown garden and broken front gate. I'm relieved to find the living-room lights on, and the faint drone of the television just audible as I tread through the long grass towards the front door. I look for a doorbell. There isn't one so I rattle the flimsy letterbox and wait. A few seconds later I hear the jangle of keys followed by the turning of the lock. The door eases open a few centimetres, constricted by the safety chain, and a small pale face belonging to a little girl peeks up at me through the gap. She has watery blue eyes and something dark, chocolate maybe, smeared round her mouth.

'What do you want?' she demands.

'Er, is Leo in?' I ask.

'Nope.'

'Tia, who is it?' a female voice calls.

'Dunno, someone for Leo,' the little girl, who I guess is Tia, calls back.

Another few seconds pass before a second face appears

above Tia's, its owner in possession of a very familiar pair of eyes. They appraise me for a moment before the safety chain is released and the door is opened fully, revealing a teenage girl dressed in a leopard print onesie with bleached blonde hair piled on top of her head.

'Can I help you?' she asks, folding her arms.

'I'm looking for Leo?' I stammer, peering behind her into the living room. I can make out an orange three-piece suite that dominates the small space, and half of a huge TV set. The girl notices me looking and puts her arm on the door-frame to block my view.

'And you are?' she asks.

'Er, David, a mate of Leo's from school.'

She raises her eyebrows. 'The one he's been spending all this time with?'

'I guess so.'

'I'm his sister, Amber.'

'Nice to meet you,' I say, extending my hand. Her arms remain folded and she stares at me, as if to say, are you for real? I drop my hand to my side and pretend to wipe it on my trousers.

'Leo's not here, by the way,' Amber says.

'He's not? Oh. Well, do you know where he is?'

'Down the baths, I think.'

I screw up my face apologetically. 'Sorry, down the where?'

'The baths? The old swimming baths. Down the bottom of Renton Road?'

I shake my head.

Amber rolls her eyes again. 'You're not from round here, are you?'

'Er, no.'

'That was a rhetorical question by the way,' she says.

'Oh.'

'Tia!' she calls.

By now Tia has scampered back into the living room and is engrossed in a noisy episode of *Horrible Histories*.

'Yeah,' Tia calls back.

'I'm going out for about ten minutes. Don't open the door to any strangers.'

'OK!'

Amber grabs a coat from the pile draped over the banister and pulls it on over her onesie.

'I don't want to be any trouble,' I say quickly. 'If you give me the road name I'm sure I could find it on my phone.'

Amber slides her feet into a pair of fluffy pink boots and straightens up.

'No offence, but a kid like you will get eaten alive around here. I'm surprised you made it this far, to be honest. Nah, best I take you.'

And with that she slams the front door shut behind us and sets off across Sycamore Gardens, leaving me with no choice but to hurry after her.

Amber walks quickly, her mass of white-blonde hair bouncing up and down on her head.

'Leo didn't tell me he had an older sister,' I say, as I scurry along beside her.

'Probably because he doesn't,' she replies.

'But you said—'

'We're twins.'

'You are?' I say in surprise. 'Leo never said so.'

Amber shrugs.

'It certainly explains it,' I continue.

'Explains what?' Amber says sharply.

'Your eyes. They're identical to Leo's.'

'Are they?' she murmurs, before taking a sharp right and leading us down a narrow alleyway. We come out on a main road.

'There they are,' she says, pointing across the road towards a large building surrounded by a tall corrugated iron fence, only its arched roof visible over the top. We cross over. Amber leads me round the perimeter of the fence. Every few metres, large signs declaring, 'Private Property – Trespassers Will be Prosecuted' are attached to the fence, pretty much all of them daubed with graffiti.

'What is this place again?' I ask, folding my arms across my chest and shivering.

'The old swimming baths,' Amber replies. 'Been here since the Victorian times. They closed down a few years ago.'

'Why?'

'Health and safety, I think.'

'And now it's just derelict?'

'Pretty much, yeah. There was talk for a while about turning the place into luxury flats but nothing's happened so far. They've probably finally figured out that anyone with enough money to buy a luxury flat wouldn't be seen dead living in Cloverdale.'

By the time we get round to the back of the building, away from the glow of street lamps, dusk has melted into actual darkness. Amber takes out her mobile phone and shines it over the fence.

'Here we go,' she murmurs, loosening one of the fence panels to reveal a small rectangular hole. She motions for me to crawl through it. I hesitate before dropping to my knees and squeezing through the narrow space. I turn, expecting to see Amber crawling after me, but instead she's pulling the fence panel back into place.

'Hey, wait! Aren't you coming in?' I ask, panic rising in my voice.

She crouches to peer through the hole and looks at me like I'm mad.

'I don't think so.'

'But where do I go now? Where's Leo?' I ask.

'Inside somewhere,' she says, motioning vaguely. 'You might need to use your phone to see. It's pretty dark in there.'

'Oh, right. Well, er, thanks for bringing me.'

'You're welcome,' she says.

And just like that, Amber is gone, leaving me all alone, crouched in the darkness, possibly about to get murdered. I straighten up and wipe muddy hands on my trousers before groping in my pocket for my phone. I adjust the straps on my backpack and begin to walk round the building. I'm shaking like crazy and several times I almost trip over the piles of rubble in my path. I dare to look around me, noticing the baths themselves are built from handsome red brick and decorated with intricate stone carvings. At the front I discover a set of stone steps sweeping up to an arched entrance held up by four fat stone pillars. I go up the steps and push at the door, not expecting it to give, but it does and I go tumbling into the foyer, landing on my hands and knees on the marble floor. As I clamber to my feet, the smell of chlorine hits me. Then the sheer quietness. It's as if all the noise in the world has been sucked out, all apart from the sound of my uneven breathing.

I stand up and begin to walk forward, my legs trembling. I shine my phone over the reception area. To my right there's an old desk, complete with till and swivel chair. To my left there's a defunct vending machine, empty. In front of me there's a set of turnstiles. I go through them and keep walking. I come to the changing rooms – ladies on the left, gents on the right. Out of habit I go into the gents, figuring this will lead me to the pool, and hopefully to Leo. Already I don't have a clue which part of the fence I crawled through and the prospect of spending the night trapped in an abandoned Victorian swimming pool doesn't exactly fill me with delight.

It's pitch-black. My phone beeps, informing me the battery is low. I decide to conserve the power and slide it back into my pocket, resorting to feeling my way round instead. I let my hands roam over the metal lockers, keys still in locks. In one locker there's a forgotten towel – stiff and sour smelling. Gradually my eyes get used to the dark and I can make out the pegs and benches lining the walls, the showers and urinals. I turn the corner and I'm greeted with a faint glow of light. I make my way towards it.

I step out on to what I quickly realise is the side of the pool. Above me the clouds have cleared, and the half-moon glows through the roof, which I can now see is made of glass, casting the entire space with a silvery sheen. Banks of flip-down wooden seats line the length of the pool on each side. At one end there is a three-tiered diving platform, at the other five windows, tall and narrow. I inch forwards and peek down. The pool is empty. Of course it is. And yet I can't help but feel disappointed. I sit on the edge, dangle my legs over the side and marvel at how far down it seems to the bottom with no water distorting the depth. I take out my dying phone and shine it towards the deep end.

'Oi!'

I drop my phone. It makes a loud clatter as it hits the floor of the pool.

This is it; I'm going to die.

'Oi!' the voice calls again. In my panic I can't identify where it's coming from immediately and it takes several seconds to trace it to a shadowy figure standing on the highest diving platform. A moment later a thin beam of torch-light hits me in the face. I stand up, squinting and shielding my eyes.

'David?' the voice says.

'Leo?'

There's an audible sigh and what sounds like a collection of about ten swear words, all strung together to make one ultimate curse, before the creak of metal as Leo descends the ladder. By the time he reaches the bottom, my heart has just about stopped threatening to burst out of my chest.

Leo strides towards me, one arm straight out in front of him, the torch aimed at my head.

'Don't shoot,' I joke.

Leo doesn't laugh.

'How did you get here?' he demands, his eyes flashing angrily.

'Your sister brought me,' I stammer. 'Amber. Hey, how come you didn't tell me you had a twin?'

He ignores my question.

'She shouldn't have brought you.'

'It's not her fault. I asked her where you were.'

'Whatever,' Leo mutters, lowering the torch.

'This place is really cool,' I say. 'Terrifying but cool. Did you used to swim here? When it was still open I mean?'

Leo doesn't answer me.

'You shouldn't be here, David,' he says.

'But I was worried about you. You haven't been at school all week.'

'I was ill. I am ill.'

I study his face in the faint moonlight.

'You don't look ill,' I point out.

He ignores me, turning and shining the torch over the bottom of the pool.

'You want me to get that?' he asks, nodding down-wards.

'Sorry?'

'Your phone.'

'No, I can get it.'

He ignores me again and jumps down to the bottom of

the pool. He picks up the phone, tossing it to me. I surprise myself by catching it.

'When are you coming back?' I ask, as Leo strides back to the metal steps, his trainers squeaking against the tiles. He doesn't answer.

'You can't stop tutoring me now,' I continue. 'I got a B on a test exam paper the other day. Can you believe that? Mr Steele almost fell off his chair he was so shocked. And it's all down to you.'

Leo pauses and sits on the top rung of the steps, his arms hooked round the frame.

'Who says I'm coming back?'

'But you've got to,' I say.

Even though Leo has only been at Eden Park for a couple of months, the thought of him not being around any more feels totally wrong.

'According to who?' Leo says.

'I don't know. Me. The authorities.'

He snorts.

I sit down next to him, my arms clasping my bent legs.

'What happened, Leo?' I ask. 'Why haven't you been at school?'

He just shakes his head.

'Is it something to do with Alicia Baker?'

He turns sharply to face me.

'Why? What's she said?'

'Nothing really. Ruby Webber and Becky Somerville were doing all the talking for her.'

'And what did they say?' he demands.

'They didn't say much either,' I admit. 'They reckon Alicia's too heartbroken to tell them what happened.'

Leo exhales deeply, frowns and nods.

'What did happen, Leo?'

'Nothing,' he growls, angling his head away from me.

'It can't be nothing. If it was nothing you wouldn't be hiding here.'

'I'm not hiding,' he says, jumping back down to the bottom of the pool. I think he lands badly because he swears sharply to himself and limps round in a circle for a moment.

'Are you OK?' I call, clambering down the ladder after him.

'I'm fine,' he snaps.

'It can't be nothing,' I repeat. 'The thing with Alicia, I mean. I saw you together at the bonfire, and you were totally into one another, and now it's all over?'

'It's none of your business, David.'

'But I want to help,' I say, glancing upwards, the sides of the pool looming high above my head.

'Believe me, you can't,' Leo replies.

'Try me,' I say, planting myself in front of him. He looks at me for a moment before shaking his head and pushing me gently backwards.

'Just go home, David,' he says, his voice tired.

'No.'

'What?'

I take a deep breath.

'No,' I repeat. 'Everyone else may have fallen for your hard-man act, but I haven't. I'm not afraid of you, Leo, not one bit.'

Leo squares up to me, his chest all puffed out.

'Oh really?' he says.

'Yes, really,' I reply, standing up straight. 'And I'm not going anywhere until you talk to me.'

Leo glares at me, his eyes cold and intense.

'I'm your friend, Leo,' I add.

He snorts again.

'You hardly know me, David,' he says.

But he's wrong. I do know him. And I want to know him more. I have no idea why. I only know that I'm drawn to him in ways I can't quite explain, and that I can't shift the sneaking suspicion that beneath it all, he gets me, that he's drawn to me too.

'Yes, I do know you,' I continue gently. 'I know you're kind and sweet and patient.'

Leo rolls his eyes towards the glass roof.

'But I mean it!' I say. 'Please tell me what happened. I'll support you, whatever it is, I promise I will.'

Leo lets out a laugh. 'That's what she said.'

'Who?' I ask. 'Alicia?'

'Forget it.'

He crouches down, his back to me. He looks small suddenly, like a little kid. I crouch down beside him. I want to fix things, make it better, but I don't know how.

'Leo,' I find myself saying in a low whisper. 'If I tell you something, a secret, something only Essie and Felix know about me, do you promise not to tell anyone?'

He shakes his head and laughs.

'I get what you're doing here,' he says. 'You tell me some

194

stupid secret and then expect me to tell you all my shit in return, right?'

'No. This is something I *want* to tell you. You don't have to tell me anything in return, honestly.'

And I mean it. Suddenly I want him to know. I want to open myself up to him, be vulnerable, with no expectations.

Leo just shrugs.

'So, do you promise?' I whisper.

'Promise what?' he says in an exaggerated whisper, making fun of me.

'Not to repeat what I'm about to tell you?' I say.

'Look, David, I don't give a toss about your stupid secret, OK?'

'Promise?' I repeat in a loud voice.

'Promise,' he mutters, rolling his eyes, not quite looking at me.

I slide on to my bottom and scoot round so I'm facing him. The floor of the pool feels cold and hard through the thin fabric of my school trousers.

'What if I told you I wasn't gay?'

'But you are gay, you said so yourself. You like that Scandi kid, what's-his-name, Olsen.'

I sigh. I need to come at this from a different angle.

'Let me start again, remember that time after our first detention together, when you asked me why Harry calls me Freak Show?'

'Yeah,' Leo replies, picking at his shoelaces.

'Well, I sort of didn't tell you the whole truth.'

He shrugs again.

'What did you want to be when you were little?' I ask.

He wrinkles his nose, 'I dunno.'

'You must have wanted to be something.'

'I said I dunno,' he says irritably. 'Look, what's this got to do with you being gay or not?'

Despite the cold, my palms are prickling with sweat. I wipe them on my trousers, but new beads of sweat appear almost immediately. I clear my throat.

'OK, when I was eight my class was asked to write about what we wanted to be when we grew up.'

I close my eyes and just like that, I'm back in Miss Box's classroom, the smell of leftover school dinners and sweat and grass stains drifting across our bowed heads as we write, my tongue twitching with concentration as my pen speeds down the page, excited by the task I've been set, unaware of what is to come.

I open my eyes. Leo is frowning slightly.

'After we'd finished writing,' I continue slowly, 'Miss Box, she was our teacher that year, went round the room in alphabetical order asking everyone to stand up and say what they wanted to be. All the other kids wanted to be footballers or actors and stuff, and I kind of got that feeling you sometimes get after an exam, when you come out and at first you're feeling pretty confident but then everyone starts discussing their answers and it suddenly dawns on you that you've totally messed up. Know what I mean?'

Leo sort of nods.

'Well, as Miss Box went round the room, it was just like that. Because I hadn't written about wanting to be a footballer or an actor or a doctor, like everyone else. I hadn't written down anything like that. I just wrote what I really wanted to be,' I can feel my face turning red. 'What I really am.'

Leo is looking at me now. Properly. I feel lightheaded.

'I wrote I wanted to be a girl,' I say, my voice cracking on girl.

When Leo doesn't say anything, I just keep talking. I tell him about my scrapbook, my box of dressing-up clothes, the endless letters to my parents I've written but never sent. I tell him about all the research I've done on the internet; the websites and forums I've pored over; the YouTube videos I've watched on loop. I even tell him about my weekly inspections and how it feels to look in the mirror and realise my inside and outside don't match up; that they don't even come close.

The entire time he doesn't interrupt. He just stares at me, barely blinking, his expression undecipherable.

'Sometimes,' I say, 'I look in the mirror and the kid who looks back; he's like a stranger to me, an alien even. It's like I know the real me is in there somewhere, but for the moment I'm trapped in this weird body that I recognise less and less every day. Does that make any sense at all?'

Leo opens his mouth as if he's about to say something but no sound comes out.

'Of course it doesn't,' I say sadly. 'How could it?'

'Why are you telling me all this?' Leo asks finally, his voice sort of croaky.

'I don't know,' I admit. 'I suppose there was just part

of me that wanted to share something important with you. Something really important.'

'Right.'

A silence hangs between us. Leo is fiddling with the frayed hems of his jeans, and I can only guess that I've totally freaked him out and he's heard enough. I was stupid to think he would react any differently. After all, it's not every day people turn round and tell you they want to be the opposite sex, least of all some kid you've known a matter of months.

'I suppose you think I'm a freak now too,' I say, my voice coming out all small and sad.

Leo looks up at me sharply. We lock eyes for a moment, Leo's amber flecks flashing in the moonlight.

'I don't think you're a freak, David,' he says, his voice slow and careful.

'You don't?'

There's this sort of glassy film over his eyes. Not tears (I don't think I can even imagine Leo crying), but something close.

'No,' he says. 'What I mean is, I get it.'

I sigh.

'That's kind, but you don't get it, Leo, you can't.'

He looks at me for a second before swearing under his breath and standing up. At first I think he's signalling that it's time for us to leave, that the conversation is over, and I make a move to stand up too. But then I realise, instead of walking away, he's taking off his hoodie. Which makes no sense because it's absolutely freezing in here, my bum's almost totally numb beneath me. I stare up at him, confused.

He tosses his hoodie aside. His hair is sticking up in messy tufts. He takes off his sweatshirt, then his shirt, the entire time not saying a word, his face blank but determined, until he's wearing just his white T-shirt. His arms goose-pimple immediately. He pauses for a second before lifting up his T-shirt, not over his head, but up to his chin. Instead of skin, his chest is covered by what might look to anyone else like a tight white crop top. But not to me. I know exactly what Leo is wearing. And Leo knows I know. And it's like the jigsaw-puzzle pieces that have been floating around in my head for the last couple of months have suddenly slotted together to form a picture.

27

'You're a girl?' David whispers, so quietly I can barely hear him.

I let my T-shirt fall back into place. The cold hits me suddenly, sharp and icy. I feel a shiver snake its way up my spine. David jumps to his feet, gathering up my clothes and thrusting them into my arms.

'Quick, get them back on or you'll freeze to death,' he says, his eyes not quite meeting mine, his forehead scrunched into a frown, like its hurting his brain to even attempt to get his head round what he's just seen.

As I pull my layers back on, I can feel him watching my every move, probably looking for all the clues he missed, those telltale signs that passed him by.

I pull my hoodie on over my head and fold my arms.

'You look like you've seen a ghost,' I say.

David nods faintly. Because I suppose, in a way, he has.

'You're a girl,' he repeats. This time it's not a question, more a declaration of a fact he now knows to be true.

'Well, technically, I actually prefer the term "natal female", "biological female" if you must,' I say.

'But you look like a boy,' David says in wonder. 'Totally and utterly like a boy.'

'What can I say, I've had a lot of practice.'

There I go again. Being a smartarse. But David doesn't seem to notice or care. He steps forward, studying my face, walking round me in a slow circle, like I'm a sculpture in an art gallery. I half expect him to reach out and prod me, just to check I'm actually real.

'Are you on hormones and stuff?' he asks.

'Hormone blockers,' I say. 'They freeze puberty.'

'I've read about them on the internet,' David murmurs. 'How long have you been on them?'

'Nearly six months now.'

'An injection?'

'Yep, every three months.'

'Does it hurt?'

I shake my head.

'And how does it feel? Different?'

'I guess.'

'Does it mean you don't have periods any more?'

I stiffen. 'Yeah. You ask a lot of questions, you know that?'

'What happens after that?' he asks. 'After hormone blockers I mean.'

'Well, next year I'm meant to move on to testosterone.'

'Testosterone,' he echoes, sounding out each syllable as if trying out the word for size.

'Two trans kids in one school,' I say. 'Who'd have thought, eh?'

I realise then that maybe I suspected David all along, but didn't properly admit it to myself until he actually told me. Because for some reason I'm not surprised, in fact it makes total sense, although now I've totally rained on his parade by whipping my top off. Shit, did I really do that?

'I read somewhere that most schools have at least two transgender pupils,' David says. 'I always assumed it was a made-up statistic, to trick kids like me into feeling less of a freak. I never in a million years guessed the other one would be you.'

I smile weakly.

'Do you think there's a transgender version of gaydar?' David continues. 'If so mine is totally off.'

I look at my feet. 'Yeah, well, no one was meant to know. It was meant to be a secret.'

I can feel David's eyes still on me, boring into me, like they want to get right inside and burrow under my skin.

'You told Alicia, didn't you?' he says slowly. 'That's why she won't talk to you. And why you haven't been coming to school.'

'Very perceptive,' I say grimly.

Just the mention of Alicia's name makes me feel sick.

'What happened?' he asks.

'What do you think happened, eh?'

David looks at his feet. 'I'm sorry.'

'Yeah, well,' I murmur, shrugging, thinking maybe if I act like I don't care, I'll stop actually caring all together.

'Is that why you left Cloverdale too?' David asks.

I don't answer.

'It is, isn't it?'

I sigh. 'Yeah, that's why I left Cloverdale.'

'What happened? Were you in disguise there too?'

202

'Disguise?' I say. 'This isn't Scooby Doo you know.'

He blushes. 'Sorry, but all this vocabulary is kind of new to me. Not to mention the fact I'm still in mild shock from, well . . . this,' he says, gesturing at me.

'It's called going stealth,' I say. 'And no, I wasn't stealth at Cloverdale. Everyone there knew, it was impossible to avoid, I went to primary school with half of them and they'd all known me as Megan.'

'Megan,' David says. 'Of course. Jesus, I'm dense.'

'What do you mean?' I ask.

'I googled you and all this stuff came up about a girl called Megan Denton. Hey, weren't you some kind of swimming champion? Is that why you hang out here?'

'Something like that,' I mutter. I don't like to talk about my life as Megan to anyone.

'And how was it?' David asks. 'At school I mean?'

I close my eyes for a second, trying to think of a suitable way to sum up life at Cloverdale.

'Hell on earth?' I offer, opening my eyes.

'In what way?'

I shake my head.

'Did something specific happen? To make you leave?' David pushes.

I start to feel hot, the way I always do when conversation turns to what happened in February.

'I don't want to talk about it.'

And I don't. If there's one thing I want to dwell on less than Alicia Baker, it's that.

'Please?' David asks.

'No, David, seriously.'

'Please. I want to know. I want to understand. I don't know, maybe I can help?'

And I don't quite know whether it's because I've said so much already I figure I've got nothing to lose, or because the clouds have moved across the moon, plunging the baths into darkness, or what. But for some reason, I start to speak.

28

It's a freezing-cold day in February, one of those grey wintry days when the sun never seems to make it quite high enough into the sky. But I don't care. Because today I'm meeting Hannah Brennan in the woods after school.

She's been giving me these looks for weeks. At first it was just a quick glance in the corridor, or a smile across the canteen. I'd glance behind me, to check she wasn't aiming them at anyone else, but quickly I realised they were meant for me. And then they got longer, more seductive. The other morning she full-on licked her lips at me. In lessons she's been making excuses to talk to me. Asking to borrow stationery and stuff, brushing her fingers against mine for a bit too long as I pass over an endless stream of pens and rulers.

I've never really fancied Hannah in particular, no more than any other girl at school. But over the past few weeks I've begun to notice how nice her bum looks in her tight school skirt, spotted the lacy outline of her bra peeking through her blouse, thought about what it might be like to kiss her. For a bit she was Alex Bonner's girlfriend, but they've been off for months now. She's got a reputation for being a bit wild. There's this rumour about her and one of the student teachers, and another about her and Clare Conroy on the overnight school trip to London . . . Amber reckons Hannah is a slut. But then that's Amber's standard opinion on anyone she doesn't like.

Anyway, yesterday I was walking to geography when Hannah appeared from nowhere and dragged me into this little alcove by the art rooms. She full-on pressed her body against mine, her tits rubbing against my chest, her cheap perfume filling my nostrils, making me dizzy.

'Meet me after school tomorrow,' she said breathlessly.

'Where?'

'The woods. Four o'clock.'

'But, why?'

She smiled this insanely sexy smile.

'Come meet me and I'll show you why.'

Then she was gone.

I spend the whole day debating whether or not to go meet Hannah, but when the bell rings for the end of the day, I tell Amber I'm staying behind to do some extra maths revision. She narrows her eyes in suspicion, but doesn't push it. I go to the disabled toilet near the staff room and check my reflection. I suck on two polo mints at once. It's still only 3.40 p.m. Already the school feels empty. I wander around the library, not really looking at the books, just killing time. At 3.55 p.m. I leave and head across the car park, towards the woods.

The woods is kind of an elaborate title for the tangle of bushes and trees at the back of the school. They're officially out of bounds. Not that anyone pays much attention. At lunch and break times

206

they're populated by Alex Bonner and his lot. Wild and overgrown, after dark they're frequented by druggies and winos. As I trudge through the undergrowth, I spot two abandoned needles and a used condom. I'm heading for the little clearing in the centre, where I'm guessing Hannah will be waiting.

I arrive to find it empty. I check the time. Four o'clock exactly. There's an old wooden crate lying on its side. I turn it upside down and sit down. I look up. Above me the daylight is melting away.

Five past four. There's a crackle of undergrowth. I stand up. I realise my heart is beating crazy-fast. At first I assume it's because I'm nervous about Hannah, but then I realise it's not nerves, it's fear. Because all of a sudden something doesn't feel right. The sound coming towards me is too loud, too heavy to be just one girl.

That's when I start to run.

'She's on the move!' someone yells. It's Robert Marriott, Alex Bonner's right-hand man.

'After her then!' Alex shouts.

I keep running. But I know I can't keep going in a straight line because if I do I'm going to hit the perimeter fence of the school. I need to veer off to the left or right if I have any hope of getting out of here without them catching me. They're gaining on me, their whoops and hollers growing louder every second. From the sound of it, there are eight of them at least, maybe more. The whole crew. I take a sharp left, but I'm not far enough ahead to do so without them noticing. I'm a decent runner, but among the gang is Tyler Williams, who runs the one hundred metres for the county, and he's the one who's gaining on me, expertly weaving through the trees, negotiating my sudden twists and turns with ease. Suddenly, he's on me, grabbing my sweatshirt and yanking me backwards, holding on to me until the taller, stronger boys are able to catch up with him and tackle me to the ground, removing my coat and tossing it aside. Among them is Alex. He takes a spool of blue plastic string from his bag and cuts off two lengths with a Stanley knife. He passes a length each to the boys at my feet and head. Their first two attempts to tie me up fail because I'm struggling so much. But then Alex kicks me hard in the stomach. I fold up in pain. The two teams leap into action, knotting the string tightly round my wrists and ankles as I writhe in the dirt. Alex stands over me.

'If you hadn't turned up today, we'd have left you alone,' he says. 'But you pushed your luck. You thought you could get your dirty tranny paws on my girlfriend, and for that you're going to have to pay.'

'Girlfriend?' I stammer.

'Wait a second, you didn't think Hannah was actually interested in you, did you? Sorry to disappoint you, mate, but she's into real men.'

Behind him, the other boys snigger.

'Let's go,' he barks.

He strides off leaving the four biggest boys to hoist me up. I squirm as much as I can, but the string only seems to get tighter, rubbing painfully against my skin. I'm dragged back to the clearing and tied against the largest tree, the string digging into my middle.

'I think it's time you remembered what you really are,' Alex says. He takes the Stanley knife from his pocket and exposes the blade. It flashes in the light.

I decide to use the only weapon I've got. I scream. I've spent so many years purposefully lowering my voice, I don't even know whether

I'll be able to do it and at first the only noise I can make is a rattling squeal. But then it switches up and this sound emits from me I had no idea I was capable of making. The boys back away in shock.

'Tape her mouth shut!' Alex yells. Tyler gropes in his bag before dashing over with a roll of duct tape. He rips off a strip with his teeth and places it over my mouth. For a second our eyes meet. Tyler and I used to play together at nursery. I try to scream again but the sound is muffled against the tape.

'Now, where was I?' Alex says.

I can see his breath in the air. He walks towards me, his eyes and the Stanley knife flashing. Why can't he just beat me up, I think. I've taken enough beatings to know I can handle them. What's another black eye? But beating me up would be boring.

He takes the Stanley knife and slices through my sweatshirt, from the neck downwards, taking care not to cut through the string holding me in place against the tree. He slices again. The material falls away, landing at my feet. He does the same with my school shirt, leaving me wearing only my white T-shirt and binder. The cold hits me then, so icy it stings.

Then Alex is cutting through my T-shirt and I realise I am crying, hot tears running down my face. I close my eyes. If they're going to do what I think they're going to do next, I don't want to see their faces. As I hear the fabric of my T-shirt torn away from my body I hear a collective jeer. Then Alex is sawing through my binder, the Stanley knife snagging on the thick material.

'Keep still,' he demands.

I squeeze my eyes shut, my body convulsing, no tears left.

'Alex Bonner!'

The voice of Mrs Hale, the Deputy Head, is unmistakable.

The knife bounces off my knee as it drops to the ground. But still I can't open my eyes. I keep them squeezed shut as I'm untied, as the tape is carefully removed from my mouth, as Mrs Hale forces my arms into her coat and phones for assistance. I finally open them to be guided back to school. The last thing I see are my tattered clothes on the ground and the gleam of Alex's knife on top of them.

I find out it was the caretaker who alerted Mrs Hale. He saw Alex and his gang heading to the woods and got suspicious. I'm later told some of the boys tried to run, but were quickly rounded up, along with Hannah.

I'm given some uniform to wear from the lost property box. Everything is too big. Mam arrives with Tia in tow to collect me. When Mrs Hale realises we don't have a car, she gives us a lift home. Mam doesn't say a word, just wears this grim look on her face the whole journey.

I don't speak for a week.

I never go back to Cloverdale School.

'So what happened? To Alex and everyone?' David whispers, breaking the silence.

I run both hands through my hair. It's the first time I've ever told anyone what happened all in one go like that. Even Jenny only got it in dribs and drabs and never the full story. I feel exhausted but oddly relieved.

'Well?' David prompts.

'Alex got excluded. The others were suspended for a week.'

'That's it?'

'What else could they do? Exclude ten kids all at once?'

'So they made you leave instead?'

'They recommended I move elsewhere. For my own safety, they said. I reckon they just couldn't do with the hassle. I had a tutor come round to my house for the rest of the school year. I'd have been quite happy going on like that but then I got the place at Eden Park. It was meant to be a fresh start. What a laugh, eh?' I say, my mouth curling into a fake smile.

'It's not too late. You can still come back,' David says, his face all hopeful.

'No I can't.'

'But you can't leave now.'

'Now is exactly when I've got to leave. Before more people find out.'

'Would that be so terrible?'

'Did you not listen to a word I just told you? The world isn't kind to people like me.'

'People like us, you mean?' David says.

We lock eyes for a moment. David's are wide, intense. They make me want to look away.

'Eden Park isn't Cloverdale. It'll be different,' he says.

'Will it? Harry makes your life hell for something you wrote years ago, when you were just a little kid. He already hates me. Imagine what he'd do if he got wind of what I just told you. He'd make it his mission to destroy me, you know it, and I can bet you he wouldn't be on his own.'

David swallows hard. 'Alicia might not tell. You might be able to keep it secret after all.'

I shake my head.

'You should call her,' David says.

'You think I haven't tried already? Her phone's switched off.

She doesn't even want to hear my voice, never mind actually talk to me.'

David looks at his feet and immediately I feel bad for snapping at him.

'Sorry,' I say.

There's a long pause.

'Leo, can I ask you something?' David asks.

I shrug,

'How did your mum react? When you first told her about wanting to live as a boy?'

I sigh. 'There was never really a moment like that. It was just always the way I was, from birth, practically. She was all dismissive at first, when I kept telling her they'd made some big mistake at the hospital. She would tell me to shut up and stuff, but eventually she must have got sick of me begging because she took me to the doctor. And when they took it seriously, and referred me to a specialist, she started taking it seriously too. For a while we were really close, but for the last few years we've just been clashing all the time. We can hardly be in the same room as each other these days without one of us losing our rag.'

'You're lucky though,' David says quietly, 'to have her just accept you like that, even if you don't get on so well any more.'

I shake my head. 'I dunno, lucky isn't the word that springs to mind when I think of Mam.'

Silence. David chews his fingernail and watches me, like he's waiting for me to say something more.

'So, what are you going to do?' he asks eventually. 'About everything.'

I don't have the words to answer.

29

Leo walks me to the bus stop. The whole time my head is swimming.

Leo is like me. I am like him.

I want to ask him about a million questions, but don't know where to start. Away from the dark safety of the pool, Leo is silent again. I keep sneaking looks at him out of the corner of my eye, looking for the evidence I've missed, my eyes trailing up and down his body for clues. But he's still the same old Leo – gruff, grumpy, complicated Leo.

By the time we reach the bus stop it's started to drizzle and there's a veil of grey mist in the air.

'Can we swap numbers maybe?' I ask.

Leo frowns.

'Unless you want me to come knocking on your door every time you go missing in action,' I say.

This does the trick and Leo reluctantly recites his number in a monotone. I immediately call it. Leo's phone lights up in his jeans pocket, his ring-tone tinny and harsh.

'And now you have mine,' I say. 'In case you need me,' I add meaningfully.

'Right,' he murmurs, not looking at me. 'Look, you all right to wait on your own?'

'Oh. Yeah, fine.'

He nods. We stand awkwardly for a second, exposed under the bright lights of the bus shelter after the shadowy darkness of the pool.

'I'm going to go then,' he says, turning away.

'Wait,' I blurt.

He turns, his brow wrinkled.

'Will I see you again?' I ask.

The words seem silly the moment they leave my mouth – overly dramatic and sentimental, like they're lines from a film or play.

Leo just shrugs and prods an empty Coke can with his foot. The lights of an approaching bus blink into view. He jerks his head towards it.

'Good timing,' he says.

'Yeah,' I murmur, fishing around in my bag for the bus fare.

'You can wait ages sometimes,' Leo adds, his eyes fixed on the road.

I stick my hand out and the bus begins to slow down.

I take a deep breath and say what I want to say quickly.

'It would be a real shame, you know, if you didn't come back to school I mean.'

Leo doesn't say a word, aiming his gaze somewhere above my eyebrows.

'I'd really miss you,' I add, immediately blushing.

Leo still doesn't reply.

The bus stops and the doors open. I climb on, dropping my money into the slot. By the time I've settled into my seat, Leo has disappeared from view, swallowed up by Cloverdale Estate.

As the bus rumbles north through the city, the image of Leo lifting his T-shirt to reveal his chest binder plays on repeat in my head. It is almost too much for me to take in and I begin to fear my brain might explode with excitement and unanswered questions. Then it hits me. Finally, I am not alone. There is someone who understands *exactly* how I feel. The revelation makes me want to shout and sing to the entire lower deck of the bus.

'How was maths?' Mum asks when I get home.

'Maths was amazing,' I reply, chucking myself on the sofa.

'Wow!' she says, 'I never thought I'd hear you use the words "maths" and "amazing" in the same sentence. Leo must be some teacher.'

'He is,' I say softly. 'He's the best.'

Before I go to bed I text him:

Will I see you at school? Dx

He doesn't reply. The idea of him not being there any more makes me feel sick. More than ever, he has to come back to school now, he just has to.

30

When I get home Tia is sitting cross-legged on the floor with Amber sitting on the settee behind her, her forehead creased with concentration as she tries to force Tia's wispy hair into a French plait. When she sees me enter the room, she raises a single eyebrow.

'What was that all about then?' she asks.

'None of your beeswax,' I mutter.

'Leo doesn't want to talk. What a surprise,' she says to no one in particular.

I ignore her, slumping down on the settee beside her, exhausted.

She secures the bottom of Tia's plait with a hair bobble and taps her on the shoulder.

'All done, T.'

Tia beams up at her before crawling over to retrieve the remote control from under the coffee table.

'Where's Mam?' I ask.

'Down the pub with Spike. They're celebrating.'

'Celebrating? Celebrating what?' I asked.

'Spike moving in.'

'Didn't he already do that?'

'Not officially, apparently.'

I pick up an old copy of the *Sun* from the arm of the settee and pretend to read it. The whole time I can feel Amber watching me.

'Your whole life can't be one massive secret, Leo,' she says.

'Why not?' I reply, continuing to scan the printed words, but taking none of them in.

'Because you're never going to enjoy any of it otherwise. You'll be too busy looking over your shoulder all the time, forever worried people are going to find out. It's no way to live.'

'So what do you expect me to do?' I ask, lowering the paper. 'Because telling the truth hasn't worked out too well for me so far.'

'I don't know, Leo, but you could start by telling me why I've been calling in sick for you all week.'

I toss the paper aside and stand up.

'I'm going out.'

'But you've only just come in.'

'Yeah, well I'm not in the mood for company somehow.'

I let the front door slam hard behind me.

I spend Friday and Saturday on the settee watching DVDs with Tia. Anything that means I don't have to think. Because thinking means making decisions. And making decisions suggests you have choices. And right now choices are something I do not have. I made sure of that when I got in too deep with Alicia.

We're about halfway through *The Lion King* when my phone beeps. I leap on it, thinking, hoping it might be Alicia, but it's David.

I spoke to A. Everything's going to be OK. She's not going to tell! Dx

I spoke to A? What is he talking about? Then I realise. A equals Alicia.

I text back, my fingers moving fast over the keys.

Wot u mean? Wot u say 2 her?

A few seconds later David's reply comes through.

I asked her if she'd told anyone and she said no. She's not planning to either. Good news!!! Dx

I slam my fists down on the settee, stirring Tia from her Disney trance and making her jump. How dare David go sticking his nose into my business, talking to Alicia like that. What if someone overheard him?

'You OK, Leo?' Tia asks, her eyes wide and frightened.

'Yeah, T, fine. Sorry I scared you,' I say absent-mindedly.

My phone beeps again.

Are you still there? Aren't you pleased? She isn't going to tell! It can all stay a secret after all! Dx

He must really think it's that simple. Maybe telling him was a total mistake.

I check my mobile credit. I'm almost out. I take the landline phone from its cradle and lift it to my ear, relieved to hear a dial tone. Mam has remembered to pay the bill at least. I take it into the hallway, shutting the living room door behind me with a click, and dial David's number.

'Hello?' he answers eagerly.

'It's Leo,' I say gruffly, settling onto the second stair.

'Oh hey, Leo! Is this your landline or something?'

'What the hell did you think you were doing?' I growl. 'Talking to Alicia like that?'

'What do you mean?' he asks, his voice small and wounded.

'You had no right to do that, David, no right at all.'

On the other side of the door I can hear Tia singing along to 'Hakuna Matata', doing all the different voices. I put my hand over my free ear and turn towards the wall in an attempt to block it out.

'But it's OK, she isn't going to tell anyone. She promised,' David says. 'I thought you'd be pleased.'

I let out a low groan. 'Just tell me what she said.'

'When I asked her, she said she hadn't told anyone and had no plans to.'

'That's it?'

'We didn't have much time. I practically had to stalk her to get her alone in the first place. Ruby and Becky have barely left her side all week.'

I breathe out. So Alicia isn't going to talk. But I don't feel relief, not even close.

'Leo?' David says. 'You still there?'

'Yeah.'

'I thought you'd be glad.'

'It's because she's ashamed,' I say flatly. 'That's the only reason she's gonna keep it secret.'

'You don't know that,' David begins.

219

I cut him off. 'Yes I do,' I say firmly.

There's a pause. I can hear Phil barking in the background.

'I'm sorry I went behind your back,' David says quietly.

'Look, I'm sorry I snapped at you, all right,' I say with a sigh. 'I just don't like people sticking their noses in my business.'

'I was just trying to help.'

'I know, I know. I just . . .' I let my voice trail off.

I don't know what to think. The only thing I'm certain of is that Alicia hates me. The fact she isn't planning to tell doesn't change that.

'Are you going to come back to school then?' David asks, his voice hopeful.

'Eh?'

'School? You've got to come back at some point.'

I rake my hands through my hair and try to visualise walking in through the school gates, eating lunch in the canteen. Sitting behind Alicia in English. The first two I can just about handle. The third . . .

'You have your mocks soon, don't you?' David adds. 'And sixth form college applications to fill out? You can't miss all that, Leo, you know you can't.'

I hate him for being right. Doing well in my exams is my ticket out of Cloverdale. If I do well, I can do 'A' levels at the big anonymous college in the city, then go to university somewhere far, far away – Scotland or Cornwall or somewhere, maybe even abroad, start again fresh. But none of that is possible without GCSEs under my belt. And for that I have to go back to Eden Park School.

I have to face Alicia.

I let out a sigh. David leaps on it.

'Does that mean I'll see you at school on Monday?' he asks.

'I dunno. Maybe. Look, I have to go.'

I hang up, rest the back of my head against the wall and close my eyes.

In the living room, Tia is still singing.

31

On Monday morning I wait for Leo at the bus stop out-side school. Opposite me, two coaches are parked outside the gates, their engines gently humming, the drivers of each standing on the pavement, chatting and smoking cigarettes. There must be a trip somewhere today.

I check the time on my mobile. The number fourteen is late. In the distance the first bell rings. I watch as the play-ground gradually empties. I can just make out Essie and Felix in the distance, Essie's newly dyed red hair practically glowing.

I rise up on my tiptoes and peer down the road looking for Leo's bus, enjoying the wintry sunshine on my face and brilliant blue sky above me. The morning feels fresh, full of optimism, and I can't help but feel hopeful on Leo's behalf that things are going to be OK after all.

My mind is still buzzing with everything he told me last week, in fact I've barely thought of anything else. I'm so full of questions I might burst, but I sense Leo will take some warming up before he's prepared to answer them all.

Finally the bus rumbles into view. I can't see Leo among the alighting passengers and for a moment I fear he's not coming back to school today after all, but then I spot him sloping down the stairs, the last person to get off. He looks tired. His hair is matted, like he's just tumbled out of bed, and he has dark circles that almost resemble bruises, purple and painful-looking, beneath his eyes. When he sees me he frowns.

'What you doing here?' he asks, shifting his backpack from one shoulder to the other.

'I just thought you might appreciate some moral support,' I say brightly.

'I do all right on my own, thanks,' he says, squinting in the sun, using his hand as a shield.

'I know you do,' I say. 'I just wanted to see you, and say hey.'

'Well, hey,' he replies, rolling his eyes.

In the distance the second bell is ringing.

He sighs. 'Come on then.'

We cross the road and go through the gates, making our way across the deserted playground.

'How was the rest of your weekend?' I ask.

'All right,' Leo says.

He doesn't return the question.

I sneak a sideways glance at him. Although he looks absolutely knackered, it suits him. It makes him look edgy, dangerous almost. It's a look I couldn't carry off in a million years.

He pushes open the main door and there's an awkward moment when I realise he's holding it open for me, playing the gentleman.

'You coming in or what?' he asks as I hesitate.

'Of course,' I say, ducking under his arm.

Leo takes an immediate left, towards the Year 11 form rooms.

'If you need me today, for anything, just ring me,' I call after him.

He shakes his head slightly and keeps walking.

I arrive at my form room just as everyone else is leaving. Harry pushes past me, crushing me against the door frame. When Mr Collins sees me he frowns and makes a big show of making a black late mark next to my name on the register. I mouth my apology and head straight to biology.

When I arrive Essie and Felix are already there, sitting side by side at our usual bench, their heads bowed together.

'Hey,' I say, dragging up a stool.

'David, we've been looking for you!' Essie says, sitting up straight. 'Where were you this morning?'

'Stuff to do,' I say, pulling my bag into my lap and taking out my pencil case.

It feels strange not elaborating further, but I feel safer saying absolutely nothing. After all, Leo's secret is not mine to share.

'Does that mean you haven't heard?' Felix asks.

'Heard what?'

The two of them exchange wide-eyed looks.

'About Leo,' Essie says.

'What are you talking about?' I ask, not in the mood for her guessing games.

'Wait, you seriously don't know?' Felix says.

I glance around me. The entire class is animated, their loud chatter punctuated with occasional gasps or squeals of laughter. I turn back to Essie and Felix.

'What exactly is going on?'

'Look,' Felix says, clearing his throat, 'it appears Leo Denton isn't quite who he says he is.'

'What do you mean?' I ask, putting my hand on the bench to steady myself.

'Becky Somerville tracked down a kid from Cloverdale School on Facebook,' Essie says. 'A cousin of a cousin or something, and they told Becky exactly why Leo left.'

I swallow. I don't need Essie to say anything else.

'There he is!' Lexi shouts, pointing out of the windows that line the opposite side of the room.

Half of the class sprint over to join her.

'Don't you mean, there *she* is?' Tom quips to a chorus of cruel laughter.

I join the scrum, pushing my way to the front. Beside me, my classmates' noses are practically pressed against the glass, their faces glowing with excitement and scandal.

Below us, oblivious to his gaping audience, Leo is making his way across the playground, heading towards the two coaches I spotted earlier.

Dr Spiers enters the room, barking at us to come away from the window and sit down. Reluctantly, we peel away and return to our benches.

I sit down on my stool, trembling. I pull out my mobile phone. Maybe if I'm quick enough I can warn him. I've halfway through composing my text when Dr Spiers' hand slams down on the desk, centimetres from my hand.

'Give it here.'

'But, sir, it's an emergency.'

'No texting in class. No excuses. Now hand it over.'

'Please, sir,' I begin to beg.

'Give me the phone Mr Piper,' Dr Spiers says in a bored voice, his arm out-stretched. 'Before I lose my temper.'

With my little finger, I manage to press send on the incomplete text before placing it in Dr Spiers' open palm. I watch as he locks it in his desk drawer.

'You can collect it after school,' he says.

I know it is useless to even try to argue with him.

As Dr Spiers starts the lesson, I close my eyes and find myself doing something I haven't done since I was a little kid and really wanted a Barbie Dream House for my birthday.

I pray.

I pray for Leo.

32

Having arrived at form room and found the classroom empty, I make my way back across the playground as instructed by Mrs Craig.

I remember taking home a letter about the trip now, weeks ago, back in October. It's to some gallery in town; a 'treat' before we have to knuckle down to revise for our mocks. I forgot to ask Mam to sign the permission slip and had to forge her signature on the bus.

Ahead of me, I can see a line of kids waiting to board a pair of coaches. I slow down. It looks like the whole year group. Great. I look for Alicia. I can't help it; my eyes seek her out before my brain can stop them. The moment I clock her it's like my heart has jumped into my mouth. She's standing with Ruby, her lips pursed and her arms folded across her chest, her mass of black curls held off her face with a silver headband.

I hang back, not wanting her to spot me, and wait to see which coach she boards before choosing the opposite one.

I'm the last to get on, Mr Toolan ticking my name off a list as I climb up the steps.

'Welcome back, Leo,' he says. 'All better now?'

'Yes thanks, sir,' I say, not looking at him.

I hesitate, searching for a seat alone.

'Come along, Leo, we haven't got all day,' Mr Toolan says. 'There are plenty of places to sit.'

Reluctantly I choose a seat near the front, next to a girl from my French class – Serena, I think her name is. She's quiet in class, only speaking up when asked to by Madame Fournier, so I'm pretty confident she won't try to talk to me on the journey. As I sit down, her eyes bulge at me before looking away again. Unable to fit my backpack under the seat in front, I stand up and shove it in the overhead compartment. As I tuck in the straps I can feel Serena's eyes on me again, only she's too quick and turns her head to look out of the window before I can catch her in the act. I glance towards the front of the coach. Mr Toolan is talking to the driver. I sit back down to discover Serena has twisted her body away from mine, one leg crossed over the other, so her back is practically facing me. What is her problem?

The other coach pulls out first, passing us on the left hand side. I scan the windows for Alicia, only the glass is tinted and all I can make out are murky shadows.

My phone vibrates in my pocket. I take it out. It's a text from David, checking up on me I expect.

Leo, whatever you do, don't get on the bus. I think

I stare at it. The message just stops there. He thinks what?

Maybe he worked out the trip would mean seeing Alicia unexpect-edly and he wanted to warn me. Too late. I try to ignore the waves of sickness in my belly and shut my eyes.

As our coach eases its way through the tail-end of the rush hour traffic, I try to switch off. I just need to focus on getting through today. I'll worry about tomorrow when it comes. One step at a time. Once we arrive at the gallery, hopefully I'll be able to slip off, keep out of everyone's way until it's time to go home again. I begin to feel a bit better.

Then I hear it. *Megan*.

My eyes snap open and I listen carefully. I tell myself I must have imagined it, but I'm not convinced. I glance at Serena. She's wearing sugary pink versions of the headphones Alicia wears. She's listening to poppy stuff, the sort of thing Tia likes to wail along to. I wish I had an iPod and headphones of my own to drown it out.

I shut my eyes again, but this time I can't ignore the sick feeling in my stomach.

We arrive at the gallery about half an hour later. It looks like a giant sugar cube; square and white and modern. As we're herded off the coaches and into the foyer, I come face-to-face with Alicia. She's been crying, I'm certain. Her eyes are red, her face blotchy. She meets my eyes for a second. They flash with panic then look away again. I want to go over and hold her, make it OK, only I know I can't.

We're being divided up into four groups. My heart sinks when I realise I'm in the same one as Alicia. I consider joining one of the other groups but Miss Jennings has her eye on me.

We're led into the first gallery by our tour guide, an animated

Chinese guy with an American accent. The room is long and white and brightly lit. The paintings on the wall are massive and just the kind of art I hate; the sort that looks like a toddler has done it. Still, I try to listen to what the tour guide is telling us, anything to distract me from the fact that a tearstained Alicia is standing only a few feet away from me.

'Freak.'

The delivery drips with venom and even though I don't know for certain, I'm pretty damn sure it's directed at me. I try to remain calm and fight the urge to turn round, find out who the voice belongs to and make them pay for it.

In front of me, the tour guide waves his hands around as he talks about the inspiration behind the painting before us. I don't give a toss, it just looks like a load of red and blue paint chucked on a canvas to me, but I try to focus on his words anyway, subtly easing my way to the front of the group, away from the voice. All the time panic is rising inside me. Because all this can only mean one thing – Alicia told and my secret is out.

'Tranny.'

This time I know who the voice belongs to. Miss Loudmouth herself, Becky Somerville. I whirl round to face her. She smiles smugly.

'What did you call me?' I demand, squaring up against her.

'Tranny,' she replies innocently. 'I'm so pleased you answered to it.'

She smiles sweetly as she clocks my clenched fists.

'You're not going to hit a girl are you? Wait, silly me, I'm forgetting it's a fair match. Just go ahead. We'll see how long you last at Eden Park.'

230

I take a deep breath and release my fists. God, I hate her.

Alicia reaches out and pulls Becky back. Becky turns and scowls at her.

'What? She deserves it, after what she did to you,' Becky says, putting extra emphasis on 'she'. 'She's nothing but a dirty lying pervert.'

The kids surrounding her make noises in agreement. Their faces are blurring. I feel lightheaded.

'So, Alicia?' a kid called Charlie says. 'How was it batting for the other side?'

'Oh fuck off,' Alicia says.

I've never heard Alicia swear before. It's one of things I like most about her, that she doesn't feel the need to show off like that, not that she's showing off now; anything but, her face red with shame.

'She doesn't bat for the other side, you moron,' Ruby says angrily. 'It's not her fault – Leo, or should I say Megan, totally tricked her.'

'Shush!' Miss Jennings says, glaring at us all.

Ruby pauses before lowering her voice.

'Alicia is the victim here.'

'Shut up, Ruby,' Alicia says.

'But it's true!'

'I said shut up!'

The whole exchange seems to happen in stereo, and I'm certain the walls are starting to spin. I want to scream and shout at them, go crazy and lash out, but I can't. Because my brain is consumed by one single thought.

She said she wouldn't tell. She promised. She's not special after all. She's just like all the rest, just like Hannah.

I need to get away. Now.

The tour guide moves on to the next painting. The moment Miss Jennings's head is turned, I duck behind another school group before turning and walking straight out of the gallery, as fast as I can.

33

It's nearly two o'clock when I get back to Cloverdale. It took three buses to get back from the gallery. I didn't have enough money for the third bus so I had to sneak on through the back doors.

The whole way home my brain is a jumble of thoughts; images of Alicia colliding with flashbacks to the woods, the gallery. It's never going to change. As long as there is a chance of being found out, I'll never be safe, I'll always be waiting. I need to get out of here, and fast.

As I approach the house I can hear the faint roar of the vacuum cleaner.

Mam is home.

I consider turning back but I'm starving and I know that Mam and Spike finally went to the supermarket the other day so the fridge has proper food in it for the first time in weeks. Plus I know Mam has a shift at the launderette at three. If I'm quick once she's gone I can be out of the house without having to run into Amber or Tia.

An unwanted picture of Tia realising I'm gone floats into my

233

head, her lower lip beginning to wobble, her eyelashes wet with the beginnings of tears. I shove it out.

As I put my key in the lock, I hear the vacuum shut off. I close the door behind me and take off my blazer, flinging it over the banister. It lands with the embroidered crest facing up. Fairness and initiative? Give me a bloody break.

I enter the living room. Mam is standing with her hands on her hips, her body angled to the door like she's been waiting for me. The telly, some American reality thing, is on mute.

'And what do you think you're doing here at this time of day?' she demands, pointing at the clock.

She's wearing an old pair of jeans and a faded T-shirt of Spike's, and she has a tea towel wrapped round her head bandana-style. I prefer her like this, when she's natural. She looks younger and prettier; not that she'd believe you if you told her.

'Well?' she says, following me through to the kitchen.

I open the bread bin and take out two slices of bread. The margarine is already out on the counter, lid off, toast crumbs clinging to the edge of the tub.

'Half inset day,' I say, rinsing off a knife.

'Liar,' she replies, not missing a beat.

Slowly I turn to face her.

'You're a liar, Leo,' she continues. 'Bare-faced. I got off the phone with that Mr Toolan a bit ago. According to him you've just done a runner from school.'

'So? What do you care?' I say, returning to the task of buttering my bread.

'Do you want to move schools again, Leo? Do you want to end up in the PRU?'

The PRU. Pupil Referral Unit. The place for the kids no one else wants. The ultimate threat. Once you're in the PRU there's no coming back, no matter what they claim.

'Because I can't handle all that palaver again,' she says. 'No way.'

I drop the knife with a clatter and turn round again.

'What palaver? All you did was come to one little meeting and sign a couple of forms. Jenny sorted the rest out.'

'Oh sorry, I forgot, let's all bow down to Saint Jenny!' Mam says, raising her hands in the air. 'With all her fancy university degrees in being bloody patronising. She talks to me like I'm about five years old half the time.'

'And why'd you reckon that is, eh, Mam?'

She comes up close, so her face is only centimetres from mine and I can make out the pores on her nose and cheeks.

'You think you're so clever, don't you?' she hisses. 'That you know exactly what goes on behind the scenes of everyone's life.'

I turn my back on her and march over to the fridge. I take out mayo, ham and tomatoes, slamming them down on the counter.

'Cos you don't, Leo,' she continues. 'You don't know the half of it.'

'I'll tell you what I do know,' I say, spooning a thick layer of mayo onto each slice of bread, my hands trembling. 'I know that at age fifteen, my life, past, present and future, was, is and always will be a pile of shit.'

I slap down the ham and start to saw at the tomatoes, but the knife I'm using is too blunt and I end up with a load of mush. I scrape it onto my sandwich anyway, not caring what it looks like, even what it tastes like any more.

235

'That's not my fault, Leo!' Mam shouts. 'I know you like to think everything is, and maybe some bits are, but you cannot blame me for every single bad thing that's ever happened to you!'

There's a beat before I burst into tears.

I think they shock me more than they do Mam. I'm not a crier, even as a kid I hardly ever cried. I'd get angry, scream, throw stuff, but I wouldn't cry. And these days I'm Leo Denton, master of the poker face. But right now I'm powerless to stop the tears from flowing and all I can do is stand there as they rock my body.

'What do you want me to do, Leo? Eh?' Mam asks desperately. 'What the hell do you expect me to do? Magic it all better? If I knew how to do that then we wouldn't be in this mess, any of us.'

I can't catch my breath to reply.

'Jesus, I can't deal with this right now, Leo, I just can't!' Mam says, pacing back and forth.

She looks up at the clock and swears under her breath.

'Shit, I've got to go.'

She rips the tea towel off her head and chucks it on the table, grabbing her handbag and keys.

I'm still crying, shaking all over. And all I want her to do is stop and hug me, make it OK, just like she used to once upon a time. But she's reapplying lipstick, fumbling for her lighter and fags, refusing to look at me. The whole time her hands are shaking.

'Look, just pull yourself together, Leo,' she says. 'Please. And, and clean this place up while you're at it.'

A few seconds later the front door slams shut and I'm alone.

I throw my sandwich at the wall. It hits the tiles with a splat, the cheap white bread sticking for a moment before the whole lot slides down the wall and into the sink.

My tears replaced by anger, I turn and charge up the stairs. I go into my room first, flinging clothes into an old sports bag. I do up the zip and haul it downstairs. I return to the kitchen and check the tin. It's got less than a fiver in it, but I pocket it anyway. I need more though, much more. I head back upstairs to Mam's room. The curtains are still closed and the bed is unmade. The whole room smells of sleep and stale perfume. I pull open her drawers. They're a mess; a jumble of knickers and tights, but I'm certain Mam must keep a bit of cash somewhere in here. I just need enough to get a train or bus that will put a decent distance between me and Cloverdale. I'll worry about what to do next when I get there. I kneel down and investigate the very bottom drawer. It's full of odds and ends: screwed-up receipts, batteries, scraps of wrapping paper, old birthday cards. But no cash. I yank at the drawer in frustration. It comes all the way out and I drop it in surprise, trapping my finger beneath it. Cursing, I pick it up and try to slide it back in. It's heavy though and I have trouble lining it up with the runners.

It's then I notice the glint of gold.

I pause and heave the drawer out of the way, placing it on the bed behind me. I lie down on my belly. The carpet is covered with Mam's hair, blonde and wiry. Gross. I reach in the gap where the drawer fitted and quickly realise the drawers are not as deep as the frame. My left hand gropes about until it strikes something cool and metal. I pull it out. It's a rectangular box; red with gold trim. It's vaguely familiar. It's got dents on each side, as if it's been dropped or thrown on more than a few occasions. The lid doesn't quite fit

237

properly, and, luckily for me, the lock is broken. I place it on my lap and lift the lid.

The box contains mostly photographs. Quite a few of them are the ones I begged Mam to take down when I transitioned from Megan to Leo: Amber and me as babies wearing matching pink babygrows; the two of us as bridesmaids in peach satin dresses, Amber beaming while I scowled, hating every second; the four of us – me, Amber, Mam and baby Tia, sitting on the settee, Tia screaming her head off, the rest of us laughing. Looking at them now, it's like I'm looking at the ghost of some girl I used to know. I put the photos aside.

There are the bracelets we wore as babies in the hospital, tiny things, not much bigger than my thumb; our baby-sized handprints – red paint on white paper; locks of our hair taped to a piece of scruffy card. Beneath these things are several bits of paper. I unfold the first. It's Tia's birth certificate, listing Tony the twit as her dad. Poor Tia.

I realise I've never actually seen my birth certificate before, I've never needed to. Quickly, I unfold the next piece of paper. It's mine.

I wince as I read my birth name, Megan Louise Denton, and see my sex listed as female, there in black and white. My eyes float down the page. Then they stop. Something is not right.

My father is listed as Jonathan Denton. Jonathan? But my dad's name is Jimmy. Jimmy Denton.

Then it dawns on me.

I've always assumed Jimmy was short for James. Never Jonathan.

I've been looking for the wrong man.

34

The Year 11 kids return to school around three o'clock, while I'm in PE. I can see the coaches arriving from where I'm standing shivering on the football pitch, freezing to death in goal, but it's too far away to pick out Leo from the steady stream of people pouring off the coaches.

After PE I head to the science labs to retrieve my phone from Dr Spiers. Before handing it over he insists on lecturing me on the general evils of mobile phones. When he finally winds up I have to fight the urge to snatch it from his hands. The moment I'm out in the corridor I check for text messages from Leo. Nothing. I can only guess he must be out of credit. I call his number but it goes straight through to a generic voicemail message. Unsure of quite what to say, I hang up.

'Sorry I'm late,' I say, as I slide into the back seat of the car after school.

'No problem,' Mum replies, starting the engine.

As we drive past, I look for Leo at the bus stop but the shelter is empty.

Livvy twists round in her seat.

'Oh my God, did you hear about that boy in Year 11?' she asks.

'What boy?' I say carefully.

'You know! The one who got kicked out of Cloverdale!'

'Cloverdale? Isn't that your friend, David?' Mum asks, eyeing me through the rearview mirror. 'Leo?'

Livvy stares at me, disgusted. 'You're friends with Leo Denton?'

'I didn't know he got *kicked out* of Cloverdale,' Mum says, frowning.

'He didn't,' I say, anger rising in my chest on Leo's behalf. 'It wasn't his fault. They made him leave for his own safety.'

'And ever since he's been at Eden Park he's been pretending to be a boy, but he's actually a girl called Megan!' Livvy finishes, triumphant.

Mum raises her eyebrows. 'Is this true, David?'

Half of me wants to defend Leo and present his side of the story, but the other half knows I'm on dangerous territory if I do. I let that half win.

'How am I supposed to know?' I snap. 'We're not even proper friends. He just helps me with maths sometimes, that's all. It's probably a load of made-up rubbish.'

I angle my body so I'm looking out of the window, but I can feel Mum's eyes on me. I'm thankful when she doesn't say anything more on the subject and turns up the radio instead.

It's after dinner. I'm lying on my bed stalking Zachary's Facebook page on my laptop, when my mobile buzzes. I lunge for it, desperate for it to be Leo. I let out a sigh of relief when I see his name blinking on the screen. His text is short.

Meet me @ the baths. 8pm.

Itching for more details, I ring him back, but it goes straight through to voicemail again.

I tell Mum I'm going over to Essie's and taking Phil with me, promising to be back by nine thirty. She frowns but agrees I can go, providing I text her when I arrive, and when I'm leaving to come back. Before I go I nab the torch we keep for emergencies from under the sink, slipping it into my backpack.

As we sit on the lower deck of the bus, Phil cowering at my feet, I try to think of what Leo could possibly want. And while I hope he's OK, I can't help but feel flattered that I'm the one he's called on in his hour of need.

A distant church bell is striking eight as I squeeze through the hole in the fence outside the baths. Phil whines a little as I drag him through after me.

'Sorry, buddy,' I whisper. 'Nearly there, I promise.'

I flick on the torch, comforted by its fat beam, and start to pick my way across the rubble.

I discover Leo sitting on the lowest of the three diving boards, his legs dangling off the edge.

'Hi!' I call, heading towards him.

Leo raises his hand in silent greeting. Beside me, Phil's paws skitter about on the slippery surface. I tie him to the metal steps before climbing up them and crawling along the diving board on my hands and knees, the torch wedged beneath my chin. Leo turns and smirks as he watches my cautious progress.

'You all right there?' he asks, the amusement in his voice clear.

I ignore him as I manoeuvre myself so I'm sitting on the edge of the board beside him, our shoulders touching.

I switch off the torch and place it behind me. I dare to shimmy forward a little, curling my fingers so they're gripping the underside of the board and trying not to fixate on the distance between me and the rock solid surface of the empty pool below.

Leo fidgets beside me, a bundle of nervous energy.

'Thanks for coming,' he says.

'Any time,' I murmur, watching his knees jig up and down in the moonlight. This is not the Leo I am used to. The Leo Denton I know is still and solid.

'So, what's up?' I ask, confused.

Leo turns to face me. His eyes won't stay still in their sockets.

'I found him,' he says.

'Found who?' I ask.

'My dad. Jimmy.'

I let out an excited gasp.

'That's amazing! But how? Did he get in contact?'

'Not quite.'

'Then how?' I ask, watching as Leo's feet get in on the act, his toes wiggling up and down, mania taking over his body.

'What's the name Jimmy short for?' he asks.

'James,' I reply automatically.

'Yeah, but it's also short for Jonathan, did you know that? Cos I sure as hell didn't. I've been searching for the wrong flipping bloke all this time.'

'You're joking!'

'Nope. I found my birth certificate and there it was in black and white. I legged it straight down the library, typed his name into Google, and there he was, fourth bloody entry down. Jonathan Denton & Co Carpenters in Tripton-on-Sea.'

'And you're sure it's the right one?'

'His picture is on the website; it's him all right.'

I take my iPhone from my pocket and type 'Jonathan Denton Carpenters' into Google. Seconds later I'm staring at a picture of Leo's dad. He's sporting a red sweatshirt with 'Jonathan Denton & Co' emblazoned across the front and wearing the same crinkled smile from the photo Leo showed me that day in the library. Leo leans in to look.

'Yep, that's him,' he says, his voice glittering with pride. 'That's my dad.'

'Where's Tripton-on-Sea?' I ask. 'I've never heard of it.'

'Kent. Some little seaside place. Which means my auntie Kerry was actually right, he did go to the coast after leaving Cloverdale.'

'So now what?' I ask.

'What do you think? I'm going to go find him.'

'How do you mean? You can't just turn up on his doorstep.'

'Why not?' Leo asks, clearly annoyed that I've dared question his distinct lack of a plan.

'Well maybe you should ring him first? Warn him?'

'Warn him? Thanks a lot.'

'I didn't mean it like that.'

Leo shakes his head firmly. 'Nah, this has to be done face-to-face. It could be any old crackpot on the phone, but if he sees me in the flesh, he'll know for sure I'm his. You said yourself how much we look alike.'

'I guess,' I murmur, unconvinced.

'Don't you see?' Leo says, shifting his position so he's facing me side-on, making the entire diving board wobble. 'It was almost like it was meant to be. I'm on the verge of running away to God knows where, and then I find my birth certificate and discover exactly where my dad is. I mean, I'm not usually into this kind of thing, fate and crap like that, but it has to mean something, right?'

'Wait, you were planning to run away? Without telling me?'

'You seriously expect me to stick around after what happened at school? In case you missed it, everyone knows, David. It's like Cloverdale all over again.'

'But you can't go, not now.'

'Are you not listening to me? I'm not setting foot in Eden Park School ever again.'

'But Leo—'

'Look, it doesn't matter, David, none of that does. What matters is that I've found my dad, which is where you come in.'

'Me?'

'Yeah. Look, the thing is, I was wondering whether I could maybe borrow some money? Just a loan, until I get settled in Tripton.'

The thought of Leo leaving feels like a sharp slap across my face. I finally find someone who truly understands what I'm feeling and almost immediately they up and leave.

'David?' Leo prompts.

I realise I haven't answered him.

'Of course,' I say, recovering myself. 'How much do you need?'

'Well, the train fare down to Tripton is seventy-nine pounds. Plus I guess I'll need a bit extra, so I'm not just turning up empty-handed. Two hundred pounds maybe? Just to keep me going for a bit while I sort myself out.'

I try to remember how much I had in my savings account when I last checked. Including my birthday money there's at least four hundred pounds in there. More than enough. I glance across at Leo. Although he's right beside me, I can feel him slipping through my fingers. His head is already in this Tripton place, filled with thoughts of Jonathan Denton.

'I'll tell you what I can do,' I say.

Leo nods eagerly.

'I'll lend you the money on one condition. That you let me come with you.'

Leo's face crumples into a deep frown. 'What?'

'Well you can't go alone.'

'And how'd you work that one out?'

'Because. You'll need moral support.'

'I'll be fine,' Leo says, folding his arms.

'I'm not saying you won't. But you can't be too careful. I mean, what if your dad turns out to be a crazy axe-murderer or something?'

'He won't. He's my dad.'

'But what if something else happens, if things don't quite go to plan,' I say quietly. 'You'll need a friend with you.'

Leo flinches at my use of the 'f' word.

'I can handle it,' he says firmly. 'Whatever happens, I'm ready for it.'

'That may be the case, but my offer is final,' I reply. 'If you're going, I'm coming too, the end.'

He stares at me. 'You're serious?'

I nod solemnly. 'I want to be there for you, Leo. Please let me.'

I reach for his hand. Leo hesitates before letting me take it.

'Please?' I repeat.

There's a pause before he lets out a huge sigh.

'OK, but while we're there we follow my rules.'

'Fine.'

'And you won't tell anyone.'

'Not even Essie and Felix?'

'Especially not Essie and Felix. This is between us, OK?'

'Deal.'

35

I choose to wait until the last minute to tell Essie and Felix, chickening out entirely by doing it over Skype. It's Thursday evening and Leo and I are due to leave for Tripton first thing in the morning. Leo hasn't been in school all week, persuading his mum's boyfriend to ring up the school and tell them he's come down with flu.

'You want us to do what?' Essie demands, her image slightly jerky on the computer screen. It settles to reveal her and Felix sitting on Felix's bed. Felix is sitting cross-legged with Essie behind him, her chin resting on his shoulder, her legs wrapped round his torso and her arms dangling down over his shoulders. It reminds me of a wildlife documentary I once watched about frogs mating.

I sigh and repeat my instructions once more.

'If my mum calls either of you for any reason this weekend, I need you to cover for me and say I'm with you, but can't get to the phone right now. And if anyone at school asks about me tomorrow, I'm at home sick. Apart from Livvy. Whatever you do, do not speak to Livvy.'

'But why?' Felix asks, his voice slightly out of sync with his lips. 'Where on earth are you going?'

'I'm sworn to secrecy.'

'By whom?'

'I can't tell you.'

'But we tell each other everything, David,' Essie wails. 'You know stuff about me no human being should know about anyone.'

'I know,' I say reluctantly. 'And I'm sorry. I just can't tell you this.'

'You're not going to meet someone off the internet, are you?' Essie asks. 'Did you not see that episode of *Hollyoaks*?'

'Look, if I tell you where I'm going, will you stop asking questions and just trust me?'

'Yes,' Felix says, at the exact same time Essie says 'no'. Felix pokes her.

I take a deep breath.

'I'm going to a town called Tripton-on-Sea for the weekend. But that's all you're getting.'

'Tripton-on-Sea? But isn't that some seaside place in Kent?' Felix says, pushing his glasses up on his nose. Trust Felix to have heard of it.

'Are you positive you're not meeting someone dodgy off the internet?' Essie asks. 'Because, I'm sorry, but this has dirty weekend written all over it.'

'Look, it's not someone off the internet. I'll have my mobile with me,' I say. 'I'll send you a text every now and again to reassure you I'm alive.'

Essie continues to frown.

'And if you don't get any texts, you have my permission to call me,' I add.

'How very generous,' she says huffily.

'Ess, please?'

'OK, OK,' she says. 'But if you don't answer, we're coming to find you.'

On Friday morning Mum drops Livvy and I off at school as usual. Livvy kisses Mum on the cheek before darting off to join her friends.

'Remember, I'm staying at Felix's until Sunday,' I say, as I clamber out of the car.

I've told my parents that Felix, Essie and I are working intensively on a science project all weekend.

'Are you sure Felix's parents don't mind having you for two whole nights?' Mum asks.

'I told you, no.'

'Do you want your dad to come and pick you up on Sunday?'

'No!' I cry.

She looks up at me in faint alarm.

'No,' I repeat, softly this time. 'Felix's dad has already said he'll drop me back on Sunday afternoon.'

'OK then. Well, have fun. And don't let Felix's mother force feed you too much quinoa or goji berries or whatever super-food she's got her cupboards stuffed with these days.'

'I won't. Bye, Mum.'

I slam the door shut and watch as Mum speeds off.

I drop down to tie my shoelaces and then, instead of going through the school gates, I take a sharp right, keeping close to the perimeter fence.

In the distance I can hear the bell ringing for registration. I take it as my cue to break into a light jog. A minute later I reach the relative safety of the mound of bushes that marks one corner of the huge fence that encloses the school. I poke my head inside first, to check it's empty. The bushes provide a hollow space in the centre popular with couples, offering both privacy (to a degree) and shelter, as long as you don't mind sharing it with at least six other people at a time. It smells of cigarette smoke and cheap aftershave and the ground is littered with cigarette butts and sweet wrappers. I set my bag down and remove my blazer. I take a navy hoodie out and pull it on over my school shirt. I remove my school shoes and replace them with trainers before stuffing them, along with my tie and rolled-up blazer, into my bag. Next I take out my mobile phone and, with suddenly shaking fingers, I dial the school reception. I select option two to report an absence and wait. There are a few bleeps before I'm put through to Miss Clay.

'Hello, this is Jo Piper and I'd like to report my son, David Piper, absent today,' I say, just like I practised last night. I wince, steeling myself for Miss Clay's immediate suspicion but it turns out my vocal practice has clearly paid off because she simply thanks me for calling and hangs up.

I exit the bushes as discreetly as possible before legging it down the road, not daring to look back. I only begin to relax when I'm safely aboard the bus heading towards the railway station.

When I arrive, Leo is waiting under the clock in the entrance hall. He looks nervous, glancing about the place like he's got a bomb strapped to his chest.

As I get closer, he notices me approaching and gives me a stiff nod.

'Morning, travel buddy,' I say.

'Morning,' he murmurs back, his eyes refusing to latch on to mine.

As we queue up to collect our tickets, Leo doesn't say a word, just keeps his eyes fixed on the departure boards over-head, his eyes wide and unblinking.

Our assigned seats are at the front of the train.

'You do know we're only going for two nights, don't you?' Leo says as we walk along the platform, pointing at my bulging backpack. 'What the hell have you got in there? A dead body?'

I look over my shoulder and lower my voice.

'It's girl stuff,' I whisper.

'Girl stuff?' he repeats, his existing frown deepening.

'You don't mind, do you? It's just that I thought this might be an ideal opportunity, seeing as there's pretty much zero chance of me bumping into anyone I know.'

'Opportunity for what exactly?'

'Some real-life experience,' I say.

I've been reading all about 'real-life experience' on the

internet. Sometimes the specialist doctors won't let you start taking medication until you can prove you're able to live in the world in your chosen gender. And so far the furthest I've managed is the bottom of the garden. But now I have an entire weekend ahead of me in a town where no one knows me. It's too perfect an opportunity to pass up. Although the expression on Leo's face doesn't exactly seem to indicate his agreement.

'I thought you of all people would be supportive,' I say huffily.

Leo frowns. 'I am, I just don't want us drawing too much attention to ourselves this weekend. It's meant to be about my dad, remember.'

'And it will be, I promise,' I say. 'I've just brought casual stuff with me. I'm not going to be strutting around Tripton dressed up like a drag queen if that's what you're worried about.'

He continues to frown, but doesn't say anything more and I persuade him to go ahead and find our seats. I board the train at the back and locate the nearest toilet. I look both ways, relieved to find my fellow passengers busy reading newspapers or talking on mobile phones. No one seems to be paying attention to the skinny boy hovering outside the toilet.

As the train begins to chug out of the station, I press the button and the toilet door slides open. I step inside and lock the door, checking it three times. I set my bag on the floor, pull down my trousers and sit down on the toilet seat. The metal is cold against my bum. I try to take a pee, but it's as if my insides are seized up with nerves and nothing happens. I give up and pull up my knickers, before taking off my trainers, trousers and socks. The air is cold and makes my skin goose-pimple. I bob down and take out a pair of tights from my bag. I gather them up in my hands before smoothing them over my legs and pulling them up high, over my belly button. I then fish a bra out of my bag and fasten it around my rib cage, twisting it to the front and hooking the straps over my shoulders, adjusting the one on the left hand side, so the padding I've carefully stitched into each cup lies flat against my chest and level with the right.

I take out my outfit, a green shirt dress with a belt and buttons up the front, another reject from Essie (from her very brief preppy stage), and pull it on over my head. It's a little rumpled from where it's been rolled up in the bottom of my bag but it will have to do. I ease my feet into a pair of grey Ugg boots, the only footwear I could find in my size.

I balance my make-up bag on the edge of the sink. The mirror is made from that strange misty sort of glass that might not be glass at all, the sort you find in scruffy public toilets and makes your reflection look like a ghost. The cloudy glass softens everything so I'm just a series of blobby shapes – a dark blob for hair, a green blob for dress, a white blob for face. To apply my make-up I use the tiny mirror in my powder compact, holding it up as I put on foundation, con-cealer, blusher and mascara. Every so often the train sways violently from side to side. Reluctantly, I veto eyeliner.

Finally I kneel down to retrieve my wig from its little netted bag. The train lurches suddenly and I have to put my hand out and hold on to the rail above my head to keep myself from falling. I lower the wig on my head. It feels different somehow; putting it on here, rather than in the privacy of my bedroom. It's not just dress-up any more; this is real.

I bundle up my boy clothes and shove them into my bag. I inspect myself in my compact and realise I have no idea whether I look like a girl or not. I have stared at myself in the mirror so hard and for so many hours at a time, I no longer know for sure which features are masculine and which aren't. I wish I could see myself as a stranger might. I think of Leo, all the way in coach A, and wonder how I'll look to him. My heart starts to race a little.

There's a sharp rap on the door, making me jump.

'Nearly finished!' I call. My voice sounds like it doesn't belong to me.

I take one last look in the toilet mirror, at the ghost girl looking back.

Another rap on the door, more urgent this time. I pick up my bag and open the door. It's a young woman with a grizzly toddler under one arm and a big pink changing bag hooked over the other. I don't meet her eyes as I squeeze past. On the way to my seat I keep waiting for people to look up at me, for them to clock my bigger-than-average feet, my jaw line, the false shine of my wig, anything that might give me away. I accidentally knock a man's arm with my bag and he glances up, briefly annoyed, only for his face to relax into forgiveness when he looks at mine.

'Sorry,' I stammer.

'No problem, love,' he smiles, returning to his newspaper.

As I continue through the train, my palms are sweating and my heart is going crazy, pounding so hard I can't help but think of those old fashioned cartoons, the ones where you can actually see the character's heart booming out of their chest. But all the nerves and fear are cancelled out by blinding happiness.

Love. That man, a complete stranger, called me 'Love'.

I finally reach coach A. It's the designated quiet coach. I creep past businessmen and women tapping away at laptops or dozing. At the far end of the coach, I spot Leo's sandy head, facing away from me. We have table seats. Opposite, an elderly couple is bent over crossword.

As I slide into my seat beside him, Leo looks up and sort of does a double take. I feel my cheeks begin to burn all over again.

'Do I look OK?' I whisper.

'Sure,' he whispers back, before shutting his eyes.

For the rest of the journey, Leo sleeps or at least pretends to. He looks peaceful and younger somehow. I try to read for a bit but keep having to read the same paragraph over and over again.

Eventually we rumble into London. Once off the train, Leo leads the way, striding confidently through the station and towards the underground entrance.

'How come you know your way around?' I ask as we squeeze into a packed tube carriage.

'I come down here for specialist appointments,' he says in a low voice.

'Does your mum come with you?' I ask.

'She used to. Not so much now.'

'But don't you get nervous? Coming all this way on your own?' I ask.

Leo meets my eyes. 'Never.'

Every few seconds I catch sight of the green material flapping round my thighs, or a strand of long hair, my hair, out of the corner of my eye, and it delights and terrifies me in equal amounts.

After two changes we get off the tube and board a second, quieter train. After about forty-five minutes, the tracks start running alongside water.

'Look,' I say, pointing, 'the sea.'

Leo nods, his face blank.

I rest my forehead against the cold glass. The tide is way out, revealing wide flats of mud and silt the same colour as the dingy grey sky.

Leo outlines the plan for the rest of the day. As he speaks his eye-line hovers somewhere above my eyebrows, as if he can't quite bring himself to look straight at me. I guess I didn't give him much warning about coming dressed in girl's clothes, but I still can't help but feel a little disappointed by his reaction. He proposes we head to the bed-and-breakfast we booked on the internet first, to drop off our things, before grabbing something to eat and heading to Jimmy's house for what Leo refers to as a recce. We'll return tomorrow morning, which is when Leo will introduce himself. Once I'm satisfied he isn't about to get chopped up into little pieces and buried in the back garden, I will go back to the B&B alone before heading home on Sunday.

'What if he's in when we go by later?' I ask. 'Won't you be tempted to knock on the door rather than wait until morning?'

'No,' Leo says firmly. 'I'm sticking to the plan.'

For the rest of the journey I try to get Leo to play games but he refuses to bite, closing his eyes and angling his body away from me. I can tell he's not properly sleeping though and I'm annoyed. Ever since we made the decision to come here, I've been envisioning a cinematic adventure full of self-discovery, bonding and life-defining moments, but so far Leo is failing to cooperate. Half an hour later a disembodied voice crackles over the tannoy.

'Next stop – Tripton-on-Sea.'

Tripton-on-Sea is a small station with only two platforms, and Leo and I are the only people to leave the train. Even though it's not yet two-thirty, the light already seems like it's dimming into dusk.

Leo digs a printed map out of his pocket, turning it round a few times to get his bearings.

'I think the B&B is this way,' he says, pointing down a steep cobbled street. We follow it to the seafront, where we stand for a few moments; the beach spread out in front of us, grey and empty, the first proper sight of the sea still giving me a hint of the thrill it used to when I was a kid. To our right stands a pier. It's not like the pier at Brighton, with its funfair and arcades and flashing lights. The Tripton-on-Sea pier is bleak in its emptiness and lack of decoration, stretching out into the water for what seems like miles.

'Sixth longest pier in Britain,' Leo says.

I look at him quizzically.

'Wikipedia.'

'Get you, Mr Trivia,' I say.

In front of the beach there's a small amusement park, closed up for the winter. It's dominated by a modest roller coaster, its twisting metal form painted ice-cream colours, exaggeratedly bright against the grey sky. The smaller rides are covered up with plastic tarpaulin.

We take a left and walk along the front. Quite a few of the places, the ice-cream stalls and rock shops, have their barriers pulled down.

'I hate seeing places shut up like that,' I say. 'I know they're only buildings, but it always makes me feel a bit sad. Do you know what I mean?'

Leo doesn't answer; he continues to study the map, looking up every so often to check the street signs. I shuffle along beside him, my Ugg boots dragging on the pavement. The toes are getting damp, forming dark half-moons on the fabric.

'My sister's got some of those,' Leo says after a moment, nodding at my feet. 'Fake ones, though.'

'They're the only things I could get that fit,' I admit.

'What size are you?' Leo asks.

'Nine,' I sigh, 'and growing. You?'

'Six,' Leo replies in a low voice.

'Swap?'

He manages a brief smile.

We take a left and head up another steep road. Sea View is a tall, narrow house in the centre of a terrace. We ring the bell and are greeted by a middle-aged woman with silvery grey hair, wearing a striped apron and a weary expression, the sort adults seem to reserve exclusively for teenagers – a mixture of suspicion and impatience. She introduces herself as Mrs Higgins.

'I have a reservation,' Leo says. 'A twin room under the names of Leo and Amber Denton?'

Mrs Higgins looks at us both briefly before going behind the reception desk to check in her book. We shuffle into the narrow hallway. The wallpaper is pink and chintzy and peeling slightly at the edges.

'Twin, you say?' Mrs Higgins says. 'You didn't specify you wanted a twin when you booked.'

'I'm pretty sure I did,' Leo says.

Mrs Higgins takes off her glasses.

'Let me assure you, if you specified a twin room, I would have given you a twin room,' she replies snootily.

For a second I think Leo's going to lose it and start yelling at her. I can tell by the way his body stiffens, his fingers splaying out like a cat stretching its paws, preparing to pounce. But he keeps his cool and if Mrs Higgins notices his simmering anger, she does a pretty good job of hiding it.

'Well, do you have any twin rooms available then?' he asks, his eyes flashing.

'No. The family room is available, that has three beds, but that'll cost you an extra thirty-five pounds for the night.'

'You're joking?' Leo says. 'But you're the one who messed up, why should we pay for it?'

Mrs Higgins gives him a long look.

'I'm afraid that's the only alternative, young man. Apart from that I'm fully booked tonight.'

Leo swears under his breath.

'It's OK, bro,' I whisper, tugging on his sleeve. 'We've shared a room for enough years to figure something out.'

Leo gives me a sharp look, clearly not appreciating my sisterly role-play.

'Payment in advance,' Mrs Higgins says, holding out her hand.

As I take out my wallet and peel out the notes, I can feel her eyes on me, possibly searching and failing to find the non-existent family resemblance between Leo and me. When I hand over the money she makes a big show of counting it.

'Room nine. Top of the stairs, turn left. No noise after ten, no smelly food in the rooms. Breakfast is served seven until nine in the dining room.'

She hands us a key on an oversized plastic key-ring before disappearing into the back office.

'Have a nice stay!' I call after her in an American accent. I turn to Leo to share the joke, but he's already halfway up the stairs.

Room nine is small and square and furnished with a tiny wardrobe, chest of drawers and double bed covered in a flowery bedspread. It smells of pot pourri and disinfectant. We stand there for a moment, both of us just staring at the bed.

'Sorry,' Leo mutters, dumping his bag on the floor. 'I'm certain I booked a twin.'

'And I'm sure you did,' I say. 'That silly cow downstairs clearly had it in for us the moment we walked in the door. Don't worry, we can put pillows down the middle or something.'

I head over to the window and yank it open to lean out. The room looks out onto the dustbins.

'Sea View, my foot!' I laugh. 'Come see.'

But Leo stays where he is.

'Let's just get out of here,' he says.

We have a late lunch of fish and chips. It's cheaper to take away so we sit on a bench overlooking the amusement park, flimsy polystyrene containers balanced on our laps as we stab at our food with tiny wooden forks. The whole time Leo doesn't say a word, just stares out to sea.

36

Beside me David is swinging his legs and wolfing down his fish and chips, every so often commenting on the cold to fill in the silences.

I can't help but get a shock every time I look at him. Not that he looks bad, because he doesn't, but it's hard to get my head round him being here, dressed like, well, like that. But the weirdest thing is that it's not actually that weird, because the clothes he's wearing suit him, way better than anything else I've seen him wear. He seems less awkward in them, less self-conscious about what his body is doing. I even start to feel a bit guilty about continuing to think of him as a 'he' at all.

I shiver and pull my beanie hat over my ears. I look down at the pavement slabs beneath my feet and wonder if Dad has stepped on this exact same spot. Or even sat where I'm sitting now. The thought that he's close by makes my stomach flip-flop a little. I put aside my fish and chips. I've barely touched them.

'You don't want them?' David says, looking at me in surprise.

'Nah, not that hungry. Finish them if you want.'

David eagerly takes my tray, polishing off the lot in less than five minutes. As soon as he's swallowed his last mouthful, I stand up.

'We should keep moving, check out Dad's before it gets dark.'

We dump our empty containers and drinks cans in the bin and continue along the front. Towards Dad's house.

When we turn into Marine Avenue, the last of the afternoon light is fading behind the houses. Dad lives at number eighteen. We count up from number two, my heart speeding up with every step. And for the first time that day I feel glad David is with me. Not that I'm not grateful he lent me the money, because I am, but his presence clouds my vision and messes with my focus. But now, only metres away from Dad's house, I'm relieved he's with me. Which, when you've spent most of your life longing to be alone, is a pretty strange feeling to experience.

'Eighteen,' David and I murmur in unison, coming to a slow stop on the pavement.

The house, big and painted white, stands in darkness and I can't help but feel relieved there isn't the temptation to forget my plan of coming back tomorrow and march up to the door right now, waving my birth certificate above my head like a lunatic. No, I've got a plan and I'm going to stick to it. I'm going to be calm and grown-up; keep the volcano dormant.

I tear my eyes away from Dad's front door.

'C'mon,' I say to David, 'let's go.'

We head back down the street. After another ten minutes of walking we turn on to what must be the high street. It's littered with chain shops and fast-food restaurants and the odd gift shop selling faded postcards and heart-shaped lollipops with 'I love Tripton' on them.

'Oooooh, look, a bingo hall!' David cries, interrupting my thoughts. 'I've always wanted to play bingo.'

I look where he is pointing. The bingo hall is housed in what must have once been an old cinema or theatre.

'Mam plays bingo,' I say flatly.

'Have you ever gone with her?' David asks.

'No.'

As if.

'Then it'll be a first for both of us!' he says, grabbing my arm and steering me towards the entrance.

I shake him off.

'David, I don't want to play bingo. Look, let's head back to the seafront or something.'

'But we've already seen the seafront. C'mon, it'll be fun.'

'I've told you, I don't want to. Anyway, I don't have any money.'

'My treat.'

'No, you're paying for everything as it is.'

'But I don't mind, honestly.'

Just then a drop of rain lands on my nose. I look up. The sky has turned a deep grey. There's a moment of quiet before the heavens open and the rain comes thrashing down in sheets. David pulls his coat up over his head to shield his hair and dashes into the foyer of the bingo hall. Reluctantly I jog after him.

'We're too young,' I hiss. 'It's over-eighteens only, look.'

I point to the sign over David's shoulder. He just shrugs, and it strikes me then that the female version of David is much bolder than the boy version I already know. It's like the wig, dress and Ugg boots contain magical powers.

'I didn't have you down as such a goodie-goodie,' he says.

'Look, if they kick us out, they kick us out, so what? Got any better ideas?'

Behind us the rain is pelting down, the high street instantly emptying as pedestrians duck into shops for shelter.

'Fine,' I say, shoving my hands into the pouch of my hoodie.

David heads to the kiosk. The guy behind the desk barely looks up from the newspaper he is reading, yawning openly as he takes David's money.

David dances back over with a set of bingo cards each and two pens.

'Look, they're proper professional bingo pens!' he says, taking off the lids and peering at the flat, fat tips with fascination.

'I know what they are,' I reply. Tia has more than a few of them in her felt-tip-pen collection; castoffs from Mam.

Beyond a pair of double doors, the bingo hall itself is cavernous, the bored voice of the unseen bingo caller echoing off the walls. The place is mostly empty. Just a cluster of elderly women sitting near the front, and a handful of solo players dotted about, their heads bent over their bingo cards.

David and I slide into a plastic booth, David clapping his hands together like a kid at a birthday party as he looks around the place.

A bored looking girl in her early twenties (boredom is clearly the theme around here) with a name badge that reveals her name is Kayleigh ambles over, holding a notebook and pen.

'Can I get you any drinks?' she asks.

'A Coke, please,' David says.

My eyes dart down the sticky drinks menu, quickly identifying the cheapest pint of beer.

'Pint of Foster's, please,' I say, figuring it's worth a chance.

Kayleigh scribbles it down without blinking.

David looks up in surprise.

'Actually, I've changed my mind, I'll have a Foster's too,' he says.

Kayleigh nods and wanders off. She returns a few minutes later with our pints, liquid slopping over the edge of the glasses as she sets them down on the scuffed plastic tabletop.

'Want to set up a tab?' she asks.

'Ooooh, yes please,' David says. Kayleigh hands us a plastic token with a number seventeen on it.

'This is *so* fun,' David says as soon as Kayleigh is out of earshot, his eyes sparkling.

I shake my head and watch as he leans forward and sips the foam off his pint. Immediately he makes a face.

'Urgh, it's rank!' he cries.

'What? You never had a beer before?'

'No,' he says, wiping his mouth on a napkin.

'It's an acquired taste I suppose,' I admit, taking a long gulp. The last time I drank beer was at Becky's party. With Alicia.

According to David it was Becky who found out and told everyone, not Alicia. Not that it makes a whole lot of difference. She still hates my guts.

Opposite me, David wrinkles his nose and takes another, more cautious sip.

The bingo caller announces the next game is about to start. Rolling my eyes, I pick up my pen. David is already poised, his pen hovering expectantly over his card, his 'eyes down', as instructed by the caller.

The game begins. David revels in everything; marking off each

266

number with his special pen; giggling at the traditional bingo calls –
'legs eleven; two fat ladies, eighty-eight; unlucky for some, thirteen'
– every sip of warm watery beer.

The first game is won by one of the solo players. He raises his
hand calmly and looks completely unenthused by his win. The
second game is won by one of the old ladies down the front, who
yells, 'here!' and waves her hanky over her head. The third time
we're going for the house; the big one, the jackpot. The game
seems to go on for ever. My eyes begin to blur. At one point another
one of the old ladies calls 'house' but it turns out to be a false alarm,
provoking lots of tutting from the other players. We keep playing,
the numbers coming faster and faster.

'C'mon thirty-six, thirty-six,' David chants. 'How many do you
need?' he whispers across the table.

'Er, just one. Fifty-two,' I reply, rubbing my eyes.

More numbers. Another false alarm.

Then, 'Danny La Rue, fifty-two.'

'Fifty-two,' David says. 'They just called fifty-two, Leo! House!'
he yells, waving his arms in the air. 'House! Over here!'

My winnings amount to one hundred pounds. It's the most
money I've ever had. I return from the kiosk in the foyer, the notes
crisp and beautiful in my hand, unable to quite believe they are
legitimately mine.

I indicate our empty pint glasses.

'Another?'

We play more rounds of bingo. David gets a line and wins a
tenner. The old ladies at the front throw us dirty looks, which make
David start giggling so hard he can't stop. And I don't know if it's the
beer, or what, because suddenly I'm giggling too. It's not even that

funny, not really, but somehow that makes us laugh even harder. They're the sort of giggles I haven't had since I was a little kid, the sort that make you clutch your stomach and gasp for breath. Eventually we're laughing so loudly we have to abandon our bingo cards and stumble out into the street where it's finally stopped raining.

We're at the end of the high street and turning onto the seafront when David clasps his hand to his mouth and lets out a gasp.

'What's up?' I ask.

'I didn't pay our tab!'

We lose it then. We have to hold on to each other we're laughing so hard.

I know then I'm officially drunk.

Considering it's a Friday night, the streets of Tripton are pretty quiet. In the distance we can hear music. We head towards it. At some point, David's arm links through mine and by the time I realise, it feels too late to shake him off. As we get closer, it's obvious the music is coming from a pub called the Mermaid Inn.

I push open the doors. The music we heard originates from the corner of the pub where a large woman is standing on a tiny stage belting out 'Beautiful' by Christina Aguilera, a glittery silver curtain twinkling behind her. As we make our way towards the bar, I can feel the punters' eyes on us. For the first time since arriving in Tripton, I can sense David's nerves as he grips my arm, his fingernails pressing into my skin, even through my multiple layers.

I guide him over to an empty table by the window.

'Are people looking?' he whispers, his eyes wide and fearful.

'Course not.'

'Do I look OK?'

'You look fine.'

I peel a twenty-pound note out of my wallet.

'No, my round,' David says. 'I insist.'

I open my mouth to protest, but then snap it shut again. I need this money, pure and simple. If I'm going to come here to live with Dad, I can't just turn up empty-handed, I need to contribute, earn my keep.

'Thank you. I'll have a pint.'

'Here,' David says, pressing the note into my hand. 'You go up.'

'No, you,' I say, passing it back. 'You've got a better chance of getting served.'

'How come?'

'Everyone knows it's easier to get served if you're a girl.'

A massive beaming grin spreads across David's face.

'What? Why are you smiling?'

'You just called me a girl,' he says, his cheeks all pink and pleased.

And I suppose I had, in a way.

'You called me a girl,' David repeats, his eyes turning all misty, and I start to worry he might cry.

'Go on then, get the drinks, I'm thirsty,' I say quickly, prodding him on the shin with my foot. He bites his lip and nods, before taking a deep breath and heading up to the bar.

My eyes wander around the pub. It's one of those old-fashioned sort of places, with lots of dark wood panelling and brass everywhere. Even though it's only November, it's already decorated for Christmas with a wonky plastic tree on the bar and fake snow sprayed unevenly all over the windows. Over on the stage an old bloke, clearly wearing a toupée, is also getting into the festive

269

spirit, ready to belt out 'The Fairytale of New York', if the intro is anything to go by.

David returns with a pint in each hand and at least five bags of crisps shoved under one arm, a huge smile plastered across his face.

'He didn't even ask me for ID!' he says. 'And he called me darling!'

I laugh. 'Told you so,' I say, relieving him of my pint. David perches on his stool and rips open the bags of crisps.

'Cheers,' I say, raising my glass.

David looks up and smiles.

'Cheers,' he says. 'Here's to . . . what?'

'I dunno. Does it have to be to something?'

'Of course it does!' he cries.

He thinks for a moment. 'Here's to us! To Leo and David!'

I roll my eyes but clink glasses with him anyway.

The old bloke on the stage reaches the chorus and as most of the pub joins in, I find myself murmuring along with them. David looks at me in surprise.

'It's my favourite Christmas song,' I say with a shrug, fiddling with a beer mat.

'Really? Don't you find it a bit depressing?'

'Nah, I like it,' I say. 'Besides, life is depressing, isn't it? It's a well known fact murder rates rise on Christmas Day.'

'But that's horrible! Christmas is meant to be a time for magic.'

I shake my head. 'You're well cheesy sometimes, you know that? You're gonna tell me you still believe in Santa next.'

David sticks his tongue out at me and sips his beer. His mouth leaves behind a lipstick mark on the glass. He holds it up to the light and admires it for a second.

'What's your favourite Christmas song then?' I ask.

'Guess.'

I think for a moment before snapping my fingers.

'Mariah Carey, "All I Want for Christmas is You",' I say.

David smiles a slow smile.

'Wrong. It's "Have Yourself a Merry Little Christmas", the Nat King Cole version.'

'Who?'

'Exactly. Don't think you know everything about me, Leo Denton,' David says, wagging his finger at me.

David using my full name like that, just like Alicia used to, reminds me of her all over again and I feel myself slipping away for a moment, back to her bedroom on Bonfire Night. It was only just over a week ago but it feels like longer.

'How do I look then?' David asks, as the song ends and the karaoke host begins to announce the next singer.

'Eh?' I say, dragging myself and my wandering thoughts back to the Mermaid Inn.

'How do I look?' David repeats.

'I told you before, fine.'

'Can you be a bit more specific?'

'You look . . . good,' I say.

'But good how? Do I, you know, pass?'

'Pass?' I ask.

'You know what I mean! As in, do I pass as female?'

'Oh, right. Well, that's a hard one.'

David's face falls a little.

'What I mean is, it's hard because I know you as a boy. But I reckon if I was a stranger and saw you on the street, I would assume you were a girl.'

271

'Really?' David says, his eyes full of wonder again.

'Sure,' I say.

He bites on his lip to stop a no-doubt massive grin spreading across his entire face.

'Because you look totally like a boy,' he says, 'and sound like one too.'

I glance over my shoulder, relieved to find all the people around us wrapped up in their own tipsy conversations.

'It's just practice,' I say with a shrug, 'knowing what works.'

'Have you met a lot of people like us?' David asks.

I shake my head.

'What? Not any?'

'Nope.'

'But how? What about the special clinic you go to? Down in London?'

I shrug. 'It's easy enough to avoid the other patients if you need to. My therapist always goes on at me to go to support groups and stuff, but it's not my bag.'

'How come?'

'Because it's not. I'm stuck in this body, for now anyway, so what's moaning about it to a roomful of people going to do to help? Nothing.'

'Don't you find this helps though?' David asks.

'What?'

'Being able to talk to me and not have to hide anything. Doesn't that feel like a relief?'

I hesitate, keen to divert the conversation away from me.

'So what's your girl name then?' I ask. 'You haven't told me yet.'

'Sorry?'

272

'You've got to have a girl name, surely. You can't seriously expect people to keep calling you David when you look like this.'

'I suppose not,' David says, looking down at his lap and carefully smoothing out his dress.

'So what is it then? You must have thought about it.'

'Of course I have,' David says. 'I take this stuff seriously, you know, it's not just a game.'

'Jesus, I know that,' I say, taking a swig of beer. 'C'mon then, don't keep me in suspense.'

'Promise you won't laugh?'

'Course I won't.'

David takes a deep breath.

'OK then. It's Kate.'

'Kate? What, as in Middleton?'

'Yes, but that's not why I picked it,' he says quickly, 'although she is amazing.'

'So why did you?'

David leans in, his elbows resting on the table.

'I once asked my mum and dad what they would have called me if I was a girl, and they said it was going to be a toss-up between Kate and Olivia. And I couldn't pick Olivia, because that's my little sister's name, so I went with Kate.'

'Kate,' I repeat. 'Kate Piper.'

'What? Don't you like it?' David asks.

'No, no, I do. I just thought you would have picked something a bit more, I dunno, jazzy.'

'Jazzy?'

'OK, maybe jazzy is the wrong word. I dunno, something a bit more out-there, quirky. Kate is nice though. It suits you.'

273

'Honestly?'

'Yeah.'

'Thank you,' he beams. 'What about you? How did you pick your name? Leo.'

I pause to fold up one of the empty crisp packets, smaller and smaller until I can't go any further, making my fingers slick with salt and grease.

'Well?' David prompts.

'Mam helped me pick it,' I say, wiping my hands on my jeans. 'Leo's my star sign, not that I'm into that stuff. But Mam suggested it and it just kind of worked.'

'That's so cool,' David says. 'I cannot imagine having that conversation with my mum, not for one second. How did you get everyone to start calling you it?'

'I refused to answer to anything else. And eventually it just stuck. I was never much of a Megan anyway.'

There's a long pause. Even though we haven't stepped a foot on the beach, there's sand under my fingernails.

'What are you going to tell Jimmy?' David asks quietly.

'What do you mean?' I ask.

'You know, about you being a boy now?'

'I'm just going to tell him straight out,' I say boldly.

'Do you have a speech planned?' David asks.

'I don't need a speech.'

The truth is, I have so many things I want to say I can't even begin to put them into a proper order. Every time I imagine the conversation we're going to have tomorrow I stall, because so much of what I'm going to say depends on Dad.

David gets hiccups then, really badly, and I'm glad of the

distraction. Thinking about tomorrow makes my head hurt. David's hiccups are so loud people start looking over at us. I try to get him to drink backwards out of his glass, but it goes all over his dress and the hiccups continue, louder than ever.

Between hiccups, we continue to chat about other stuff – music, films, TV – our conversation sound-tracked by Tripton-on-Sea's residents belting out song after song, some more tunefully than others. And for a bit I can block out the uncertainty of tomorrow and just live in the moment. And it's a good moment, it's fun, and I feel almost free in a way that seems brand new. It takes me a little while to work out that David was right earlier (not that I'd ever tell him so); it's because I'm not having to lie. For once I'm able to talk to someone without having to edit each sentence before it leaves my mouth, just in case it drops me in it. Being with Alicia was amazing and exciting and all that, but there was always this fear bubbling just under the surface, always the feeling I was walking on a tight-rope, likely to fall at any time.

The conversation moves on to school and David is talking about Zachary, the blond kid he likes, and how he won some all-county athletics thing last week.

'You really like him, don't you?' I say.

David goes red instantly.

'Yeah,' he says, running his finger round the top of his glass. 'It's hopeless though.'

'Definitely?'

'Of course. Do you really think someone as popular and amazing as Zachary would fancy someone like me? That's what's so frustrating sometimes. Being like this. It shuts down all these possibilities.'

'It might not . . .' I say, but my lack of conviction shows in my voice as it trails off. After all, it was being like this that killed stuff with Alicia.

'Yes, it does,' David says. 'It has already. God, I long to be normal sometimes, and to be able to do normal teenage stuff.'

'Like what?'

'Oh, nothing major. Just, I don't know, dance with a boy at the Christmas Ball or something.'

The ball. I was meant to be taking Alicia.

'But normal is such a stupid word,' I say, anger suddenly rising in my belly. 'What does it even mean?'

'It means fitting in,' David replies simply.

'And that's what you really want? To fit in?'

'Not all the time perhaps. But a lot of the time, yes, I think it would be a lot easier to just blend into the crowd. Isn't that why you don't tell people?'

'That's different.'

'Is it though?'

I don't answer.

'What about Alicia?' David asks. 'You think you're going to be able to sort stuff out with her?'

'No way. It's over,' I say, flipping my beer mat off the edge of the table and watching it arc in the air before catching it. 'Well and truly.'

'Are you sure?'

'Oh yeah,' I say, downing the rest of my pint.

David needs to go to the loo then and I'm glad as it means we don't have to keep talking about Alicia. Only it's got her back on my brain. I check my phone on the off-chance there might be a message or missed call from her, but there's nothing, and even though I'm not surprised, I feel the sharp sting of disappointment.

When David returns, his lipstick freshly applied, he has more drinks in his hands and a mischievous look on his face.

'Bloody hell,' I say, taking the drinks from him and setting them down on the table. 'What are these?'

I take a sniff at the unidentifiable liquid in the glass closest to me, almost poking myself in the eye with the umbrella decorating the glass in the process.

'I asked the barman for a surprise,' David says, slamming down on his stool hard and almost tumbling off backwards. I take a long sip. Whatever it is, it's sweet and strong and goes straight to my head. Opposite me, David's face looms larger, then smaller, than larger again, as if I'm looking at him in a wall of mirrors at the funfair. His voice too seems to have faulty volume control, going up and down, up and down. Soon we're both laughing, over what I'm not too sure, but it's contagious and we can't stop and soon the people on the tables around us are laughing as well. David asks someone to take a photo of the two of us on his phone.

'No,' I protest. 'I look shit in photos.'

But it's too late, David is putting his arm round my shoulder and yelling 'cheese' as the flash goes off, super bright, white dots dancing in front of my eyes.

At one point David does actually fall off his stool, slipping off the edge and landing in a heap on the carpet. I'm laughing so hard I can barely help him up. It's as I'm crawling back to my own stool, tears rolling down my cheeks, that I hear my name being called.

'Leo? Can we have Leo up on stage, please?' the compere, a round little man wearing a spangly waistcoat, calls hopefully over the microphone.

'Over here!' David yelps. 'He's over here!'

'No! No way, David,' I slur, trying to back away against the wall.

'Please!' David begs, putting his hands together as if praying. 'Pretty please, Leonardo!'

'That's not my name,' I say.

'Come on, lad, don't disappoint your girlfriend,' a bloke to my left says.

'She's not my girlfriend,' I begin to say, but my voice is swallowed up as I'm pushed through the crowd. The pub is suddenly packed, as if the entire population of Tripton-on-Sea has turned out to witness my stage debut.

I don't know how I get up on stage, but somehow I find myself being passed the microphone from the compere as the introduction starts. I squint at the crowd. David has managed to make his way to the front and is sitting on a stool, clapping his hands together in excitement.

'Go, Leo!' he yells, cupping his hands round his mouth.

I try to focus on the screen in front of me but the words are dancing about, refusing to stay still. I don't know the verse so I just stand as still as I can and speak the words in rhythm with the white dot bouncing across the screen. But then the chorus kicks in and I realise I know the tune and it's like I'm having an out-of-body experience as I find myself singing louder and louder until, by the time the chorus kicks in for a second time, I'm belting out the words and strutting up and down the stage like a wannabe rock star.

'Right now, the time is ours! So let's fly higher!' I bellow. 'Light the stars on fire! Together we'll shine!'

And suddenly some old bloke has got his lighter out and a few seconds later there are at least five lighters waving in the air and people swaying along to the music. And I am drunk, so, so drunk. And all the time David is whooping his head off and it's so bizarre I start laughing and end up half-singing, half-laughing my way through the rest of the song. Then it's over and David is dragging me down from the stage and throwing his arms round me.

'You were like Justin Bieber up there!' he cries in my ear.

'Piss off,' I say, pushing him off me.

I'm laughing though. We both are. We stumble back to our table, punters thumping me on the back with congratulations as we go.

'I should kill you for that,' I say.

'But you're not going to, are you?' David says, grinning wildly. And he's right. Because I'm grinning too.

'Your turn!' I say, leaning across to the table next to us to grab hold of the song catalogue.

'No way,' David says, snatching it out of my hands. 'Believe me, no one wants to hear me sing. I'm tone deaf.'

'No you're not.'

'Yes I am. I discovered this at the age of nine when I was tactfully dropped from the school choir.'

'The bastards,' I growl.

'I know! It was pretty devastating. Up till then I was convinced my destiny was to be the white Beyoncé.'

I snort with laughter.

'I don't blame them though,' David continues. 'I was, am, pretty dreadful.'

'So what's the dream now?' I ask. 'Now that being the next Beyoncé is off the cards.'

'I want to work in fashion,' he replies. 'To be a designer maybe. Or a buyer.'

'I can picture that,' I murmur.

'What about you?'

'Me?'

'Yeah, what do you want to do?'

'God, I dunno.'

'But you must have some kind of idea?'

But the future is just like it's always been for me, cloudy, full of obstacles.

'Look, I'm feeling kind of hot, I'm going to get some air,' I say, standing up.

David jumps up too. 'I'll come with you.'

We step into the cold, past the smokers gathered outside, huddled together on picnic tables.

'I've got the bestest idea ever,' David whispers in my ear, his breath warm with booze. 'Let's go swimming!'

'Are you mental? It's November.'

'So? Where is your sense of adventure? You're meant to be the crazy one, remember? The junior-hacksaw killer!' he slurs, jabbing me in the chest.

'Shut up,' I hiss. 'People are looking.'

I take him by the arm and lead him away from the pub. David shakes me off and grabs my arm instead, dragging me across the road and towards the beach. I'm too floppy with drunkenness to do anything but let myself be dragged, stumbling, over the wet beach. The tide has come in and only a few metres of beach remain. David collapses breathless on the sand, yanking off his Ugg boots before wriggling out of his tights. I turn my head away.

'C'mon, Leo!' he cries, pushing me down on the sand. And before I know it I'm taking off my trainers and socks and rolling up my jeans to the knee and following David to the shore.

He takes my hand and looks at me, his eyes shining.

'After three?'

'This is insane. You're insane.'

'Shush! After three?'

I find myself nodding.

'One, two, three!'

We run into the surf, the icy water hitting our ankles.

We scream in unison.

'It's freezing!' I yell.

'Oh my God! Oh my God!' David cries, holding on to both my hands and hopping from foot to foot.

'You're officially mental!' I yell.

'Good!' he yells back.

We splash about for about five minutes, every few seconds screaming our heads off at the cold, until an unexpected wave hits us, soaking us from the waist down and sending us scrambling back to shore in wet defeat.

We fall on to the sand, shivering as we hunt for socks, tights and shoes in the darkness. David finds his phone and shines it over the sand.

'Aw, look at your feet!' he says, shining the phone over them like a spotlight. 'They're so tiny!'

I bat him away.

'Hey, I was still looking!' he says. 'They're well cute.'

'Pack it in, will you?' I say, pushing him away. I catch him off guard and he goes toppling over on his side. He gurgles with laugher and rolls on to his back.

'Look, I'm a sand angel!' he crows, opening and closing his arms and legs.

I stand up.

'C'mon, Kate,' I say, folding my arms across my chest. 'I'm dying of hypothermia here.'

David stops flapping his arms and gazes up at me.

'What?' I ask. 'Why are you looking at me like that?'

He closes his eyes, a blissed-out expression on his face.

'You called me Kate.'

37

I'm dying. I've got to be. There's no other explanation. My head is throbbing and my throat feels like it's lined with razor blades. I groan and roll over. It takes me a few seconds to realise where I am, that I'm not in my bunk bed at number seven, Sycamore Gardens, but on a lumpy mattress in a bed-and-breakfast in Tripton-on-Sea. I open my eyes. The flimsy curtains hanging at the windows do nothing to stop the room flooding with light. I wince and bury my head in the pillow before daring to open them again, more slowly this time. On the radiator our things – my jeans and socks, and David's tights and dress – are draped haphazardly. I turn over. David is curled up with his back to me, snoring softly. Last night, just after he'd informed me he was having the best night of his life, he threw up in the toilet of our tiny en suite bathroom. He then staggered around the room getting undressed, crashing into the wardrobe before finally collapsing into bed.

I fumble on the floor for my phone. Last night I set an alarm for seven so that we could have breakfast and be camped out at Dad's house by eight. I rub my eyes and squint at the display. It's blank. I frown and stab at the buttons. Nothing. The battery is dead.

'David,' I say, poking him in the back. 'David, wake up.'

David groans and pulls the duvet more tightly around him.

'Not finished,' he moans, yanking a pillow over his head.

Panic rising in my chest, I scramble over his dozing body, snatching up his mobile from the chest of drawers on his side of the bed. I press the button. The display blinks into life. 11.46 a.m. I drop the phone on the floor and leap out of bed, grabbing my clothes.

We've missed breakfast by nearly three hours, not that it matters. Mrs Higgins tuts loudly as I tear down the stairs, past the reception desk, David chasing after me, yelling my name.

I run down to the seafront, dodging pedestrians, my lungs and calves on fire, my head still banging from the hangover of my life. I only slow down when I turn into Dad's street, jogging along the pavement, counting down the numbers until I reach number eighteen. There is no car in front of the house. I press my face up to the window, looking for signs of life.

'Shit,' I cry.

'Who you after?' a voice calls.

I jump away from the window.

An elderly man holding a watering can is standing in the front garden of the house next door.

'Er, Jimmy, I mean, Jonathan, Jonathan Denton,' I say. It feels weird saying Dad's name out loud to a stranger.

'You just missed him. Back later, I imagine.'

'Right, thanks.'

The man smiles and nods before going into his house.

I wait until he's out of sight before kicking Dad's door.

'You heard what he said, he'll be back,' David says, having finally caught up with me, wheezing heavily. 'Stitch,' he adds, massaging his stomach.

'He doesn't know that for sure though, does he?' I spit. 'He could be out all day and night for all he knows.'

'But probably not,' David says, continuing to rub his stomach.

I glare at him. 'I should never have drunk so much last night. What was I even thinking? The night before something as massive as this, how stupid can you get?'

'You were having fun, Leo. It was a really good night. Actually, scratch that, it was a great night, it was one of the best I've ever had.'

'But it shouldn't have been!' I yell. 'Don't you get it?'

David backs away, and for a second I think he's going to cry. He doesn't though, carefully adjusting his wig instead. It's flat on one side from where he slept on it, and his day-old make-up is smudged and creased.

'So what are we going to do?' he asks.

'We're going to wait.'

I sit down on the wall of the house, directly opposite Dad's, David reluctantly perching beside me. It's cold, colder even than yesterday, and in the mad rush of leaving the B&B, I didn't bring my gloves or hat with me. To pass the time, David tries to encourage me to play games with him – I spy, and animal, vegetable, mineral – but I refuse to join in. I'm not in the mood. Plus I'm too angry with him. If I'd come alone, I'd never have got myself in that state. I'd have been here at eight o'clock on the dot, fresh and prepared and focused. I block out David's voice and stare at Dad's house, scared if I take my eyes off it, it might crumble away to nothing. Finally David stops trying to talk to me and plays Candy Crush Saga on his mobile instead.

After an hour my stomach begins to rumble. After two hours, the sound is almost deafening.

'We need to eat, Leo,' David says quietly.

'I'm fine.'

'I know you like to think you're superhuman, but you're not. Besides which, if I don't eat soon I might faint, or be sick.'

'Do what you like.'

David stands up and heads up Marine Avenue in the opposite direction from the sea. He returns a few minutes later.

'Look, there's a café literally at the end of the road. Come get warm for a few minutes, have something to eat and come back refreshed.'

My stomach lets out another angry rumble.

The café is warm and steamy with red-and-white checked plastic cloths on the tables and ketchup and mustard in oversized squeezy bottles. We order a mountain of cheese on toast and mugs of scorching hot chocolate. Although I'm starving, I have to force the food into my mouth, barely tasting it. While I'm picking at the last few crusts, David goes to the toilet to fix his hair and make-up. He overdoes the blusher, but I don't have the energy to tell him so.

When we return to our spot, a shiny blue Volvo is parked outside Dad's house.

He's back.

I stare at the house.

'You ready?' David asks.

286

I stand up and begin to cross the road, David close behind. Even though I've been imagining versions of this moment for years and years, I still have no idea what I'm going to find behind the front door of number eighteen. I've got my fantasy version of what happens, of course. Dad recognises me immediately, flinging his arms round me in joy. Straight away he accepts his baby girl is now a teenage boy and invites me to live with him, and I get to start my life all over again, fresh and clean. That's what would happen if my life was a feel-good family film; one with a plinky-plonky piano soundtrack and good-looking actors playing all the parts. But my life's never been a feel-good family film. Not even close. So perhaps this is my time. Maybe it's finally my turn for something good to happen.

I open the front gate and it's like I'm a puppet and some puppet master in the sky is controlling my movements and steering me up the short path towards the front door, like I'm floating almost. Somehow I make it to the door. I raise my hand to knock but before my knuckles have connected with the glass, the door opens.

I know it's him straight away. It's like he's stepped right out of the photograph in my wallet. He's piggy-backing a little boy, who is about four years old and wearing a Spider-Man costume beneath a navy duffel coat with fat red toggles. Whenever I've thought of Dad over the years, I've never ever thought of him with a family, not once. I've spent my whole life imagining him as a bit of a wanderer, going from place to place, a free spirit. I've never once pictured him with a wife or kids. I feel stupid.

'Can I help you?' he asks. His voice is deep and far posher than I was expecting. I search for some recognition in his eyes but find none.

287

I open my mouth to speak but no sound comes out. David, who I'd forgotten was beside me, jumps in.

'Are you Jonathan Denton?' he asks, although we all know the answer.

'Yes. Who wants to know?' Dad asks, a slight frown on his face.

This must be what it's like to see someone famous out and about. You convince yourself you know them because you've seen them on telly and in magazines, but it doesn't prepare you for seeing them up close. And you think you know exactly how you'll act when you do, but when the actual time comes, you sort of fall apart.

I finally find my voice but it sounds like it doesn't quite belong to me.

'You used to know Samantha Binley?' I say.

Dad's face changes then, sort of darkens. He lets Spider-Man slide down his body. Spider-Man looks up at me. He has babyish versions of Dad's eyes. Green with amber flecks. My eyes. My half-brother.

'Babe, have you got the keys?' a female voice says. Dad moves to the side and a woman appears beside him. She's pretty with tanned skin and dark-brown curly hair. The next thing I notice is that she's pregnant. When she spots us on the doorstep she rests her hands protectively on her bump. A ring sparkles on her left hand.

'What's all this then?' she asks, not unkindly.

'Collecting for charity, aren't you?' Dad says smoothly.

'Ooh, what charity?' the woman asks.

'Animals,' David says. 'Endangered species.'

'You get Archie in the car,' Dad says to the woman, 'I'll sort this out.'

'OK, babe,' she says. 'Come on, Archie, sweetheart.'

Archie gives me one last curious look before scampering after his mum to the shiny blue Volvo. The Ford Fiesta from the photograph is clearly long gone.

As soon as the woman's back is turned, Dad's mask falls.

'C'mon then,' he says grimly, leading us into the hallway. I can see through into the kitchen. It's bright and modern. The fridge is plastered with pictures Archie must have painted, all of them featuring brightly coloured stick people, the same set of three over and over again – Mum, Dad and Archie. A perfect little family.

'You said you were here about Sammy?' he says, his voice brisk and business like. He directs his question at David, still clearly totally unaware who I am.

'I'm her kid,' I blurt.

Dad's eyes narrow and move across to me.

'You're one of Sammy's kids?' he says slowly.

I nod. 'I'm Leo. Leo Denton.'

Me saying Denton makes him flinch that tiniest bit.

'I'm one of the twins,' I add, my voice almost a whisper, 'Megan and Amber. I'm Megan. Only I'm not Megan any more, I'm Leo.'

I recite my date of birth. All the time Dad's expression stays neutral, unnaturally so, like he's trying his very hardest not to react to a word I say.

'I'm sorry, but I have no idea what you're talking about,' he says, folding his arms across his chest, smiling this smile that doesn't go anywhere near his eyes, his voice artificially calm and cold.

'But you must. I'm telling you the truth, I swear. I can show you my birth certificate if you want.' I start to fish in the pocket of my hoodie, my hands shaking, but I can't find it. I must have put it in another pocket. I start to turn them out, panicking I've lost it.

'No need for any of that,' Dad says briskly, resting his hand on my arm. 'Now I don't know why you're here, kid, if it's money you're after or what, but I'm really not interested.'

Fresh panic starts to rise in my belly.

'Look, this has nothing to do with money, or my mum, I swear. She has no idea I'm even here. I'm yours, I promise you I am. I'm transgender; it means I was born in the wrong body. I'm Leo now, but I was born Megan, one of the twins, your twins.'

Dad rubs his forehead and swears under his breath. 'Look, I think it's time for the two of you to leave,' he says, looking up and making a move towards the door.

'But you can see he's yours!' David chimes in desperately. 'Any idiot can see he is. Look at his eyes; they're exactly like yours. They're identical. Just look at them!'

And for a second Dad does look at me and I can see that he sees it too. That he knows. But then he's rearranging his features and pushing us towards the door, his hand on the small of my back.

I shake him off, and turn around. Red hot rage is building up inside me, only this is different to the usual sort; it's loaded with something extra – desperation piled on top of the anger.

'But I've come all this way!' I cry. 'You've got to let me talk to you. I'll come back tomorrow if you like. Or we could meet in town or something. I don't want money, or to cause trouble or anything like that, I just want to know you, and for you to know me.'

Because right now I'll take anything I can get.

Dad takes me by the shoulders and for a hopeful split-second I think he's going to have a change of heart.

'Please?' I say.

Dad's entire face is dark and mean, his mouth set in a firm line.

'Look, you've got the wrong man,' he says roughly, 'so I'm going to tell you what's going to happen next. You two little freaks are going to walk out this door and never come back. Got me?'

Freaks. He practically spits the word.

'Babe, is everything all right?' the woman calls from outside.

'Yep, just coming,' he calls back over his shoulder; from ice cold to sunny in the blink of an eye.

He opens the door and breaks into this big showman smile. And the penny drops then that this woman, his wife, has no idea about me and Amber, or Mam, or Cloverdale. Of course she doesn't. It's like that bit of Dad's life has been erased from his history.

The kid, Archie, is sitting in a booster seat in the back of the car, bouncing up and down. And in that moment I hate him. I hate this little innocent kid who hasn't done a thing wrong. And I hate the baby in the woman's belly too. I hate them so much I could burst.

Dad is behind us, forcing us out of the door, on to the path. He locks the door behind him and overtakes us, striding down the path and climbing into the car. He starts the engine and drives off, his eyes looking resolutely ahead the whole time, leaving David and me standing in his little front garden, frozen to the spot. The only person who looks at us is Archie. He twists round in his seat and stares right at me – his babyish eyes locked on to my grown-up version – until the car snakes round the corner and out of sight.

38

'Leo?' I whisper.

But Leo doesn't look at me. He just stands there, perfectly still apart from his fists, which clench and unclench, slowly at first, then faster and faster. There's a moment of absolute quiet before he lets out this terrible howl and takes off round the garden, tearing it up like a wild animal. He drags the wheelie bin and turns it upside down, scattering rubbish all over the neat paving stones. He takes the terracotta plant pots that sit in a neat row under the windowsill and smashes them in turn against the wall, before stamping on the rose bushes so they bend and snap. He kicks the front door repeatedly and for a moment I'm worried he might kick it right in. Then he's thumping it, his fists hammering against the wood. And all the time he continues to howl and I'm pleading for him to stop, screaming, begging him. A neighbour from across the road opens her window and yells at us, saying she's going to call the police. Leo raises his head and swears at her. She gasps and shuts her window.

'Leo, please!' I cry. He takes one final kick at the front door before pushing me out the way and charging down the path, flinging open the front gate so hard I think it's going to come off its hinges. He begins to stride down the road, towards the sea.

'Leo, wait!' I yell. 'Wait!'

But he keeps walking, faster and faster, taking advantage of my handicapped speed due to my stupid Ugg boots as I half-run, half-shuffle after him.

I finally reach his side outside a boarded-up gift shop on the seafront, my chest heaving with exhaustion.

'Leo!' I cry breathlessly. 'Talk to me, please!'

He doesn't answer me. He doesn't even look at me.

'Leo,' I say, grabbing hold of his hand. He shakes me off, but stops walking at least and raises his eyes to meet mine. I can't help but shrink back in fear. They're gleaming with fury – black and murderous. He holds my gaze for a few seconds before breaking away and continuing along the front. As I run after him, I almost wish he would cry instead. I would know better what to do then, I could hold him, comfort him, contain him somehow. But he doesn't do anything but walk, his hands shoved deep in his pockets, his eyes trained on the wet ground in front of him.

'Leo, where are you going?' I plead again. But he ignores me and all I can do is try to keep him in sight as he increases the pace.

Ten minutes later we're at the other end of the promenade. Neon-lit signs for amusement arcades called things like 'Flamingo' and 'Magic Land' flash wearily, some of the bulbs faded or missing altogether.

Leo strides down the main aisle of the biggest arcade. He comes to a stop at a change machine and feeds a ten-pound note, one of the ten he won yesterday afternoon at the bingo, through the slot. Coins come tumbling out. He scoops them up and shovels them into the pocket of his hoodie before heading for the fruit machines. He comes to a stop in front of one and jams coins into the slot. I don't know how the machines work so I just watch the blinking lights chase up and down, and every so often sneak a look at Leo's face. He's staring at the machine so hard his eyes almost look like they're on fire, like they could rip a hole in the machine if they wanted to, Superman-style.

At one point the machine starts flashing all over and making lots of high-pitched bleeping noises. A few seconds later a cascade of coins comes hammering down into the pan at the bottom of the machine, making it overflow. A group of kids in the corner, crowded round a shooting game, look over enviously, hungrily eyeing the gleam of coins. I want to clap or cheer, but despite his win, Leo's expression remains the same and I can only watch as he proceeds to feed the coins back in, every last one of them, until it's game over and the bright lights on the front fall dark. He stops, gripping the edge of the machine, his knuckles turning white, like if he were to let go he might fly off into the atmosphere and be lost for ever. He lowers his head and I think he's finally going to cry, but he doesn't. Instead he's off again, striding out of the arcade, and I'm scampering after him once more. Outside he crosses the road diagonally without looking. A car has to brake suddenly, its driver winding down his window and swearing. But Leo barely blinks. I raise my hand in apology on Leo's behalf and dash after him.

As I reach the other side of the road, I realise Leo is heading for the pier. It stretches out towards the horizon. There are big signs saying you have to pay to use the walkway but there's no one patrolling the gate so we go straight through.

'Leo, it's going to get dark soon, they'll be shutting the pier,' I say. 'We don't want to get locked in.'

He doesn't answer. Visible through the gaps in the wooden slats beneath our feet, the murky green sea swills over the muddy seabed. The further we walk, the quieter it gets, the lights and sounds of Tripton fading behind us, until it feels like Leo and I are the only two people in the universe. More than once I almost slip and have to grab Leo to steady myself. He stiffens at my touch but lets me regain my balance before continuing.

'Leo, where are we going?' I ask for about the tenth time.

At this stage it's a fairly stupid question because there is nowhere *to* go apart from the end of the pier, or else turn round and head back. But either Leo can't hear me or he chooses to ignore me, because he just keeps walking, his rhythm never faltering. It takes us ten minutes to reach the end of the pier and the whole time he doesn't utter a single word.

The end of the pier opens up into a rectangular space dotted with metal benches and old-fashioned viewfinders.

Leo walks to the edge, rests his hands on the metal rail and stares out to sea. I hover behind him, unsure what to do next. Out here the sea is a little choppier but it's still eerily quiet – the only sound coming from the lapping waves below us. I can't help thinking the weather ought to be wilder – stormy and dramatic – not this strange version of silence. One of the metal benches has several bunches of drooping flowers fastened to it. I wonder what terrible thing might have happened in this very spot and pull my coat tighter around my body as a shiver dances up my spine.

We stand like that for several minutes, Leo staring out to sea while I stand behind him.

'When I was little,' he begins, his voice hoarse, 'I wanted this toy garage really badly.'

I dare to move in beside him.

'It had like five storeys,' he continues, indicating the height by motioning in the air, 'and a lift and I thought it was just amazing. I cut out a picture of it from the Argos catalogue and taped it to my headboard and I'd lie in bed for hours and just stare at it. I think I even dreamed about it, I wanted it that much. And because I wanted it so badly I sort of convinced myself that if I got it, everything would be OK. It was like all the other crap would disappear, just because I had this garage. Anyway, I woke up on Christmas morning and went downstairs and there it was under the tree with a massive red bow on it, this thing I'd been dreaming about for months. And I was so excited and for like two days I thought it had worked, that everything was going to be OK, just because this load of plastic I'd wished for was actually mine. But then Mam's boyfriend at the time, Tony, Tia's dad, tripped over it and broke the ramp and didn't even say he was sorry. And Tia, who was just a baby really, she kept putting her sticky hands all over it and losing the cars, and broke the lift by being too rough with it, and by the New Year it was ruined and I realised it hadn't made things better, not even close. And most of all I hated myself for being so stupid, for ever believing it would really make things better. But that's the story of my life. Everything I want turns to crap, I should have learned that by now.'

'You can't talk that way,' I say urgently. 'You've got so much going for you, Leo.'

'I don't want to hear it. Just leave me alone, David.'

I'm David today. Kate is clearly forgotten.

'I'm not leaving you,' I tell him, 'not while you're like this.'

'I'm not about to chuck myself over the railings if that's what you're worried about,' he mutters darkly.

'I know you're not,' I bluff. 'I'm still not leaving though. Friends don't do that.'

He spins round to face me.

'How many times do I have to say this? I don't want to be friends with you, or with anyone else. I just want to be left alone.'

I open my mouth to argue back but he gets in first.

'I mean it, just get lost, David, go.'

I remain where I am.

'Go!' he yells, tears building in his eyes. 'Leave me alone, David, just, please, piss off!'

I take a step towards him.

'Go away!' he yells one final time, before turning his back on me, gripping onto the railings hard. I move in, put my hands on his shoulders and try to turn him to face me. At first he resists, thrashing angrily against me. Undeterred I try again, and this time I can feel his exhausted body slowly giving in, going limp in my arms, his head collapsing on my shoulder.

I hold on to him tight and let him cry.

We walk back to Sea View in silence. Along the way, I steal a few glances at Leo's face, pale and stern. He doesn't return them, staring straight ahead the entire time. We stop for takeaway pizza. I have to smuggle it upstairs past Mrs Higgins. We eat it in bed and watch rubbish telly – *The X Factor*, then half of some stupid action film from the eighties with really bad special effects. The whole time Leo barely speaks.

'Is it all right if we go to sleep now?' he asks, as the credits of the film begin to roll. It's the most he's spoken since we were on the pier.

'Of course,' I say. 'Whatever you want.'

We take turns using the bathroom. As we negotiate our way round the tiny bedroom, collecting toiletry bags and night clothes, it feels like we're doing an awkward little dance together.

When we're done, I turn out the light and climb into bed beside Leo. It shifts as he rolls over to face away from me. I roll over too so I'm facing the same way, my face inches away from his curved back. I long to reach out and touch it, to let him know I am here for him, but I feel scared to do so, unsure of what might be pushing it too far.

'Leo?' I whisper.

'Yeah?'

'Are you OK?'

He makes a sound that I can't decipher.

'Leo, can I tell you something?'

The covers rustle. I choose to take it as an OK.

'I think you're the bravest person I've ever met, you know,' I say.

Leo lets out a sharp laugh.

'You haven't met all that many people then.'

'I'm serious, you are,' I say. 'And your dad is mad for not wanting to know you, bonkers. Cos you're amazing.'

I pause, worrying I've made a serious error by mentioning Jimmy.

'You sure you're not drunk again?' Leo says after a beat.

I take his joke as a good sign and poke him gently in the ribs.

'I mean it,' I add after a moment. 'He isn't half the man you already are.'

The sentence hangs in the air like an echo.

Then silence.

'Thanks, David,' Leo murmurs eventually, his voice cracking a little, 'that's a really nice thing to say.'

My fingers search tentatively for Leo's in the darkness. I find them, my fingers daring to curl round his. I hear Leo take a deep breath before allowing his hand to relax into mine. His hand feels small and soft in my big paddles; like a child's almost.

We lie in silence for a bit, our breathing falling into rhythm.

'Leo?'

'Yeah?'

'I think I'm going to tell them.'

'Who? Your parents?'

'Yeah. I think I'm going to tell them tomorrow, when I get home. Before I do anything else.'

'You're doing the right thing.'

'You think?'

'Course. Your mum seemed really sound when she drove me home that time.'

'I hope so. I'm still terrified though.'

'What's your dad like?' Leo asks quietly.

'I look like him apparently, not ideal as he's pretty much a giant.'

'No, I meant what's he like as a person.'

'He's just kind of a typical dad, I guess.'

As soon as the words leave my mouth I regret them.

'Shit, sorry,' I say quickly, 'I didn't mean it like that. God, that was so stupid of me.'

'It's OK,' Leo says. 'Go on.'

I visualise my dad – big and goofy and embarrassing.

'Well, he likes football and golf and beer and cars and stuff like that,' I say carefully. 'And when I was a kid he used to try and get me to kick a ball about with him in the garden and stuff, but when I made it clear I wasn't into all that, he never put pressure on me, or made me feel like it was a big problem. And when I was asking for dolls for Christmas and wanting to paint my bedroom girly colours, he never batted an eyelid, or at least if he did, he didn't let me see. He's always just let me be me, I guess.'

'He sounds pretty great,' Leo says.

'Yeah,' I murmur, realising that describing him out loud like that, he sort of does.

'Why are you so scared of telling them if they're so cool?' Leo asks, practically reading my mind.

'Because I'm pretty sure they have no idea this is coming. It's going to knock them sideways and I have no idea how they're going to react. I mean, they're hardly going to be letting off party poppers and unfurling banners, are they?'

'They'll be OK, I know it. Even if they're shocked at first, they'll come round eventually, I bet.'

My grip on Leo's hand tightens.

'Thanks, Leo, that means a lot.'

We lie there in silence for a few moments.

'Are you going to tell your family about what happened today? Amber or your mum or anyone?' I ask.

'I don't know. I don't think so. What good would it do? It's funny, Amber had him sussed from the beginning, but I could never see it. I was just blinded by this idea of him. Jimmy the hero . . .'

Leo's voice trails off.

'Look, I'm knackered, I'm going to go to sleep now,' he says.

'OK.'

'Night, David.'

'Night, Leo.'

I lie there for ages before I drop off. And although he doesn't say another word, I can tell Leo is awake too. The whole time he doesn't let go of my hand.

39

We wake up at dawn and creep out of Sea View before breakfast.

David travels back in his boy clothes.

'You still gonna tell them today?' I ask.

After two days as Kate, he looks strange back in a baggy hoodie and skinny jeans, with his boy's haircut.

'Yes,' David replies firmly.

He looks petrified though.

We don't talk much for the rest of the journey. I think we've said enough the past few days to last us a lifetime.

We say goodbye at the station, outside the taxi rank.

'Will I see you at school tomorrow?' David asks.

'I don't know yet,' I admit.

'You'll be old news by now, I bet,' he says brightly.

'Sure,' I say, rolling my eyes, not believing it for one second.

'All we need is for someone to release a sex tape to take the heat off and we're home and dry,' he adds with a grin.

I fake a smile.

David looks at his feet for a moment. The laces of his Converse are too long and drag on the pavement.

'Stupid jokes aside, I really hope you do come back.'

'Yeah, well, we'll see.'

David nods and adjusts his scarf.

'Well, bye, I suppose,' I say.

I turn to go and David grabs hold of my hand and pulls me into a hug. I find myself returning it. We break apart and nod at each other before going our separate ways. And it's weird, because as I head across the street and towards the bus stop, I sort of miss him.

As I cross the estate, the whole place seems changed somehow in a way I can't quite put my finger on. I've been away just over forty-eight hours but it seems longer. I feel different too; raw, like I've had a layer of skin ripped off and underneath is all red and delicate and painful to the touch.

It's past noon, but I expect everyone will be in bed. Apart from Tia maybe, who still rises at dawn like a newborn, and will have been glued to the telly for hours by now.

I'm digging about in the bottom of my bag for my keys when the door flies open and Tia flings her tiny body at me.

'He's back!' she screams. 'Leo's back!'

'Steady on, Tia,' I say. 'Let me get in the bloody house at least.'

I'm kicking off my trainers when I notice a figure in the doorway to the lounge. At first I think it's Mam. It takes me a moment to realise it's Auntie Kerry, puffing furiously on a cigarette and glaring at me.

'What are you doing here?' I ask, disentangling myself from Tia, who still has her skinny little arms round my waist. There's a wet patch on my hoodie from her tears.

'Tia, go upstairs,' Kerry says.

'But I want to watch cartoons with Leo,' Tia protests, lacing her fingers through mine.

'I said upstairs!' Kerry shouts, setting Tia's lower lip wobbling.

'Go on, T,' I say.

Tia nods and heads up the stairs, her head bowed.

'Give your mam and Spike a call,' Kerry calls after her, 'and your big sister. Tell them they can come home now.'

She turns and walks into the living room. I can tell she expects me to follow. She waits until we're in the centre of the room before spinning round and slapping me across the cheek. It shocks more than it hurts.

'Where the hell have you been?' she barks.

'What the hell was that for?' I cry, holding on to my cheek.

'Answer the bloody question, Leo, before I really do lose my patience.'

'Away,' I mutter.

'Away? What d'you mean, away? Away bloody where?'

'Why the drama?' I ask, 'I left a note.'

'What note? No one's seen a note.'

'I left it on top of the telly,' I say, crossing over to the television set. But the spot where I left my note is bare. I hunt around, eventually finding it down the back of the set, tucked under the radiator. I fish it out and hand it to Kerry. She doesn't bother to read it, flinging it onto the coffee table instead.

'That's it? You go gallivanting off for two whole bloody days and all we get is a sodding note?'

'I thought someone would see it,' I mutter.

'Do you know where your mam and Spike are right now?' she

asks, jabbing a finger in my chest. 'Where they've been for the past two nights?'

I shake my head.

'Driving around looking for you, that's where. Tia's been in tears since yesterday morning, Amber and Carl have been all over the estate searching for you. The police, well they've been no help at all.'

'The police? What did you call them for?'

'What did you expect us to do? We had no bloody idea where you were. Your phone was off.'

'I forgot my charger,' I say, looking at my feet.

Kerry just glares at me.

'I didn't think Mam would care,' I say. 'I didn't even think she'd notice.'

Kerry's face turns a fresh shade of red.

'Your mam may not be winning any prizes for the world's best mother any time soon, but I would think very carefully before accusing her of not noticing her own kid is missing.'

'She seems to do a pretty good job of not noticing me when I am around, so what am I supposed to think?' I retort.

'Raising three kids alone isn't a walk in the park, you know.'

'It's not our fault she can't hold on to a bloke.'

Kerry slaps me again. Hard. This time it hurts.

'You have no idea, Leo,' she says, pointing a shaking finger right up in my face. 'Until you've walked in your mam's shoes, you will have no bloody idea what her life has been like, bringing up the three of you alone, so don't you even pretend you do.'

I slump down on the settee, my arms folded. In front of me Kerry fumbles in the pocket of her jeans for a packet of cigarettes. She takes one out and swipes a plastic pink lighter from the coffee table, lighting up with still-trembling hands. She does the whole thing without taking her eyes off me for a second.

'Leo, remember that weekend when your mam came home with a black eye?'

I frown.

'It was just after all that bother at school,' she prompts.

All that bother. Whenever anyone talks about what happened back in February, they always seem to speak in some weird code.

'Yeah,' I say, 'what about it?'

'What was his name again? The ringleader?' Kerry asks.

'Alex Bonner,' I murmur, my voice flat. Just saying his name out loud makes me feel dizzy and sick.

'That's him, nasty little beggar. Your mam went to have it out with Alex but he wasn't in. His mam was though, giving a load of lip.'

'What?'

I know Alex's mother, everyone does. She's one of those people on the estate you just can't miss. Annette, her name is. She looks just like Alex, with the same jet-black hair, hard face, and terminator build.

'Hang on, Annette Bonner gave Mam that black eye?'

'You should have seen Annette. She was in a right state once your mam had finished with her. People had to drag your mam off her in the end.'

I stare at Kerry. I can't believe what I'm hearing. Mam went up against Annette Bonner for me?

'Why didn't she tell me?' I ask.

'God knows. God knows why your mam does a lot of the stuff she does.'

Silence. I can sense Kerry watching me as she smokes.

'Come on then, where were you?' she says, taking a deep breath and folding her arms. Like Mam, she's tiny, built like a sparrow. Which makes it all the more incredible Mam beat up big old Annette Bonner. Jesus.

'Come on, don't keep me in bloody suspense,' Kerry says, taking another long drag on her cigarette, the smoke misting the air between us. 'Where have you been?'

'You really want to know?' I ask.

'Yes, I do.'

I take a deep breath.

'I was in Kent.'

Kerry's forehead creases in confusion.

'Kent? But that's bloody miles away. What the hell's in Kent?'

I take out my wallet and slide out the photograph of Dad. She takes it between her fingers, her eyes bulging. She looks down at me.

'Where'd you get this, Leo?'

'Does it matter?'

'Where did you get this, Leo?' she repeats.

'Mam's bedroom. I've had it for years.'

'We turned the house upside down looking for this,' she says softly. 'Your mam ended up thinking she must have thrown it out by accident.'

I look up. I always assumed Mam never missed it. She certainly never said anything about it.

'That was his first car,' Kerry says, her fingers tracing its outline.

'Drives a brand new Volvo these days. Midnight blue. Very smart,' I say.

308

Kerry's head snaps up.

'You saw him?'

'Oh yeah. We had a great chat, me and old Jimmy,' I say with a bitter laugh.

She just stares at me, her mouth hanging open slightly.

'Didn't like me turning up on his doorstep very much,' I say. 'Didn't like it at all in fact. You probably knew as much though, didn't you?'

Kerry sinks on to the settee beside me, the photograph fluttering to the floor.

'How did he look?' she asks.

'Like this I suppose, but older,' I say, leaning forward to pick up the photograph.

'Me and Amber got his eyes,' I add.

'I know you did,' Kerry says.

'He's got a wife and kids of his own now,' I say. 'Posh house and that.'

'Has he now?' she murmurs, her face white. It's not a proper question though.

'Didn't want to know, of course. Called me a freak.'

'Oh, Leo.'

I crumple up the photograph in my hand and let it drop. I don't cry though. I'm not planning on wasting any more tears on Jonathan Denton.

'What happened, Kerry? Why did he leave?'

'You mean, what did your mam do to make him leave?' she snaps. 'I know that's what you're thinking, Leo.'

I look down at my feet. Because she's right, that's exactly what I was thinking.

'Me and your mam are well aware that you've always had her down as the bad guy and your dad as the hero,' Kerry continues. 'We may not have done well at school and passed many exams, but we know that much.'

She picks up her fag again. It's burned down to nothing. She tuts to herself and lights another.

'Then tell me the truth,' I say.

She raises her eyebrows.

'The truth, eh? You want the truth?'

I nod.

'You sure?'

'For God's sake, Kerry.'

She takes a deep drag on her cigarette and lets her eyes fall shut as she exhales. Her eyelids are waxy and shiny. She opens them again.

'Your mam met Jimmy when she was twenty-one. He was twenty-three and drop-dead gorgeous. All the girls in Cloverdale fancied him, but he chose your mam. Anyway, they'd been going out for six months when she found out she was pregnant with twins. And at first Jimmy was all excited, telling everyone he met. He even proposed, brought her home this flashy ring. Everyone on the estate was green with envy, including me a bit.'

'So then what happened?'

'He started getting distant, staying out late. Your mam just put it down to him being a bit stressed about money being tight. Anyway, one day, about six weeks before she was going to pop, your mam got home from doing the food shopping and found a note on the coffee table.'

I glance at my note, nestled among the ashtrays and mugs.

'We thought it was a joke at first,' Kerry continues. 'But then we went upstairs and all his clothes were gone from the wardrobe and he wasn't answering his phone. I assumed he'd just got cold feet and would come back, but he never did. Your mam never heard from him again.'

'But that can't be right. I remember him. I remember him changing my nappy,' I say.

Kerry shakes her head.

'You can't, Leo. He was gone over a month before you were born.'

I squeeze my eyes shut and try to conjure up the image in my head, of Dad singing as he bent over me.

'It must be my ex, Chris, that you remember. He helped out quite a bit when you and Amber were little. Or your granddad maybe, before he died.'

I shake my head firmly.

'No, I'm certain it was him, Kerry, I can picture his face.'

But already it's fading, his features growing hazier by the second.

Kerry puts down her cigarette and takes my hand, looking right into my eyes. Her fingers are rough and freezing cold.

'It wasn't him, Leo. Trust me, it wasn't.'

I stare hard at the carpet, so hard my vision blurs.

'Why didn't she just tell us?'

'What, tell a couple of little kids their dad buggered off before they were even born? Easier said than done, Leo.'

'Better that than not telling us anything at all.'

'Your gran told your mam to tell you and Amber he was dead, but she couldn't bring herself to do it. And anyway, as soon as you could talk you were obsessed with the idea of him. It was easier to let you dream, easier for your mam to be the villain who drove him away.'

'Did she love him?' I ask.

She sighs and shakes her head.

'She really did, the fool that she is.'

I stare at the carpet.

'I always assumed she'd driven him away, like she did all the rest.'

'No, Leo.'

'That's why she does it though,' I murmur.

'Does what?'

I look up. Because it all makes weird, messed-up sense now.

'Pushes them away. So they won't leave her like Jimmy did.'

Not Dad. Not any more. Jimmy.

Kerry lets out a heavy sigh.

'You and your mam have let that man haunt you for too long now. It's time to move on, Leo, for both of you.'

40

I turn my key carefully in the lock and ease the front door open. The hallway is empty. I creep forwards and press my ear up against the kitchen door.

I can hear my family on the other side; the rustle of newspapers, muffled voices, the occasional clink of glasses and cutlery, Radio 4 playing in the background. A perfect family scene. And I'm about to turn it upside down.

I back away and head upstairs to my bedroom where I dump my bag on the floor and remove my coat. I hunt around in my desk for the unsent letter to my parents, the one I almost posted under their bedroom door way back in August. I take it out of its envelope and read it through before smoothing it out and carefully gluing it on to the next available page of my scrapbook.

Mum and Dad look up in surprise as I enter the kitchen.

'You're back early,' Dad says. 'We didn't expect you until dinner time.'

'You look like shit,' Livvy observes.

'Livvy!' Mum scolds. 'Language.'

'But he does!' Livvy protests, pointing at me with her yoghurt spoon.

'That's no excuse.'

Livvy drops the spoon with a clatter and stands up to leave the table.

'Excuse me, madam, we clear up after ourselves in this household,' Dad says.

Livvy rolls her eyes but heads over to the dishwasher with her dirty brunch dishes, loading them noisily before wandering into the living room and switching on the TV. The whole time I just stand there, clutching my scrapbook so hard my fingers start to feel numb.

Mum peers up at me.

'You do look on the tired side, David,' she admits. 'Up chatting all night I expect. Now, do you want some scrambled eggs or something? I think there might even be some smoked salmon left if you're lucky.'

I don't say anything.

I simply walk over, put my scrapbook down on the table, and walk out again, shutting the kitchen door behind me.

I go upstairs, curl up on my bed and wait.

It's only an hour before I hear the knock at the door, but it feels like days. And even though I've been expecting to hear it, it still makes me jump.

'Come in,' I say, sitting up.

The door opens and in step Mum and Dad, the scrapbook tucked under Dad's arm, their faces serious.

I stare up at them and realise my whole body is quaking all over. I wonder whether there'll ever be a time when my body does what I want it to.

Dad clears his throat.

'David,' he says, 'before we say anything more, we want you to know one important thing. And that's that your mum and I love you very much. We always have and we always will. But we also need a bit of time to digest this, OK?'

I nod.

'Now, are you certain this is what you want, David?' Mum asks, edging forward. 'You're not just confused?'

'No, I'm sure, Mum. I've been sure for ages now.'

'Yes,' she says quietly, lowering her eyes.

As I watch her move across the room, it's almost like I can see all the plans she had for my future slowly crumbling inside her head.

'Why didn't you tell us earlier?' she asks, her eyes glistening with tears as she sits down on the bed beside me. Dad reaches across and squeezes her hand.

'I don't know,' I say. 'I was scared I think. I was worried you would disown me or something.'

Mum starts crying properly then. Of course that sets me off, and then Dad too, which is miraculous in itself because I haven't seen Dad cry over anything non-football related since his parents died. Noisy crying must be genetic because we're so loud Livvy comes barging in assuming Granny must have just died. Mum whisks her out of the room, reassuring her Granny is very much alive. She ends up dropping her off at Cressy's for the afternoon, leaving the three of us to talk without interruption.

We go through my scrapbook, page by page. I show Mum and Dad the videos I've been watching on YouTube, the forums I've visited, the websites I've pored over. I tell them about the specialist clinic in London, the one where Leo goes. I monitor their faces out of the corner of my eye as they stare at the computer screen, their eyes wide, and I can almost see the cogs in their heads whirring at a speed of one hundred revolutions per second as they try to process everything they're seeing and hearing. Some of the more explicit stuff makes them frown and wince and I can tell Mum is fighting back more tears. But they keep watching, reading, listening. All the time I have to keep reminding myself I've had pretty much my whole life to slowly get used to the idea, while they've only had a few hours.

Dad goes off to make tea. He comes back with a tray packed with biscuits (the nice ones we usually only get out when we have guests), cheese and pickle sandwiches and massive mugs of tea. We sit on my floor and have a sort of picnic, sitting in a triangle, our knees touching.

'I'm sorry,' I say, as we slurp tea, my throat exhausted, my tear ducts sore.

Mum frowns. 'What do you mean, David?'

'For not being normal. I know it would be easier for everyone if I was.'

She and Dad exchange looks.

'I'm not going to lie to you,' she says. 'Of course I'd prefer it if things were more straightforward. I love you and I don't want to have to see you have a hard time unnecessarily. And the road ahead, if this is what you really want to do . . .'

'It is,' I say firmly.

'Well then, the road ahead is going to be tough. It's going to be long and painful and frustrating and you're going to encounter people who don't understand it. I'm not even sure I understand it right now.'

'I know. But I'm ready, I promise I am.'

'What I'm trying to articulate, David,' she says, 'is that we love you and we're going to support you.'

'Besides,' Dad says, 'who wants to be normal anyway? Fancy that on your gravestone. "Here lies so-and-so. They were entirely normal".'

I smile. But I can tell he's putting on a brave face with all the fake jolliness. It reminds me of when his mum died and he was all lively and together at the wake, making jokes and filling up everyone's drinks, and later I overheard him crying alone in the bathroom.

The phone rings. Mum and Dad both claim it must be for them, leaving me alone among the remnants of our picnic.

When Livvy gets home from Cressy's, we all eat dinner round the table and Mum and Dad act like nothing has changed, when really, three out of four of us know that everything has.

I go to bed early. Mum tucks me in, something she hasn't done in years. She's been crying some more, I can tell because her face is covered in fresh blotches.

'Can I show you something?' I ask as she turns to leave.

'Of course,' she says, although she looks a little fearful.

I pick up my phone and scroll through the camera roll until I find the shot of Leo and me from the other night in Tripton. Despite his protests, Leo is grinning at the camera, his eyes sparkling. Next to him I'm beaming away, rosy-cheeked, high on alcohol and life. I pass the phone over to Mum and hold my breath. She stares at the screen for ages.

'When was this taken?' she asks, not taking her eyes off it.

'Not long ago,' I reply, biting my lip.

I try to read her expression, but I can't quite work it out.

'You look really happy,' she says finally.

'Thank you,' I whisper.

She peers closer at the photograph and her expression changes a little. She looks up at me, a different kind of frown on her face from the one she's been wearing for the majority of the day.

'Was this taken in a pub?' she asks.

'Course not,' I lie. 'You know I don't drink.'

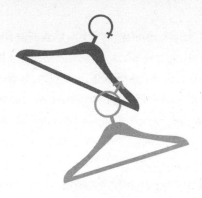

41

The next day I go back to school.

David ignores my protests and meets me at the bus stop. The moment I step through the school gates, kids are staring at me, their mouths hanging open like goldfish. I now know for sure what zoo animals must feel like. At lunch time Essie screeches at any kid who looks our way to 'get a life', which I don't think really helps. I appreciate the thought though.

On Tuesday I have English. Alicia isn't in class because of rehearsals for *Oh! What A Lovely War*. The sight of her empty chair is still enough to make my insides twist though.

On Wednesday I eat lunch with David, Essie and Felix in the canteen. Harry comes over to our table and calls us 'the mutant, the geek, and the two super freaks' and asks us whether we've thought about opening our own travelling carnival. Essie tells him to 'curl up and die'. I go to stand up. David grabs hold of my wrist and pulls me back down. Harry saunters off, smirking.

On Thursday Becky keeps calling me Megan during form room.

I don't bite and keep staring straight ahead until the bell rings and I can escape.

Later that morning, I'm walking down the corridor alone when some sixth former stops me and asks if I'd be interested in joining the Maths Challenge team. At first I assume it's a trick and he's about to follow up with some nasty insult, but he doesn't, handing me a flyer instead.

'We need some new blood,' he says, 'and Mr Steele gave me your name. Think about it?'

I find myself promising I will.

On Friday I make it down the corridor without anyone saying anything nasty. It's only a small triumph but one I'm prepared to take.

The bottom line is, I survive the week. And if I can survive one week, I can survive more.

When I get home from school Mam summons Amber and me to the lounge. At first she doesn't say anything, chain smoking as she fiddles with her hoop earrings and not looking us in the eye. Eventually though, she sets her fags and lighter down, takes a deep breath and starts to talk.

And finally we get to hear everything, right from the very beginning with no gaps – Mam's story in her own words.

42

Four weeks later

It's the last Friday of term before the Christmas holidays and Essie and Felix have been acting weird all week; lots of urgent whispering when they think I'm not looking, and fixed smiles when they think I am. At first I put it down to boyfriend/girlfriend stuff but something tells me it's more than that.

Today is definitely the pinnacle of their weirdness. In history Essie is totally manic, babbling non-stop. Even Felix seems on edge.

'What's going on, guys?' I ask, for at least the one-hundredth time this week.

'Nothing,' they reply in unison.

'We're still on for tonight, aren't we?' I ask.

'Of course we are,' Essie replies. 'Why wouldn't we be?'

'Just checking,' I murmur.

For the first time ever we've decided to boycott the Christmas Ball. Instead we're going to hang out at mine, gorge on pizza (Essie and I anyway, Felix will be bringing his own cauliflower-crust alternative) and watch Christmas films. And although I know we'll have fun and everything, and even though the Christmas Ball has proved the most disappointing night of the year every year for the past three, I can't help but feel a small ache of regret that tonight it's going ahead without me.

The final lesson before lunch is maths. Mr Steele hosts a maths quiz. I'm pretty sure 'quiz' is just a slightly friendlier word for test, but I surprise myself by actually doing OK, not good enough for a prize, but OK. After the lesson I head to the canteen. I'm unloading my tray when I sense someone by my side. I look up. It's Leo.

Upon his return to school following our weekend in Tripton, the teachers quickly figured out what was going on and a series of special assemblies was arranged, explaining Leo's situation and what being transgender means, and making it clear that anyone found guilty of bullying would face a harsh punishment. Although the name-calling and cruel whispers haven't stopped altogether, they've certainly died down.

Leo and I have steadily been hanging out more. We've been to the cinema a couple of times, sometimes to McDonald's or Nando's afterwards. He's been over to my house a few times too, and charmed the pants off my mum and, to my surprise, Livvy. A couple of times a week he eats lunch with Essie, Felix and me. He never says a lot; just listens and occasionally chips in with a sarcastic comment. Earlier in the week, the four of us went to see the drama club's production of *Oh! What a Lovely War* in the school hall. Alicia was in it. She looked very beautiful and sang two solos. While she was singing Leo's eyes looked all dreamy and sad.

He emailed his therapist, Jenny, about me, and she gave him the details of some support groups to pass on to me that might be helpful while I'm waiting for my referral to the specialist clinic in London to be accepted. Leo promises he'll come with me in the New Year, although I'm not sure he will when the time comes. He avoids the subject of his gender whenever possible, even with me.

'Hey,' I say, opening my can of Coke.

I notice Leo's lack of food.

'Don't tell me you weren't tempted by the driest turkey in the land,' I say, presenting my plate as if it's the top prize in a game show.

'I can't stay,' he replies. 'I just came by to give you this.'

He hands me a note.

I frown and open it, immediately recognising Essie's spidery handwriting.

If anyone asks, you don't know where we are. See you at yours tonight. E & F x

I look up at Leo.

'You know what's going on?' I ask.

'No idea. They just asked me to make sure you got this. Why, what does it say?'

'That they're bunking,' I say. 'But they never bunk.'

For all Essie's claims to be a rebel, she never misses school unless she's close to dying.

Leo shrugs. 'I dunno. Like I said, they didn't say anything else.'

He stands up and turns to go.

'Hey,' I call after him. 'Are you going to the ball tonight?'

'What do you think?'

'Me, Essie and Felix are hanging out at my house if you fancy it?'

'Thanks for the offer, but I reckon I'm just going to stay in tonight.'

I can't help but feel disappointed.

'That's too bad. In that case, I guess I won't see you until next term?'

'I suppose not.'

'Merry Christmas then.'

He smiles.

'Yeah, Merry Christmas.'

I watch him leave.

That afternoon, usual lessons are cancelled and replaced by DVDs or games, which makes Essie and Felix's disappearing act even more puzzling.

On the way home, Mum plays Christmas songs in the car.

In the back seat Livvy jigs up and down.

'Excited about your first ball then, Liv?' I ask over my shoulder.

'Duh?' she replies. 'Of course I am. It's going to be epic. Mum, did I tell you there's going to be an actual snow machine?'

'You did, darling,' Mum says, winking at me.

'Ten of us are going to Cressy's to get ready. Cressy's mum has hired a limo and everything, a white one.'

'Sounds great,' I murmur.

'Not just great, epic,' Livvy says dreamily.

After an initial freak-out, Livvy has taken the news of what my parents are referring to as my 'gender issues' far better than expected, the blow possibly softened by my parents' promise to coincide my first clinic appointment in London with a trip to see *Wicked* afterwards. I often sense Livvy looking at me though, through narrowed eyes, as if she's trying to figure me out by telepathy or some other cosmic means, rather than just coming out and asking me.

'Did you get ice cream in for tonight?' I ask Mum.

'Of course.'

'What flavours?'

'Oh, you know, a variety,' she says vaguely.

'And did you get the non-dairy stuff for Felix?'

'I think so . . .'

We pull into the driveway. As I'm climbing out of the car I'm certain I see the curtain twitch, which is odd as Dad doesn't normally get home from work until at least five-thirty, if not later.

Mum opens the door, nudging me through it first, to reveal Essie and Felix in a tableau on the stairs, Essie with her arms outstretched, Felix crouching beside her.

'Surprise!' they yell.

I notice Essie is wearing a pair of fairy wings and has glitter smeared on her cheeks, and Felix is sporting plastic mouse ears and an all-in-one garment that looks suspiciously like a silver unitard.

'Don't ask,' he says.

'What are you guys doing here?' I ask. 'You're not meant to be coming over until seven.'

'We were fibbing!' Essie sing-songs with delight.

I turn to Mum.

'Did you know about this?'

She just shrugs innocently and ushers Livvy into the kitchen.

Essie scampers down the stairs, followed by Felix, his hands hovering awkwardly over his crotch.

'What's going on?' I ask.

'She's got a thing planned,' Felix whispers.

'Oh. OK.'

Essie produces a wand from behind her back and starts swinging it about above her head.

'Do not fear, sweet thing, for tonight, Cinderella, you shall go to the ball!' she cries in a theatrical voice.

She points her wand at Felix, almost poking him in the eye. He scampers up the stairs, returning a few seconds later with a shiny black box in his hands. I peer at it, realising it's a brand new make-up kit.

'It's Mac,' I say, looking up. 'But this stuff costs a fortune.'

'My dad's wife works at the head office,' Essie says with a shrug.

'But you can't stand her,' I say.

'She's been tolerable the last few times I've seen her,' Essie mutters sheepishly.

Essie waves her wand again and Felix hurtles back up the stairs. He returns with a wig on a polystyrene head.

'Is that *my* wig?' I ask. It's been styled into soft waves and has a small tiara nestled on top.

'Yep,' Essie says proudly. 'Hats off to your mum for smuggling it out of your room without you noticing.'

I peer down the hallway, but Mum has shut the kitchen door.

'And now for the pièce de résistance!' Essie cries.

She waves her wand a final time. Felix goes dashing up the stairs once more, emerging a few seconds later carrying a dress bag.

'Open it,' Essie whispers, her eyes glittering.

Slowly I unzip the dress bag to reveal just about the most beautiful dress I've ever seen. It's light blue with delicate shoulder straps, a full skirt and a gauzy sash round the waist.

'It's just like the movie star dresses in my scrapbook,' I breathe, running my fingers over the silky fabric.

'I know,' Essie says excitedly.

'It's incredible, it really is. But I can't wear it,' I say, doing up the zip.

Essie's face drops.

'What do you mean, you can't wear it?' she demands.

'Are you serious? Wear this to the ball? With a wig and make-up and stuff? Can you imagine what Harry would do?

I'd be a laughing stock until the end of time. Look, I'm really touched you've done all this for me, I'm bowled over, but I can't go to the ball wearing this, I'm sorry.' I shove the dress back into Felix's arms, tears in my eyes.

'When Ess said "you shall go to the ball", she didn't specify which ball,' Felix says gently.

'What do you mean?'

'We mean we're not going to the Eden Park Christmas Ball,' he says.

'Then where are we going? We're not crashing some other school's ball are we?'

'Not exactly.'

'Then where are we going?'

'You're just going to have to trust us,' Essie says.

I hesitate.

'Look, just start getting ready,' she continues. 'All will become clear, I promise. Oh, wait, one last thing.'

She runs up into my bedroom, returning a minute later with a shoebox. I take off the lid to discover a pair of silver sequined Converse.

'Trainers?' I say.

She smiles mysteriously.

'I told you; all will become clear.'

Having my mum do my make-up is probably one of the most surreal episodes in my life so far (and probably hers). It's almost as surreal as having Felix sitting on my bed dressed as a mouse watching. Dad arrives home from work and orders us pizzas (salad for Felix) before dropping Livvy off at Cressy's house. Things get even more surreal as I sit round the kitchen table in my bathrobe wearing full make-up, chomping on a slice of Hawaiian pizza with my parents as if it's the most normal thing in the world.

At six-thirty I am standing alone in my bedroom staring at myself in the full-length mirror on the back of my door, not entirely sure of what to make of the person staring back at me.

There's a knock at the door.

'C'mon out!' Essie calls. 'We wanna see.'

'Hang on,' I yell back.

Because I want this moment to last a few seconds longer. Just me and the mirror. And me finally liking what I see in the reflection, even if it also makes me feel like I might faint or vomit or both at any second.

More knocking.

'All right, all right, I'm coming,' I say, taking one final look. 'But first, close your eyes.'

'They're closed!' Essie and Felix call back in unison.

I take a deep breath and cautiously step out on to the landing. Essie and Felix are poised, holding hands, their eyes screwed shut, Felix dressed in a slightly too-large tuxedo, Essie in a very short purple dress and artfully ripped fishnet tights.

'OK, you can open them now,' I instruct.

Essie opens hers first, gasps, hugs me and promptly bursts into tears.

'I'm hoping they're happy tears,' I say as she sobs on my shoulder.

'Of course they are!' she wails, breaking away and clinging on to the banister as mascara pours down her cheeks.

Felix passes her a fresh toilet roll before breaking into a grin and pulling me into a hug.

'You look amazing,' he whispers. 'Proper fit.'

I laugh and hug him even harder than I already was.

The doorbell goes.

'That'll be Leo,' Felix says. 'I'll get it.'

'Leo?' I say.

'Well you can't go to the ball without a date,' Essie says, blinking away her tears.

'Wait,' I begin to protest. But Felix is already bounding down the stairs. Dad beats him to the door. Essie and I hang over the banister and watch as Leo steps into the hallway, looking self-conscious in a grey suit and a blue tie.

Essie wolf-whistles. 'Nice threads, Denton!' she calls.

He rolls his eyes in response.

'Aw, check out Leo's tie,' Essie whispers, as Dad takes Leo's jacket and offers him a slice of leftover pizza. 'It matches your dress!'

'Don't even go there,' I warn her.

'Why not? You're single, he's single . . .'

'We're just friends, Ess.'

'But you guys would be so cute together!'

'Ess, I mean it,' I say firmly.

'You're no fun at all,' she says. She's smiling too though.

I kept my promise to Leo. I haven't told Essie or Felix I was with him the weekend I went to Tripton. They suspect though, and have probably been driving themselves insane trying to figure out what we were up to down there. And maybe one day, with Leo's permission, I'll tell them, but for now that weekend is our secret – just Leo's and mine.

Essie takes my hand and we head downstairs. I trip on my dress on the bottom step and Leo has to jump up to steady me, but apart from that it's a perfectly graceful descent.

'You totally lied to me this afternoon,' I say lightly.

'I've had a lot of practice,' Leo replies, one eyebrow raised.

We smile at each other.

'You look nice,' he says.

'Honestly? I can't decide whether I feel amazing or ridiculous.'

'Go for the former.'

'Thanks. You look nice too. It *suits* you. Get it?'

'Ha ha.'

'I do try. Hey, do you know where we're going tonight?'

'I might.'

'But you're not going to tell me, are you?'

'Nope.'

Mum and Dad swoop in then, armed with a camera each, and make us pose for a series of photographs in the hallway. As they snap away, calling out instructions, I wonder what they're thinking; whether they're silently freaking out at sending their only son off to a phantom ball dressed up as girl. Whatever their feelings are, they're keeping them well hidden, covered up with wild enthusiasm. Since telling them, their behaviour has been slightly hysterical, the two of them torn between acceptance and horror; trying to make up for the horror bit with overt support. Only the other night I heard Mum crying again, Dad soothing her, so I get the feeling we still have a long way to go. But I love them for trying so hard, so much it makes my heart ache sometimes.

As we pose for my parents I notice instead of wearing smart shoes or high heels, all four of us are wearing trainers. I'm about to ask why when there's a loud beep from outside. Essie runs into the living room and sticks her head under the curtains.

'The limo's here!' she calls.

Leo frowns. 'A limo, Essie, are you serious? You do remember where we're going, don't you?'

'Oh relax, I couldn't resist,' Essie says, shooing him away. 'C'mon, everyone, time to go!'

I'm the last to leave.

'Be safe kiddo,' Dad says, hugging me.

'I will.'

Mum takes me in her arms then, hugging me close.

'You look really wonderful,' she whispers in my ear.

'Thank you, Mum.'

We pull apart. Her eyes are all wet.

'Now look after each other and have fun,' she says, wiping her cheek with her sleeve. 'That's an order by the way!'

The limo is pink with leopard-print upholstery and flashing lights. It is the ugliest vehicle I have ever seen.

'It's so tacky! I adore it!' Essie proclaims, sprawling over the seats. 'I asked the company for the most disgusting limo they had and they have not let me down!'

'I feel like I'm in an incredibly low-rent music video,' Felix murmurs, gingerly sliding in beside her.

Leo is still frowning. 'We're not meant to be drawing attention to ourselves, remember?' he hisses.

'So?' Essie says, pouting.

'I hate to say it, but I think Leo's right,' Felix says. 'We're going to stick out like a sore thumb in this thing.'

'Can someone *please* tell me where we're going?' I ask.

Everyone ignores me.

Essie sighs. 'How about we get out round the corner from the venue and do the last bit on foot?'

'That'll have to do,' Leo says grimly.

As the limo creeps through the evening traffic, I try to narrow down our likely destination. We head out of Eden Park, on our way passing several limousines heading in the opposite direction, towards school.

'Suckers!' Essie yells out of the sunroof.

After that we head south through the city centre, then over the bridge. It's only then it dawns on me where we're going.

We're heading for Cloverdale.

Leo guides the limo driver round the back of the estate, avoiding the main streets and dropping us off on the corner of Renton Road. Home of the old Cloverdale swimming baths. As Leo helps me climb out of the limo, I notice the queue of people snaking down the side of the fence. I begin to feel nervous, holding on tight to Leo's hand. He squeezes back.

'Oh my God!' Essie cries, grabbing Felix's arm and jumping up and down. 'People have come! They've actually come!'

As we move closer, I realise I recognise most of the people in the queue. There are a couple of girls from my textiles class, some emo kids from Year 11, a lesbian couple from Year 9 holding hands, a large group of goths, from Year 7 kids up to sixth formers. As we walk past them I can feel their eyes on me, their nudges and whispers tumbling down the line like dominoes. My legs feel like they're made of paper.

'I've got you,' Leo whispers as he steers me towards the front of the queue.

We get there to find Amber holding a clipboard, her hair scraped back in a tight don't-mess-with-me ponytail, accompanied by a burly boy wearing black who is introduced as her boyfriend, Carl.

'AKA the muscle,' Essie says, her eyes lingering on Carl's arms.

'What's going on?' I ask, as Essie turns to speak to Amber. 'You keep saying "all will become clear", but so far absolutely nothing is.'

'Just trust us,' Felix says.

I glance at Leo.

'What he said,' he adds.

Essie gives Carl the nod. He pulls aside the loose fence panel. Essie bangs the fence three times with her elbow. The crowd quiets down.

'I now declare the very first Alternative Eden Park Christmas Ball open!' she yells to polite applause.

I don't have chance to ask any questions because I'm then being pushed down on my hands and knees. One by one we crawl through the hole which has been carefully lined with plastic sheeting. Once through the hole and standing upright again, I can see the route to the baths has been lit with hundreds of tea lights in jam jars. We follow it up in to the foyer where there are more lights, guiding us towards the pool itself. The four of us lead the way, the excited murmurs of our classmates humming behind us.

'How did you get all these people here?' I ask, glancing behind me.

'We just conducted a rather militant underground advertising campaign,' Felix says casually.

'Consisting of what?'

'Oh, it was very easy,' Essie says. 'The second Leo described this place we knew we had a venue. We then simply gave people an alternative; spend another Christmas Ball hating the human race and all it stands for, or have some fun for a change and come to this one instead.'

As we get closer I realise I can hear music.

'Is that a DJ?' I ask.

'It might be,' Felix says, his face twitching.

As we turn the corner on to the poolside, I can't help but let out a gasp. Because it looks amazing. There are more lights, as well as white balloons and silver streamers everywhere. Plus, suspended from the top diving board, there's a slowly turning disco ball, casting millions of dots of light around the space.

'This is what you were doing,' I say, 'this afternoon.'

'And last night. And the night before that,' Essie says. 'Getting a generator in here was no picnic, you know.'

At the other end of the pool, near the shallow end, there are proper decks blasting music out of a set of massive speakers. The DJ himself looks suspiciously like one of Felix's older brothers.

'Felix, is that Nick?' I ask, squinting at the slight figure behind the decks.

'It is.'

'He doesn't mind DJing a high school ball?'

Felix turns to me, his face grave.

'I won't lie to you, I've promised to be his slave for the duration of Christmas Day in return.'

I look at the three of them; their faces aglow from the flickering candles dotted everywhere.

'I can't believe you've gone to all this trouble,' I say, 'just for me.'

I can feel myself welling up for about the fifth time this evening.

'Oh no you don't!' Essie cries. 'You are not crying tonight. It's not allowed, for one thing it will totally ruin your make-up. And for another, your emotion is misplaced; it's not just for you. Take a look around.'

I do as I'm told. Gradually the bottom of the pool, for tonight re-christened the dance floor, is filling up with awestruck kids; the oddballs of Eden Park High. But then I realise it's not just the goths and the emos and the nerds out there on the slippery surface. There are other kids out there too, kids I've always dismissed as normal, kids who I never dreamed would choose a ball in an abandoned swimming pool in Cloverdale over Harry Beaumont's snow machine extravaganza.

Nick begins to play a Bruno Mars song.

'Come on,' Essie says, 'let's dance.'

'I don't know,' I say, planting my feet firmly on the ground.

I can't forget the fact I'm here as a girl, as Kate. And down on the dance floor are a ton of kids whose reaction to my appearance I have yet to properly gauge.

'Go,' Leo whispers in my ear. I hesitate before letting Essie guide me towards the ladder. We clamber down on to the dance floor, the surface of which slopes gently downwards towards the deep end.

'I get the Converse now,' I say, nodding down at my feet.

'See, I told you all would become clear,' she says, grinning, pulling me into the centre.

As the chorus kicks in I can feel people looking at me. Essie immediately begins to dance, flinging her arms in the air and singing along. But I'm rooted to the spot, too afraid to make any sudden movements. Even though Leo has paved the way at school in some respects, I'm still a boy in a dress to most people; David Piper in drag.

Essie grabs hold of my hands.

'What's wrong?' she asks, shaking them.

'I don't think I can do this, Ess, everyone's looking.'

She yells something I don't catch over the music.

'What?' I yell back.

'Dance like no one is watching!' she shouts in my ear. 'Pretend it's just you and me!'

I shut my eyes for a second and try to imagine it's just Essie and me dancing around her bedroom. I begin to move, just my arms at first, slowly introducing the rest of my body. After twenty seconds I dare to open my eyes and although half of the kids on the dance floor are still gawping at me, I manage to more or less block them out for the rest of the song, just concentrating on my mad best friend's grinning face as she bounces up and down in front of me.

We've danced to a couple of songs and I'm almost in the swing of things when I hear it.

'Freak Show.'

I look over my shoulder, but the dance floor is crowded and I can't work out where it came from, I stop dancing.

'You OK?' Essie asks, tugging at my arm.

I nod. But I'm not OK. This is too much too soon. I try to keep moving but my limbs feel heavy and clumsy.

The next time I hear it clearly. I spin round. A group of kids from the year below are standing in a semicircle, staring at me, their lips curled in disgust.

'Tranny,' one of them says.

The others dissolve into giggles.

'Yeah, are you like a drag queen?' another asks.

Leo appears as if from nowhere and cuts them off.

'Piss off, why don't you. If you can't be cool then you may as well go to the other ball.'

'Yeah,' Essie chimes in. 'If you've got a problem with anything you see, then you're not wanted here.'

'Well?' Leo growls. 'Got anything more to say?'

The Year 9 kids look at one another before wandering off, throwing us dirty glances over their shoulders.

'Idiots,' Essie mutters. 'You OK?'

'Fine,' I say, although I'm shaking.

'Thanks,' I murmur to Leo, as the next song kicks in.

He shrugs.

'Is it always going to be like this?' I ask.

'For a while, yeah. But it'll get better, I promise, it already has for me. And this comes from someone with a bit of experience.'

I nod gratefully, relieved to find I've stopped trembling.

As Felix joins us we start to dance again and Leo surprises me by not being all that bad a dancer, although he does bow out of some of Essie's more outrageous dance move suggestions. We dance to song after song and slowly I look around to find fewer kids are staring at me; they're too busy dancing themselves. Our dance circle slowly expands until I find I'm dancing alongside kids I've never even spoken to before.

At one point I'm conscious of Simon Allen shuffling about beside me, still smelling distinctly of plasticine despite wearing what appears to be a hired tuxedo.

'Hey, Simon,' I say.

'Hey,' he replies. 'Look, I, er, just wanted to say, I think you've got proper balls.'

The second the words leave his mouth, he goes bright red, like tomato red.

'Oh my God, sorry, bad choice of words,' he stammers. 'What I mean is, I think you're really, really brave.'

I'm a little taken aback. In all our years of sitting next to each other in form room, Simon and I have barely spoken. There's always been this non-verbal agreement between us that associating with each other may draw unwanted attention to our individual oddness.

'Thank you, Simon,' I say. 'I really appreciate you saying that.'

'You're welcome,' he says, looking at his feet before turning to shuffle off again.

'Wait,' I say.

He turns, his face still pink.

'Dance with us?'

He hesitates before nodding, and ends up staying for another two songs.

Nick has been instructed to play as many requests as possible, so the music lurches from rock to pop to punk to folk.

'Wanna drink?' Leo asks when a particularly obscure goth rock song starts to play.

'Good idea.'

We sit on the edge of the pool with cans of Coke, watching our classmates dance below us. A group of Year 7 kids are staring up at us, their mouths hanging open.

'Just block them out,' Leo instructs, as if he can read my mind.

'Is it weird?' I ask after a few seconds. 'Having your special place invaded like this?'

I can hardly believe this is the same space Leo and I spent that freezing cold evening, sitting on what is now a dance floor teeming with kids.

'A bit,' Leo admits. 'Not that it's going to be mine for much longer. They're bulldozing it in the New Year.'

'No way?'

'Yup. They're going to flatten it to the ground,' he takes a long sip of Coke. 'Nah, it's good it's going out in style.'

'I wonder how the real ball is going?' I muse.

'Did you know I was meant to take Alicia, once upon a time?' Leo says, fiddling with the ring-pull on his can.

'Really?'

He nods and looks really sad for a second.

'For what's it's worth, she tweeted that she was boycotting it this year,' I say.

'Doesn't make much difference though really, does it?'

'I suppose not.'

I pause. Leo is looking deep into his Coke can.

'You still really like her, don't you?'

He shrugs and looks away.

Just then the music stops abruptly, resulting in a collective groan from the Goth kids on the dance floor. It takes me just a few seconds to recognise the introduction to the next song. 'Have Yourself a Merry Little Christmas' – the Nat King Cole version. It's the first proper slow number of the night and quickly kids start shyly partnering off.

'Your favourite Christmas song, right?' Leo says.

I nod.

He jumps down on to the surface of the pool.

'Wanna dance then?' he asks, holding out his hand.

'Seriously?' I ask, glancing around me.

'No one is looking,' he lies. 'C'mon.'

I let him help me down on to the dance floor. Even though we've shared a bed, and hugged and held hands, and told one another some pretty personal stuff, somehow negotiating where our hands should go while we are dancing is suddenly the most awkward thing in the world. Eventually we get into position and begin to sway back and forth with the music. I keep my eyes on Leo in an effort to drown out the whispers and nudges coming at us from every angle. Not that I blame them in some ways, it's kind of a scoop; the two of us slow dancing together.

'I'm sorry I'm not Zachary,' Leo says as we reach the second verse.

'What do you mean?'

'You know, your fantasy? Dancing with a boy at the Christmas Ball? I'm kind of guessing this wasn't quite what you had in mind.'

I look up at Leo and smile.

'You're right, it's not. But this is better. One hundred times better.'

And I swear Leo, king of the poker-face, is blushing.

It's as we're dancing to the final chorus I notice her; standing on the side of the pool, combing the packed dance floor, her face all tear-stained.

Livvy.

'Excuse me,' I say to Leo.

He frowns but lets me go.

'Livvy!' I call. When her eyes finally latch on to me, there's a moment of confusion before her face melts into recognition.

'What are you doing here?' I ask as I climb up the ladder on to the side of the pool.

'I got a taxi,' she replies.

'But why? Why aren't you at school?'

She looks at her feet.

'Cressy and I had a fight.'

'What about?'

'She started it,' she says. 'She danced with Daniel Addison. She doesn't even like him! And she knows how much I do, I've told her so like a million times.'

Her eyes start to well up with tears all over again.

'Come here,' I say.

She lets me hold her.

'I'm sorry, Liv,' I say, stroking her hair. 'That's a sucky thing of Cressy to do.'

She nods fiercely, a bubble of snot protruding out of her right nostril.

'Here,' I say, passing her a napkin from the refreshment table.

She blows her nose hard.

'How was the ball apart from that?' I ask.

She shrugs. 'Not like I imagined it.'

'Yeah, they're kind of like that,' I say.

'The snow machine didn't work,' she says. 'It snowed for

about three seconds then got clogged up. When I left, Harry Beaumont was outside screaming about it to someone on his mobile.'

I grin. 'I'm glad you're here, Liv.'

She nods and looks out on to the dance floor.

'I like your dress,' she says, peeking at it out of the corner of her eye.

'Thanks, Liv. I like yours too.'

She bites her lip to stop herself from smiling.

'Why don't you come dance?' I say.

'I don't know. I might just sit and watch,' she says, motioning to the fold-down seats behind her.

'Don't be stupid. Come on, dancing will make you feel better, I promise. Only you'd better take off your heels first.'

And this is how I end up spending most of the ball dancing with my baby sister.

It's almost the end of the night when I hear the opening chords of a familiar song. And for a moment I'm back in the Mermaid Inn, Tripton-on-Sea, high on life, as Leo nervously shuffles about the tiny stage in front of me, clinging to the microphone and looking like he would quite like to kill me.

'I'll be back, Liv,' I say.

She waves me away, happily dancing with a group of Year 8 kids. I wade across the dance floor, scouring the bobbing heads for his. As the chorus kicks in, I swear under my breath. I turn round in a slow circle. He's got to be here somewhere. Then I see him, fighting his way across the dance floor towards me. I break into a grin and push my way through the crowd. We collide in the middle of the dance floor.

'It's your song!' I yell.

'No it isn't,' Leo yells back. 'It's ours.'

Essie and Felix join us then. We put our arms round each other and jump around in a circle, bellowing the lyrics in each other's ears.

Right now, the time is ours
So let's fly higher
Light the stars on fire
Together we'll shine

And even though I know that there's a ton of stuff ahead I'm so terrified about I can't breathe sometimes, tonight I can't help but feel like no matter how hard it gets, everything might just be OK in the end.

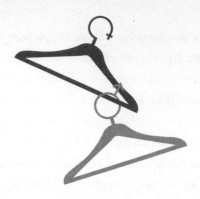

43

It's Boxing Day. Amber is round at Carl's house. Mam and Spike, in matching onesies, are passed out on the settee, crumpled paper hats perched wonkily on their heads. In front of them on the coffee table are the remains of lunch – turkey sandwiches, Pringles, pickled onions and mince pies. Tia is sitting cross-legged on the floor watching *Brave* on DVD, a pair of glittery fairy wings on her back. The living room is still a mess from yesterday, wrapping paper and pulled crackers strewn all over the carpet, and dirty glasses and bowls of crisp crumbs dotted on every surface.

It was an all right day in the end. It turns out Spike is half decent in the kitchen, so he took care of Christmas dinner while Amber and Tia made a huge raspberry trifle for dessert. The jelly layer hadn't set properly so it was a bit runny, but it still tasted nice. Mam was in a good mood and even agreed to a game of Tia's Junior Monopoly after lunch (we let Tia win). In the evening Auntie Kerry and her boyfriend and a few mates of Spike's came over. One of them brought his ukulele with him and played loads of Christmas songs on it,

Spike joining in by drumming on the coffee table. We all joined in the choruses and Mam sang so loudly she lost her voice. When we did 'The Fairytale of New York' I thought of being in the Mermaid Inn in Tripton with David. It feels like years ago. Whenever I think of Tripton now, it's this stuff – winning at the bingo, splashing around in the freezing cold sea, holding back David's hair as he threw up in the en suite of the B&B – that pops into my head. The other bits, the bad stuff with my dad, I keep buried. Jenny reckons I need to work through it. And I will. But for now, I just want to forget him and move on.

The letterbox rattles. I glance at Mam and Spike but they're comatose. I sigh and heave myself out of the armchair.

It's Kate, bundled up under loads of layers. She's wearing make-up and I can see her wig peeking out from beneath her green bobble hat.

'Hey, someone cut the grass,' she says, gesturing at the lawn behind her.

'Oh yeah,' I say. 'Spike and a couple of his mates did it the other week. Took them the whole day.'

'Looks good.'

'Yeah. We've got an actual front path again.'

'I almost forgot, Merry Christmas,' she says, doing jazz hands.

'Merry Christmas,' I reply.' 'You, er, want to come in or something?'

'Best not, everyone's waiting,' she says. Over her shoulder I can see her mum and dad and Livvy in the car. They wave. I raise my hand in greeting back.

'So, how's your Christmas been?' I ask.

'Weird but good. We told my gran yesterday.'

'Wow. And? How'd she react?'

'Um, OK, I think. Shocked. I'm pretty sure she almost choked on her Christmas pudding. She clearly thinks it's a phase but, hey, she hasn't disowned me yet so that's something, right?'

I nod and laugh.

'Oh, and guess what else?'

'What?'

'My referral to the clinic in London was accepted. The letter came on Christmas Eve, would you believe.'

'That's wicked news,' I say. And I mean it.

'I know,' Kate says, beaming. 'It still might be another three months before I get an appointment, but it's a step in the right direction. I feel like things are finally happening, you know?'

'Definitely.'

'And we've got an appointment to see Mr Toolan in the new year, to maybe talk about me coming to school in role, maybe even as early as Easter.'

'Wow.'

'I know, right? So far so terrifying.'

She's grinning ear-to-ear though.

'Anyway, the real reason I'm here is to drop this off,' she says, reaching inside her coat and pulling out a slim package wrapped in silver paper. She thrusts it into my hands.

'What is it?' I ask.

'Duh. What do you think it is? It's a Christmas present.'

'But I don't have anything for you.'

'That's OK. It's only small. Well, aren't you going to open it?'

'You want me to open it now?'

She nods.

I rip off the paper to reveal a paperback book. I turn it over and study the front cover.

'*Alan Turing: The Enigma*,' I read aloud.

'He was a really amazing mathematician apparently,' Kate says. 'He cracked codes during the Second World War and then went mad.'

'I think I've heard of him,' I say, flicking through the pages.

'It got loads of good reviews on Amazon,' she adds.

'It's great, thank you,' I say, closing it.

'You're not just saying that? I was worried it might be a bit boring.'

'Nah, it looks brilliant.'

She smiles and relaxes back on her heels.

'What about you? How's your Christmas been?' she asks.

I glance behind me, at the scene of relative peace in the lounge.

'It's been . . . OK actually.'

'Have you heard from Alicia?'

'No. I think that ship has definitely sailed,' I say, smiling tightly.

There's a sudden gust of cold wind. I zip up my hoodie all the way to my chin.

'For what it's worth, she's really missing out,' Kate says, not quite looking me in the eye.

'Yeah, well, that's life I guess. You don't always get what you want.'

'You can say that again,' she says.

Her dad beeps the car horn.

'I'd better go. We're going to see *The Nutcracker* at the theatre tonight. Family Boxing Day tradition.'

'Nice. Enjoy it.'

'Blokes in tights! What's not to enjoy?' Kate quips.

'Thanks again for the present,' I say, clearing my throat and holding the book up. 'I might read some tonight.'

'You're very welcome,' she replies. 'So, see you next year?'

'God yeah, see you next year.'

'Harry's going to have it in for us big time, I bet.'

'Maybe, maybe not. What's he going to do though? Realistically?'

It turns out the snow machine failure was the very least of Harry's problems on the night of the ball. After a massive overspend on the budget, poor attendance has left the ball planning committee in debt to the school. Not that any of this was our fault directly, but I have no doubt Harry is going to find a way to place the blame on us. It was worth it though. One hundred per cent.

We stand there for a moment, smiling, not really needing to say anything.

Kate's dad beeps the horn once more.

'You better go,' I say.

'Yeah, you're right.'

She hugs me hard, before dashing down the path.

I stand on the doorstep in my socks and watch as the car disappears down Sycamore Gardens.

About an hour later, just as it's getting dark, it begins to snow. Mam and Spike have headed out to the pub for the night, and Amber is still round at Carl's, so it's just me and Tia at home.

As soon as she sees the snow she goes mental, tearing around the lounge and begging me to come out into the back yard and make a snowman with her.

'There's not enough snow for that,' I tell her.

'Snowballs then!' she says.

In the end I watch from the doorway. Not enough snow has fallen yet to scrape up a decent snowball, so after a few failed tries Tia just stands there instead, her arms outstretched and her head lifted up to the sky, trying to catch snowflakes in her sticky little open mouth.

'Get your coat at least,' I call after her. But she doesn't listen. It's like the snow has put a spell on her.

I quickly get cold just standing there watching, so I pull the door to and go back inside. But Tia's outside for another ten minutes, just in her crocs, jeans, T-shirt and fairy wings. When she eventually comes in, her face is bright red and her teeth are chattering. When I touch her hands, they're like ice-blocks, but she doesn't even seem to notice. Sometimes I do wonder if Tia is wired up right. I make her some cocoa and leave her curled up on the sofa watching *Beauty and the Beast*, an old picnic blanket draped over her tiny body.

I head upstairs and sit up on Amber's bunk where I watch the snow fall through the window, the flakes getting increasingly fat, settling fast. As I'm watching them fall, faster and faster still, I get this weird feeling, sort of like déjà vu, of being in the snow with Jimmy, when I was really, really tiny. Of course I now know this is impossible; just my mind playing tricks on me. In the past I would have tried to cling to this thing that may or may not be a memory, but tonight I let it dissolve into nothingness, just like the snowflakes on Tia's tongue.

As I look out of the window, if I blur my eyes a bit, I can imagine that I'm not in Cloverdale at all – but somewhere far, far away instead. It's funny how snow changes that, takes everything ugly and grey

– the dustbins and piles of rubbish and rusty cars – and hides them all under a sparkling white blanket. It won't last. By tomorrow night the snow will have turned slushy and stained. But for tonight, with not a soul in sight, it's perfect. I push open the window a crack and listen to the absolute stillness. I shimmy down the bed so I'm lying on my back, and all I can see is the sky, the falling snowflakes lit up in orange by the street lamp outside the window.

I don't know how long I've been lying there like that, when I hear someone knocking at the door. It'll be Mam I expect, having forgotten her keys. Or belated carol singers out for a few quid.

I sit up and listen as Tia opens the letterbox and calls, 'What do you want?'

A few seconds later she yells my name up the stairs. I climb down the ladder.

'It's for you,' Tia says, blinking up at me from the hallway, her fairy wings all crooked from where she's been lying on the settee.

'I gathered that,' I say impatiently. 'Who is it?'

She just shrugs and wanders back into the living room.

I pad down the stairs. Behind the glass of the front door, there's a shadowy figure. I open it.

It's Alicia. She's wearing a purple coat and fluffy white earmuffs. There's snow on her shoulders and in her hair. I stare at her. I'm pretty sure my mouth is hanging open.

She takes a deep breath.

'I want you to know it wasn't me,' she blurts. 'I didn't tell a soul about what you told me, I wouldn't have. But then Becky went digging on the internet and blabbed. She's not my favourite person right now, if that's any consolation. Look, what I'm trying to say is, I'm sorry. For everything, but mostly for taking so long to say so.'

352

She says all this quickly, her eyes wide and startled, as if she's surprised she wound up on my doorstep in the first place.

'No, I'm sorry,' I say. 'I should have told you from the start, I shouldn't have let things go that far.'

She puts her finger to my lips to silence me and looks into my eyes.

'Leo, can I ask you something?'

I nod.

'Can we please forget about all that and, I don't know, start again?'

'Start again?'

'As friends.'

'Friends,' I repeat.

She holds out her hand and takes another deep breath.

'Hi. I'm Alicia Baker. Nice to meet you.'

I hesitate before taking her hand in mine and shaking it.

'And I'm Leo, Leo Denton.'

She breaks into a smile. That smile.

'Merry Christmas, Leo Denton.'

Acknowledgements

A huge thank you to everyone and anyone who supported me during the writing of this book, but especially:

Bella Pearson, for not only being an incredible editor, but for having faith in me from the very start. I couldn't have got there without you.

The entire team at David Fickling Books, including but not limited to, David Fickling for his invaluable editorial input, wise words and warm welcome into the fold, Linda Sargent for her fantastic notes, Phil Earle for making me feel like a bit of a superstar, and Rosie Fickling for answering my endless questions! I consider myself very privileged to be a DFB author.

Alice Todd, for coming up with the perfect cover. And Ness Wood at DFB for finding her!

Margaret Ferguson at Farrar, Straus and Giroux in New York for her wonderfully thoughtful editorial notes and for keeping my wandering timeline in check! I'm so excited to work with you further.

My hands-down amazing agent, Catherine Clarke, for making me feel I'm in safe hands every step of the way.

Imogen Cooper and the fantastic team at The Golden Egg Academy for being exactly what I needed at exactly the right time. I am very proud to call myself an 'egger'.

The lovely folk at Curtis Brown Creative (CBC), especially Anna Davis and Chris Wakling, for spotting my potential and gently suggesting I should try writing for young adults (light bulb moment!).

Each and every one of my fellow CBC classmates, especially the Monday night crew – Paul Golden, James Hall, Michael Hines,

Dan MacDonald, Fiona Perrin, Christina Pishiris, Maria Realf and Sara-Mae Tuson. An extra shout-out to Fiona for 'lending' me her daughters and their mates for an afternoon's crash course in all things 'teenage'. Chloe Atkinson, Elyse Emanuel, Sienna Emanuel, Jacob Grosvenor-Brown, Bryony Ingram, Lewis Lehrfreund, Georgina Martin, Will Murray, Alex Pritchard, Lizzi Shearing, Kat Smith and Will Taylor – thank you for educating me so brilliantly!

Jake Dorothy and Stef Williams for inviting me into their homes and being so generous, candid and honest. Your input was vital.

The magnificent Gender Identity Development Service team at The Tavistock Centre, past and present but especially Polly Carmichael, Sarah Davidson, Domenico de Ceglie, Keyur Joshi and Elin Skagerberg.

Nikki Gibbard, Winnie Tang, Katherine Watson and David Whitfield (aka the besties) for being generally awesome. An extra special bow-down to Nikki for being my head-cheerleader from the very beginning – it meant a lot then and even more now. Much love to you all.

My family for not totally freaking out when I announced, after ten years as an actor, I was planning to give the equally stable career of writing a go! Your quiet pride in me means so much and ensures my feet stay firmly on the ground.

The following lovely people for helping shape the book in ways big and small (but all important!); Gregory Ashton/Lesley Ross, Chloe Austin, Andrew Clarke, Barry Cunningham, Julia Green, Lisa Heathfield, Jill McLay and Anna Ramberg. You are all brilliant!

And finally thank you to Matt for his patience, superiority on all things SPAG and all-round good energy. I'm so glad to be sharing this adventure with you.

Amnesty International UK Endorses This Book

Amnesty International UK endorses this book because it reminds us that we are all born equal and we should celebrate our human differences.

'All human beings are born free and equal in dignity and rights.'
Article 1, Universal Declaration of Human Rights

The Universal Declaration of Human Rights was signed by world leaders in 1948, but it is a sad truth that all around the world sexual minority groups continue to suffer discrimination, abuse and often extreme violence simply because of who they are.

Sexuality and gender identity are often confused. Sexual orientation is the way you identify yourself – through desires, feelings and sexual activity, whether that's towards people of the same sex or opposite sex from you. Gender identity is rooted less in physical identity, and refers to the way you identify with and express yourself in masculine and/or feminine notions of identity.

In the UK, research shows that as a group transgender people are the most likely to live in fear of hate crime and most likely to have suicidal thoughts due to hate crimes and incidents against them.

····· *The Art of Being Normal* ·····
Now that you have read this book,
Amnesty suggests thinking about these questions:

· *Why is it called* The Art of Being Normal?
· *What assumptions did you make about David and Leo as you were reading?*
· *Having read the book, is there anything you would do*
or say differently in your life?

It was the appalling revelations about the Nazi Holocaust that prompted the creation of the Universal Declaration of Human Rights (UDHR), the first global document to agree terms for what we know to be right and just.
It's because of the UDHR that we now all have human rights, no matter who we are or where we live. They help us to live lives that are fair and truthful; free from abuse, fear and want and respectful of other people's rights.
But human rights are often abused and we need to stand up for them, for ourselves and for other people.
Amnesty International is rooted in the UDHR. It is a movement of ordinary people from across the world standing up for humanity and human rights. Its purpose is to protect individuals wherever justice, fairness, freedom and truth are denied.

If you are interested in taking action on human rights, you can find out how to join our network of active Amnesty youth groups at:
www.amnesty.org.uk/youth
You can find out more about LGBTI issues at:
www.amnesty.org.uk/lgbti

If you are a teacher, take a look at Amnesty's many free resources for schools, including our 'Using Fiction to Teach About Human Rights' classroom notes on a range of novels with human rights themes, at:
www.amnesty.org.uk/education

Amnesty International UK,
The Human Rights Action Centre,
17–15 New Inn Yard, London EC2A 3EA
Tel: 020 7033 1500
Email: sct@amnesty.org.uk,
www.amnesty.org.uk

Help & Support

If you or anyone close to you has been affected by any of the issues in *The Art of Being Normal*, here are some organizations in the UK and Ireland that offer help, advice and support.

All About Trans is a media project looking at creative ways to encourage greater understanding between trans people and media professionals to support better, more sensitive representation in the UK media.
www.allabouttrans.org.uk

Allsorts Youth Project listens to, supports and connects children and young people under 26 who are LGBT or unsure about their sexual orientation and/or gender identity.
www.allsortsyouth.org.uk

Galop is the LGBT+ anti-violence charity, offering support for victims of hate crime, sexual violence or domestic abuse.
www.galop.org.uk

Gendered Intelligence is a highly creative and innovative charity that works with the trans community and those who impact on trans lives. They particularly specialize in supporting young trans people under the age of 21.
www.genderedintelligence.co.uk

LGBT Youth Scotland is Scotland's national charity for LGBT+ young people, working with 13–25 year olds across the country.
www.lgbtyouth.org.uk

Mermaids UK supports and empowers young trans people and their families/carers.
www.mermaidsuk.org.uk

National Trans Youth Network is a network of trans youth groups from around the UK.
www.ntyn.org.uk/network/

The Proud Trust is a life-saving and life-enhancing organization that helps young people empower themselves to make a positive change for themselves and their communities.
www.theproudtrust.org

School's Out UK is an education charity with an overarching goal to make schools and educational institutions safe spaces for LGBT+ people.
www.schools-out.org.uk

Stonewall is the largest lesbian, gay, bisexual and transgender rights charity in Europe.
www.stonewall.org.uk

Transgender Equality Network Ireland is a non-profit organization that seeks to improve the situation and advance the rights and equality of trans people and their families in Ireland.
www.teni.ie

Transgender NI is a not-for-profit organization dedicated to improving the lives of trans people across Northern Ireland.
www.transgenderni.org.uk

About the author

Lisa was born in Nottingham in 1980. She spent most of her childhood drawing, daydreaming and making up stories in her head (but never getting round to writing them down). As a teenager she was bitten by the acting bug and at 19 moved to London to study drama at university.

Following graduation, Lisa adopted the stage name of Lisa Cassidy and spent several happy and chaotic years occasionally getting paid to pretend to be other people. Between acting roles she worked as an office temp and started making up stories all over again, only this time she had a go at writing them down. One such job was at The Gender Identity Development Service – a specialist NHS service for young people struggling with their gender identity.

The stories Lisa heard inspired her to create a fictional teenage character exploring these issues in her debut novel. *The Art of Being Normal* went on to win the Waterstones Children's Book Prize for Best Older Fiction in 2016.

Lisa is also the author of *Paper Avalanche*, *All About Mia*, *Malala (Yousafzai – First Names)* and was one of the seven authors for the collaborative YA novel, *Floored*. When she's not writing, Lisa loves long walks, long talks, dessert, good books and bad TV. She lives in London.

LISA WILLIAMSON

FIRST DAY OF MY LIFE

It's results day. Frankie's best friend, Jojo, is missing.
And a baby has been stolen.

Everything is about to change.

Read on for an extract from Lisa's next book
First Day of My Life.

Prologue

OPERATOR: Emergency services operator, which service do you require? Fire, police or ambulance?

CALLER: (*breathless*) Police!

OPERATOR: Connecting you now.

POLICE CALL HANDLER: You're through to the police. What is the address or location of your emergency?

CALLER: (*hysterical*) Someone's taken her! Someone's taken my baby!

POLICE CALL HANDLER: Can you repeat that please?

CALLER: My baby! She's gone! Please, you need to help me!

Caller breaks down in tears.

POLICE CALL HANDLER: OK, I need you to listen to me. Can you tell me your exact location?

CALLER: (*inaudible – voice muffled*)

POLICE CALL HANDLER: I'm sorry, I didn't quite catch that. Can you say that again, please?

CALLER: I'm in Newfield. Newfield, Nottingham. The BP garage on Larwood Avenue. Please, you need to do something. They've got my baby.

POLICE CALL HANDLER: A unit is on their way. Can I get some more details from you? What's your name?

CALLER: It's Caroline, Caroline Sinclair.

POLICE CALL HANDLER: OK, Caroline. When did you realize your baby was missing?

CALLER: Just now. I came back to the car and she was gone. I was only inside for a few minutes. Oh God . . .

Caller starts crying again.

POLICE CALL HANDLER: How old is the baby?

CALLER: (*inaudible*)

POLICE CALL HANDLER: Caroline, how old is the baby?

CALLER: She's twelve weeks.

POLICE CALL HANDLER: And what's her name?

CALLER: It's Olivia.

Caller becomes hysterical again.

POLICE CALL HANDLER: Try not to panic, Caroline. A unit will be with you very soon.

CALLER: Tell them to hurry, please! I just want my baby back. I just want my baby.

PART ONE
Frankie

Chapter 1

'Jojo, it's me. Where the flip are you? I've got to be at the salon by midday, remember. If you're not here by eleven, I'm going without you, OK?'

I hang up and place my phone face down on the table.

'Still here?' my eighteen-year-old brother Luca asks, making me jump.

'It's not polite to sneak up on people,' I tell him as he lumbers into the kitchen, wearing nothing but a pair of grimy-looking boxer shorts.

'As if I'd waste my time,' he retorts, opening the fridge, then letting out a lingering belch as he peruses the contents.

'You could at least put a T-shirt on,' I say, scrunching up my nose in disgust.

'Are you joking? It's thirty-three degrees already,' he replies, shutting the fridge and opening the freezer below. He sticks his hand into the almost-empty bag of ice cubes and pulls out a fistful, stuffing them into his cheeks.

'I hope you washed your hands.'

'Maybe. Maybe not,' he says, grinning as he crunches down on the ice.

'You're disgusting.'

'Why, thank you,' he says, performing a little bow.

I drag one of Mum's rubbish magazines across the table towards me and pretend to concentrate on an article about a woman who's convinced her goldfish is actually her dead husband, while Luca bangs about making toast.

Mum and Dad purposefully had Luca and I close together (there's just eighteen months between us), in the hope we'd get on. Their plan backfired spectacularly. In fact, Mum reckons if bickering were an Olympic sport, the two of us would have a clutch of gold medals by now.

I didn't think it was possible, but just lately Luca's been even more of a pain than usual. He picked up his A level results last week, and despite barely revising got more than enough points to secure his place at Bristol. He's been lording it about ever since, making out he's God's gift to academia.

'You know what your problem is, Frankie?' he says, leaning against the sink while he waits for his toast to pop up.

'Enlighten me,' I say, rolling my eyes.

'You've got no tolerance.'

'Now that's where you're wrong. I've got no tolerance for you, Luca Ricci.'

'Nah, you're the same with everyone. No wonder Jojo's ditched you.'

'Erm, excuse me?'

'I heard you leaving that arsey voicemail just now.'

I close the magazine. 'So you *were* eavesdropping on me?'

'Don't flatter yourself, Frankie, you're not that interesting. I had no choice. You've got a voice like a foghorn.'

'It's called projection,' I snap. 'And for your information, I wasn't being arsey, Luca, I was being direct. Jojo's nearly an hour late.'

I gesture at the oven clock. 10:59.

'Maybe she went to school without you,' Luca suggests, slathering butter on his toast.

'And why would she do that? We had an arrangement.'

Jojo was due to call for me at 10 a.m. From here, we were going to walk to school together, pick up our GCSE results, then celebrate/commiserate* (*delete as appropriate) over a McDonald's breakfast before my shift at the hair salon, reconvening in the early evening for a party at our classmate Theo's house.

'*We had an arrangement*,' Luca repeats in a high-pitched voice.

I chuck the magazine at him. He dodges out of the way just in time, leaving it to land in the sink.

'When are you going to uni again?' I ask, standing up.

'You'll miss me when I'm gone.'

'Yeah, right,' I mutter, hoisting the slightly soggy magazine out of the washing-up bowl.

I deposit it on the table and glance back at the oven. 11:00.

'Looks like you're on your own,' Luca says, wiping his buttery fingers on his boxer shorts.

'Oh, piss off,' I reply, picking up my phone and marching out of the kitchen.

'Good luck!' he yells after me. 'Something tells me you're gonna need it!'

Swearing under my breath, I slam the front door behind me and set out across the green that separates our row of houses from the main road. Not that it's especially green right now. We're in the midst of a massive heatwave and every patch of publicly owned grass in Newfield, the town where I live, has been bleached a dirty shade of yellow.

I thought it was amazing at first. After a damp, miserable start to the summer, I rejoiced at the rocketing temperatures and record hours of sunshine. Fast-forward seventeen days and I'm well and truly over it. I'm over waking up every morning covered in a sticky layer of sweat. I'm over the constant noisy whir of the fan next to my bed. I'm over wearing the same shorts and vest-top combinations. But most of all, I'm over feeling knackered all the time. I've only been walking for a few minutes and already my breathing is heavy and laboured, sweat trickling down the back of my neck. I stop walking and remove a bobble from around my wrist, sweeping my already damp long dark-brown hair into a messy topknot.

Today must be one of the hottest days so far. The air is thick and syrupy and the tarmac so hot it shines like liquid. I squint up at the sky, an ominous shade of dull blue dotted with sickly yellow clouds, and wonder if today might be the day when it finally breaks and we get the thunderstorm the weather fore-casters keep promising is just around the corner.

I cross the road, and then take a left down Temple Street, before turning onto Larwood Avenue.

Only it's blocked off by a length of police cordon tape.

I frown. If I don't go down Larwood, I'll have to go the long way round and I'm cutting it fine as it is.

I glance behind me to check no one is looking before diving under the cordon.

I've walked maybe two house lengths when I hear footsteps behind me.

'Oi! Where do you think you're going?' a voice calls.

Reluctantly, I turn round.

A police officer is striding towards me wearing a deep frown. 'And what do you think you're playing at?' he asks.

'I'm going to school,' I reply with a shrug.

'In August?'

'It's GCSE results day.'

'I don't care what day it is. Did you not see the cordon?'

'The cordon?'

'Yes, the cordon.'

He points. I turn around and pretend to notice the cordon tape for the first time.

'Oh my God, I totally didn't see it there,' I say, shaking my head in wonderment.

The police officer folds his arms across his chest and sighs. 'Funny that, considering I watched you duck right under it less than thirty seconds ago.'

'Did you really?' I say, blinking in confusion. 'Wow, I literally have no recollection of doing that.' I laugh a tinkling laugh. 'I must be more preoccupied with my results than I thought.'

I give him my very best smile. (For the record, I have a great smile. 'Dangerous', according to my ex-boyfriend Ram. Like Julia Roberts in *Pretty Woman*, according to Maxine, my boss at the salon.) The police officer just glares back, somehow immune to its usual powers.

'Can I go now?' I ask. 'It's just that I'm kind of running late.'

He sighs. 'Go on, then.'

I smile – maybe he's not so bad after all – and thank him, before continuing up the street.

'Er, what do you think you're doing?' he calls after me.

I turn back to face him. 'You said I could go.'

'Yes. Back the way you've come. This street is a crime scene.'

'A crime scene?' I ask, screwing up my face.

'Yes.'

I peer up Larwood Avenue. Apart from the cordon tape, a few police cars and some official-looking people milling about, nothing appears to be out of the ordinary. No blood splatters or chalk outlines or Forensics tents.

'What sort of crime scene?' I ask.

'None of your business.'

'But if I don't cut down here, I have to go all the way around.'

'Not my problem,' the police officer says, walking me back towards the cordon.

Chapter 2

By the time I get to school, most people have been and gone and the foyer is empty apart from Mr Devi, the head of Year Eleven, and Mrs Schulman, the deputy head.

They're sitting at a table in front of the entrance to the main hall. They look weird in their off-duty summer clothes. I can see Mrs Schulman's lacy bra straps peeking from beneath the straps of her sundress, while Mr Devi is wearing a pair of truly hideous salmon-coloured shorts and some Velcro sandals so ugly I can barely bring myself to look at them.

'Frankie,' he says as I approach. 'Great to see you. Having a good summer?'

'Yes, thanks, sir,' I reply automatically.

The truth is, although I'm not having a bad summer exactly, it's far from the life-defining fun-fest I imagined it would be. It hasn't helped that for three weeks of it, Jojo has been ill with a horribly contagious virus. I hadn't realized just how many of my summer plans revolved around her until she suddenly wasn't available.

There are two boxes on the table. One marked A–M, a second marked N–Z. While Mrs Schulman delves into the second box, I attempt to peer into the first. Only three envelopes remain, but the box is too deep for me to make out whether one of them is addressed to Jojo or not.

'Here we are,' Mrs Schulman says, handing me my envelope. 'Ricci, Francesca.'

I thank her and take it outside, sitting down on the steps. The concrete is hot against the back of my thighs.

As I turn the envelope over in my hands, I can't help but think back to the last time I opened something so official-looking.

It was back in April and I'd just got home from school. The letter was propped up against the fruit bowl on the kitchen table, the Arts Academy's distinctive logo printed next to the postmark. My heart racing, I rang Jojo straightaway to check if she'd got her letter too, then we put our phones on speaker and opened them together on the count of three.

I can still remember the growing heat in my cheeks as I read the contents, my disappointment red-hot. And the cooling numbness that quickly replaced it when Jojo said the three little words that I'd been so sure were destined to be part of *my* script.

I got in.

I shove the memory away and slide my finger under the flap of the brown envelope, pulling out the computer printout tucked inside.

My eyes scan the list of grades.

A three in maths.

Fours, fives and sixes in everything else.

Except drama.

For drama, I got a nine.

The very top grade. Literally, the best you can get.

'Typical,' a familiar voice says. 'The second I finally nip off for a loo break, you turn up.'

I look up. My drama teacher, Ms Abraham, is standing over me, wearing a denim pinafore dress over a white vest top and a pair of canary yellow flip-flops.

I like Ms Abraham a lot. She's older than she looks (I know for a fact she's at least forty), but she still manages to be cool and fun at the same time as being a really good teacher. Before she did her teacher training, she was a professional actor in London although she claims she never quite hit the big time. She reckons the closest she got was understudying Naomie Harris at the National Theatre.

'But that's massive,' I said when she told us one lesson. 'Why didn't you just keep going?'

She just shrugged. 'Dreams change, Frankie.'

I looked around the draughty drama studio and pulled a face. 'No offence, miss, but this is not my idea of a dream.'

That earned me a poke in the ribs from Jojo. Not that Ms Abraham seemed to mind what I'd said. She just smiled an enigmatic smile and told me I'd get it one day.

'What are you doing here, miss?' I ask as she sits down beside me, tucking her dress between her legs.

'Just helping out,' she says. 'It was absolute bedlam earlier.' She nods at the piece of paper on my lap. 'Congratulations on that nine, by the way.'

'Oh, thanks,' I say, shoving it back in the envelope, suddenly self-conscious.

'You should be really proud,' she adds. 'You worked bloody hard for that.'

I don't say anything.

'I mean it, Frankie,' she insists. 'Do you know what percentage of students manage a nine in drama?'

'No.'

'I'll tell you. It's five. Five per cent.'

'Is Jojo also one of them?' The question leaves my lips before I can stop it.

Ms Abraham tilts her head to one side. 'Does it make a difference if she is or isn't?' she asks.

I shrug. 'No.'

Yes.

There's a pause. Ms Abraham has painted her toenails coral. She must have done it at home herself because it's a bit messy, specks of polish clinging to her cuticles.

'Frankie,' she says. 'I know you may not want to hear this, but I'm really looking forward to having you in my A level class this coming term. Seriously, the Arts Academy's loss is my gain.'

'Thanks, miss,' I say. 'But you really don't have to do this.'

She raises an eyebrow as if to say, 'Don't I?'

'Honestly, miss, I'm not bothered. It was ages ago now. And yeah, I wanted to get in at the time, but I've had the summer to think about things and the truth is, I'm not sure it's the right place for me anyway.'

'Really?' she says, continuing to look doubtful.

The Arts Academy is a free specialist arts college, the only one of its kind in the whole of the Midlands. Entrance for the acting strand is ultra-competitive and by audition only. Ms Abraham was the one who told Jojo and me about it in the first place; the one who encouraged us to apply for a place in Year Twelve; the one who wrote our references, and helped us pick out audition pieces.

'Really,' I say. 'I mean, I'm sure Jojo will get on just fine there, but, I dunno, it just struck me as a bit regimented, you know? A bit stuck up its own arse.'

'Oh,' Ms Abraham says, blinking. 'Right. Well, I have to say, I'm a bit relieved.'

I frown. 'Relieved? Why relieved?'

'Well, to be honest, I've been a bit worried about you, Frankie.'

'Me?' I say, screwing up my face.

'Yes. You.'

'Why?'

'I know how badly you wanted to get in. I hated the idea of you getting despondent based on this one disappointment. Especially when you've got so much talent.'

Have I, though? Surely if I was that talented we wouldn't even be having this conversation right now. I'd be too busy preparing for my first term at the Arts Academy.

'Yeah, well that was then and this is now, and I'm totally over it,' I say.

Ms Abraham continues to look unsure.

I laugh. 'Seriously, miss, there's no need to look so worried. It's ancient history, I swear.'

Finally her face melts into a smile. 'Well, that's great to hear, Frankie,' she says, nudging my shoulder with hers. 'Really bloody fantastic.'

My phone buzzes in my bag.

''Scuse me, miss,' I say, getting it out.

It's a WhatsApp message from Mum.

> Well???

My eyes drift to the time in the top right-hand corner of the screen. I'm supposed to be at the salon in less than ten minutes. Maxine's usually pretty good if I'm ever a bit late but I don't want to take the piss when she's already given me the morning off as paid leave.

'I'd better get going,' I say, clambering to my feet. 'Work.'

Ms Abraham stands up to join me. 'Is Jojo on her way, do you know?' she asks.

'Why? Has she not come in yet?'

'No. Her envelope's still here. I assumed you'd come together.'

'Yeah, well, that was the plan . . .'

Ms Abraham's expression turns serious once more. 'Everything's OK between the two of you now, isn't it?'

''Course,' I say. 'Fine. Something must have come up, that's all. I'll give her a ring on my way to work and see what's up.' I pull my backpack onto my shoulders. The canvas straps are damp with sweat from where they've been wedged under my armpits.

'I'm really glad we got the chance to chat, Frankie,' Ms

Abraham says. 'I'm so pleased you haven't taken the Arts Academy thing to heart.'

''Course I haven't,' I say. 'I mean, at the end of the day, it's just a school, right?'

She nods and smiles and I know I've said the right thing.

We say our goodbyes and I walk briskly towards the gates, my lie reverberating in my ears.

Because it's not just a school.

It's *the* school.

And Jojo is going and I'm not.

Find out what happens next by getting yourself a copy of Lisa's highly anticipated new book *First Day of My Life*.

Publishing July 2020.